Marius' Mules

The Invasion of Gaul

by S. J. A. Turney

1st Edition

"Marius' Mules: nickname acquired by the legions after the general Marius made it standard practice for the soldier to carry all of his kit about his person."

For my beautiful wife Tracey, who has done nothing but encourage me. So it's mostly her fault!

Also for my grandfather Douglas, who is responsible for my irrepressible love of history.

I would like to thank those people instrumental in bringing Marius' Mules to fruition and making it the success it has been, and those who have contributed to the production of the Second Edition, in particular Leni, Jules, Barry, Robin, Kate, Alun, Nick, two Daves, a Garry and a Paul. Also a special thanks to Ben Kane and Anthony Riches, who have greatly encouraged me towards the improvements in this edition.

Cover photos courtesy of Paul and Garry of the Deva Victrix Legio XX. Visit http://www.romantoursuk.com/ to see their excellent work.

Cover design by Dave Slaney.

Frontispiece Coin Image creative commons, courtesy of Classical Numismatic Group, Inc

Many thanks to all three for their skill and generosity.

Published in this format 2021 by Victrix Books

Second Edition

Dramatis Personae

(List of Principal Characters)

❖ Marcus Falerius Fronto – Legate of the Tenth Legion

❖ Gaius Longinus – Legate of the Ninth Legion

❖ Gnaeus Vinicius Priscus – Primus pilus of the Tenth Legion

❖ Lucius Velius – Centurion & chief training officer of Tenth Legion

❖ Quintus Lucilius Balbus – Legate of the Eighth Legion

❖ Aulus Crispus – Legate of the Eleventh Legion

❖ Titus Balventius – Primus pilus of the Eighth Legion

❖ Aulus Ingenuus – Lesser officer of Eighth Legion's cavalry wing

❖ Tetricus – Junior Tribune attached to the Seventh Legion

❖ Florus – Young legionary in the Tenth Legion

❖ Quintus Atius Varus – Prefect of the Ninth Legion's cavalry wing

❖ Quintus Titurius Sabinus – Senior staff officer

❖ Titus Atius Labienus – Senior staff officer and lieutenant of Caesar

The maps of Marius' Mules

The campaign against the Helvetii

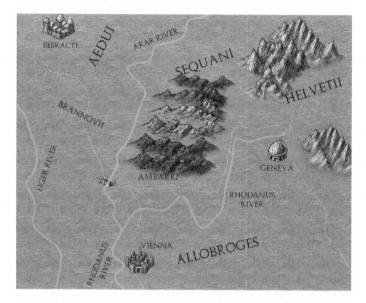

The Battle of Bibracte

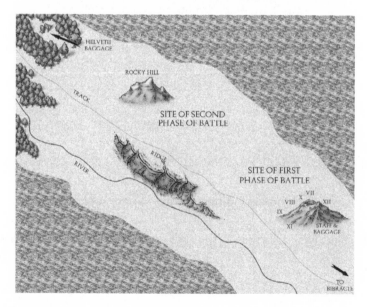

The campaign against Ariovistus

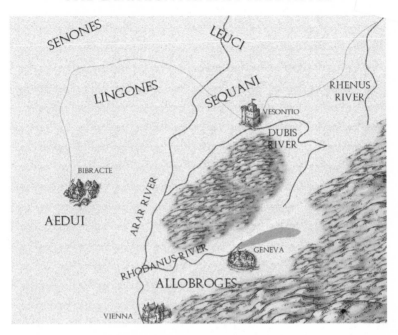

The battle of Vesontio

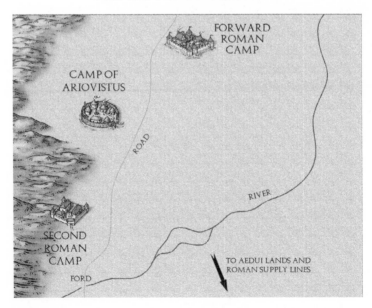

Also available online at:
http://simonturney.com/downloads/marius-mules-maps/

PART ONE

ACTS OF AGGRESSION

CHAPTER 1

(TENTH LEGION'S SUMMER CAMP AT CREMONA)

'Cursus Honorum: The ladder of political and military positions a noble Roman is expected to ascend.'

'Tarpeian Rock: Cliff on the Capitoline Hill of Rome from which traitors were hurled.'

'Latrunculi: Roman board game involving stones of two colours on a board, resembling the Chinese game of Go.'

M arcus Falerius Fronto trudged through the mud between the headquarters pavilion and his tent, kicking in irritation at errant stones, which disappeared into the dark with a skittering sound. He would have given good money to be back at the winter quarters in Aquileia, on the warm Adriatic. For all that Cremona was a reasonably sized town with all the facilities and amenities a Roman gentleman could enjoy, the camp itself, almost a mile away, was much the same as any practice camp throughout the empire: cold, damp and dirty. Like many of the mighty general's senior officers, Fronto's quarters were considerably closer to the centre of command than he would truly wish. Though the concentration of the officers made for better organisation and a certain camaraderie, the great Caesar slept little and late and had a tendency, when thoughts occurred in the dark of night, to wander among the tents of his officers and seek out their opinions of grand designs and obscure schemes. It was said by some of the men that Caesar never slept, though Fronto knew the truth, having just removed the cup from the general's hand, emptied the dregs outside the tent and draped a blanket over the figure slumbering in the folding campaign chair.

Fronto's mind wandered back over the briefing earlier in the evening and the array of maps on the campaign table that he had tidied and gathered up before he left. Some of the officers present had had the foresight to heavily water their wine, knowing how generals tended to drag out these meetings for many hours, considering every minute detail. Those who were unprepared had begun to doze hours ago and would be looking to the security of their careers in the morning. The general himself, as always, drank a half and half mixture of good Latin wine and water, remaining sober until most of his officers had left, and never drinking enough to lose control of his tongue. This was a man with many secrets, Fronto was reminded.

There had been much speculation among the officers over the last couple of days as to why Caesar had come to Aquileia at all, yet alone to a practice camp for three legions in the hinterland. He had been quietly settled in Rome ever since his governorship had been confirmed and had shown no significant interest in the troops under his command. Then suddenly he had arrived in camp with an entourage of his favourite staff officers and a wagon full of maps and supplies. Fronto had been apprised of the imminent arrival of a party of soldiers by the sentries, had immediately recognised the standards and the man in the red cloak on the white horse, and had alerted the other officers without delay. He had his own theories concerning the general's presence.

Caesar had had a command tent raised and with barely a nod of recognition to the officers with whom he had served before, called for a meeting and disappeared within. An hour later, the general had briefed all present on the nature, geography and politics of Gaul and the Gaulish tribes, though still no one had been enlightened as to the reason for this meeting and the information divulged.

The ordinary civilian back in Rome tended to label anyone from north or west of Roman territory a 'Gaul' though, in truth, the land to the north was held by the Helvetii, above them the Belgae and the Germanic tribes and to the far west, by the sea, the Aquitani peoples. The Gauls consisted the tribes that lay between these others.

Still, sometimes a sweeping generalisation made things easier. And no true Roman could think of the Gauls without a thread of bitterness weaving into his heart. Even the two and a half centuries that had passed since those barbarians had broken the walls of Rome and desecrated the holy places had not dampened the ardour of many a Roman nobleman. Fronto had a suspicion. He would not dare voice it yet, but the nagging feeling remained that the general planned to take the legions into Gaul and, despite the worries and implications of such an act, he could not ignore the quickening of his pulse when he thought of Romans wreaking long awaited vengeance on these uncivilised brutes. These days people said that the Gauls were a different people; that they had a culture. To Fronto, they were just another enemy; to Caesar, a stepping stone.

His mind wandering from subject to subject, deep in concentration, Fronto realised with a sudden jolt that he had walked far past the officers' quarters and almost to the edge of the camp. There were very few soldiers outside at this time, and most of those were going about their various night time duties. None of them, of course, caught the eye of the senior officer walking in their midst. Fronto looked up at the moon. Late. Very late. By rights he should be abed now like the rest of the officers and yet sleep was far off. Reasoning that lying staring at the roof of the tent was unlikely to help him pass into the arms of Morpheus, Fronto reached out and grasped a passing legionary by the arm. The startled boy, who could not have been more than eighteen, stammered a respectful greeting that the officer waved casually aside.

'Is there anywhere open in the town that serves a reasonable wine at this time?'

The young soldier's brow creased. 'I believe there's an inn down near the river sir, which stays open almost 'til dawn.' He suddenly pulled himself to a semblance of attention. 'Not that I've been in such a place of course, sir.'

Fronto smiled. 'Relax, lad. I'm not looking for infractions of the rules, just a drink.' He patted the boy on the shoulder and flipped a small coin into his hand. 'Next time you get there, have a drink on me. I have a feeling you won't be seeing the place for much longer.'

He walked off in the direction of the west gate, leaving the puzzled-looking soldier standing in the street, staring at the coin in his hand.

Passing through the gate with only a brief question from the duty centurion, Fronto left the camp and started down the hill toward Cremona and its warm and friendly drinking establishments. There were few locals around at this time, and those that he encountered were generally drunk and semi-conscious. He made his way down to the river, his mind once more on the great general he had left a mere quarter of an hour ago.

Caesar was a man who had been acclaimed as a hero and an advocate of Roman expansion for his deeds in Spain. Indeed, to the general himself none of the officers would say differently. Many personal journals, however, would give another impression. Those who had had the dubious honour of accompanying the general on his rise through the cursus honorum could see a side of the great man of which the public would never learn. The man was a genius; of that, there could be no doubt. A modern-day Scipio, or Gracchus, matched today only by the great Pompey or Crassus. He had come from a noble family, though not a particularly wealthy one, and had risen rapidly through the shrewd borrowing of money and the skilful manipulation of the general mass at Rome. In this Fronto could see unlimited ambition; had seen it time and time again in the general's plans and actions. It was largely this ambition, smouldering scarcely concealed beneath the surface that led Fronto to suspect what was coming. Like a number of the other officers in Caesar's command, Fronto had served with the general in Spain, on the campaign that had given Caesar a piece in the great game, and yet put him in extreme danger of prosecution for war crimes. There was no doubt in his mind that Caesar's campaigns could be a path to glory, but they could also be a path to damnation.

Fronto turned a corner and saw a sign for a tavern. Here in Cisalpine Gaul, the influence of Roman civilisation had all but wiped the Gaulish culture from the land, and the street and tavern could easily have been on the outskirts of Misenum or Puteoli, his home town. After three days of almost constant rain, one could only wade through these badly paved streets and, as Fronto reached the front door, under the swinging, rusty sign, he took advantage of the boot scraper by the door, leaving large clods of earth. The inside, lit only by three small oil lamps, was dingy and only four men sat around the room, sipping wine or swigging beer. Fronto ordered a good wine and took a seat in a dark corner. His thoughts turned once more to the people known as the Gauls. It was a misnomer really. The innkeeper who had served Fronto's drink was *theoretically* a Gaul, though Fronto could hardly compare this Latinised man with his slight Etrurian accent to the Gauls that had broken Rome so long ago. Nor, for that matter, with the feared Belgae or Helvetii, hardened by centuries of war among themselves and against the Germans across the Rhine.

Still, the Helvetii would be the ones to watch. Not only were they just over the border from here, but there had been rumours emanating from their territory for a long time now. Roman merchants had made a killing there, buying up food stocks and carts and pack animals and all manner of other goods. Each officer had his own opinion on the activities of the Helvetii, ranging from an expansion into Sequani territory, to crossing the Rhine and claiming land in Germany, to invading Gaul. There was no doubt that the Helvetii loved to make war, and the only question really was against whom. One thing that all were sure of was that the Helvetii, warlike as they were, would never consider attacking the might of Rome. And yet two things nagged at Fronto. First was Caesar's sudden fascination with Further Gaul and its tribes, and the other was a conversation he had had yesterday with a local merchant. The man, from whom many of the officers had been purchasing items for months, had been packing all his worldly goods onto a cart when Fronto came across him. Upon being asked why, the man had replied 'Have you never seen the birds fleeing the forest when a predator enters?' and had refused to be pressed further.

Matters to think on; Fronto pondered as he drained the glass. He purchased another at the bar and then returned to his dingy table. The general was renowned for his ability to think problems through obliquely. Was it possible that the general had already taken stock of what had happened and used it to create a hypothesis of events in the near future? Did Caesar actually think that the Helvetii would invade Roman territory? Were it from anyone else Fronto would have laughed off such an idea, but from the general? Fronto had played the man at Latrunculi several times and considered it a personal mark of glory that he had once won a game.

Fronto was at least as well versed in the rules of the game as any other well-bred Roman, and better than most, but Caesar was another matter entirely. He had a disturbingly clever habit of having calculated every possible combination of moves at least seven turns ahead. It was this gift for strategy that made Caesar as dangerous in the field as he was on the board.

In response to his unsettled feeling, Fronto had put his command, the Tenth, on a state of alert within moments of Caesar's arrival at the camp. There had been plenty of complaints from the senior centurions of course, but Fronto had silenced them with a look. He had commanded legions before, under this general and others. The senior men of the Tenth knew that; they also knew that something was in the wind. Fronto also had a habit of being prepared.

He sighed and wondered whether he would be a legionary officer all his life. He had served in a number of theatres and commanded a number of legions as and when he had been required. Commanding a legion had always been a temporary post at the whim of the army's general, and in those days Fronto had been keen and continually seeking a new challenge. Caesar had broken tradition in many ways, including his tendency to leave an officer in command of a legion for long periods. Thus in Spain, Fronto had commanded the Ninth for a considerable time, becoming very familiar with its officers and their quirks. In fact long-term command had permanently changed Fronto's views and attitudes toward the military, and he could see the benefit of building a rapport with a legion.

His command in Spain had perhaps tied him a little too closely to Caesar, and he had narrowly escaped prosecution along with the general, after which he had tried to dabble in political circles at Rome as the cursus honorum demanded. A dull and incomprehensible two years in Rome had given Fronto enough of a taste of Rome's political life to know that his place was in the field, and he had applied to the senate once more for a command. For over a year he served in various locations, never tied to a unit for more than a month, his reputation constantly growing, until he heard of his old patron's appointment as governor of Illyricum and Cisalpine Gaul. Sure of his path, he had visited Caesar and asked the general if there was a place in Gaul for him. Caesar had smiled and, without hesitation, sent him to Aquileia to command the Tenth, whose current commander was returning to Rome.

He was fated to the soldier's life. He would never sit in the senate; he may never make a provincial governor, and he was resigned to that. Only two things still ate away at him late at night. Firstly there were the young, go-getting officers, just starting off on the cursus honorum, who could not comprehend why a man would backtrack down the rungs of the ladder. Fronto suspected that they laughed about him behind his back. The other was, of course, his family. Neither his mother nor his sister had ever forgiven him for his abortive political career, when he had been expected to make Senator at least. He knew he was bright enough, as did the womenfolk, but he preferred the clear-cut blacks and whites of military command to the soul-destroying greys of politics. Throwing back the last of his second unwatered cup faster than he probably should, Fronto stood, thanked the barman, and made his way out of the tavern.

The streets of the town were muddy, dark and deserted, and Fronto carefully picked his way through the murky alleys until he came out near the bridge. So deep in thought was he that he almost knocked down the figure entering the alley as he left it. Gnaeus Vinicius Priscus, the Tenth's leading centurion, staggered against the wall, righted himself quickly and saluted Fronto. The officer waved the salute aside and growled, covering his own embarrassment.

'Priscus, what the hell are you doing sneaking around down here at this time of night? Haven't you got duties in camp?' He grasped the centurion by the shoulder fastenings of his mail shirt and turned him around, walking him out of the alley.

Priscus looked momentarily taken aback and for a moment a fleeting and knowing smile crossed his face before professionalism took over. 'Sir. I was, in fact, looking for you. One of the gate guards told me you had come down here. We intercepted a messenger coming to the camp. I thought you would want to know before word reached the other officers.'

'A messenger?' Visions of Gaulish hordes sweeping south across the empire's borders ran unbidden through his mind. 'A messenger from whom?'

Priscus stumbled on the dark road; looked up in time to see that they were emerging into the faint circle of light cast by the torches on the camp's walls.

'One of our friendly merchants, up on the frontier, near the Helvetii. It seems big things are happening over the border. His message was for the officer commanding, but I got a few hints. There's been some kind of failed coup in the tribe's leadership.' Priscus held up his hand and signalled to the guards, who swung open the great wooden gates to allow them entry.

Fronto smiled. 'You did well, Gnaeus; very well. Caesar will almost certainly call another staff meeting, and it stands the Tenth in good stead if we appear to be well prepared. Get back to the others and call up all the officers of the Tenth. As soon as I've seen the general, I'll want to call a private meeting.'

Priscus saluted again and turned as they reached the gate, giving the agreed password to the guards. As the gates swung shut and the centurion made for the Tenth, Fronto called out after him 'Oh, and Gnaeus, get some of the good wine out of storage. This might be a long meeting and a long night.' Priscus grinned and set off at a jog.

Fronto made his way through to the commanders' tents and, reaching his own, examined himself in the large bronze mirror he had recently purchased from a vendor in the village. Generally presentable, though with muddy boots and some decidedly serious-smelling horse dung on the hem of his red cloak. He looked around the tent for his spare boots and laid eyes on them where he had left them beneath his small table. Muddy, but better and, with a bit of hasty rubbing, the dried mud would come off. The sounds of activity outside heralded the fact that the news had reached the general. Fronto hastily cleared off the worst of his boots and contemplated what to do about the cloak. He could not present himself to the general smelling like a livery stable. In a rush now, he opened his travel chest and retrieved a crimson cloak from inside, neatly folded the way only his sister could have done. How long had it been since he had worn it? So few occasions to dress up these days. Needless to say, some of the others would take every opportunity to rib him about this over the next few days, but the smell of horse shit would be a stronger fuel for their jibes.

Moments later a breathless messenger reached his tent and knocked on the wooden post at the door. 'Sir, the general...'

Before he could finish the summons, Fronto was out of his quarters in full dress and marching toward the command tent. Over his shoulder he called back 'Yes soldier, I know.'

Fronto had been the first to arrive at Caesar's tent by a clear margin and, though he was now waiting outside the flaps, he knew that his promptness would have been noted. As several of the lower ranks passed by in the torchlight, the officer was sure he heard a few badly-concealed sniggers. Ignoring them, he kept his eyes on the tent's entrance, waiting for Caesar's attendant to call him. Footsteps behind told him that the other senior officers had arrived.

A jolly voice behind him said 'Why, who is this joining us for the briefing? Could it be the great Scipio? Or perhaps Apollo himself is deigning to lighten our lives with his *radiant* presence.' Slightly subdued laughter rippled down the line behind Fronto.

Without turning his head, Fronto addressed the voice.

'Longinus, you missed your chance for a career on the stage. What are you doing here, among these serious and talented military types? Have you tired of talking to your mule?'

He heard Longinus' intake of breath, ready to launch into a diatribe on the nature of Fronto's family and their resemblance to certain species of amphibian. The new commander of the Ninth resorted to this subject in every one of their arguments whenever he ran out of clever things to say. Fronto suspected that the slightly portly officer resented the fact that his command of the Ninth had come only because Fronto had resigned his commission with that unit on his return with Caesar to Rome. Moreover, the Ninth still held Fronto in esteem since he had been with them throughout their time in Spain.

Before Longinus could get his comment out, Caesar's servant appeared at the doorway.

'Gentlemen, the general will see you now.'

As the officers filed into the tent, Fronto took the only seat he knew to be comfortable. Once the eleven men were seated, a curtain to the left was pulled aside, and Caesar himself strode in. The officers stood as one, saluting and bowing. Caesar acknowledged them and sat, followed by the others. As his servant poured a glass of wine, the general opened his mouth to speak and then closed it again. His eyes had fallen on Fronto. A warm smile spread across Caesar's face.

'My dear Fronto, did my summons catch you on your way to anywhere glamorous and important? How inconvenient of me.' Fronto could feel the colour rising in his cheeks as laughter filled the room.

He carefully folded back the sides of the cloak so that the red lining covered the worst of the golden images on the outside. His sister had had the cloak made to order by one of the best men in Rome to celebrate Fronto's triumphant return from Spain a few years ago. The golden Gods and victories cavorted with mythical creatures and horses, covering most of the plain red. A single gold thread hung from one shoulder where Fronto had, after one particularly drunken evening, unsuccessfully tried to unpick a representation of Pegasus. He gratefully accepted the proffered glass from Caesar's servant and sank his face into it. After a moment's steadying he lowered the glass and, in a gesture that he felt sure few of the other officers would dare match, fixed Caesar with a warming smile, holding his eyes.

'General, as you know the history of this cloak, you know it has only ever been worn once in public, and it places upon your revered self a mark of great distinction that I would don it for your presence.'

Caesar's smile faltered and Fronto wondered for a moment if he had gone too far. A moment later, however, the general laughed uproariously. Some of the officers joined in, though Longinus retained a frustrated silence. The general slapped his knee and wiped a tear from his cheek.

'Fronto, you are well named. You have more front about you than any man I know. Very well, honour me with your priceless cloak and pray that the next time I see your charming sister I do not tell her what you really think of this ostentatious piece of apparel.' He took a sip of wine and sat up straighter.

'To business gentlemen. Your orders and your explanation. You will immediately, upon leaving this briefing, return to your legions or other duties, and see that the entire camp stands to. I want all three legions ready to march at an hour's notice. Paetus, you will have the camp made ready for the army's march. Cita, get all the necessary provisions and pack animals for two weeks in the field. Almost the entire camp will be leaving, including the cavalry.'

Looking around, Fronto counted the faces registering surprise with satisfaction. He returned his eyes to the general.

'Now, I expect you're all aware by now that a messenger reached the camp tonight. He has come from the north, where he was accompanying a trader dealing with the Helvetii. There has been something of a disturbance among the tribe's leadership. Some of you may remember the name of Orgetorix from earlier briefings. He has evidently tried to arrange a coup for control of the tribe, in association with other ambitious men of the Aedui and Sequani tribes. I rather gather that this failed, as Orgetorix committed suicide four days ago while on trial for the attempt. In the normal flow of events, this would stand well for Rome. The man was obviously a rabble-rouser and could conceivably have united three tribes into a confederation on our border. Unfortunately the latest news, from two days ago, is that villages and towns of the Helvetii are burning across the length and breadth of the mountains. Those of you who have studied this particular tribal area will be aware that the Helvetii are by far the strongest group, and are unlikely to have been bested very quickly by anyone bar us.' He paused for a moment, smiling.

'However, it is a strange custom of these peoples to destroy what they leave behind. Not, like us, to prevent them being used by erstwhile enemies, but to help bind the tribe together and provide the added impetus needed to keep such a group collected and moving with purpose.' Again the general paused to make sure he was being followed.

'Gentlemen, the Helvetii are moving. The whole tribe.' At a gesture from Caesar, his servant unrolled a map on the low table between them all. The map covered the territories of Cisalpine and Transalpine Gaul and the surrounding areas.

'As you can see, the Helvetii are bordered to the east by Lake Geneva. To the north lie the Rhine and the powerful German tribes. To the west there is only a narrow route between the Jura Mountain and the Rhone, through unstable territory held by other tribes. And of course, to the south: Rome. Wherever the Helvetii plan to go, if they are bringing their whole tribe and all of their possessions, they cannot realistically attempt any route other than through our lands. They have two days' advantage on us if we want to meet them in battle in open land, but they are burdened and slow. I will be leaving for Geneva some time tomorrow morning, and taking a few key personnel with me. I have sent word to Massilia to have the Eighth Legion march and they will meet me there. The three legions here will move out two days after I do, and will make for Vienna on the Rhone. They will wait there as long as necessary until I send the signal. The force I shall take to Geneva should be more than sufficient to turn the Helvetii away, given the terrain. I want the other legions in reserve at Vienna as a reserve in case the Helvetii make their way around us, and in such as position as to be able to move anywhere along or across the border in the shortest time possible.' Caesar sat back, while the others continued to pore over the map.

Fronto frowned and leaned forward.

'Sir. If, as you say, the Helvetii are coming south, why do we need to keep reserves? Surely we would be better on the forced march to Geneva with you. Then we could meet them in open battle straight away and finish them.'

Caesar smiled.

'Fronto, I have planned ahead. One legion and associated auxiliaries should be able to hold them off at Geneva should they not acquiesce to our demands. After that, they will have no choice but to head west along the river and the Roman military will be waiting there for them too. I shouldn't worry too much about missing all the fun, Marcus, as you're one of the key personnel I'm taking with me to Geneva.' He turned back to the others.

'On a more personal note, the Helvetii are one of the most powerful tribes in all the Gauls, and have become complacent and over-familiar in recent years. They constantly cross our border in small groups for mercantile reasons. They seem to have no respect for the frontier and no fear of the might of Rome. Regardless of the tribe's intentions, I will not countenance their crossing into Roman territory and, should they make any attempt to do so, I will meet such a move with equal force.'

Caesar's voice began to drone in the ears of Fronto. He spent some time calculating the hours he had now spent awake. It was, by his rough estimate, somewhere around four in the morning. He had been up at dawn to oversee the drill on the siege engines and had eaten only once, at lunchtime, despite the tasty morsels being offered at the briefing. Moreover, the other officers had caught up on at least an hour, as had the general himself. Almost twenty four hours solid. No wonder things were starting to run together. With a start, Fronto realised his hand had slipped sideways and dark wine had dripped onto his cloak. Prying his eyes open, he forced himself to concentrate on the commander. With a second jolt, he realised that the general had finished.

Caesar leaned back in his chair and steepled his fingers. 'I think that's all, gentlemen... unless there's anything you wish to ask?' The officers remained silent, some shaking their heads until, at a dismissive gesture from the general, they bowed in turn and made their way out of the tent.

As Fronto stood and bowed, trying hard not to let the ornate cloak fall over his head, Caesar gestured to one side. Obediently, Fronto stepped to the side of the tent and waited until the other officers had filed out. With a word, the general also dismissed the two servants, who left through a different flap and into separate quarters. Once they were alone, Caesar heaved a sigh of relief and gestured Fronto back to a chair.

'For the sake of all that's good and sacred, Fronto, please take that cloak off. It's as distracting for me as it is annoying for you.' Caesar reached down to the table by his side and poured two more goblets of wine. Fronto set his eyes on the goblet as he unfastened the last catch of the cloak, and wondered exactly how much wine he had drunk tonight. Certainly more than he should have done on a duty night. And yet his head felt surprisingly clear, if tired, perhaps due to all the exercise, concentration and fresh air. With a smile, he let the cloak drop to the floor and accepted the goblet. Almost as an afterthought, and with pictures of an irate sister swimming in his head, he retrieved the cloak, folded it carefully and placed it by his side.

'Caesar, I appreciate, as always, your private invitation to talk, but I really should be returning to the Tenth and having them stand to.'

The general cast his eyes over the slightly ruffled officer and a smile played around his lips.

'Marcus, how long have we known each other now? I would think the best part of ten years, yes?'

Fronto nodded. 'I would think so sir, yes.'

'In all the time I have seen you in command of a unit, that unit has never been unprepared for anything. I would lay a hefty wager that the Tenth are already standing to. It's not entirely unreasonable to suspect that your juniors are already having the tents pulled down and stowed. I'm well aware that you were half expecting something like this tonight, especially since you were standing outside in answer to my summons almost before I had sent it. That Priscus is a good man. If only he were a man of standing and property, he would be a good choice, I think, to step into your shoes when you try for Senatorial power.'

Fronto growled; a low growl, but nevertheless, Caesar must have heard it. 'I'll never make a politician. I don't have your gift with people.'

Caesar smiled. 'No, perhaps not. But your family will never rest until you achieve some kind of position. Still, in time we may be able to do something about that. You stick with me Marcus, and we'll both go a long way.'

The general stood for a moment and wandered around the tent, casually pausing by the main door and glancing out into the night, before letting the flap fall closed.

'There is no doubt in my mind Marcus that you are exceptionally intelligent and astute for a 'career' soldier. I tend to keep an eye on your behaviour, as it tells me whether I am being too open or too closed, too friendly or too harsh. I also understand that you either know or suspect a great many things that have flown like a flock of geese over the heads of the rest of my command. The time has come to be very frank in our discussions, Marcus. If you will talk straight with me, I will extend you the same courtesy.'

Fronto's eyes darted around the tent nervously. This was the sort of situation that had seen a number of loud-mouthed officers fall from grace in the past few decades. Still, he *had* known Caesar for a long time, and better to open oneself than to be thought secretive.

'Very well sir.'

Caesar once more took his seat and refilled the goblets. 'Tell me what you suspect and I will confirm and clarify for you.'

Fronto swallowed and took a deep breath. 'Here we go,' he thought, 'time to leap from the Tarpeian Rock.' He leaned forward to narrow the distance between the general and himself and spoke in a low, conspiratorial voice.

'General, we go to war against the Helvetians tomorrow, do we not? I know there is a thin veil of embassy over the campaign, but let's see this as soldiers. I cannot believe that you have set up this elaborate trap for anything less than a definitive military action. Permit me to speak *very* freely, sir?'

Caesar nodded.

'You have more ambition than I. Possibly more than anyone alive in the state, including the great Pompey; ambition that could carry Rome to the limits of the earth. I mean no insult by this; I'm merely stating the facts the way I see them. I believe you will find a reason to wage war on the Helvetii, even if they go home in peace. I think you need it for your own personal self-worth, you need it to win the support of those in Rome who currently favour others, and you need it in order to create further opportunities.'

'Further opportunities, Marcus?' Caesar smiled a grim smile and Fronto swallowed again, aware of the danger in which he had just placed himself.

'The Gauls sir. The Helvetii are not important enough for you. Certainly not enough to keep the four legions you have in these provinces busy. No, you want the big fish, sir, don't you? You want the Gauls. It'd be a massive campaign, but that doesn't matter, does it sir? The Gauls are famous. All Romans know them. Many fear them. Most hate them. To destroy the Gauls would be to earn a place in history, sir. Or am I far from the mark?'

Caesar sat silently for a while, swilling the wine around in his cup. After a disturbingly long pause, he once more raised his head and fixed Fronto with his mesmerising stare.

'I was right about you Fronto. You could be exceptionally useful to me, but you could be a dangerous man. Few others have ever spoken to me like that, and none of them have come away better off for the experience. But you? You're career military, with absolutely no pretensions to politics and no designs on Rome, and I find that, against all odds, I actually trust you. Do you know how many people there are in the whole of the empire that I feel I could actually trust? Very few indeed, even in my own family. Very well; you have had your say, and I shall explain.'

'You are, of course, entirely correct in so far as you go. I have no intention of letting the Helvetii go, though we must not be seen to go wading into Gaulish territory unbidden. If we want Gaul, we have to manufacture a reason that will put all of Rome behind us. The Helvetii are merely the key. That idiot noble of theirs, Orgetorix, had worked so hard to bring himself to sole power over the Helvetii, and to create a union with a number of other tribes. If he had succeeded, we would have our reason now.'

Fronto frowned, mulling through the information. He suddenly looked up, his eyes glinting.

'You don't want to destroy the Helvetii at all, do you sir? The legions by the Rhone aren't there to trap them, but to divert them and drive them on. You want them to go west, into Gaul, where they become enough of a danger for you to take the battle to them, yes?'

'Very good, Marcus. Very good indeed. Yes, we need the Helvetii to become enough of a threat to warrant Senatorial approval of our intervention. And once we're deep into Gaul...'

'Nothing can stop us, sir?' Fronto smiled.

'Exactly! I know you have no interest in politics, Marcus, and I know that you're only truly happy when you're involved in a bloodbath, so I trust you won't cause me any trouble?'

'Trouble, sir?'

'Marcus, there are a lot of people who would consider this plan as dangerous; even reckless; and the greatest benefit at the end will be felt by myself and my army. Senators and fat noblemen get very testy when so many resources are put into something with so little visible benefit to them. There are few I can take on campaign with me that I can trust to do everything within their power to achieve the goals we set. I think you are one of them. The Tenth Legion will take prime position among the forces in Further Gaul. I want you and yours to show the Helvetii what it means to face the world's greatest fighting force, and I want the other legions to look at the Tenth and marvel so much that they strain to be like them. Do you understand?'

Fronto's face fell into his usual sour and serious cast. He mulled over, only for moments, what his commander had just implied.

'Caesar, as always, I and the Tenth are at your command.' A small grin passed across his face. 'Although I would respectfully submit that the Tenth already have that effect on their enemies and friends, sir.'

His eyes narrowed again as a thought struck him.

'By the way, sir, I may have drifted off a little toward the end, and I don't remember hearing who was coming with you to Geneva.'

Caesar sighed.

'Longinus, yourself and Tetricus, a tribune from the Seventh. Oh, and that vicious-sounding training officer from your Tenth will be staying behind.'

'Why sir? Why us, when you'll have the commander of the Eighth there with you? Who'll command these three legions on the march? And why is Velius staying here?'

Caesar leaned forward.

'Sometimes I wish you'd listen so that I didn't have to go over the same things twice. Longinus is a good man with cavalry, and we may want his advice on skirmishers and scouts. I'm sure you remember some of his cavalry actions in Spain. Tetricus because he's an old hand at planning defensive earthworks. You because I need you for advice on a command level at the least. And Velius is staying here because of the training needs of the two new legions.'

Fronto's elbow slipped from the chair arm.

'What new legions?'

Another sigh.

'Good grief Marcus, how long were you asleep? I've already had Sabinus out tonight setting up the recruiting staff. I want enough men to create two legions within the week. They will then march to Geneva to meet us with your training officer in command. I hear good things about him.'

Fronto leaned back and then levered himself out of the chair.

'Very well sir. If you would excuse me, I would like to get back and see what Priscus has done in my absence. Our legion insignia's probably pink now. Thank you very much for the wine and your confidence.'

The general nodded as Fronto retrieved his cloak, stood, bowed, and left the tent.

The camp of the Tenth was a flurry of activity as Fronto returned. As he made his way between the cookhouse and the latrines, a legionary wearing only his tunic and covered in pig-grease stains came smartly to attention, almost concussing himself with the tool he carried.

'At ease, soldier. Have you any idea where centurion Priscus is?'

The soldier relaxed and swung the heavy head of the pick-axe to the ground.

'Sir, the centurion is over near the granaries, giving out orders sir.'

With a nod of thanks, Fronto made his way toward the wooden granaries that stood at one end of the Tenth's quarters. Priscus was standing on two of the projecting beams at the base of the granary itself, around two feet off the floor. A standard bearer and three legionaries with excused-duty status stood around his feet with wax tablets, checking and marking as the centurion called out. As Fronto approached with a smile on his face, Priscus waved an arm toward one of the most complex areas of activity. Over the hubbub, he bellowed

'Arius, you piece of horse excrement! Wet side OUT, damn it, wet side OUT!'

Arius, a recent addition to the officer class and the most junior optio of the legion, jumped at hearing his name and dropped the huge, half-folded tent into the mire that was the result of so many pairs of hobnailed boots. The tent fabric landed in the brown liquid with a sucking sound and Arius turned to face Priscus, his face slowly turning purple. The other soldiers laughed raucously as they went about their own efficient business.

Priscus' eyes flashed momentarily and he held his vine staff, one of the centurion's badges of office, in the air. 'There's a vicious battering with this awaiting the next man who laughs at an officer. D'you understand, you swine?'

The soldiers immediately went quietly back to work, and Priscus looked down at one of his helpers.

'How many does that make so far, Nonus?'

The legionary drew the stylus down the list and looked up. 'Twenty eight down and stowed, seven in progress sir.'

As Priscus opened his mouth again, he noticed Fronto standing next to one of the supply wagons with an amused look on his face. He glowered.

'With all respect sir, if you think this is funny, perhaps you'd care to have a try?'

Fronto grinned and stepped forward.

'I've had my fair share of this, Priscus, don't you worry. Oh, and I think you can relax the pace a little. I've just been past the Ninth and they haven't struck a single tent yet. I daresay the Tenth will be eating a hearty breakfast and relaxing on the grass while the other legions are still working. They may complain now, but they'll be happy in the morning.'

'It *is* the morning. Do I take it you'd like the others rounded up sir, for a briefing?'

Fronto nodded. 'I'll be at the bath house on the edge of town. No one else here will have time to use it at the moment, and the locals don't go at this time of night, so it seems a good place for us to have our little meeting. Get them rounded up and in the changing room in about half an hour.'

Priscus returned the nod. 'Nonus, you take charge of this rabble for the time being. I'm going to find the other officers and go meet the legate.'

A quarter of an hour later the officers and senior NCOs of the Tenth met at the changing room of Cremona's secondary bath house. The main baths were in the centre of town, in constant use by the citizens and closed late at night, but another bath had been constructed outside civic limits largely for the use of the military when they came here during the summer months. This one was never closed and rarely visited by civilians, staffed only by soldiers in need of extra pay. Fronto was already lounging in the hot bath when his officers entered. At the sound of their arrival, he raised himself from the steaming water and, wrapping a towel around his waist and shuffling his feet into wooden sandals, made his way through to the steam room, beckoning to Priscus as he did.

Priscus gestured in return with the small amphora of wine he carried. 'Didn't bring any goblets sir. I presume there are some hereabouts?'

'On the table near the entrance, next to the strigils.'

The officers stripped out of their uniforms, none of them wearing armour due to the nature of their current labours and, each pouring himself a goblet of wine, made their way into the baths. No urban complex this; no perfumed Greeks here to scrape the day's dirt away with a strigil. Three of the officers collected the scrapers from a table on their way into the steam room. Within moments all were present among the clouds of steam, seated around the walls, with their eyes on Fronto.

'Gentlemen, you are all aware that we are about to break camp. All the legions and support units will be on the march in a couple of days. I realise that this is relatively short notice after such a prolonged period of inactivity, but it is the intention of our illustrious general to meet the Helvetii, who are of a mind to cross the borders of mighty Rome on their way to another part of Gods-forsaken Gaul and are already on the move. Caesar, along with the Eighth, who are coming up from Massilia, and a few of the senior officers, will be heading for Geneva tomorrow for the initial negotiations and conflicts. The three legions here will make for Vienna and will stay there and await the almost certain arrival of the Helvetii.'

One of the centurions from the Seventh Cohort leaned forward.

'Sir, if he expects a big fight, why not take all the legions to Geneva and finish it there.'

Fronto swallowed. He knew the truth of course, but could not allow word of the general's future plans to leak out. He hated lying to his men.

'The general does not want to meet them in a defensive situation by the river. Siege warfare has rarely been a bonus for the legions. He would much rather drive them into open land and then meet them on a field where our full tactics can come into play. Caesar feels they might need to meet the full force of Rome in order to deter them and, if they will not be deterred, to chastise them appropriately. Do you all get my drift?'

The rest of the room's occupants nodded their understanding, the gestures half-lost in the increasing steaminess of the room. Priscus was the only one to speak.

'Sir, you've heard about these Helvetii. They say they're the fiercest of all the tribes in the east. They're not going to turn round and go home, even if we put all the legions in their way. This is going to come down to a hard fight, and you know it. And I'm sure Caesar will know it. That's why he's preparing a trap, isn't it?'

Fronto smiled a grim smile.

'Very astute Priscus. Yes. I think it's safe to say there's a fair fight coming our way in a few weeks, and I intend the Tenth to be ready for it and to do our traditional job of showing up any other unit in the campaign. To this end, I want all drills doubled, even while on the march. Every evening in camp, the men will be put through their paces. I'm afraid, however, that I'll have to leave the details to you, Priscus. I am one of the people the general intends to take to Geneva, so you'll all be reporting to Priscus here as senior officer. There's a lot of upheaval coming, but I have procured for the legion twenty amphorae of good Campanian wine and two cows for butchering. At the end of every day's march and at the end of the training sessions, the top three men will dine on choice beef and drink good wine as a reward for their efforts.'

Velius, renowned for his crude and occasionally brutal humour and his heartless training techniques, and the only officer to have brought his vine staff into the baths, looked up at his commander.

'Sir. What else? You're not the sort of man to call a meeting in the middle of important work to give us orders you could have given in front of the men and in the morning. What's the murderous bastard got planned for us?'

'Velius,' Fronto replied through gritted teeth, 'your mouth is going to be the death of you. Regardless of your opinions, that is no way to speak of the general, and I'll caution you against doing it again.'

He sighed and looked around.

'You are, on the other hand, entirely correct.'

'This is on a strictly need to know basis, and I believe Caesar would not consider it necessary for you to know. You will not, under any circumstance, pass this information on to another living soul.'

The tension in the room was tangible.

'I can't say too much at this time, but prepare yourselves for a long and drawn-out campaign. I believe it is very unlikely indeed that we will return to Cremona in the near future, or even at all. Sell anything you can't take tonight, and make sure the men aren't carrying useless extras with them.'

'We'll be going on beyond the Helvetii then? Perhaps having a go at the Gauls?' Priscus was nearing the edge of his seat, anticipation clearly audible in his voice.

'I'll give you nothing further, but mark what I said. I don't care if the other legions aren't prepared and have to leave their accumulated goodies to rot in a camp they won't be returning to, but the Tenth will be prepared for anything the general cares to throw us into.'

He turned his gaze to Velius.

'You, however, have a different job. Your optio will be commanding your century on the march. I'm afraid your training talents have been brought to the general's attention. He's raising two new legions here within the week. You will be assigned both of them for training. They will each be given only a partial officer staff for the time being, so you'll be effectively in charge. As soon as you've got them assembled, they're to march on Geneva and meet up with the general's forces there. You'll have to train them on the move and in action, I'm afraid. They'll only receive a senior command unit when they reach Geneva.'

Velius opened his mouth to object, his face already taking on a slightly purple colour. Fronto waved his hand at the centurion; a gesture for silence.

'Now, gentlemen, I'm going to oil down and get clean, then have a refreshing cold bath. Would one of you like to be a bootlicker and get a strigil to help me?'

CHAPTER 2

(AROUND THE CITY OF GENEVA AND THE FORT OF THE 8ᵀᴴ LEGION)

'Honesta Missio: A soldier's honourable discharge from the legions, with grants of land and money, after a term of service of varied length but rarely less than 5 years.'

'Optio: A legionary centurion's second in command.'

'Decurion: 1) The civil council of a Roman town. 2) Lesser cavalry officer, serving under a cavalry prefect, with command of thirty two men.'

It had been a long and gruelling march to this outpost on the edge of the empire. Fronto wandered around the ditch and among the defences outside the ramparts and stockade of the regular summer training camp of the Eighth. They were taking great care to make the camp secure, as the general belief among the common soldiery was that the legion might be staying here for some time. The Eighth, though based in Narbonensis, close to Massilia, were the only legion assigned to Transalpine Gaul and, as such, they were required to make their presence felt along the entirety of the Rhone's east bank, from the Mediterranean to the lake at Geneva. Their summer training quarters were occupied as regularly as their base near Massilia and had all the facilities of a permanent installation.

He glanced over at the frightening form of Balventius, the scarred and partially blinded primus pilus of the Eighth, standing on a wagon and directing a unit of men deepening the defensive ditch. Behind him, the civilian settlement lay sprawled from the river up the slope of the valley, with the summer fort of the Eighth built up against the walls of the town.

Glancing east, Fronto could see small detachments of the legion building a new temporary camp less than a mile distant, and he knew, even though he could not see them, that more soldiers were following suit on the other side of the town. Caesar had decided, quite rightly, that it would save a lot of training time for the two new legions if they arrived to find their camps already prepared. All in all, when the Eleventh and Twelfth turned up, the best part of fifteen thousand heavy infantry would lay in a line a mile and a half to either side of the town of Geneva.

It had been hard to ignore the droves of locals flooding the roads leading south out of Further Gaul, their worldly possessions crammed in carts or strapped to their backs. The legion had been in Geneva for only a few hours, after meeting up with the general's party near Ocelum, but the atmosphere was already tight and nervous. Legions were at their best in open territory, with full scope for manoeuvre. Sieges rendered the heavy shock tactics of the Roman army impossible, and made the officers and the men equally uneasy.

Fronto glanced across the bridge and at the mountains beyond. Somewhere beyond sight, the entire Helvetii tribe was moving and, if Caesar and the fleeing locals were correct in their surmise, the tribe would be coming this way; to this very bridge. The sound of hoof beats behind startled him from his chain of thought.

Caesar reined his white charger in beside his officer and looked down.

'Fronto, I'm going to need you at the headquarters building within the next half an hour. Leave someone else in charge here.'

'Sir.' Fronto nodded, tearing his eyes from the ongoing work.

As the general rode back toward the headquarters building he had commandeered from the legate of the Eighth, Fronto wandered up to the cart.

'Balventius, you're in charge here unless your commander appears.'

Fronto turned his eyes to the bridge once more as he walked toward the fort's west gate. He could not shake off the feeling that the Helvetii were already there, watching him. He amused himself for a few moments watching the engineers working on digging lilia by the gate. Unaware that there was an officer nearby, their language was crude and violent, and shovelfuls of mud and clods of earth flew in seemingly random arcs from the depths of the ditch. The Eighth had been raised almost sixty years ago for the protection of Cisalpine Gaul and the Northern provinces after the victories of Rome over the Allobroges and the founding of Geneva as a Roman city. With the civil wars earlier in the century and the frantic raising and disbanding of legions throughout this turbulent time, few legions could claim a heritage that long. The Seventh, Ninth and Tenth were of much the same age, and Fronto had seen a marked similarity between the men of the Ninth and Tenth between commands. There was such a similarity again between his own Tenth and this Eighth Legion. He had heard tales of the commander of the Eighth, an old career soldier who had managed to achieve a remarkably long period in command of one unit. The men around Fronto now could just as easily have been his men. He smiled. Despite having commanded the Tenth for little over a year, Fronto already felt very close to his men and, he thought with more than a little pride, his men seemed to feel a similar bond with their commander. A clod of earth landed on the toe of his boot.

A short while later, the commander of the Tenth arrived at the headquarters building at the centre of the Eighth Legion's summer base. Standards, flags and pennants stood and hung outside. A staff officer Fronto did not know came to the door and waved them inside. Fronto removed his helmet, placing it in the crook of his arm and falling into step behind the unknown staff officer.

Caesar sat in his own campaign chair behind a desk littered with records. Standing around him were various secretaries and officials of the city and, seated to one side were Longinus and Tetricus, along with Balbus, the legate of the Eighth. Although he and Fronto had never met, the Eighth was an experienced and decorated legion, and Balbus' reputation preceded him. Fronto gave him a respectful nod, which was returned as Balbus stood to acknowledge their arrival. The other legion commander was a lot older than Fronto, with a receding hairline and a round face. He looked rather jolly to Fronto, as though he should really be sitting at the theatre in a toga, rather than here in a cuirass. Tetricus was middle-aged with a shock of dark hair above a pale and serious face. Longinus had the same disapproving expression he habitually wore.

Caesar was deeply involved with one of the secretaries, and Fronto waited what seemed an age before the general closed his wax tablet and the attendants hurried from the room.

'Ah Fronto, sorry about that. Would you take a seat, please?'

The officer made his way to one of the chairs around the large central table, while Caesar continued to put the documents away in order.

'I'm very busy this morning, so this will have to be brief. I have sent a request out this morning to the decurions of Geneva and the surrounding settlements, asking them to furnish me with every available able-bodied man. I intend to raise a number of auxiliary units here, some of which will become attached to the Eleventh and Twelfth, who should be arriving in two days, according to my latest information. A legion will not be necessary to look after this area once the Helvetii leave. Therefore, I intend to leave several auxiliary units here under the command of the decurions of Geneva once we move.'

Balbus nodded at the general thoughtfully.

'Things are heating up here,' Caesar continued, 'and they will only get worse. The Seventh, Eighth, Ninth and Tenth, along with the two new legions, have to be available to cover other areas of our northern border and to campaign wherever necessary, and so I must raise troops here as long as the manpower is available. I will, of course, need men from the Eighth to begin the training of the new units as soon as they are assembled. I would think we will have enough for two or three within the next week.'

Longinus sat silently, and Tetricus looked distinctly uncomfortable in the combined presence of so many superior officers. Fronto opened his mouth to speak, but Balbus pitched in before him.

'Caesar, I appreciate that there has been no problem with the raising of your two legions at Aquileia, and that there may be no problem with raising auxiliary units here, but there are a couple of factors I would like to draw to your attention.'

Caesar nodded at him.

'Go ahead Balbus.'

'Firstly, it will cost us to raise any troops here. Geneva is not a wealthy city, so any funding of units and extra equipment they need will have to come from us. Also, we are expecting the Helvetii any time now. We will not have time to give the auxiliaries anything more than the most basic of training, and they will remain in that state when we leave, which is dangerous for the security of the frontier.'

Caesar frowned.

'Funding will not be a problem. My retinue brought a chest of denarii with them, raised in Rome for the very purpose of support of my governorship. This is to be used sparingly, as it has to last, but should certainly be enough to cover these units.'

Balbus nodded approvingly, and the general continued.

'I had not fully appreciated the problem of training time, this is true. However, I will find a way to delay them. Would two weeks extra be enough to get them through the basic drills do you think gentlemen?'

Fronto nodded. 'Given the training manpower, three to four weeks in total should be enough to at least make them useful, if not competent. We would obviously have to devote their training specifically to the type of work and warfare we are expecting here. I think that gives us a little edge. I'll confirm everything with Velius when he arrives.'

'Good.' Caesar smiled at the Tenth's legate.

As the general continued talking, he leaned down to the table and began to write furiously. 'Fronto, I am placing Velius in charge of the training of all new units we can furnish in Further Gaul while still in the province. When he arrives, have him quarter the legions and then report to me.'

Caesar cast his eyes over the records and then looked up once more, this time focusing on Tetricus.

'Tribune, I want you to take charge of the engineering works here. Regardless of our defensive position behind the river, there are ways the Helvetii could outflank or otherwise outmanoeuvre us. The land between the lake and Mount Jura is unsecured, so I want a wall and ditch constructed between the two, close to the river's south bank.'

Tetricus' eyes widened. 'Sir, that's nearly twenty miles!'

'Yes, but the army has embarked on more ambitious projects than that before and succeeded. I want you to take the best engineers from the Eighth, along with as many labourers as you need, and start surveying for the best sites. There's plenty of time, but I want the initial construction to be underway by the end of tomorrow. I will leave it to the discretion of you two as to how many men you can reasonably take for the job. I just want it done as quickly as possible.'

Caesar's eyes moved on to Fronto.

'That means that you get the other engineering project, Marcus. I want the bridge completely dismantled. It's a weak spot in our defences, and I need it removed. It'll be a large task, as it's a Roman bridge and not one of the local ramshackle constructions. Go with Tetricus and select some of the engineers for the task. In fact, I want you to liaise with the tribune on every aspect of the defences. Tetricus may be very clever and experienced with fortifications, but you will need to make sure that anything he comes up with is suitable for the disposition of the men.'

Fronto nodded.

'Of course, sir.'

He turned to Tetricus.

'I suggest we take a walk down by the bridge and the river before we go and sort the personnel out.'

Tetricus nodded respectfully.

'Perhaps sir, but I will need a little time first. I need to take stock of all our assets before we begin planning. I do think perhaps it would be better if we found our engineers first. They may have useful suggestions.'

Fronto shrugged.

'You're the expert.'

Smiling benignly, the general turned to face the older commander of the group.

'Balbus, you know this territory and its people better than anyone here. I need you to liaise between all the more senior officers here and myself. I want you to give a great deal of attention to the maps and find any holes in our strategy, any weak spots, or anything else of which I have not taken account. Moreover, I want you and Fronto to come up with a reasonable plan for the disposition of the Eighth Legion and two training legions along the river and the defences Tetricus will be constructing. This brings me to you, Longinus.'

The commander of the Ninth frowned.

'Sir, I can't really understand why I'm here and not with my legion.'

Caesar leaned back in his chair.

'I want you to command the cavalry attached to the Eighth, separately, along with the mounted auxiliary units. You will be in charge of placing scouts and running mounted patrols on the other side of the river and along the lake shore. Should there be a serious engagement, I will want you commanding the cavalry there too.'

He smiled with satisfaction.

'I will continue to base myself here, and the four of you will have access day or night. If I am asleep and you need me for anything, speak to one of my adjutants and they will wake me. I think that just about covers it unless any of you have a question or comment?'

As the four officers in the room remained silent, shaking their heads, Caesar nodded and dismissed them.

At the front door of the headquarters building Longinus split off to find the Eighth's cavalry prefect, and Balbus spoke directly to Fronto for the first time; his voice deep, soft and weary.

'I get the impression from what Caesar says that your man Velius is a fair asset. He's obviously not even considering my training officer.'

Fronto nodded, examining Balbus' face for signs of disapproval, but the older man appeared to be stating it as fact rather than making a complaint.

'He's a good man. A little too straight talking some times, but that can be useful. Caesar knows what he can do. The Tenth was undermanned when I took control and around a third of the legion were new recruits a month ago. Velius had them working together like veterans in no time. We have some good men in the Tenth.'

He smiled. 'If it's alright with you, I'll head off with Tetricus now and find some men.'

Tetricus, following the other two at a respectful distance, cleared his throat. Fronto turned.

'Tetricus, we're not Senators; we're soldiers. If we're going to work together this next couple of weeks, you're going to have to relax a little. For a start, you can call me Marcus, and you can walk *with* us, rather than behind us.'

31

'Yes Marcus. It just feels a bit odd. Crassus doesn't approve of his tribunes addressing him as anything other than sir.'

Balbus smiled.

'Crassus is very young. Once he's fought across the continent and acquired arthritis in two or three joints, he'll settle down like Marcus and I. And call me Quintus, too.'

Tetricus smiled. 'I'm Gaius.'

Balbus patted Tetricus on the shoulder. 'We have some good men in the Eighth too, but they're used to being the only ones in the province. You'll have to put your foot down with them. They may be a little put out at being assigned to another officer, even if he's appointed by Caesar. They're proud of the Eighth and of being the guardians of civilisation here in the north.'

Fronto grinned.

'And so they should be, legate. The Eighth has a fairly fearsome reputation. I remember when I went to Spain and later joined the Ninth, the Eighth were regularly reported to be involved in some sort of action up here, and the name Balbus was already spoken of highly in command circles that long ago. You must have been with them a long time. Have you never considered taking political office?'

Balbus smiled one of his rare smiles.

'Marcus, my officers have been jumping for a week, ever since we knew Caesar was coming. The men stand in awe of the general but, though you may not be aware, your reputation carries at least as far and as fast as mine. Our career centurions already know who to watch for. Things tend to shake up wherever you go, and those in the know say you have the ear of Caesar beyond all others.'

'I don't know about that, but the general and I have known each other a long time, and he seems to trust me. I think I'm just too set in my ways to be unpredictable and dangerous. Mark my words, Quintus, that man is dangerous. Brilliant and charismatic, but dangerous. There's one legion here, with two on the way, which is fine, but there are three more legions gathering at Vienna and more auxiliaries being raised. That kind of force is not used to swat flies. He's building an invasion army, and that should be plainly obvious to anyone with a strategic background. He'll either lead us to glorious victory, or to an unprecedented bloodbath. Likely a little of both.'

Fronto suddenly remembered that Tetricus was with them. Turning, he narrowed his eyes.

'Needless to say, this is all in strict confidence, Gaius.'

Balbus shrugged. 'What will be, will be, Marcus.' He paused for a moment at the crossroads by the granaries and collared an optio, who came immediately to attention.

'Optio, find Helvius and bring him to me at my quarters.'

He turned to the other two. 'Care for a drink while we wait for my chief engineer?'

'Why not,' Fronto grinned.

Tetricus shook his head.

'Thank you for the offer sir, but I really must run a survey of our resources if we're going to plan any works. Perhaps you could have someone find me at the stores when you've spoken to your senior engineer?'

Balbus nodded and the young tribune jogged off toward the storehouses.

As the two legates entered the commander's house, Fronto admired the building. The summer training base of the Eighth had been in use now for well over a decade and had become a second home for the legion. Certainly, it seemed to have become a such for their commander. Essentially a small villa, Balbus' quarters were an oasis of peace in the middle of a muddy military base.

'Must be nice to be based somewhere often enough to make something of it. We use a different training site every time we leave Aquileia, so they're always the same old muddy shit-holes. You've got walls around you and a ceiling above. We seem to spend around eight months sweating under leather tents and then four months in winter quarters. Nice place you have.'

Balbus smiled again. 'A nice little 'home away from Rome', you might say. Corvinia lives in Massilia, but she comes here with me during the summer. I think she does her best to pretend she doesn't live in a fort, though I don't believe she's ever considered living in Rome either. She's a country girl from Campania, and I think she likes the open spaces too much.' He ducked to avoid a plant trailing from a basket on the wall. 'You've never married, have you Marcus?'

'I never had the time. Perhaps if I'd followed the cursus honorum, I might have done. I don't think I'm much of a catch these days, frankly.'

They reached the dining room, and Fronto was surprised to see a decent repast already set out on the table, with wine at the ready. Balbus registered the look on Fronto's face and smiled.

'My wife thought the general might grace us with a visit, so she's permanently prepared. I daresay she won't mind if we dig in.' The legate pulled a dish of sweet meats toward them across the table.

'Anyway Marcus, I think you're putting yourself down. I never tried to climb the political ladder myself, and yet I caught a wife and ended up with three children. A good solid military man is worth ten young lunatics who command a legion as merely a step to bleeding Rome dry in a political role. Take that Longinus of the Ninth. In a year or two, he'll be in Rome, probably making policy decisions that affect the rest of us, and the man couldn't command a cohort, let alone a legion.'

Fronto stopped, mid-mouthful.

'I didn't realise you knew Longinus? But I suppose you must do to have formed such an accurate opinion of him. He's never been very happy with having had to replace me in the Ninth. I think it took the best part of a year for his officers to stop laughing at him. As an infantry commander he's a bit of a donkey; doesn't know one end of a pilum from the other. Pretty good with cavalry though, Caesar's right about that. Do you know Crassus too?'

Balbus frowned. 'Legate of the Seventh eh? I've heard of him, of course. The son of one of Caesar's most rich and influential friends, given a command through pure nepotism. I don't like that much, but it's the way of things.'

'He's the one my sister likes to compare me with, because he actually cares about climbing the political ladder. He's using his command to catapult himself into politics. Although he's a competent enough officer, I suppose, I doubt he'll ever make a great commander. Too indecisive.'

'Ah, a ditherer.' Balbus took a drink of wine and then looked up as a slave coughed politely on the threshold.

'Yes?'

'Centurion Helvius here to see you sir' the slave said, in good Latin, with a hint of a Greek accent.

'Show him in.'

Helvius was an impossibly tall and thin man, with a receding hairline and a nose that had been broken badly at some time in the distant past. He ducked as he crossed into the dining room and remained low for a moment in a bow. Standing, his eyes fell on Fronto. Balbus waved an arm expansively toward Fronto, a chicken leg in his grip.

'Helvius, this is Marcus Fronto, legate of the Tenth.'

'I suspected as much, sir.' The centurion turned and bowed to Fronto. 'I'm honoured to make your acquaintance, legate.'

'Pleased to meet you too, Helvius.' He glanced at Balbus, who waved him on, taking another mouthful of bread.

'I don't want to disrupt things too much for you, Helvius, but I'm afraid I need to take the best of your engineers and sappers for a time.'

Helvius' brow creased. 'Sir?'

'Here's what I want...'

The morning was bright and crisp; chilly, but not quite freezing. Fronto stamped his feet and blew into his hands until a little colour returned to them. Standing where he was, on the end of the earth embankment that projected out into the lake, he could see down the almost perfectly straight line of ditch and rampart into the distance. He could not see the other end, of course, not now, but he knew it was extending at a backbreaking pace. He had left Helvius in charge of that end now, and had come to trust the competent engineer of the Eighth enough to leave him be. He instead had returned to the length of defences near Geneva to oversee the next stage. The construction of the palisade formed from nine foot-tall sharpened logs was beginning. Fronto had split the remaining men at this end into four groups. One was spending most of its time on the hills behind Geneva to which Tetricus had directed him, cutting down trees and shaping them into useful timber. The second had begun the palisade. The third were taking shortened stakes, sharpening them to a vicious point and sinking them into the ditch. The final group were constructing a redoubt, the first of several, in the form of a small, square fort near the water's edge. Fully supplied with ditch and mound and their own palisade, these forts would be focal points for the disposition of troops that Balbus had ordered. Indeed, the locations of the forts had been chosen by the Eighth's legate in line with his plan.

Tetricus stood not far away, holding a map that threatened to escape, fluttering in the wind. He was explaining to an engineer from the Eighth Legion where the forts were to be constructed and to what size and composition. Fronto put his hands around his mouth to amplify his voice.

'Gaius! Don't forget the gate. I think it needs to be about a mile from the lake.'

Tetricus waved back, acknowledging him, exchanged a few more brief words with the engineer and then began to trudge up toward the embankment.

By the time he reached the legate, he was breathing hard, the plumes of air frosting in the morning chill.

'Word's come down from Helvius sir. He's almost in Sequani territory. Fourteen miles now, and he thinks only five to go before the territory doesn't warrant ditch and ridge. Six days for fourteen miles so far, so he should be finished in two or three, then they'll start palisading back this way until we meet. The majority of the work now is going to be palisading and fort building.'

Fronto grinned. 'The old man's going to be happy with us, Gaius. We're ahead of schedule, and the defences are a step up on what he asked for. I think we need to take the wall down about a hundred paces into the lake, until it's too deep for wading. Also, keep the palisade in sections and held down behind the embankment. That's the last thing to put in place, and if it's held in sections with troops nearby, they can be hoisted up and hammered in along the entire length in moments.'

Tetricus nodded, glancing out into the lake, his hand sheltering his eyes from the bright, cold light. Scanning the horizon, as he had taken to doing for the last three days, his gaze settled on a century of men jogging round the end of the lake, coming their way and wearing full kit; new recruits freshly arrived with the Tenth's training officer yesterday.

'Velius seems to be having fun sir.'

Fronto followed his gaze and spotted the exhausted trainees carrying their sacks full of rocks. The training centurion ran alongside them. To his credit, he was carrying nearly twice the weight they were.

'He takes everything so personally. Running recruits until they throw up is a job he could easily have delegated to one of the lesser training officers.'

Tetricus laughed. 'I think he just likes to watch recruits vomit.'

'You may be right.' Fronto held up a hand and waved to Velius. The centurion saluted back, barked an order at the front row of victims and turned to run up the embankment.

'Morning, sir.' Velius was as red faced as if he had come straight out of the warm room of a bath house. He dropped the pack to the ground and hoisted his vine staff under his arm.

Fronto cast an appraising glance over the training officer. Velius was old enough to have received his honesta missio from the Tenth several times over, but the other officers generally held that the centurion would remain the legion's training officer until he dropped dead on duty. A lot of people were unsure as to how to deal with Velius, though Fronto liked his gruff no-nonsense attitude.

'Velius, how's it going? Will they be capable of manning the wall in a week or two and frightening the Helvetii away?'

Velius made a sour face and spat on the ground.

'I reckon it'll take a fortnight to teach them to walk in the same bloody direction. Did you see that run, sir? Two of them fell in the lake. In armour! Have you any idea how difficult it is to haul a fully armoured and equipped man out of four feet of water?'

'I thought you'd have them accurate on a ballista by now, Velius. You've trained more men than I've had dinners.'

'I don't know about that, sir. You eat every meal like it was a condemned man's last. I've never tried training more than a cohort's worth of men at a time, and now we're talking twenty times that many, with half the training staff I normally have. And they're all soft boys sir. Still, I reckon another week and we'll see a bit of a change in them.'

Fronto glanced with subconscious unease toward the mountains on the other side of the earthworks.

'I hope so, Velius. I really hope so. I don't like siege warfare in any conditions, but being trapped and forced to defend is a situation I would rather avoid.'

'I think…' Velius faltered as he realised Fronto was no longer listening to him and, sheltering his eyes, looked in the same direction as his commander. Tetricus followed suit immediately.

A single rider was charging full pelt down the hill toward the camps.

Fronto grimaced. 'I feel I should be shouting 'Open the Gate', but we don't have any gates yet!'

Tetricus began madly waving the horseman to the very eastern end of the embankment, to avoid a mad dash into the dangerous ditch. The horseman complied at the last moment, pushing his exhausted horse through the ankle deep water and dismounting on the beach behind the embankment. The horseman, one of the scouts Longinus had set in commanding positions around the lake end, staggered up to Fronto, as the highest ranking officer present.

'Sir, I have to report the Helvetii on the move sir.' With that, he collapsed to a seated position on the ground, breathing heavily and in bursts.

Fronto crouched opposite him.

'How many, man?'

The scout looked up at him, plumes of frosted breath momentarily obscuring his face.

'All of them, I would say sir.'

Tetricus called down from the top of the embankment, where he had remained.

'Sir, two more riders on the way. I'd say from the directions they're coming that we can assume the Helvetii are less than an hour away.'

Fronto sprang into action.

'Tetricus, send someone over to Helvius. Let him know what's happening and then form up all the units of the Eighth we've got working here. I'll find Balbus and get him to send the Second Cohort over and give the engineers any protection they need. When you're done, come and find me at Caesar's headquarters.'

He turned to the training officer.

'Velius. Get both the new units into full dress and parade formation right where I'm standing. They don't have to be veterans; they just have to look like them. Oh, and when these scouts and their horses have recovered for a moment, send them to Longinus with a message to form up.'

With that he was off at a run toward the town and the garrison fort of the Eighth Legion. As he approached the north gate of the fort, a legionary stepped out into the gateway, challenging Fronto.

Fighting to restrain his irritation, Fronto slowed to a stop and gave the password, identifying his name, rank and unit. The soldier immediately stepped aside, and he ran on toward the headquarters building at the centre of the fort.

Inside, the building had changed tremendously since Fronto and his men had had their briefing here less than a week ago. The rooms that had before been occupied by pay staff and accounts clerks had been cleared out, with all such mundane offices now located in the small annexe to the west of the fort. The rooms were now occupied by staff officers and the senior officers of the Eighth. Two large rooms had been devoted entirely to the officers of the newly raised Eleventh and Twelfth, there being a large amount of organisation and records involved in such a task. The officers had been drawn from the centurionate of the current four legions or the general staff. Aquilius, the Eighth's chief training officer (and Velius' current second in command) occupied the same room, trying to organise the newly raised officers into an effective command unit. From what Fronto had heard, Balbus himself had been giving advice and pointers to the new officers, which could only help, given the legate's lengthy experience in command.

Maps and documents lined the walls as Fronto made his way through the busy, hectic and overcrowded headquarters to Caesar's office.

A Greek-speaking slave attempted to arrest Fronto's progress at the general's door, but Fronto ignored him and banged loudly twice on the door.

'General?'

Caesar's clear and commanding voice came from within.

'Fronto? Come in.'

Angrily pushing the Greek slave to one side, Fronto hammered the catch up and, swinging the door back, stepped in. Remembering his etiquette just in time, he skidded to a halt on the marble and came up straight, saluting. Caesar had not even looked up. From his campaign chair, with his eyes scanning a document, the general addressed his officer.

'Yes, legate?'

'The Helvetii sir. They're approaching the lake. I would estimate less than an hour away. I've made all the arrangements I could on the way sir.'

A second voice asked 'How are the new recruits looking, Marcus?'

Fronto swung around to see Balbus sitting in a dark corner.

'They'll be useful enough, Quintus, never fear about that.'

Caesar finally looked up.

'Take a seat, man, for heavens' sake. If they're an hour away and you've informed everyone that needs to be organised, then we have a few moments yet.' He turned to Balbus. 'Do go on.'

Balbus cleared his throat. 'Not much left to say, Caesar. The first two cohorts of the Eighth will continue to occupy this site until we are faced with immediate confrontation, at which point they can be through the north gate and at the wall in about the time it takes to lace a pair of boots, where they will spread out and occupy the three miles closest to the lake. The Third Cohort will play rearguard, covering the eastern end of the settled area, from the lakeshore up to the mountain road. The Fourth to Seventh Cohorts will be given the six miles of defences at the far end, near Mount Jura, and the Eighth to Tenth will take the central section. The Eleventh and Twelfth Legions will be positioned to overlap. They will be split by cohort but never too far from the rest of their legion and close to a more experienced unit. This defence may be eighteen miles or so, but that way we'll have fifteen thousand men covering it. If all else fails, the Third Cohort will be within an hour's march of the defences, should we need them. I cannot foresee a circumstance in which the Helvetii, even if they come full force, can break such a defence. And by the way, sir; Fronto's excelled himself with the quality of the defences.'

'Has he indeed?' Caesar smiled. 'I know how much you hate taking a defensive position, Fronto. I also know that that means you will put together the best possible system. Why on earth do you think I assigned an engineer's job to you otherwise? You know what you want and Tetricus knows how to put it together for you.'

Fronto blinked and Caesar continued.

'If I'd given it to Longinus, who loves standing high in a fortified position and looking down on assailants, the defences would have been average at best, if not substandard.'

Balbus laughed out loud.

'Caesar, all this aside, my disposition reports can wait. We should head to the lake and prepare to meet the Helvetii.'

'Indeed, legate; indeed. Very well, Fronto? Lead us to your magnificent defences.' With that the other two officers rose and followed Fronto from the room.

Word of the messenger must have spread quickly for, as Fronto and his two companions passed through the headquarters and the fort, various high-ranking officers came out to join them, falling in behind Caesar and the two legates.

Fronto was impressed to note that Balventius had assembled the Eighth's officers and given out the call to fall in before Balbus had even left the headquarters building. Here, he thought, was a legion who could actually give the Tenth a run for their money.

Once they had left the fort's gate and were moving down toward the defences, he was equally pleased to see that Tetricus had managed to get the engineers from the Eighth back into their units and in position near the lake and that the still slightly disorganised Eleventh and Twelfth were forming up on either side of the Eighth under the direction of Velius. The four short lengths of palisade that had been constructed lay in place on the slope, ready to be hoisted into position at short notice. To all intents and purpose the defences looked to be a mere ditch and embankment. The mass of troops forming in the area of the ridge, on the other hand, suggested differently.

Another scout had arrived shortly before the officers reached the wall, confirming that the Helvetii were around a quarter of an hour away.

Caesar smiled and looked around at the army massing.

'Splendid. All our forces will be marshalled and in formation by the time they get here. Fronto, have all the senior officers report to me. Let's show these barbarians who they're up against.'

Fronto jogged down to Balbus, positioned with the standard bearers of the Eighth, and had a word with him before running back up to join the general. Moments later, a horn call rang out in the still air.

When the Helvetii came, they came in their thousands, pouring through the valley mouth at the other side of the river, and flooding onto the plain before the defences. With many an indrawn breath, the three legions stood firm and in formation, themselves covering a vast area between the lake, the defensive bank and the town itself. In front, on top of the embankment stood the general himself, Julius Caesar, with his echelons of command.

The Helvetii spread out as they came to more level ground. Their movement was slow and steady and made no suggestion of an attack or, indeed, a provocative move of any sort. As the remnants at the back of the tribe began the descent toward the lake, the front ranks opened up and two men came forward, backed by a small group of high-ranking tribesmen.

The two men were very well dressed for barbarians, Fronto thought. Their clothes were not dissimilar to those worn by the people of Cisalpine or Transalpine Gaul, within the empire. Their tunics, which were of an obviously Roman cut, their cloaks, and much of their jewellery had obviously been purchased from Roman merchants. The man on the left wore a gladius, the Roman short sword, and a pugio dagger at his other hip, in the manner of a legionary. The chain mail shirts they wore were of high quality manufacture, probably again from within the empire. While their breeches were of a Gaulish cut and pattern, the overall effect was far more disturbingly civilised than Fronto had expected. From the low mumbling among the ranks, others had drawn similar conclusions. Balbus turned his head slightly and made a cut-throat motion at Balventius, standing in command position of the Eighth.

Balventius turned to face the men and raised his voice only slightly above the unavoidable noise of armour and cold men.

'Be quiet lads. Can't you see there are officers present?'

Balbus turned his head back to face the advancing embassy. The two men ran to the highest piece of land available close to the Romans, a slight rise on the shore of the lake, where a tree overhung the water. They stepped as high as possible, though they were still forced to look up at the Roman officers. Their 'honour guard', presuming that is what they were, stopped just short of the raised ground.

The man on the left called out in a clear and powerful voice. Fronto was surprised to hear reasonably well-spoken Latin, though he should really have expected it. He could not think what they would have hoped to achieve if they spoke only barbarian tongues.

'I am Numeius of the Helvetii. My companion is Verudoctius. We are chieftains and men of note.' The one called Verudoctius bowed and, straightening, saluted Caesar with a Roman gesture. 'We do not wish to make war on Rome or its esteemed generals. All we ask is leave to pass through the territory of your mighty empire to the lands of our brothers that you call the Gauls.'

Numeius in turn bowed and gave a Roman salute.

Caesar glanced at Balbus for a moment, then at Fronto. Very quietly; far too quietly for the Helvetii to hear, he said 'If I said Gauls to you, what would your reply be?'

Balbus and Fronto looked at each other. Balbus spoke first. 'The Gauls destroyed Rome. They cannot be trusted.' Fronto nodded, adding 'defilers and vandals.'

Caesar smiled at them both. Fronto had seen that smile once in a Northern Spanish winter, on the face of a wolf starved half to death, and coming upon an injured legionary. He shuddered. Caesar was gauging his officers before his reaction.

The general stood for the first time since the emissaries had arrived.

'You call the Gauls your brothers, and well you might. The Gauls once destroyed our city; defecated in our holy places. Kinship with these people is unlikely to advance your case, barbarian.'

The two ambassadors glanced at each other for only a moment before Numeius came back with a formulaic excuse.

'That was centuries ago, Roman, and different tribes. We are not Gauls, and even those Gauls that now live are different, after centuries of peace, to the ones you speak of.'

Caesar laughed. Laughed so hard he sat back down in a carefully positioned command chair.

'Peace? You dare speak to me of peace? Rome had a Consul named Lucius Cassius. Are you familiar with the name?'

For a moment, the two conferred, a look of worry passing between them.

'This name is not familiar to us, Roman.'

Caesar stood once more, the colour rising in his cheeks.

'Damn you barbarian for a liar. Of course you know him. It wasn't that long ago your people killed him and tortured and enslaved many a Roman in his army! Cassius was beloved of the Roman people, and you murdered him. You claim you are a peaceful people. Pah! I have no time for this.' Standing, Caesar made to walk away, winking at Fronto as he turned away from the speakers.

The two conferred again, but only for a moment.

'Roman, there have been many confrontations between our peoples in the past. We are here now only in peace. We request only the time to pass through to our allies.'

Caesar wheeled on the spot.

'Go through the Jura pass, through your other allies. Begone!'

The increasing desperation of the ambassadors was evident not only in Numeius' voice, but also in the speed with which the reply came back.

'We cannot pass that way because of many tribal differences and the difficulty of the route. We vouchsafe Roman lands and would cause no trouble or mischief upon our crossing.' With an urgent tone, Verudoctius spoke up for the first time, earning him an evil glare from his counterpart.

'Great general, we have brought with us on this journey everything we have; everything we are. For your assurances of safe passage, we can give gifts to the Roman people that would earn you a place in their heart.'

For a moment, and just for a moment, Caesar was actually speechless. Fronto could understand. He was under no illusion. This plan of the general's was not greatly for the good of Rome, or even the legions, but for the good of Caesar. What he wished to achieve with a war was being handed to him on a plate by the barbarians, but he would lose face if he came this far and relented. The other officers held their breath.

Caesar turned to the officers, gave them a meaningful look, and then addressed the Helvetii once again, this time loud enough for the whole tribe to hear.

'Chieftains, I will deliberate on this matter. Go away from this place, where trouble will brew between our two armies, to a place of refuge and return, if you still require passage, on the day before the ides of Aprilis, which is the twelfth day to you.'

With that the general turned away from the ambassadors and marched down the embankment. The officers turned and followed him, leaving only sentries on the raised earth.

'That should give them something to think about, and give us time to train the new legions and complete the defences gentlemen, yes?'

Longinus' jaw dropped.

'Caesar, you cannot be suggesting we refuse their offer? Think of the booty we can take back to Rome for a simple two weeks' escort duty!'

The general gave Longinus a distasteful look. 'You would bargain with the murderers of a Roman Consul, Longinus? I thought you had more about you than that. Pull yourself together and stop thinking of money. Revenge is the order of the day.'

The general turned to look up at the sentry who was still standing atop the mound. 'Soldier! What is happening among the Helvetii?'

The sentry turned and saluted. 'There's some heated conversation going on sir. I think they're confused.'

'Good. Keep an eye on them. If they move away, send someone to inform me and have the scouts placed back in position. If they move in this direction, sound the alarm. Fronto? Balbus? Come with me.'

Chapter 3

(Along the bank of the Rhone)

'Primus Pilus: The chief centurion of a legion. Essentially the second in command of a legion.'

'Capsarius: Legionary soldiers trained as combat medics, whose job was to patch men up in the field until they could reach a hospital.'

'Vienna: Latin name for the modern town of Vienne, in the Rhone Valley.'

Fronto and Tetricus surveyed their handiwork. The green embankment continued nineteen miles to the west from here. The height inevitably varied but was generally around fifteen feet. Only a single pace lay between the wall and a ditch six feet deep which, itself, was only five or ten paces from the river bank. Such was the defensive system that Caesar had ordered. Fronto and Tetricus had gone a step beyond with their handiwork. The ditch was lined with a deadly carpet of sharpened points, and the lilia, small concealed pits each housing a pointed stake, were strategically placed between the bank and ditch. On the top of the bank, an eight foot palisade covered the entire length of the system, with only three gates, set five or six miles apart. Fort-like structures lay at regular intervals along the wall, small redoubts in which a large number of soldiers could be based. All in all it was a system any Roman commander would be happy with. Any commander except Fronto, at least. He turned to Tetricus.

'What happens if they come across the lake in boats?'

Tetricus sighed. He was getting a little sick of Fronto's pessimism.

'Sir, there aren't enough boats in the whole province to get a tribe that big across a lake this size.'

'And if they go *round* the lake?'

'Through territory hostile to them? Then the Third Cohort can earn their pay, can't they sir.'

Fronto cleared his throat with an irritated twitch and stamped his feet. The morning was cold, and weeks of chill had penetrated so deep into his bones that he felt he might never be warm again. He was already wearing his thick woollen tunic, scarf and cloak. His breeches were the special heavy and slightly longer ones than he usually wore, and he had taken to wearing the heavier of his pairs of boots.

A soldier came running up the embankment, the frosty grass crunching under his feet. At the top he came to attention, breathing heavily.

'Sir, centurion Velius requests permission to bring a detachment onto the defences.'

Fronto eyed the soldier, one of Velius' raw recruits, surely. He was correctly equipped and well turned out, had come to attention particularly formally, and only his accent betrayed him. He could easily have been a soldier from the Tenth. There was no doubt; Velius knew his job and had performed it excellently.

'Very well soldier, tell Velius his unit has permission to approach.'

'Sir!' The soldier turned sharply and began pounding back down the hill, leaving an arcing trail of footprints on the whitened grass.

Tetricus watched him go and turned to the commander.

'I think we should send Velius on a tour round the empire. Within a month we'd have several million well-trained men.'

Fronto smiled. 'Yes, but who'd make the wine and ferry it to us if everyone was a soldier?'

Moments later, Velius came round the corner of the nearest redoubt. Following him were two detachments of troops, each with a centurion. One unit bore the standard of the Eleventh, and one the Twelfth. The units marched at double speed and in good formation to the embankment, where they drew up sharply. Velius addressed the two officers on the wall.

'Sir, request permission to demonstrate the techniques of Roman defensive engineering to these men who've been selected as the first engineer units of the Eleventh and Twelfth.'

Fronto smiled at Tetricus and then turned, straight faced, to address the training officer.

'Go ahead centurion, we're just leaving anyway.'

As the two began a gentle walk down the slope, Velius barked out a few orders to the new units, who fell into a more relaxed stance.

'You will notice the height of the bank, and the gradient that has been achieved...'

Velius' voice faded into the distance as the two made their way back toward the fort.

Fronto shaded his eyes and looked ahead to the camp.

'Are the Eighth nearly ready to move, I can't see well in this light, but it looks like everything is still in position.'

Tetricus squinted in the same direction.

'They're almost ready to move sir. Give them an hour and they'll have all those tents down. Problem is: half the men who organise these things are still babysitting the Eleventh and Twelfth. I presume those men will be back with their unit as soon as all the legions are in position.'

Fronto made a low grumbling noise deep in his throat.

'I hope so, Gaius. Caesar hasn't committed himself to anything yet, or at least isn't admitting to it. Any time I ask him about the next move he just taps the side of that enormous nose and winks. He doesn't like to be anticipated in anything.'

Passing through the gate into the camp, Fronto was pleased to see that he had been mistaken at a distance. The tents were, indeed, all still up, but the weapons and equipment were all stowed ready for transport, and everything was maybe an hour away from departure. He saw the Eighth's primus pilus gesturing with his vine staff near the latrines.

'Good work, Balventius.'

The senior centurion nodded. 'We're basically ready. I've tried to get permission to strike the tents and get underway sir, but I can't get to see our legate. He's busy with the general.'

Fronto returned the nod. 'Get it all prepared, tents struck and everything, but don't actually get them underway until you get word from Balbus or myself. I have to go and see Caesar first.'

Fronto half-walked, half-ran off in the direction of the headquarters. Tetricus watched him go, a smile plastered across his face. The commander was getting edgy, like most of the officers and men. It was the tenth day of Aprilis today, and the Helvetii were due to return in the next two days. That meant the legions had to be in place by tomorrow morning at the latest, and Fronto hated having to wait in a defensive position. Tetricus smiled again. He had not known the commander long, but he liked him a lot. By tonight, the Eighth would be in place, with two green legions in support, in a highly defensible position on the wall. Tetricus had been assigned to Fronto as an aide, and the legate had immediately put him and Velius in command of the Eleventh and Twelfth. He was looking forward to it. He had never commanded a full legion and, although he technically outranked Velius, he was happy to defer to the older man in terms of command. Velius had received his first battle scar before Tetricus was born. The men of the new legions were starting to get tense and argumentative, but a good fight always took that out of them.

'Ah well. A couple of hours and we'll be ready to move.' Tetricus strode off in the direction of the camp of the Eleventh, who would be awaiting his orders.

A quarter of an hour later, Fronto strode into the Headquarters of the Eighth's garrison fort. The building was bustling and busy. Despite the absence of the newly commissioned officers of the Eleventh and Twelfth, who were now at their own camps and preparing their legions for later in the day, a large number of officers, administrators and other personnel charged around the building, carrying piles of parchments, wax tablets and lists. Caesar's door stood open, people rushing in and out almost constantly. Fronto waited impatiently by the opposite wall for the line of incoming and outgoing scribes to thin out, tapping his fingers on his crossed arms and making a throaty harrumphing sound.

A hand on his shoulder made him start. He turned to see the worn but smiling countenance of Balbus.

'You look like a man who's ready to charge the barbarians all by yourself. What's got at you?'

Fronto sighed. 'Just one of those days I suppose. I see the Eighth is ready to move. Balventius has been trying to get hold of you, but I gave him permission to strike tents and make ready. I assume that's alright?'

'Yes indeed. Things have been a little hectic here, and I've not had the chance to get away. I saw Longinus earlier. He's already sent all my cavalry and the auxiliary riders off to the far end of the wall. I can't decide whether he's being tactical or just trying to stay out of the way of the action.'

Fronto nodded.

'Probably the latter.'

He gestured at the door, the traffic having fallen to a sensible level, and the two legates entered.

Caesar stood, his campaign chair folded against the back wall. He was, for a change, in full armour with a servant tying the ribbon around the cuirass. Fronto, who spent most of his life in full armour, could never see the attraction of the glamorous looking efforts that generals habitually wore. The whitened chest piece with the embossed decoration was very impressive but impractical in a combat situation. Fronto had been given a very ornate cuirass after the Spanish campaign, though he had left that back in Puteoli in a chest. The armour he currently wore was a bronze-finished steel cuirass with the traditional soldier's decoration of a Medusa head on the chest. Comfortable and practical.

Caesar glanced up at them as they entered.

'Ah, gentlemen. I assume manoeuvres are underway?'

Fronto and Balbus nodded. 'The Eighth are striking tents and will be in position by sunset, fully encamped. The Eleventh and Twelfth have maybe an hour on us and will be in position in time for the men to eat lunch sir.'

'Good. Good. I want all available senior officers with me when the Helvetii arrive so, Balbus, you'll have to leave your primus pilus in charge of the Eighth for now. On the bright side gentlemen, that means that the two of you and Longinus will get the next two days in luxurious quarters in Geneva with myself and the other staff officers.'

Balbus merely nodded, but Fronto's fear that the day would turn nasty was gradually being borne out.

'Sir? The Eighth is still lacking its major training officers due to the inexperience of the two new legions. Balventius is good, but he could have trouble holding a widely-spread legion together without a solid command structure around him. To keep us here will not help. Balbus should be with the Eighth, and I should be with the new legions, helping Tetricus and Velius when they need it. I'm not an ambassador, sir; I'm a soldier.'

A slightly peeved look passed across Caesar's face. The servant tying the ribbon finished and stepped back abruptly.

'Legate, tell the Eighth's primus pilus to call his training officers back in. They can aid the Eleventh from where they'll be on the wall. I'm sure he can manage.' With a sigh, Caesar sat down on the corner of a large table.

'Fronto, I know you hate this, but you need to be aware that an officer has a number of tasks above and beyond fighting and commanding a unit. We need to present these barbarians with a united and terrifying front, and all the legions, in the day or two to come, will need officers who are fully informed of the situation. You *will* come with me to the meeting, and you *will* allow the more junior officers the chance to do their jobs. Tetricus will be moved to the staff in a year or two and he will need command experience in case he has to command a legion then. Velius and Balventius have over a hundred years of command experience between them. I'm sure they can handle anything that's thrown at them.' He saw Fronto open his mouth and draw breath to speak, so he gestured pointedly.

'Don't make me argue, Marcus, just do as you're told!'

———————————

Fronto sat by the warming fire of Balbus' quarters. He was once again profoundly grateful to the legate of the Eighth for the hospitality he had shown during the last two days. Longinus and many of the staff had, in the way of insecure officers everywhere, spent their entire time hanging around Caesar's feet like lapdogs and attempting to get themselves into his good books. Fronto had known Caesar long enough, and Balbus was secure enough, to know that the best way to get on the general's good side was to be there just before he realised he needed you, and be conspicuously absent the rest of the time. Thus, the legates of the Eighth and Tenth had been prompt at all four of Caesar's dinners and strategy meetings, and had spent the rest of the time at Balbus' house, talking over old campaigns and discussing the generalities and the specifics of life in the military.

Fronto had been embarrassed on his first evening here to be eating one of the very tasty cakes Balbus' wife had made for the general when she had walked in on them. He had mumbled some excuses about deprivations around a mouthful of crumbs, and Corvinia had, surprisingly, immediately taken to the gruff legate. Apparently he reminded her of Balbus twenty years ago; a comment that had made the older legate wince. Since then, Corvinia had apparently given up any hope that Caesar might grace her household and had instead taken to looking after Fronto. He had not been allowed to return to the quarters in town, spending his nights instead in a spare room. She had fed him to within an inch of his life, and Fronto was convinced he would have to run the length of the wall twice just to wear off two days' worth of eating. Finally, she had confided in Fronto that she did not like to see such a brave, handsome and intelligent man without a good wife, and had made sure that every time he needed anything, one of her two daughters was on hand. He had asked, foolishly, after the third daughter and been told that she had been married two years ago to a soldier of some importance.

Despite feeling as though he were trying to digest a signal tower, and having to avoid and frustrate the attentions of the two teenage girls and their insistent mother, Fronto was at the most relaxed he could remember being in many years.

A runner had arrived to inform the two legates that the legions were in position and that lookouts had been placed. Balventius, Velius and Tetricus had apparently taken good care of them, and Fronto was surprised to realise that he had not spared a thought for the men during their travel and manning of the defences. That would change soon enough of course.

Today, in fact. It was a little after dawn, and Caesar had informed all of the officers that they must be in position at the town's north gate an hour after sunup. Balbus sat on the other side of the fireplace, one slave tying the ribbon around his cuirass, another lacing up his boots. Fronto eyed him up and down. Balbus looked every inch the hard bitten soldier. Much, he suspected, like he would look not long from now. Probably how he looked now, in fact.

Fronto had been all for taking a glass of watered wine with his morning repast, which his father had always claimed was good for the blood, though Corvinia had clucked over that decision and supplied the two legates with a glass of warm goat's milk each.

Fronto sat in his military garb, with the red cloak folded and ready to don when he stood. He was profoundly grateful to Corvinia for having washed and dried his good red military cloak. Caesar had made it clear that full dress was required, but had grasped Fronto by the shoulder as he left and whispered into his ear 'not *that* cloak though.'

He had made another attempt last night to unpick one of the cherubs from *that* cloak, and had accidentally torn a small hole by one leg. He sighed. The cloak would be with him until he died and, knowing his sister, he would be buried with it and would have to suffer it throughout eternity.

Balbus stood and dismissed the slave with a gesture.

'Alright, Marcus. Are you ready to face the barbarian?'

'As ready as I'll ever be, Quintus. It's about time we moved anyway. A week here at the mercy of Corvinia and I'll be a lazy, rotund man with as much energy as a sponge!'

Balbus laughed and slapped his colleague on the back.

'Come on. Let's move before one of my harpy-like daughters corners you.'

On the way through the town, the streets were eerily quiet. Fronto had always assumed that civil townsfolk awoke at a more leisurely time than the army but had found, with the early morning noise of the last few days, that the military did not have the monopoly on early. However, today the normal tradesmen, craftsmen and hawkers were absent. No surprise really, as word of Caesar's deadline with the Helvetii had leaked out almost immediately. Surely the townsfolk could not be worried about the Helvetii. They must know that no tribe could walk through such defences, held by three legions. Indeed, the increase in the local military presence had heralded a boom time for many of the local merchants and shopkeepers.

The problem was that the people of Geneva were aware of the distinct possibility that, once Caesar had his victory, he would take most of the army and head south, leaving Geneva open to revenge attacks. It was a reasonable assumption in the circumstances, and Fronto could quite understand the people not wanting to be seen to be a part of this.

At the north gate, Balbus and Fronto were the first to arrive. The two stood for a moment, enjoying the morning. The temperature had improved dramatically over the last two days, and spring appeared finally to have arrived. Perfect soldiering weather, Balbus had called it. Not cold enough to discomfort the troops, but not hot enough to exhaust them. The ground was hard, but dry, which looked suitable for military action.

They stood in silence for long moments, watching the Eighth Legion moving around the near end of the defensive embankment and admiring the beauty of the landscape beyond.

The sound of hoof beats brought them back to the task at hand. Caesar came at a trot along the main street of the town; Longinus and Sabinus, one of the staff officers, behind him among a knot of other staff. Fronto and Balbus saluted as the general arrived and then fell into step alongside the other officers.

The gathering of officers left the town with Caesar at the head on his white charger and the rest behind, a glimmer of red, burnished bronze and polished steel. The group passed down from the gate, along the shore of the lake and to the redoubt that had been constructed under Fronto's guidance near the end of the bridge that had been dismantled.

Once at the fortification, the officers were admitted by the soldiers of the Eighth that were already in position. Balbus nodded at the centurion in charge, who replied with a bow.

Caesar made his way to the centre of the redoubt and dismounted, an optio of the Eighth rushing to help him. Climbing onto a raised stand, the general looked down at his officers.

'You are all aware that the Helvetii will likely be returning today. We have no way to tell when, and they may even be a day or two late. Thus, the army will have to wait in position, and we, gentlemen, will stay at this fortification for the duration. Scouts have been placed so we will have at least an hour's warning of the enemy's arrival.'

The general then turned to Longinus. 'I want dispatch riders ready at this place to warn all the legions as soon as the Helvetii are on the move. I also want a horse brought for Fronto. Marcus, you're going to need to be highly mobile during this action, present among all the legions and being my eyes and ears and controlling the strategy of the army.'

In a louder voice, so as to be heard by the officers and all the men of the Eighth stationed close to the lake, Caesar called 'and now we wait. Look to your comrades and to your arms. Remember that you are Roman and that Rome stands in need of you now. They are barbarians, and barbarians will never again trample the soil of our lands beneath their stinking boots. Jupiter and Mars protect the men of the Eighth and the other great legions here today, serving Rome!'

A cheer rose around the redoubt, rippled along the length of the wall and into the distance like a wave. Fronto smiled. 'This is what he's good at' he thought. 'This is why he's a great leader, not just a great strategist.' Even Fronto's blood was pumping now, and he sensed the eagerness around him. Even that donkey Longinus had his sword out and was inspecting the edge. A swell of pride flowed through the legate. He was Roman, as were all the men around him, and if the mountains themselves moved against the wall, the legions would hold them back.

Velius stood on the raised platform behind the palisade and looked along the wall toward the lake. That would probably be where they hit first. They might even be fighting for control of that now. With the lake being eight or nine miles away, he could see nothing but quiet and peaceful countryside. The word had come down with a rider a short while ago that Caesar had refused access to the Helvetii and that they had threatened the Eighth before pulling back and gathering the tribe. Velius could not believe that in the face of such defences any army would try to take them, let alone a bunch of unwashed, hairy barbarians. The officers seemed to think they would come, and they should know their business. Still, Fronto had said that he would try and spend as much time as possible with the two new legions, and Velius wished that he would hurry up and get here.

The grizzled centurion knew how to command the unit; knew what to do and that the legion would obey his orders, but he knew they wanted a legate here. *He* wanted a legate here. Deep in a reverie, it took Velius a moment to realise that one of the centurions of the Twelfth was waving and shouting from a few hundred paces upriver. Shading his eyes and looking in that direction, Velius saw the centurion alternately waving at him and pointing down into the river. Following his pointing digit, Priscus felt a quickening of his pulse. A thin, diluted stream of red appeared in the centre of the river and, as he watched the icy Alpine water rush past, the pigment filled out and diluted more until the river in its entirety was tinted a rosy pink.

The training centurion drew himself up and took a deep breath. 'This is it lads. It's started upriver, but it won't be long before it comes our way. The legate will be here with us as soon as he can, but the barbarians might just get here first.'

Velius looked back along the line toward the lake again.

Hooves thundering beneath him, Fronto felt a mix of excitement he had not experienced for some time and trepidation over the delay he had suffered at Caesar's command post. The Eleventh and Twelfth awaited him only a few miles away, and some of the Helvetii were busily engaged with the Eighth, hurling missiles across the river, generally harmlessly, against the palisade; occasionally trying in small groups to swim across, despite the icy cold of the water. A large group of the barbarians had split off early on and made their way downriver, out of missile range of the Roman defences. In general Fronto found the barbarians' position laughable. Unprepared, they had no hope of tackling such a force as Caesar had gathered. Regardless of Caesar's orders to maintain a presence everywhere along the wall, Fronto intended to ride straight to the new legions and help Velius and Tetricus with any serious tactical decisions. Balbus would have no trouble commanding this end of the wall.

Riding at full pelt down the slight slope of a seasonal stream and then back up the other side, Fronto suddenly registered the activity around him. The sounds of shouting and the clash of metal weapons gradually reached him over the din of the horse. Reining in, Fronto cast his eyes around the site. One of the redoubts, filled with soldiers of the Eleventh, lay about five hundred paces ahead, and the previous, occupied by the Eighth, lay around a mile behind. Here was just a knot of soldiers based on the embankment itself, men of the newly raised Eleventh. It would be a good few miles before he reached any of the Twelfth, or even the command unit of the Eleventh. Balbus had assumed that a four mile gap between the cohorts of the fully trained legion was reasonable and could be covered by the green legions under view of the units on either side.

Fronto trotted up to the embankment just as a flurry of missiles whistled over the top of the palisade. Hurling himself from the horse just as a spear covered the intervening space, the legate landed in wet, slightly muddy grass and came rolling to his feet. One of the legionaries reached for his horse's reins and led the beast back toward the redoubt and safety. Two more legionaries came to help Fronto to his feet, but he shrugged them aside.

'Where's your centurion. What's going on?'

A figure appeared from the top of the bank, chain mail remnants hanging in tatters all that remained of his armour. His helmet was gone and not all of the blood in which he was drenched was his own, despite gaping wounds in his arm and side.

'Sir, I'm Bassianus, commanding this century.'

'What the hell is happening?'

Bassianus stood straight, wiping a stream of blood out of his eye. 'We didn't get no warning sir. They got archers. Damn good ones too, better than them Numidians we used to have with us, sir. They're in the scrub on the other bank. Must've been there since last night. They took more than half my men on the wall with the first volley, before we even knew they was there. Then, while we was ducked down and sortin' out the troops, a whole bunch of 'em came across in small boats, under cover of the arrows. This whole thing's a bastard setup sir. They'd no intention of arguing with Caesar!'

'How does it stand now, Bassianus, and where's tribune Tetricus?'

'I dunno where the tribune is sir. The bastards is under the wall sir, on this side of the river. We got 'em pinned down for now, but them archers is still thinnin' out my men, and they're still ferrying theirs across. Sooner or later we'll be outnumbered. We could call in other centuries from the Eleventh, but that'd stretch us somewhere else. We've stationed about sixty per cent of the legion close by the Eighth's redoubt on Caesar's orders, so we're a bit thinner here than we're supposed to be.'

The centurion lowered his voice to a whisper.

'And beggin' your pardon sir, I know they're new men, good lads all of 'em, but they're not strong enough trained to handle dirty fighting sir.'

Fronto nodded. He shouted to the man leading his horse.

'Soldier, get on that horse and ride upstream to the first fort. Find the centurion in charge there and tell him to send help. Any surplus troops they have from the Eighth, and the unit of Cretan auxiliary archers and Spanish slingers I saw in reserve. Tell him legate Fronto of the Tenth requested it.'

He turned back to Bassianus. 'Here's what you're going to do. Get every reserve man here to collect the shields from the dead. You're going to get your men back up onto that wall, with every second man using two shields, protecting the ones in between. The soldiers in between are going to take all these long spears that have been thrown over the wall and use them to stab down at the barbarians below. You only have to keep them occupied and keep their numbers down, and your own men protected until the archers from the Eighth get here. Then use them in the same way to take out their archers on the other bank. I'm going to head on toward the Twelfth. If I find anyone else that can help, I'll send them back. If the Twelfth aren't too pressed, I'll arrange relief.'

As Fronto set off west at a jog, the men of the Eleventh around him began collecting up spears and shields.

Velius was beginning to wonder if the legate would be turning up at all. He was starting to become extremely tense. About a quarter of an hour ago, a whole load of Helvetii had been seen on the other bank, moving between the trees and undergrowth. There was something going on, and it must be going on all the way down the line. The tint in the water was still going strong, and it was far too concentrated to be coming from miles away by the lake.

There must be a fight going on somewhere upstream, but not too far. Velius gripped his sword until his knuckles whitened. Please don't let it be the flank of the Twelfth. If there was a fight going on there, then there must be something happening up by Caesar's encampment near the lake. Now that there was activity here, Velius would be prepared to wager money there was action further downriver too. There were fords down there, and the fringes of the Twelfth, along with two cohorts of the Eighth, would have to defend them well. Somewhere out on that end was Longinus with his cavalry. The man had ridden past at high speed not long after Velius had received word that it had begun. He hoped Longinus was up to it; hoped he was even still here and not lost out in the woods.

What was happening with the Eleventh? He had not had a report from anyone recently. Suddenly there was a creaking noise and a tremendous splash. Glancing over the top of the wall, Velius saw a tall tree bobbing on the water, reaching halfway across the river. As he watched, another tree came down with a crash, parallel with the first. What the hell were they up to? The centurion was fairly sure he was not alone in having assumed that these barbarians were the sort to charge blindly against an enemy. He certainly had not expected engineering.

His worst fears were born out when, a moment later, wooden rafts began to slide down the impromptu ramp; rafts that were tied together with rope. They were building a bloody bridge! Anger rose rapidly in Velius. They were using Roman techniques, against the legions. Were barbarians not supposed to be stupid? He ran to the highest point.

'Get all the pila up here, and bring the archers in from the redoubt. I want every missile we have dropped in those thickets on the other bank, now! Before they get that bridge across. I don't much care for this type of fighting, but I'm damned if they're going to get past the Twelfth. I want men packed shoulder-deep on the wall, and all reserves up in four solid rows on the bank ready to take their place or, at the worst, take care of incursions. I...'

Velius fell silent and his head dropped to stare at the shaft sticking out of his chest. With a deep reverberating noise, the arrow had struck home just beneath his collar bone and driven in until it touched the inside of his shoulder blade. He touched it gingerly, his face registering neither pain nor fear but merely surprise. Blood welled up around the shaft as it moved. Using his other arm to take off his scarf, he wound it round the arrow shaft and tied it around his arm and neck to hold the arrow steady. Having temporarily secured it, he looked up.

No one had moved.

'What the hell do you think you're staring at? Get moving. I gave you orders.'

As the men moved to obey, a capsarius, drafted in from the Tenth at Aquileia to the new legion, came running up the slope to Velius.

'Looks deep sir. It's not near anything vital, but we should get you to the hospital tent as soon as possible to avoid excessive blood loss.'

Velius flashed a humourless smile at the capsarius.

'Just pad it and we'll break it off a few finger-widths out. There's no way I can go anywhere while there's no legate here. You really want me to put an untrained junior in command?'

The capsarius sighed. 'I do wish you officers would occasionally trust our judgement. We don't do this for a laugh, you know, sir?'

'Hmph!'

Another sigh. 'You'll suffer some fairly severe discomfort sir, and I strongly recommend that as soon as the legate gets here, you get down to a medicus.'

A short while later, Velius was back on the top of the wall, waving his vine staff with his one good arm, the other strapped to his side. Looking down over the side, he could see that the raft bridge had almost reached the bank, though the fire from the scrub and trees had all but disappeared under the constant hail of missiles from the wall.

As the centurion watched, a tall and powerfully built man, red hair and beard flowing behind him like a mane, came running out of the brush and onto the raft bridge, his long strides taking him from one vessel to the other easily. Velius held up his hand and the shooting stopped.

'One shot from one man. In the head. Let's give these hairy bastards something to think about.'

There was a moment of muttering among the legionaries on the wall, and then an optio, one of the precious few veterans in the Twelfth, stepped up to the front, carrying a pilum. Weighing it carefully and squinting along the line to the point, he hefted the weapon and raised it, standing sidelong with the point close to his chin.

'Give the word sir.'

The barbarian was getting close to the shore by now, a sword in each hand, one Roman gladius, and one Gaulish blade.

'Now, I would say.'

The missile arced out over the wall and caught the barbarian mid-leap between two rafts. Striking him just beneath the jaw, the point drove the man bodily backwards in mid-air, to pin him to the raft behind. A small crowd of Helvetii that had massed near the other end of the rafts pulled hurriedly back beneath cover.

Velius laughed. 'Good man. Go tell the quartermaster that I want any heavy rocks he can lay his hands on brought up to the wall as soon as possible. And while you're there, draw some wine from supplies. Tonight you're excused duty and you'll need it.'

'Rocks, Sir?'

Velius' grin had turned vicious. 'I'll need heavy rocks to collapse that thing while they come across it. No fun doing it now.'

Night was beginning its descent when Fronto finally arrived at the command redoubt of the Twelfth. A cheer went up as he jogged past the first of the main detachments from the legion, puffing and panting for all he was worth. He saw a square of guttering torches near the centre of the tents, by the bottom of the slope. Velius stood with three other centurions and a number of soldiers gathered around him. Fronto could hear him doling out orders in a clear, no-nonsense voice as he approached. Smiling, he ducked behind the last tent and watched Velius as he concluded his briefing. He was glad he was not one of those who had just had a chewing out for not reporting their situations regularly. He wondered for a moment whether he sounded like that when he gave briefings.

Probably.

Velius finished the briefing and gave the others permission to withdraw. As Fronto was about to come out and declare himself, the centurion turned toward him and called out softly enough to be heard by only the two of them.

'It's bad enough for a legate to be absent for an entire afternoon of fighting, but it really makes him look like a prat when he skulks around behind tents like a teenage girl listening at a door.'

'Nice to see you too Lucius.' Fronto came out from behind the tent and walked into the circle of light.

'I see you've had fun' he said, gesturing at the flower of red blooming on the white bandages around the centurion's chest and shoulders. 'A new scar to show the ladies?'

'I don't think anyone was prepared for this fight, and it shows. They were distinctly cunning and tactical. They used rafts, bridges and bows. I think we lost about a hundred men. Doesn't sound many, but it certainly bloody felt like it.'

Fronto nodded, moving toward the command tent.

'You should have seen it a few miles upstream. They actually managed to get to the wall, and the Eleventh were stuck fast trying to cope with them. They were under attack too. As soon as I reached the Twelfth, I sent a detachment from Herculius' century to give them some support. He had archers stationed down there, so they should hold, especially if the Eighth send someone too.'

Velius nodded. 'I suppose I should give you a report.'

'Save the bulk for later, just the important facts. I can guess most of it anyway. Important thing is that you've held firm and everything's under control. Would you like to explain that now?' Fronto pointed meaningfully at the bandaging.

'Arrow. Pretty deep. Capsarius fixed me up and I've been told I'm not allowed to leave the medical tent. I told him to stick it up his arse. Too much to do to convalesce.'

He sighed. 'I know you don't want to hear it all now, but suffice it to say they used missiles to cover the building of a raft bridge. We picked quite a few of them off and then dropped heavy rocks on the rafts when they were crossing in bulk. I don't think they'll try that again.'

He frowned at his commander. 'Anyway, what the hell kept you so long? Longinus passed us on the way to the cavalry a few hours before you got back.'

Fronto glowered at his training officer.

'Caesar wanted a 'quiet word' with me and it took ages. He seems to be under the disturbing impression that you're very competent and able to run a legion without me. There's a whole long-term plan unfolding here, Lucius.' He lowered his voice again as they passed within earshot of a couple of legionaries stacking shields. 'This doesn't go anywhere else but between us two, alright?'

Velius nodded.

'I kind of wish Priscus was here for you to confide in. It makes me nervous when you confide in me. I'm more used to you shouting at me.'

Fronto smiled. 'You should learn to filter some of what you say through your brain first, then I wouldn't need to tell you off so regularly! Anyway, the general's quite sure that the Helvetii will give up soon and go through the other pass into Gaul instead. He's way ahead of us on that score. All three legions will be moving out as soon as he's sure the Helvetii are gone. He's taking us west, Lucius, into Gaul itself. That's why he brought all this huge force with him. Not to frighten a few barbarians, but so that we're mobile and ready to act. The Eighth, Eleventh and Twelfth will be coming with us and we'll be meeting back up with the Seventh, Ninth and Tenth at Vienna. Anyway, that's a job for after we've dealt with the immediate problems.'

The centurion stood, deep in thought and staring into the middle distance. Fronto's voice pulled his mind back, and he shifted his eyes again to the legate.

'Has there been any news from the end of the wall?'

Velius grinned. 'Occasional reports filter down. I gather the Sixth and Seventh Cohorts of the Eighth Legion are holding their own, and babysitting the outlying units of the Twelfth. Our far flank's been under the general command of the primus pilus of this legion, a man called Baculus.'

'I've heard that name. He's a good man from the Ninth, if it's the same one.'

'Well anyway, this Baculus has managed all the work down there so far.'

Fronto sighed. 'Where the hell's Longinus been then?'

'Longinus, if you believe it, has been running a skirmishing group of cavalry beyond the end of the wall, keeping them from flanking us.'

Fronto frowned and scratched his ear.

'Longinus is an idiot when it comes to command and strategy, but I remember him in Spain, when he was just a military tribune. He was a good horseman. One of the best actually. Good place for the man to be. If he keeps running things like this, he might actually be a benefit, not a liability.'

The command tent appeared out of the gloom, burning torches lighting the front, and the flap pegged open.

'Let's get inside, Lucius. I need a drink, and if the medici catch you out here, they might forget about convalescence and just have you put down.'

The two made their way inside and a short while later the noise of concerted drinking was joined by the sound of laughter. Outside in the night, Gaulish voices whispered along the bank of the Rhone.

The first anyone knew about the second attack was when it was already too late. One of the legionaries on watch along the top of the palisade suddenly burst into flame and dropped like a falling star, bouncing down the bank and into the ditch.

By the time the alarm had been sounded, others had been struck. Several had fallen, pierced and on fire, into the stake-filled ditch. Others had gone backwards, rolling down the bank and into the camp. A couple who had been unlucky enough to survive the initial blow from the arrows now blundered, blind and on fire, igniting tents and ropes. Chaos reigned.

Fronto, still dressed only in his tunic, breeches and boots, came running around a corner and into the central space, unsheathing his sword as he ran. Velius appeared from a side alley, also unarmoured.

'When the hell did they start using fire arrows? What's it going to be next? Ballista? Catapults?'

Velius unsheathed his own sword. 'Up to the wall, sir.'

Throwing a glance over his shoulder as he ran, the centurion cried 'someone get water and put those fires out.'

Running up the slope to the wall, Fronto almost fell headlong over a smouldering body. He grabbed an optio by the arm. 'Get everyone back behind cover, and make sure they all have a shield with them.'

The rain of blazing missiles had subsided a little, with the occasional arrow whistling over the wall, and a lot more hitting deep into the outer face of the palisade with a 'thunk'.

Velius and Fronto reached the top of the bank and climbed to the parapet, keeping their heads down. A quick glance over the wall gave a clear view of the situation.

Velius shrugged. 'What can they be hoping for? They're not going to burn the wall down, and they know that once they reach this side, they'll be in close with at least one legion.'

'Shit.' Fronto grabbed Velius by the shoulders, his eyes blazing like the fires surrounding him.

'It's a diversion. It's got to be. The troops will see this miles away. It's a dazzling bloody distraction. I'll give you ten to one they're about to hit the Eleventh where I left them yesterday.'

He grabbed a passing legionary.

'Get a horse and ride down to the Eleventh straight away. Warn them they might be in trouble.'

A young optio appeared at the top of the ramp. 'Sir, we've just seen a whole mass of the enemy moving upriver on the other side.'

As the legionary ran to find a horse, Fronto and Velius took another look over the parapet. A flaming arrow whistled by, close enough to light up the centurion's face.

'Look sir. Over there. Must be a thousand of them.'

Fronto followed his gesture and saw the huddles of men, moving low to the ground.

'They're probably pushing the other side, at the hill where the line ends. They've got to be disheartened after yesterday, and they must realise that they'll never get through picking at us bit by bit. They've got to make one big push; all or nothing. I'd lay bets most of the tribe is gathering near the point where the Eleventh are weakest and at the far end, while the Eleventh are sending as many men as they can spare to help us here. I'd love to know what's happening elsewhere. They might be trying to get across the fords down by the end of the wall. I hope Longinus is on top of it. I'll bet something impressive like this is happening up by the lake too. They'll have to keep Caesar distracted.'

Velius drew himself up as best he could while staying below the defences. 'You can cope with anything they throw at you here, sir. The centurions know what to do as well as you. Let me take everyone we can spare and help the Eleventh. Tetricus may be a senior officer, but he's no battle experience. They're my responsibility until they're fully trained and can carry their own eagle.'

Fronto deliberated for only a moment.

'Alright, centurion. Do it.'

Velius charged off in the wake of the dispatch rider, shouting the names of various centurions and optios, gathering whatever force he felt the legion could spare. A number of men were moving around the camp putting out fires, dousing everything flammable with buckets of water, and removing bodies from sight.

The wall was now packed with legionaries, all fully equipped and crouched below the top. Fronto looked around and saw the young optio who had addressed him earlier giving out orders to the men in a highly professional fashion, ducking every now and then as a missile whistled over his head. He reached out and tapped the man on the shoulder.

'What's your name optio?'

'Hortius, sir.'

'You seem to be remarkably together considering the situation.'

The optio nodded.

'I travelled everywhere with the legions when I was young sir. My father was a retired centurion, and he made a living as a blacksmith wherever the army settled for a year or more. I've seen pretty much everything sir.'

Fronto grinned.

'Stick close to me, Hortius. I may need your help.'

The two officers took another opportunity to peek over the palisade. The light and fast-moving barbarian force had gone from sight now, heading toward the defences of the Eleventh. The archers were still here and, judging by the increased flow of missiles, they were settling in for the night. Fronto glanced down. As yet they were making no attempt to cross the river.

'Hortius, keep everyone down, and return shots where possible, but on no account do we want to look like we're besting them.'

'What?'

'We have a great opportunity here. We want to look pinned down, because they don't know we're reinforcing the Eleventh and that they're walking into a trap. If we stop this lot too early, they'll start to wonder if we know. The Eleventh need to look unprepared or the Helvetii might just give up and this'll drag on for a lot longer.'

Hortius' brows knitted above his nose, a worried look that Fronto recognised. 'I hope you're right, sir. If we send a sizeable part of our force to help the Eleventh and then they come at us, we're in deep trouble.'

Fronto nodded. 'I'm pretty sure. It's what I'd do.'

Glancing back at the flaming arrows around the camp, he thought to himself 'You'd just better be as bright as Caesar thinks you are.'

The fire in Caesar's tent burned bright and the light reflected off the goblet in the general's hand. Apart from the man himself, the tent's only occupants were the two staff officers, Sabinus and Labienus, and legate Balbus, breathing heavily after his jog from the wall.

'Legate, what's the latest news?'

Balbus relaxed into his chair. The last day or so had put an unusual physical strain on him and his legs were feeling a little shaky.

'There have been a number of attempts on the fords defended by the Sixth and Seventh Cohorts, though they've held firm. Longinus is spending most of his time with the cavalry on the other side of the river causing havoc among the enemy.'

'Good.' Caesar smiled. 'And?'

'We're having to deal with a small flotilla of boats attempting to cross the lake and come round behind us. Very flashy, but nothing to seriously worry about. I've sent a number of men under a centurion to bolster the Eleventh. I have a sneaking suspicion something's up there. I gather Fronto had the same thought. My scout I sent with them for a report said that nearly a quarter of the Twelfth had been sent to support the Eleventh.'

Caesar steepled his fingers and smiled at Balbus. 'And the Third Cohort up by the lake?'

'There's been no signal from them, so no trouble there. Looks like they're out of it completely.'

'Good. I expect the enemy will give up after tonight and try another way out.'

Baculus, the primus pilus of the Twelfth Legion, frowned worriedly. With half the legion under his direct command and a series of fords in the area, he had been expecting a serious fight. His troops, green though they were, had been primed and ready and itching for bloodshed. He could understand that. They were new, and they wanted to prove their worth. They had seen a few barbarians moving on the opposite bank, and had deflected or dodged the odd missile over the last few hours, but they seemed to have been forgotten. He sighed and returned to watching the river intently for any movement.

Fronto and Hortius sat below the level of the wall, playing with a pair of dice. The camp was now well organised, and twenty men patrolled with buckets of water, protected by shields. There was no fire in the camp, and the missile volleys had slowed again. Every half hour, Fronto ordered another concerted attack on the knot of Helvetii, to remind them they were still here, but all they could do now was wait. Once word was received that the Helvetii attack had failed, the Twelfth could mop up the archers across the river in moments.

Balbus, sick of stalking the wall and watching the occasional Roman or barbarian die, made his way down to the lakeshore. Here, the contingent of siege engines from the Eighth had been active for quarter of an hour now, picking off boats crossing the lake. Almost every shot from ballista and catapult had hit directly. The legate addressed the centurion in charge.

'How's it going?'

'Easy as target practice sir. Not one of them's come within three hundred paces of the shore. I think there's only about half a dozen left. Got to admire their spirit. They just keep coming, not giving up.'

'Let the others get to the beach. It'd do troop morale good if they got to have a proper fight. This to-ing and fro-ing is driving us all crazy.'

The Sixth and Seventh Cohorts of the Eighth Legion were being hard pushed by the fords. The Fourth and Fifth Cohorts upriver had suffered minor actions, but had sent more and more troops down to bolster their comrades. Even Marcus Petreius, the senior centurion on site had been surprised by the number and the sheer bravery of the barbarians who had swept into view as soon as he had received word that the Twelfth was under attack. They had been fighting for the fords and had been winning ground all night. Petreius' men kept fighting them back, but the defences were slowly becoming compromised. The barbarians kept throwing their dead into the ditch and now the sharpened stakes in the bottom were all but gone beneath the pile of bodies. Petreius knew his tactics and his men well enough to know that the Helvetii still did not stand a chance, but the Eighth was losing a lot of men and, at this rate the legion would be thinned out considerably before the barbarians gave up.

He was just considering pushing some kind of offensive, sending a couple of centuries out across the ford to try and relieve some of the pressure, when one of the legionaries nearby called out and pointed across the river. Following his direction, Petreius twitched with excitement.

Longinus and his skirmish cavalry had arrived. Not only that, but they had come through light forest and fallen upon the rear ranks of the Helvetii before the barbarians even knew they were there. In an instant the barbarians turned from fierce pride to panic and fear. Petreius ordered a concerted volley of pila and arrows from the wall, and the Helvetii, trapped between the cavalry and the wall, fell like wheat before the scythe. Those that could escape east or west along the bank of the river did so, fleeing with no sense of order. The rest would never make it back to their comrades. Petreius turned to face the tired and beleaguered men of the Eighth Legion, a mad grin on his face.

'This is it lads. Open the gate and let's get onto those fords and draw some serious blood.'

He turned once more to glance across the river. In the flickering light, Longinus and his cavalrymen moved like birds in flight, their blades raising and swooping, red and gleaming.

Velius and the primus pilus of the Eleventh surveyed the scene in front of them from the top of the wall. A senior centurion of the Eighth stood a couple of paces away.

There had been no sign of Tetricus when he had arrived and, when Velius had questioned the leading centurion, he had been told that no one had seen the tribune for over an hour.

The initial flurry of missiles from the opposite shore had been astounding. Like a swarm of hornets, the arrows and spears filled the sky, black against the dark blue curtain of night. A fair number of soldiers had fallen foul of the barrage and had continued to do so, even though the strength of the volleys had begun to wane. A defensive force three or four times the size of that the Helvetii expected waited patiently and quietly beneath the walls, shields interlocked above their heads. Waiting for the attack.

The eyes of the Eleventh's leading centurion kept straying to the blood-soaked bandage around Velius' arm and chest. He seemed to be fascinated.

'What's the matter, centurion?'

The man jolted and met the eyes of the Tenth's training officer. Despite the fact that he officially outranked Velius, he had been nothing but polite and deferential since they had arrived.

'I've been in plenty of battles in my time, and I've seen wounds like that put a man out of action for a month. Yet here you are, hours later and still on your feet directing the men. I'm just impressed is all.'

Velius sneered, though without real feeling.

'I haven't got time to be wounded. Got to show the men that you're impregnable. Only way they'll ever follow you into the lion's mouth.'

Velius ducked his head very slightly for another volley; then another; and finally, as a hail of arrows punched their way into the palisade, a mass of barbarian shapes plunged out of the scrub and into the river. There were so many that they bore a resemblance to ants from the top of the wall.

Velius was wondering what they hoped to achieve when he saw the ropes. A large number of warriors were swimming the river, but they held ropes that trailed off up the opposite bank and out of sight in the bushes.

Finally, the other ends of the ropes appeared, four of them hauling an entire tree trunk. A battering ram, as Velius immediately realised. The rest pulled smaller branches and roughly-hewn planks. He turned to the primus pilus.

'They're going to fill in the ditch with wood and try to barge a hole in the palisade. What are your orders, sir?'

The primus pilus of the Eleventh, newly raised from the centurionate of the Seventh looked up in surprise. 'What do *you* think we need to do? You're the man who trained this lot. What *can* we do?'

Velius grabbed the primus pilus by the scarf beneath his chin and hauled him up until their noses almost touched.

'The tribune's vanished and you're the senior centurion. That means you're in charge of this bloody legion. You're supposed to be a leader. Now *lead!*' he growled.

The primus pilus raised his voice, trying to cover the slight tremble in it.

'All missiles on the wall pick off those swimmers.'

Velius' eyes rolled skywards.

'Alright. Here's what you do. Form everyone who's not on the wall into three units, and make sure they're armed to the teeth and carry full body shields. Keep them ready and out of sight. As soon as you know where they're going to cross the ditch and punch through the wall, let them. As soon as they have a gap, they'll come through, and you can box them in with three units of heavy infantry. The phrase is 'rats in a trap'. It's just about over.'

The primus pilus grinned. 'You see? That's thinking. We must talk, Velius, when this is over.' Velius looked up to see the centurion from the Eighth smiling over at him, and that was the last thing Velius saw before everything went black, and the waking world slid away from him.

CHAPTER 4

(ON THE WESTERN ROAD FROM GENEVA)

'Furca: T-shaped pole carried by legionaries which held all their standard travelling kit.'

'Scorpion, ballista & onager: Siege engines. The scorpion was a large crossbow on a stand, the ballista a giant missile throwing crossbow, and the onager a stone hurling catapult.'

The road was dusty and dry. Despite a late start to the spring, the weather had been kind. The storms of Martis had given way to rain and then gentle showers during early Aprilis. These had now abated and the last week had been dry, the sun gradually growing in heat and strength. Since the legions had foiled the advance of the Helvetii and the barbarians had been forced to find another route, the three legions had marched for the last week and a half, out of the Alps, and down toward the lower lands nearer the mouth of the Rhone. Then, one morning, the scouts had reported back that the Seventh, Ninth and Tenth Legions were less than three miles away and marching on a path of convergence. North of the Rhone, they had met and the six legions had turned, a fearsome army, to march west toward the Saone and the crossings into Gaul. The heavy drum of footsteps in perfect time, stretching simultaneously over nearly four miles of road with close to forty thousand men had become a constant drone, and the choking clouds of dust and grit thrown up by the marching feet had formed a steady haze through which the army moved.

There was another fight coming their way, and everyone knew it. To begin with, Caesar and the senior officers had tried to keep the situation confined to planning sessions and strategy meetings but by now even the common soldiery could not be kept blind to the groups of tribesmen moving among the hills and keeping pace with the army. Three of the local tribes had allied with the Helvetii who, by ingratiating flattery and by use of familial connections, had gained passage through the narrow pass in the mountains.

For the last four days, the legions had been ordered to march in tighter formation with full equipment and the artillery and support wagons for each legion following up directly. Every night now the army spent two hours creating a well-defended and neatly organised marching camp.

Fronto made a point of travelling at the head of the Tenth, close to Priscus who, as primus pilus, marched at the front of the legion. Fronto could not help but smile. There was a fight coming, but this time he would be back with the Tenth, and it would be the Roman way. Open ground, fully manoeuvrable legions in proper formation. No skulking behind walls and hiding from archers. Any battles the army engaged in on this journey would be ten to one in favour of Rome; five to one at worst. With Longinus leading mounted scouts out and about within five miles of the army, there was no likelihood of the army being taken by surprise. They would have at a minimum half hour warning of an enemy attack. May Fortune help any barbarian force brave enough to challenge them.

His mind wandering, he thought of the night after the battle at Geneva and smiled. While the Eighth celebrated, Fronto had spent his time rushing around, occupied with many tasks.

He had visited the medicus at the Eighth's hospital to check on Velius. The centurion was unconscious but stable. The arrow had finally been removed and rebound, but a missile had split his skull not far above the ear. Luckily it had whistled on past and not become embedded, which would have spelled certain death. Fronto smiled. Velius *was* indestructible. Not even a ballista could stop him. The medical staff were concerned as to any damage done to his brain. They would not know how severe the wounding was until or unless he awoke, but they were hopeful.

It had been three days before the centurion had finally surfaced. Fronto and the primus pilus of both the Eleventh and Twelfth had been present as he awoke. His first words were directed at the three of them.

'It's only blood. Haven't you got anything more important to do?'

He had then been to visit Caesar at the headquarters. The general was relaxed and happy and admitted Fronto with a wide grin.

'Marcus. What can I do for you this evening?'

Fronto sagged against the wall, exhaustion beginning to settle in.

'Caesar, without Velius in active condition the Eleventh and Twelfth are in a bit of a dithering state. The primus pilus of the Eleventh keeps trying to find a superior for advice. Have you decided on who is taking command of the legions?'

Caesar smiled.

'Yes. I've appointed Aulus Crispus to the Eleventh and Servius Galba to the Twelfth.'

'I don't think I know either of them.'

'You'll have seen them around at the staff meetings. They should serve quite nicely. They're both involved with preparation at the moment, so would you mind kindly looking after the Eleventh and Twelfth until they're ready to take command?'

Fronto sighed.

'Alright. I've already got them repairing and replacing weapons and armour. You can probably see the smoke from all the temporary forges if you look out of the window. I'll go and issue orders for the day.'

He bowed and turned to leave, stopping momentarily by the door.

'I don't suppose there's been any word of Tetricus yet?'

Caesar shook his head.

'Nothing yet, but the battlefield is still being cleared. Unless he deserted or he was captured, we'll find him.'

Fronto nodded sadly and left the headquarters, making for the south gate of the Eleventh's temporary camp.

Spotting two centurions talking by the standards, he turned straight for them.

'You two.'

The men straightened instantly.

'Get every able-bodied man from both of your centuries and meet me at the redoubt by the lake. They don't need to be armoured and they can leave their furca behind. Now hurry.'

As the two centurions ran off, Fronto had wandered down to the lake, past the Eighth Legion, who appeared to be having some kind of party. Every time he walked past a small group of seated soldiers and they saw a superior officer, they sprang to their feet and saluted and, by the time he reached the redoubt, he was rather sick of saluting. He surveyed the damage done to both Helvetian and Roman armies from the vantage point and shook his head. He was still reflecting on the attrition rate of siege warfare when he became aware of the thump of booted feet not far away. The two centurions approached with over a hundred men. Fronto turned to face them, a determined look on his face.

'Alright gentlemen, we're going to head from here down to where the first units of the Eleventh were stationed. From there we're going to split into three groups. One lot will search on our side of the stockade. One will cover the stockade to the river. The other will search across the river. We'll search as long as the light lasts until we find a sign of what happened to tribune Tetricus.'

There was an equally determined look of the faces of the men as they set off at a fast march to the first position of the Eleventh.

It was, in fact only an hour or so into the search when a legionary gave a shout.

'I think it's him sir!'

Fronto ran up to the stockade and hauled himself to the top, where he could see a small knot of soldiers and one of the centurions huddled close to the water's edge. In the centre, he could just make out a small pile of bodies with spears sticking out of them, resembling some sort of hedgehog.

Fronto carefully clambered over the parapet and dropped the bone-jarring distance at the other side. He rushed toward them as they carefully hauled the extraneous bodies from the tribune, the soldiers making way for him as he arrived.

'Is he dead?'

One of the legionaries, presumably a capsarius, was kneeling, examining the body closely. A spear rose from the man's stomach, pointing accusingly at the sky. Tetricus looked remarkably white and a pool of dark, congealed blood had collected near his stomach.

'He's breathing sir, but won't be for long. I'm going to need three people's help here, and the rest of you need to clear out and give us space. We might be able to help him, but he might already have lost too much blood.'

Fronto unfastened his armour and let it drop into the water. One of the centurions and one of the legionaries stayed, while the others joined the steadily growing ranks of observers by the shore.

'What can we do?'

The capsarius looked up at him doubtfully as he tore a long strip from his tunic hem.

'I need two of you to hold that spear *very* steady, and one of you to take this cloth and hold it extremely gently but very steadily around the entry point. Do NOT press down under any circumstances. While you all do that, I will very carefully cut through the spear.'

It took a long, gruelling time to remove the bulk of the spear without rupturing any more of the tribune's insides. Even so, far too much more dark blood welled up around the shaft for Fronto's liking.

'Alright.' The capsarius threw the spear out into the river, where it bobbed away with the current in the cool, clear water, and pointed at the man with the cloth.

'Now you're going to keep that cloth over the wound, but with only very slight pressure. You two are going to very slowly and gently lift him from the ground, while I look underneath. Alright? Now go.'

As Fronto and the centurion gingerly lifted Tetricus as gently as they could, the capsarius put his head level with the ground and, as soon as the body was slightly clear, he reached underneath.

'The point was still in the ground, so the shaft went right through. The point's diamond-shaped and quite narrow, so it shouldn't have done too much internal damage. I don't want to draw it out though. We should get him to a medicus as soon as possible now.'

He looked over at the group on the bank.

'Make yourselves useful. Put together a makeshift stretcher. It needs to have a hole in the centre of the fabric so we don't drive the spear any further in. Once that's done, get him as fast as possible to the chief medicus of the Eighth, but carry him gently. Any more blood loss and he's gone for sure.'

The capsarius washed his hands in the water.

Fronto leaned down toward him.

'If you ever want to transfer unit, you'd be an asset to the Tenth.'

And now, two weeks later, Velius was back in his accustomed place, though still with a tender shoulder and a broken cranium. He would be unable to lift anything with that arm or to wear headgear for several weeks yet. Despite his injuries, he seemed to have picked up exactly where he left off and ignored any discomfort he felt. Tetricus had lived through the first four days and was hopefully still alive now, but had been far too delicate to travel. He had not woken during all that time, and had remained in the camp at Geneva, with a medicus to look after him. If he regained his strength and healed, he would take charge of the local auxiliary force.

All in all, things had worked out better that they had initially seemed. Regardless, he had been happy to see Priscus and the Tenth. It was like reuniting with a family. The three reserve legions had reached a prearranged point just north of the river a day ahead of the force moving from Geneva and had made camp overnight. Just before lunchtime the next day, Caesar and the command unit had crested the hill and come down to find Crassus in overall command of the three legions. Crassus had bowed to Caesar and formally greeted him, while the lesser ranks' reunions were considerably less formal. Following Fronto and Balbus' advice, Caesar had agreed to spend one day camped to allow the legions to unite properly before they moved on.

Priscus had clasped hands with Fronto and then walked with him.

'Why were we kept there, Marcus? The Helvetii have gone past toward Gaul days ago on this side of the river, while we were all too far south to do anything about it. Level with me.'

Fronto sighed and looked around to make sure they were alone.

'Gnaeus, we're heading deep into Gaul. You're absolutely right. We couldn't spring a trap and stop the Helvetii, or we'd have no excuse to chase them into new and fresh territory. We have to prepare for a long campaign. Which reminds me,..'

Walking over to the small pen set aside for the animals, Fronto scanned the beasts.

'Priscus!' he shouted. 'Where's my horse?'

Priscus turned to look at him and shrugged. 'I put it to work helping carry the wooden frame for the mess.'

Fronto stared. 'You did *what*? That's a thoroughbred mare that I've had with me for years. *And* it's an officer's steed, not a bloody carthorse.'

Priscus grinned an evil grin and looked around to make sure that there was no one within earshot.

'Sir, in the last year, you've ridden that horse a grand total of three times, and two of those were when you had that hip wound last Septembris. How the hell am I expected to know when you're going to want it next? You're quite lucky really. The cook wanted to serve it up at the last do we had.'

Fronto stood for a moment, his jaw opening and closing, but no words coming out. It was true. He hated riding. He was good at it, but it made him feel like an idiot trotting along gently on a horse, when five thousand others were walking. Truth be told, Fronto had not actually laid eyes on the mare in weeks, and if Priscus had not been keeping it fed and groomed, no one would have done.

'Gnaeus?'

'Yes sir?'

'I've missed you.'

Balbus rode proudly at the head of the Eighth. Throughout the journey, he had periodically ridden forward to join Fronto at the head of the Tenth, and once back to join Longinus and the Ninth. Caesar and his staff officers had ridden at the head of the column, and Fronto was often called to join them. Balbus had laughed as his fellow legate had trotted off forward, muttering and grumbling under his breath. Fronto had even, apparently, tried to persuade Caesar that Balbus would make a better staff officer and strategist, though the general had remained adamant.

79

The legate of the Eighth was happier than he had been for a long time. Oh there were downsides of course, but they were outweighed by the positives. There had been the parting with his wife; tears and pride mixed, as she had set off in the carriage toward Massilia and the Mediterranean coast, to their villa close by the Eighth's permanent installation. His two girls, the light of his life, had dealt with the news in their own way. The eldest had cried and refused to talk to her father until the carriage was ready to leave, but had rushed into his arms at the last moment. His youngest had saluted him and told him that she was proud of him before kissing him and climbing into the carriage. She would be telling all her friends that her father was conquering the barbarians by now.

The only other irritation of joining Caesar's army was the constant reminder of his advancing years. His joints ached with the morning dew, and his backside felt lashed raw every night after riding for a day. He was beginning to understand Fronto's views on riding, though he had to admit it was better to be on horseback, with his head above the dust cloud created by the stamping feet of thousands of men.

Still, life was good. Here he was riding to glory with the Eighth at his back. The officers and men of the legion had been equally pleased to be moving out on campaign. Of course, a lot of that had to do with the potential for spoils of war and other personal gain at the whim of Caesar, though there was a genuine spirit of camaraderie and many of the traditional military marching songs had rung out in the dusty air on the journey.

The Eighth had been in a rut for a long time now. Their situation at Massilia and Geneva with no aggressive or dangerous enemies to face had made them a little soft. The legate had done what he could with them, instituting daily training, exercises in the mountains and valleys, mock gladiatorial combats and many other regular activities. And yet the legion had felt as though it were atrophying, wasting away through lack of use. The recent flurry of activity and the spirit of the men had confirmed Balbus' suspicion that the sense of neglect was not through choice, but rather through lack of choice.

The battle at the lakeshore had done a lot to improve the spirit of the Eighth, and Fronto and Caesar had both commented on the strength and

80

spirit of the unit, complimenting Balbus on keeping a legion in such impeccable fighting order despite the many years of peaceful policing they had endured.

The morning after the battle, the Eighth had been in a fine mood. They had not returned to their camp at Geneva, but had gathered around the redoubt nearest the lakeshore gate. With their legate's permission, a huge feast had subsequently taken place, nearly five thousand men eating in the open air and on the beach by the lake.

Balbus had never fought alongside any of these other officers, and yet he felt as though he had known both Caesar and Fronto all his life. Fronto was a man cast in much the same mould as himself, and the general was much like any of the great figures of Rome's military history. He was gracious while being hard; supported his officers and troops as any man could, while nailing to the post anyone who crossed him or endangered the army. And yet, Balbus could not shake the feeling that the general would sacrifice each and every one of them if it were required for his personal advancement. As long as the army was his willing and useful tool, they would be well positioned. He just wondered what would happen to the legions when Caesar no longer needed them.

Last night at their rest stop, Balbus had invited Fronto and Longinus to join him for a drink and a meal in his own tent. He had briefly considered inviting Crassus, but had decided against it, keeping the group to a veteran level. The night had started a little stiffly, with the other two legates polite and distant, but wine had brought them closer together and, by the end of the evening, the three of them had laughed so loud that the animals in their pens had woken and begun to bellow.

Longinus was an enigma. Balbus had heard of the Ninth's legate a number of times before they had met, and the opinion the entire military seemed to share of him was uniformly unflattering. Furthermore, the man obviously had a history with Fronto. Still, he had distinguished himself on the field of combat and everyone had recognised it. The man was obviously a born cavalry commander, and would be forever wasted as a legionary legate. And yet he was unlikely to relinquish his control of the legion in favour of a less prestigious and less well-paid position as a cavalry prefect. Longinus had, in fact, confided with them on the matter of his strengths. He had always been a good cavalry man, and had been woefully unprepared for command of a legion, especially a legion who had just lost one of the great legionary commanders of the modern Roman military. There had been no way he was ever going to impress them with his abilities as a legate after Fronto, and so he had not really tried.

After the battle at the wall, Longinus had made a command decision and called his primus pilus to a private meeting. The legate would continue to make general command decisions for the legion and would take permanent command of a unit of cavalry formed from the Ninth and the auxiliary horsemen. Day to day control he would leave in the hands of Grattius, including full command during combat while the legate was with the cavalry. The primus pilus would then relinquish control whenever the legate returned to the legion. Grattius had agreed and would make all decisions in the name of Longinus. The legion had a newfound respect for their legate, and he would not allow that to fall away.

In fact, Balbus had come to find that he quite liked the man. He seemed to be different now somehow. Perhaps he had achieved a hitherto unknown degree of self-respect. Whatever the cause, he had lost a lot of the bluster that he had exhibited on his arrival at Geneva, replacing it with a much more level attitude. In return, Balbus had begun to treat Longinus like the equal he should be, and even Fronto had joked a little with the man. The longstanding antagonism between them seemed not to have disappeared, more to have changed into something else. Last night had made that clear. The two legates had hurled many of the same comments and insults at each other that they had before, though often through a smile. The insults had become more and more lewd and outlandish as the night wore on until Fronto's comment comparing Longinus' face with Crassus' rear end had caused them both to collapse into hysterics.

All in all, things felt lighter and clearer now and Balbus planned to get Aulus Crispus and Servius Galba, the newly installed legates of the Eleventh and Twelfth, to a get-together. He had discussed them with Fronto yesterday and they had come to the conclusion that the two new legates had been treated as inferiors by Crassus, while Fronto, Balbus and Longinus had not offered them much support. They should be treated as full legates, in order to help them gain the respect of the troops. He had only met Crispus, a fair haired and tall young man with a fixed, serious expression, and Galba, a stocky man in his mid-twenties with a barrel chest and a permanent five o'clock shadow, a few times and was consequently unsure of their talent, though they had carried out their duties adequately during the journey from Geneva.

Balbus smiled and, looking ahead at the rear ranks of the Tenth, saw the horseman coming along the line toward them. With a nod to his primus pilus, Balbus trotted his horse out of the line and off to the grass by the side of the dirt road. In moments the rider, one of Caesar's staff officers, reached him.

'Legate, the general requests that you move the Eighth out at double speed to the right and onto the grass verge. Keep your column length and formation as it is now, but move forward and form up alongside the Tenth. Longinus has reported a sizeable force of barbarians off the road about six miles ahead. The other four legions will be pulling forward and moving three abreast directly behind you. The baggage trains and siege wagons will be placed between your two legions and the other four to protect them from raiders.'

The officer pointed off ahead and into the distance.

'Can you see that tall hill with the double point to the right?'

Balbus nodded.

'That's where they are at the moment. We'll have to pass quite close to them and they'll almost certainly try to use both surprise and the advantage of height to hit us hard and fast. Thanks to the cavalry we'll be prepared. The Eighth and the Eleventh can hold the centre, with the Seventh and Twelfth behind them. The Tenth will move ahead at the last moment and turn the flank on them, as will the Ninth from the rear. We'll have them between the horns of the bull, and Longinus will bring his cavalry in from behind to trap them. Are you in agreement?'

Once more, Balbus nodded.

'We'll hold the centre well enough; the men are itching for more action. A good plan, I think. The general's determined not to play the defensive game anymore, isn't he?'

With a grim smile, the staff officer wheeled his horse and cantered off along the line in the direction of the Eleventh.

Balbus pulled his horse in alongside his primus pilus.

'Centurion, send word down the line. We're moving at double pace and pulling out to the right alongside the Tenth. The Gauls are coming, and I'll give you the details once we're in our allocated position.'

The primus pilus saluted and began to bellow orders out to the troops following him. In the blink of an eye the entire legion was moving out beside the Fronto's unit. The officers and men of the Tenth cheered them on as they ran past, armour clinking and crashing, dust clouds filling the air.

Balbus saw Fronto on the hill to the right hand side of the saddle, standing next to his horse and watching the legions move with his hand to his brow, shading his eyes from the glaring sun. Knowing that he had only moments until the Eighth was in position, Balbus rode up the grassy slope to meet the other legate.

'Balbus. Come to watch the fun?'

The older man swung himself off the horse and, holding the reins, stood next to Fronto.

'Nice day for it.'

He looked down from the slope and saw the legions moving. The manoeuvre was so slick and fluid, it resembled a choreographed dance. The Eighth was moving alongside the Tenth at double speed. The wagons were already moving toward their allocated space in the centre with the various auxiliary units gathered around them as guards. The Seventh, Eleventh and Twelfth were moving up at double speed to march just behind the carts, and Longinus' Ninth, again under the command of Grattius, held back to play rearguard. The dust cloud was increasing in size and density every heartbeat. The organisation had to be completed now. If the manoeuvres were carried out in sight of the enemy, they would know they had lost the element of surprise and the plan would not work.

Balbus looked down at the centre and a thought struck him. 'Fronto, I presume the Scorpions will be in place with each legion, but do you think the four ballistae that'll be at the centre will loose from the top of the carts?'

Fronto scratched his chin.

'I remember some trials we had when I was with the Ninth in Spain. The ballista would work, but the cart needs to be fairly well anchored, and the crew would have to be protected by a shield wall on the top. We tried shooting an onager from a cart once, but the movement threw the cart over forward. My advice would be to put baggage carts on either side of the ballista carts. It would give it better stability and allow a base for a number of soldiers to protect the crew.'

He turned and grinned at Balbus.

'It would certainly frighten the hell out of the enemy.'

Balbus smiled back.

'We'd have to keep them covered with tent leather until the last moment, of course, and not attack with them until the flanking legions are in place, or the game would be up.'

Fronto straightened and stretched his shoulders.

'I think I'll pop back to the command unit and have a little word with Caesar. Would you like to arrange that little surprise? I hear your siege crews were rather good at the lakeshore, so let's give them the opportunity to show off a little.'

The barbarians were not Helvetii, but their local allies, though at first glance Fronto could not tell the difference. A confederation of the Centrones, Graioceli and Caturiges, the Gauls came rushing down the hill like a landslide. There were several thousand of them and, with the advantage of charging downhill and a falsely perceived element of surprise on their side, they closed the gap with the Roman column in surprising time. The Gauls had forsaken the mounted element of their army, which would be dangerous to both their riders and the rest of the army when manoeuvring down such a slope, just their few chieftains remaining on horseback and carefully navigating the terrain.

The legates were well primed for the onslaught, however, and the barbarian cries of rage and victory soon turned to shouts of alarm as the Ninth and Tenth Legions came around like closing doors, boxing the charging Gauls in. There was precious little the attackers could do, their momentum carrying them inevitably forward and into the waiting arms of Caesar's army.

The legions were a lot more prepared than they had initially appeared. By the time the Gauls were a hundred paces from the lines of the Seventh and the Eighth, the front ranks had locked themselves into a shield wall. Their pila were raised to shoulder height and, at fifty paces, cast. A thousand pila rained down into the mass of Gauls, causing chaos and panic. At the same time, though a few of the barbarians had managed to peel off and engage the enfolding arms of the Ninth and Tenth, the pila cast from their ranks kept the confused mass moving generally forward.

By the time the Gauls had begun to reorganise themselves, the army pouring over the bodies of their own dead, they were entirely within the enfolding 'U' shape of Caesar's bull horn formation. The Gauls hit the front ranks of the legions like a bull to a red cloth, buckling the shield wall in a number of places, though failing to punch through it. In the intervening moments, the legions had drawn their short, thrusting swords and began their bloody and efficient business.

The butchery at the front caused panic to ripple through the ranks of the Gauls. The rear of the barbarian army began to stumble and drift apart, some of the Gauls turning and attempting to flee the field. Within moments, they were a mess; the front ranks fighting for their lives, unable to retreat or manoeuvre due to the press of their own army at their back and the tightly packed legions to each side. The centre of the mass pushed this way and that, confused and able to reach neither enemy nor safety. The rear of the army was now in full retreat, staggering up the steep slope as fast as they could.

Not giving the Gauls time to pull their army into a sense of order, Balbus spoke quietly but hurriedly to the trumpeter by his side. The signal blared out across the field and crews in the centre of the Roman army pulled the leather covers off the ballistae, anchored to four wagons for stability. The crews took positions, protected by their own personal shield walls provided by the Eleventh and Twelfth. Long iron bolts began to whiz through the air, pounding into the Gauls, pinning warriors to the ground and occasionally to other men.

Another horn blast rang out and, as the first of the fleeing Gauls reached the top of the rise, Longinus' cavalry hove into view, swords out and swinging; spears levelled. With nearly four hundred mounted legionaries and over a thousand auxiliaries drawn from Cisalpine Gaul, armed and armoured in much the same manner as the enemy, Longinus' unit was an awesome sight. Moving like heated metal through snow, the cavalry cut their way through the fleeing barbarians, though not pushing down too far into the mass for fear of rendering the Roman missiles ineffective. Longinus had been clear; his job was to prevent the army fleeing the field.

In the centre of the army, three Gauls clearly showed above the mass, mounted on powerful horses. Fronto singled them out from his position by the Tenth. With a shout, he had a runner take a message to Balbus. The messenger reached the legate and there was a sudden bout of activity below the siege engines. Balbus climbed up onto a baggage cart behind the shield wall.

'The leaders are in the centre, on the horses. Earn your pay, men, and pick those barbarians off before they can do anything.'

The ballista crews reloaded and began to loose with more accuracy and less speed, gradually gauging the distance and drop to reach the mounted men, picking off a number of warriors in the process.

After a few moments of shooting, the deadly iron bolts found their first target, the barbarian chieftain plucked from his horse with the strength of the blow and hurled ten feet back into the mess. Cries of dismay rose among the remaining Gauls, doubling in force and volume as a second bolt struck its target. Another chieftain, caught in the shoulder, was spun bodily into the air and thrown from his horse.

Fronto and Balbus both looked up to a crag behind the Tenth, where Caesar and the staff officers stood surveying the battle. Fronto waved an arm above his head, a red scarf clutched in his hand.

Caesar nodded and a staff officer next to him repeated the gesture. Fronto turned to his trumpeter and issued another order. As the short call rang out over the battlefield, the ballistae ceased their deadly rain, Longinus reined his cavalry in on the crest of the hill, and the legions broke off their brutal task and pulled back in a line.

Caesar surveyed the battlefield. There had been hardly any loss among the legions, and all the shield walls had held. The Gauls were a different matter entirely. With perhaps a third of their army intact, they had nowhere to turn and no way to escape. Their one surviving chieftain sat astride his horse, desperately issuing commands and trying to pull his force into order.

The general smiled. His legions and their commanders had worked well together, and Balbus and Fronto had even come up with the idea of using the siege engines in situ, which Caesar had not even considered. He climbed onto his white charger and rode to the edge of the hill. The field was now deep in an eerie silence: the only sound the moaning of the wounded and dying.

Raising his voice so high that his throat gave him discomfort, he addressed the Gauls.

'Barbarians, you have lost the battle. Must the butchery continue until no one is left, or will you surrender your arms?'

The Gaulish chief shouted back.

'What assurances would you give us if we surrender?'

Caesar smiled. He had been ready for this.

'Many of your countrymen will be mobilising against us, though many others fight for us. You chose to side with the Helvetii, a people who launched an attack on the forces of Rome. That was your mistake. We do not have the time or the resources to make prisoners or slaves of you, and I will not set you free to rouse your allies against us. There are only two paths open to you. Join us, or die where you stand.'

A groan rose from the Gauls as Caesar went on.

'If you hold this recent alliance with the Helvetii so dear to your hearts, you must accept what honour demands and die on this field. If you are willing to accept Roman command, you will be divided and dispersed between our existing auxiliary units. You will fight for us, among units of Gauls who follow the path of Roman civilisation, and you will have the honour of fighting under trusted Gaulish commanders. You have a count of fifty to make the choice before I order the slaughter to begin. Choose wisely, Gaul, for not only your life, but the lives of your people rest on your shoulders.'

To emphasise Caesars words, Fronto and Balbus gave signals. The front ranks of the legions locked shields once more and levelled their swords. The artillery crews reloaded the ballistae and aimed them into the centre of the army. The rear ranks of the legions hefted their pila and stood poised ready for the throw. And on the crest of the hill, Longinus' cavalry formed up in a line four deep. The Gauls knew; had to know that they were staring death in the face, with no uncertainty.

The Gaulish army shuffled their feet and muttered among themselves. Tense heartbeats passed. Caesar held his hand up, his ornately decorated sword in hand, ready to drop and give the signal.

With moments to go, the Gaulish chief held his spear and his broad bladed sword high in the air.

'Death to Rome!'

The Gaulish army surged in four directions at once, slamming into the Roman legions and sweeping toward the deadly cavalry.

Shaking his head sadly, Caesar let his arm fall. Four thousand pila swept through the air and into the mass. Bolts from five heavy ballistae flew into the crowd, two taking the leader from his horse, the other three carving a path through both flesh and metal, often taking more than one target at a time in the press of warriors. The initial volley thinned the crowd by about ten per cent, felling men across the field. The Seventh and Eighth Legions pressed forward between the arms of the other legions, carving their way and pushing the mass of Gauls into the waiting cavalry of Longinus on the hill. The Eleventh and Twelfth Legions came behind them, surrounding the artillery and the baggage trains and taking the place of the shield wall, pila at the ready.

Fronto, leaving the mop up to Priscus, joined Balbus and the two of them rode up the hill to where Caesar stood sadly, watching the obliteration of the barbarian army.

'Such a waste' he sighed. 'Why will they not accept the inevitable? We must make more of an effort to win them over.'

Fronto smiled a grim smile.

'Don't waste your sympathy, sir. They had their chance, but the Gods are with us. This is a glorious victory. It'll enhance our reputation at home, strike fear into the hearts of the Gauls, and make our legions proud and strong. That's value beyond a few auxiliary troops.'

Balbus nodded, standing next to Fronto.

Caesar sighed. 'I suppose you're right Fronto, but I don't like to waste resources.'

Words shared in other times made Fronto and Balbus cast a sidelong glance at each other. This was a man who thought of the military as a tool. Would he be as cold when it came to his own?

Balbus shook his head as if clearing it from a daze.

'Caesar, I must go.' He mounted his horse in a swift move, belying his advanced years.

Fronto and Caesar stared at him.

Balbus tapped his temple. 'Idiocy. We have to leave a few survivors to spread the word to the other tribes.' With the hastiest of salutes, he galloped off in the direction of Longinus and his cavalry.

Fronto and Caesar looked at each other.

The legate was the first to break the silence. 'Balbus is wasted as a legionary commander. He's good, but he should be with you, planning strategy.'

Caesar smiled back at him. 'It totally escaped me too, Fronto, and you know how much I hate not having covered every angle. Such as basic thing.'

Watching the last of the resisting Gauls perish in the press between the legions and the cavalry, Fronto sighed contentedly.

'That's it then sir. From here on in, it should be easy all the way over to the other side of the Rhone. The Gauls will be much more cautious about making a move now, and we know we can handle anything they throw at us here. I was pleased at how the Eleventh and Twelfth handled this. Professional; like they had been doing it for decades. I think it might be a good idea to get all the legates and higher level centurions together for a feast tonight. They deserve a celebration. Oh, and we should make wine and extra meat available for the rest of the centurions in their camps tonight.'

Caesar smiled at the legate. 'That, Fronto, is why I wanted you on the staff. Very well, issue the word to the officers. Tonight we celebrate.'

Deep in the centre of the battlefield, Longinus, now dismounted, pulled the golden torque from the neck of the chieftain. He wandered over to the body of the chieftain's horse, stepping over a tangle of corpses.

Longinus had a love of horses. It was his one talent and his one passion. He had ridden over the plains and hills of Latium since he was very young, tending his father's stable on a daily basis. He had seen the magnificent black stallion from his vantage point at the top of the hill and had marvelled. Of all the bodies on the field, this was the one he would regret most. Wiping an unbidden tear from his cheek, he pulled the iron bolt from the body and draped his own expensive saddle blanket over the horse.

CHAPTER 5

(NEAR THE CONVERGENCE OF THE RIVERS SAONE & RHONE)

'Galician: Breed of horse from the north of the Spanish peninsula, strong, hardy and short, bred from a mix of Roman and native Iberian horses.'

'Tolosa: Roman town in southwest France conquered at the end of the second century BC, now Toulouse.'

Longinus stood in the stables, stroking Bucephalus' nose. He had named his own black Galician after the famous steed of the conqueror Alexander. In much the same way, this horse had been wild and untameable when Longinus had been assigned to Spain as a young cavalry officer. His own horse that he had brought from Italy had been past his prime by that time, and Longinus had regretfully put the beast out to pasture and taken the black as a project of his own. Now the stallion was the envy of the officer class. Reaching within his cloak, he produced an apple and held it out on the flat of his hand. Bucephalus nuzzled his wrist and took the fruit from his hand gently with a brushing of his soft lips.

A voice from behind startled him and he turned sharply.

Fronto grinned.

'Passing time with a distant cousin, Longinus?'

Struggling for words, Longinus patted Fronto on the shoulder, leaving a trail of the saliva from the horse's mouth on the red cloak.

'Just trying to find someone above your level to talk to.'

Fronto grinned. A month ago he might have taken offence at the comment. Now, he was considerably more at ease with the legate.

'We're getting together at Balbus' tent. I've been speaking to the general. I've a plan, and there's a lot to discuss.'

Longinus nodded.

'I'll be there shortly. Just got to go back to my tent and change.'

'Yes, you do smell a bit like a horse's rear end.'

Smiling, Fronto walked off before Longinus could get in the last word.

Balbus' tent was warm and flickered with the light of oil lamps and burning braziers. Couches had been set around the edge so that the officers could sit in a comfortable environment to discuss the campaign.

When Longinus arrived, Fronto was already there, along with Balbus, Crispus, Galba and Priscus. Wine stood on a low table in the centre, a spare goblet already full.

As Longinus took the glass and sat, Balbus gestured at Fronto, who cleared his throat.

'Gentlemen. I don't know how much any of you know about the tribes of central Gaul. I don't personally know a great deal, but I've been sort of forced to study a lot of maps since Caesar put me on the staff. Have any of you heard of the Aedui?'

They all shook their heads except Balbus, whose brow creased in deep thought.

'I've heard of them. They're one of the larger peoples unless I'm mistaken. Lots of connections with other tribes. Don't think we've ever had any trouble with them, have we?'

Fronto shook his head, unrolling a map on the table.

Prodding various positions on the map, he outlined the situation to the other officers.

'The Aedui have long been allies of Rome, trading with our people and maintaining a comfortable border with Roman lands. The problem is that the Helvetii are currently passing through the lands of the Aedui and are looting and burning as they go. We cannot allow them to ravage the lands of our allies. Moreover, if they are allowed to move any further in the direction they are heading, they will be within raiding distance of our lands again, and the town of Tolosa will be in danger. If we do not defend the Aedui who, by the way, have sent messages to Caesar asking for our aid, we both endanger Tolosa and any other alliances we hold with Gaulish tribes. If we go to help the Aedui, we have our opportunity and motive to destroy a large portion of the Helvetii, and we stand the chance of expanding our alliances among the tribes. The Aedui are not a long way off accepting Roman status. I assume the potential benefits of this will not escape any of you.'

Murmurs of assent among the officers.

'The problem is that the Helvetii have almost reached the River Saone, and they will be hard to trap once they're crossed. Caesar has authorised an attack on the Helvetii.'

He pored over the map for a moment and then stabbed down with his finger.

'This is the only place where they can feasibly cross the Saone, and the army could reach them in a matter of a few hours. I have already passed the word to the deputies to get the necessary legions mobilised. Only three of the legions are moving to take them out. The other three will remain here.'

He glanced at Crispus. 'I'm sorry, but the Eleventh are still getting the camps in order, and they and the Eighth will be required by Caesar. The Seventh are a good, established legion, but I'm not sure how much I can rely on young Crassus' command ability, so I don't want him with me. We've beaten these local tribes four times now, but they seem to keep coming, and Caesar will want at least half of the legions in case of a further attack before we leave their territory. So, the Ninth, Tenth and Twelfth will sortie in a little over an hour, under my command, along with as much of the auxiliary cavalry as we can bring.'

Galba leaned forward scratching his bristly chin.

'So Caesar isn't going to be commanding the army?'

Fronto smiled at the other legate, a smile that was cold yet hopeful.

'Caesar doesn't think we can catch them. He intends to march the army on in the morning when they're rested and try to catch the Helvetii on lower ground. I have persuaded him to give me the chance, though. He still wants a considerable force to move on with, but has authorised three legions under my command. This is why you're here, Priscus. I want you to take full command of the Tenth in this action. I'm no accomplished general, and I'll have my hands full controlling the field. You'll have to be legate for the day.'

Priscus snorted suddenly, coughing as the wine went up his nose. Wiping his face, he sat forward.

'You can't be serious. I'm fine controlling them in camp and I can march the legion across country, but the Tenth know you're their legate. They won't be happy following me into battle.'

Fronto rounded on Priscus.

'Don't be an idiot, Gnaeus. Who do you think held them together while I was in Geneva? A battle's easier to control than a hundred mile march! You're quite capable, and you'll bloody well do as you're told. You're not taking a primus pilus' pay for sitting on your fat arse.'

For a few moments, Fronto and Priscus locked eyes until, calming down, Fronto smiled again.

'Sorry. Been away for a while and I'm a bit tense.'

'Balbus, you're going to be the senior man remaining here. You're going to have to look after all our baggage train and siege engines. We have to move fast and we can't take all the traditional accoutrements. I'm sorry to dump this administrative nightmare on you, Balbus, but I don't want young Crassus handling my legion's gear, so who else could do it?'

He turned then to Galba.

'The Twelfth are going to have the opportunity to distinguish themselves here. This is your first chance, and I want you to look good for Caesar. When we move out, you're the vanguard. I'm going to have the Ninth and Tenth pulling out to the sides. When we find them, I want to trap them against the river with a horseshoe of troops. The Twelfth will be the centre, and probably the hardest hit. Think your lads can handle it, Galba?'

The newly appointed legate smiled a grim smile.

'Oh, we'll do you proud sir.'

Fronto stopped for a moment. He had never been called 'sir' by a legate before. He was opening his mouth to point out that it was inappropriate between equals when he remembered that he was not only a staff officer, but the effective general in the field and would have overall command.

'Good.' Rather lame, he thought.

He turned to Crispus.

'I'm sorry you won't be getting the chance here, but there'll be other battles for your men. In the meantime, you'll be a third of Caesar's direct army. You'll be right under the general's eye, and this is your chance to impress him with your efficiency. Good luck, man.'

Crispus nodded, his serious face betraying nothing of his disappointment.

'That's it, I think.' Fronto stood and made to leave.

'Oh,' he said, turning again, 'Longinus, I want you to stretch your cavalry out in a wide horseshoe behind the three legions. We need to keep it closed. You'll have to plug any gaps and prevent anyone from getting away.'

'I want all three legions ready to move within the hour. We'll form up near that copse on the hill. Balbus, we'll re-join you late tomorrow. I know the route Caesar's taking. If we hit any real trouble, I'll send a rider to catch up with you.'

Balbus stood, locking forearms with Fronto in an age-old gesture of comradeship.

'Good luck Marcus. I think you're right; he's being too cautious. Make some history for us.'

Fronto smiled grimly.

'Oh I intend to, Quintus. I intend to.'

As the officers moved off quickly, heading to their commands, Priscus caught up with Fronto.

'Don't you think it's a little risky sir? I'd feel better taking six legions against them. I don't like thinking we've come all this way to walk into something unprepared.'

Fronto patted him on the shoulder.

'We sometimes have to take a chance, or we'll never achieve our goals. Don't worry. The three legions can handle it, and I've studied the maps. We can make the ground work for us.'

'I hope to hell you're right sir. Are you coming back to the Tenth?'

'No, you'll have to get them mobilised. I have other fish to fry. When I met with Caesar, Crassus was there. He suggested that one of the staff be assigned to baby sit the Eleventh while we were away. I'm damned if I'm going to let Crispus suffer the indignity of being constantly overruled by a chinless idiot. He's a legate and will be treated as such. I just need to have another quiet word with Caesar once Crassus has gone, that's all.'

Half an hour later Fronto left Caesar's tent, an air of satisfaction about him, and rode up the hill to where the legions were already assembled. Trotting to the highest ground in the centre, he motioned Priscus, Longinus and Galba to join him. Priscus looked decidedly uncomfortable on a horse and had, after much consideration, left his vine staff and centurion's crest with his gear. Clearing his throat, Fronto addressed the crowd.

'Gentlemen, we are going to engage the Helvetii. Gods willing, we'll send the whole lot of them to their barbarian Gods. If not, we want to make them suffer so much they'll never think of crossing us again. You're all travelling very light, and I want you all to break speed records on the march tonight. We won't have the support of artillery or auxiliaries, and we're attacking at only half our full strength. Still, we are better equipped, better trained, and better in every way than the Helvetii. We should be able to catch them in an uncomfortable situation and cut them to pieces. If we lose here, Caesar will likely have to turn back and head for home, and I know none of you want that. On the other hand, if we are successful, we'll be the envy of the world, and Caesar will be grateful. I know you know what that means, so give it everything you've got tonight. Think of the victor's wreath.'

A cheer rose up from the crowd. Fronto turned to the other three and lowered his voice a little.

'Longinus, your legion will take the left flank, Galba the centre, Priscus the right. The cavalry will stretch out in a horseshoe behind us all. I want the legions within sight of each other and close enough that they can close up and form a solid line when we sight the enemy. Everyone's moving at double time tonight. I want to reach the Saone in two hours at most.'

The others saluted and returned to their units.

Gulping in air, aware of the risk and the awesome responsibility he had taken on, Fronto raised his arm and dropped it as his signal.

'Move out.'

Longinus was, as usual, the first to find the enemy, riding out ahead with a scout party of twenty cavalry. He crested the rise at a gallop and reined in alongside Fronto, his horse sweating.

'They're just ahead, on the other side of that hill. We came in from the side and almost blundered straight into them. Didn't realise they were so close. They're crossing at the narrowest point in boats, but they've only got a dozen, so it's taking them a hell of a long time.'

He sighed. 'We appear to have arrived a little late. Most of the army's across, but there's maybe a quarter of the tribe still on this side. They're in a dip, so we could turn this into a slaughter. Permission to alert the other legates and get the ball rolling sir?'

Fronto grinned a wicked grin.

'A quarter of the tribe will do nicely, Longinus. They should present no real problem, and we'll thin their army out by a quarter. Caesar will be pleased. By all means let the others know. I don't want anyone cresting the hill until the horn sounds, so get them in position, but make sure they stay out of sight. Tell them to fan out and form a solid line. We want to trap them, remember?'

Longinus saluted and kicked his horse into movement, taking half his scouts toward the Ninth, while the other half went to inform the Twelfth.

Fronto turned and trotted down the hill to Priscus.

'Legate...'

Priscus bridled.

'I asked you not to call me that.'

'Tough. That's the job you're doing, so that's what I'll call you. Spread the line out to meet up with the other legions, and march up to the crest of the hill. I want you to stop before you're visible down below. We've got a quarter of the tribe trapped before the river. Time to cull some barbarians.'

Priscus nodded and turned to face the Tenth while Fronto rode to the top of the hill and dismounted. Creeping forward, he took a brief look.

The Helvetii were marshalled in a huge force on the other side of the river, though a large group remained on the near shore.

He could see why the Helvetii had chosen this as their crossing point. While other parts of the Saone would have been narrower, here the river flowed so slowly that the wake from the boats was the only disturbance he could see on the surface. He looked up. A few clouds dotted the night sky, but the moon was bright and late, hanging over the horizon like a distant lighthouse. Dawn was not far off, and the light would be useful, but by the time the conditions were perfect, the tribe would be across the river and gone. Now or never, he thought.

Looking back, he surveyed the landscape and saw the last of the troops falling into position. Waiting for the line to join, he waved a signal at the trumpeter close by. The horn sounded and the legions moved forward at a fast but steady pace, the line solid as they advanced.

The panic among the Helvetii was phenomenal and expected. The sight of over fifteen thousand heavily armed men moving in perfect unison over the crest of the hill would terrify any adversary, but the Helvetii had more to fear than most. The legions came down in a horseshoe shape, advancing on the tribe from all three sides, pressing them toward the river. Those boats that had reached the far side were sent back urgently, and the archers and spearmen among the Helvetii began to cast their missiles across the river to aid their unfortunate, abandoned colleagues; a useless gesture at best since few of the shots actually managed to cross the river and those that did occasionally found a target among their own tribe. The army on the near bank hurriedly formed a battle line, chanting and shouting. Searching for a weakness in the Roman attack, a small group of them broke formation and ran for the woods.

Longinus' cavalry spotted them and made for the trees.

The legions picked up speed as they descended the slope, casting their pila and then drawing their swords. They hit the defending line of barbarians with incredible force, sending men hurtling into the air, flailing arms broken by the heavy shield bosses. Once the initial charge was over, the Roman front line broke up into personal, brutal combat, allowing the next few ranks to move between them and into the fray. Fronto surveyed the scene and was pleased with what he saw. He had never commanded an army before, and could see now how much of the individual tactics became the province of the legate and the centurions. Scanning the combat and looking for a way to usefully influence the action, he smiled. Calling one of the dispatch riders over, he pointed to the far side of the battlefield.

'Most of their baggage train is already across, but there's still a sizeable amount here. They're trying to get it loaded onto rafts. Get to Longinus. Tell him to get cavalry over to those rafts and stop them taking the packs. He can bring up the infantry afterwards and secure them for us.'

The rider nodded, saluted and rode off in search of Longinus.

Things were going well. The Twelfth had already carved an arrowhead through the tribe and the entire legion was now engaged. Roman outnumbered barbarian by around six to one, and the outcome was inevitable. In a few moments more, the Twelfth would reach the riverbank, and the Helvetii would be divided in two. Moreover, at that point the boats could no longer continue their transport.

A cavalry officer rode up to Fronto.

'Sir, about a hundred or so of them made it into those woods, and the cavalry can't manoeuvre well enough in there to catch them. What do you want us to do?'

Fronto scratched his chin.

'How big is that wood?'

'It goes on for about a half mile, sir.'

'Alright, take the unengaged cavalrymen and keep the woods covered from every direction. They have to come out sooner or later. As soon as your legate is finished with the baggage trains, I'll get him to come and help with the rest of the cavalry.'

'Sir.' The soldier saluted and rode back in the direction of his unit.

Looking back at the field, Fronto could see that it was all but over. Few pockets of barbarians remained on the field. A few were surrendering; others were unaware that their army had gone and were fighting on in the face of hopeless odds. How would Caesar handle this?

A figure on horseback rode up the hill toward him. In the first glimmering light of dawn, Fronto recognised the stocky shape and dark features of Galba, legate of the Twelfth.

'Glorious morning sir. What shall we do with them? Do we kill them or take slaves?'

Fronto smiled his most wicked of smiles. 'Round them all up and disarm them. I have an idea.'

As Galba rode off, Longinus reined in his horse. Steam rose from its flanks and from the blood spattered legate. All done sir.'

Fronto smiled. 'I need you to go and join the rest of your cavalry and pen in the group that fled into the woods. Don't kill them. I might need them shortly.'

Longinus smiled back. 'Very well, but I think you should see this.' He handed a standard to Fronto, a staff with a burnished bronze dragon at the top and various streamers attached to it. Examining the decoration below the dragon, Fronto's eyes widened.

'Is that what I think it is?'

Longinus grinned. 'Oh yes. And the rest is in those carts. I'll leave you to preen if you don't mind while I go check on my unit.'

Fronto stared, stunned, at the standard in his hand. Shaking his head, he turned to the remaining four dispatch riders as Longinus left.

'Ride hard to Caesar and tell him what's happened.' He handed the standard to one of the riders. 'Give him this, and tell him that his advance on what remains of the Helvetii will be much faster accomplished if he comes this way.'

The riders saluted and rode off.

'What was that then?'

Fronto started. He had not realised that Priscus had joined him.

'That, my friend, is payback. A Helvetii standard maybe, but made from a Roman one. One of the standards of Cassius' army to be exact. There are several different sub tribes of the Helvetii, and these ones are the miserable bastards that murdered Cassius. Caesar will want to see what else we dig up from their baggage.'

Priscus gawped.

'Hell, we're going to be heroes. Is that why we're taking prisoners? You know we can't keep them on the march.'

Fronto gritted his teeth.

'That's part of it, certainly, but we're going to need a lot of free labour.'

'Why?'

'For the bridge.'

Priscus was totally lost.

'What bridge?'

Fronto pointed out toward the river.

'The one we're building there. We've got at least five or six hours until Caesar and the army get here. We've got some damn good engineers right here, a copse of solid building lumber, and a whole bunch of slaves that we don't know what to do with. The Helvetii have all their worldly goods with them, so we should find axes, saws and so on in their baggage, hopefully.'

He pointed into the distance, where the rest of the Helvetii were moving away from the river as fast as possible.

'We can have a bridge well under construction by the time he gets here and if we work fast we can have the entire army on the other side of the river by sunset. We'll be a day behind the enemy at most. I think Caesar's going to change his plans when he sees that standard, and we need to be prepared when he gets here. Get the prisoners roped up and ready to cut wood. Make sure they have a guard, but don't hamper their work. You can promise them they won't be harmed while they're under my command, so long as they work. Tell Galba to get their baggage train searched thoroughly and separate all the usable goods out for us. I'm going to see Longinus.'

Priscus saluted and, rather inexpertly, wheeled his horse before riding off in the direction of Galba and the Twelfth.

Fronto rode down toward the woods that were now green and lush in the early dawn light.

Finding Longinus on a slight rise with a good view of the woodland, Fronto reined in beside him.

'Would you like to do the honours? If they surrender, they'll be put to work cutting trees and otherwise unharmed.'

Longinus nodded and rode down to the edge of the woods.

Fronto took a heavy breath and wheeled, riding off toward the Tenth.

Reining in on the mud-and-blood-churned plain close to where the Tenth was roping prisoners together at the ankle, Fronto raised his voice and called over the mass.

'Pomponius. centurion Pomponius, report.'

Gaius Pomponius, the Tenth's chief engineer stood and stepped forward from where he was teaching a legionary to tie a specific knot.

'Sir.'

Fronto dismounted. Walking the horse down to where Pomponius stood to attention, he gazed thoughtfully out over the river.

'Walk with me, Pomponius. And for heavens' sake come down from attention. You'll rupture yourself standing like that, and I need you at the moment.'

Pomponius smiled and fell into step beside Fronto, his hands clasped behind his back, clutching his vine staff of office.

'What can I do for you sir?'

Pomponius was a young man for a centurion, remarkably young to have achieved such an office. He had joined the Tenth not long before Fronto, and the legate could remember the Tenth's previous chief engineer receiving his honesta missio, and the promotion of the young and endlessly enthusiastic Pomponius to centurion. Still, there was no denying that he was good at his job. He seemed to have a knack for military engineering, bordering on an art form.

'Pomponius, how many bridges have you built?'

Pomponius scratched his mousy ruffled hair.

'I dunno sir. Maybe six or seven temporary pontoon bridges and three more permanent wooden structures.'

Fronto smiled. He could remember nine pontoon bridges and four wooden ones himself, and his memory was not that good.

'What's your opinion of this place for a bridge?'

As they reached the shore, Pomponius knelt, took a boulder and hurled it out into the river. It disappeared with a satisfying 'plop'.

'Somewhere between nine and twelve feet deep in the centre. About fifty feet wide. Current on the surface is negligible; current below is probably quite strong. Good wood nearby. Can't see it being a problem. We've got three legions' worth of engineers and a lot of helpers.'

Fronto cast an appraising glance at the young engineer.

'How long do you think, given enough labour and three legions' worth of experts?'

Pomponius scratched his chin and looked about.

'I would think half a day, working at a full pace. The men won't be fit for a full day's march straight after that though, not after being up most of last night.'

Fronto smiled. 'You let me worry about that, Pomponius. I want you to gather all the engineers from all the legions together and start planning a bridge here. I'll get Priscus and Longinus to sort out all the prisoners as labour for you, and in about a quarter of an hour all three legions will be reporting to you and Priscus at the waterfront. Do your stuff, centurion.'

'Yes sir.'

Pomponius left, rubbing his hands together in a business-like fashion.

The rest of the army arrived just after noon. Caesar rode in the vanguard, with Crassus and the staff officers. Balbus rode at the rear with Crispus and the Eleventh, who came along behind the other two legions as rearguard. It irked Fronto that Crassus and Caesar still seemed to be treating Crispus as an inferior, and only Balbus deigned to join him. They all, to Fronto's mind, looked far too rested, eager and healthy. While he stood on the hill waiting for the general to reach him, he glanced quickly back down toward the river. The three legions of whom he was about to relinquish command looked like peasants, slaves and lowlifes. Only the centurions and the small groups guarding the prisoners while they worked were wearing their armour. They were covered in mud and sweaty, mostly stripped down to their waist. The difference was vast, though with good reason. The three legions beside the river had managed only about three hours sleep in the last thirty. On top of this, they had marched at high speed into a battle and then immediately begun to construct a bridge.

The crossing was well underway by now. The huge timbers that had erstwhile been some of the largest trees in the riverside woodland now stood vertically in the river, planed straight and flat-topped and stretching out most of the way across. The first of the horizontal beams had just been nailed and roped in place, and a unit of legionaries was bringing flat slats across from the woods in large numbers now. Most of the materials had now been cut and were being shaped and put in place. Three units of legionaries stood on hastily-constructed rafts in the middle of the river, placing beams and piles in place, their rafts roped to the banks on either side and held in place by captive Helvetii. It looked barely started to Fronto's inexpert eye. He had quizzed Pomponius over it about an hour ago, and the young engineer had replied 'With respect sir, you know nothing about bridges. We're about four hours from complete if work continues at this pace. Let us do our job.'

Fronto had given up at that point and gone up the hill to wait for a sign of Caesar and the army.

The vanguard came to a halt at the top of the hill before Fronto, while the Seventh, Eighth and Eleventh Legions continued on down the hill toward the river.

Ahead of Caesar in the vanguard came Crassus, who drew his horse to a halt in front of the grimy legate of the Tenth and sniffed.

'Your men are a state, Fronto. A disgrace.'

Fronto's eyes widened. As the colour crept into his face and he struggled in his tired state to formulate an appropriate reply, Crassus merely wheeled his horse and rode away. Caesar nimbly slipped from his magnificent white steed and landed lightly in front of the legate.

'Alright Fronto, you got your way. I'm here.'

He snapped his fingers and reached out behind him. A staff officer passed him the standard that Fronto's army had recovered.

Gesturing at Fronto with it, the general continued.

'I know you know what this is; otherwise you wouldn't have sent me it. Tell me everything you know and what you have planned.'

He began to stride purposefully down the hill.

Fronto jogged for a moment to catch up and then fell into step beside him.

'We caught maybe a quarter of the tribe on this side of the river. They must have been ferrying their men across for days in their little boats. We've got prisoners now and we're using them to help build a bridge. We should have the thing finished by mid-afternoon, and I figure the entire army could be across the river and in close pursuit of the Helvetii by dusk.'

Caesar stopped suddenly, and Fronto had to pull himself up short, as he almost kept walking.

'Also, we've searched all the tribal baggage we captured and have found a wealth of items that have been taken from Roman military hands. Some of it's directly attributable to the army of Lucius Cassius. Most of it's of indeterminate origin, though it seems very likely that all of it comes from that source. I think you could say that Cassius is avenged, sir.'

Caesar frowned and looked down toward the baggage train.

'The Helvetii may have destroyed Cassius' army and murdered the man himself, but it was one of their cantons; their sub tribes that was directly responsible: the Tigurine. The standard that you captured was of that people. I want to confirm this with some of the surviving prisoners.'

Fronto nodded.

'If you'd like to follow me sir, down to the waterfront, you'll find all the prisoners have been put to work.'

Caesar, once they were on their own and out of earshot of the staff officers, leaned closer to Fronto and spoke in low tones.

'The Tigurine are not to be trusted or bargained with. My father-in-law's grandfather was Lucius Piso, one of Cassius' chief officers, and he also was murdered by the swine.'

As they arrived at water's edge, the largest group of prisoners, over a hundred in all, sat cross-legged on the grass, stripping branches of their leaves and shoots. They continued to do so as Caesar and Fronto stood looking down on them, surrounded by legionaries with their swords out.

Caesar cleared his throat. In a deep, loud and clear voice, he spoke to the prisoners.

'You are the Tigurine.' Not a question. A statement.

Mutters of confirmation greeted him from the seated group.

'You were the last to cross, caught unawares by a sizeable Roman army under a great general. Fortunate for your fellow tribesmen that they were on the other side and out of danger. Not for long, though. By the end of today or early in the morning we will be chasing them down like dogs on the hunt. I am a man who does not like to waste men or resources and generally despises unnecessary brutality. Sometimes, however...'

He turned his back on the tribesmen and stepped next to Fronto. In a voice loud enough to be heard by every man present, he spoke.

'Kill them all. Every last one of them, but don't do it too quickly. I want them to have time to appreciate it.'

As the tribesmen behind him dropped the branches and stood, trying to move toward Caesar, but held at bay by guards with swords and shields, the general raised his voice above the shouting and hollering of the crowd.

'Replace them with proper men drawn from the Seventh, Eighth and the Eleventh. I want the other legions involved, and the current three can stand down for two hours and rest.'

'Yes sir.'

As the general strode away and the legionaries began to carry out his orders, Fronto tried to keep his eyes on Caesar and not watch the gruesome activity taking place over his shoulder. He could keep his eyes away, but he could not shut out the screams or the sounds of carving meat. He was a soldier and could deal with any horror that battle could throw at him, but this simple butchery and torture was not to his taste. Turning his back, he was grateful to follow Caesar away from the scene. Once again he wondered how far the general would be prepared to go for personal ambition.

Balbus found Fronto in the woods, seated on a stump left by one of the workers. He had been looking for his fellow legate for almost an hour. No one had seemed to know where he was, until he eventually tracked down a centurion he recognised, called Velius. Velius had seen his legate disappear into the woods with a large jug and had thought better than to ask.

Fronto had not seen Balbus enter the man-made clearing and gave a start when the older man coughed politely. Looking up, he recognised the shape and movement of his colleague in the dusk.

'Quintus. What're you doing here? I tried hard to find a place no one would find me.'

Balbus smiled and sat on a stump opposite.

'I gathered that from how hard you were to find. I brought more wine, though I'm not at all sure you really need it.'

Fronto's head slipped forward again.

'He had no call to do that. No reason at all. I can appreciate as much as anyone that you can't always hold prisoners and that death can be the only option on occasion. But not like that. Not carving people up for the sake of bitterness. They were warriors who lost a battle. I doubt that these so-called 'barbarians' would treat Roman prisoners that way. As far as I can remember, they put an end to Cassius and his army in a swift, no-nonsense way. Caesar had no call to do it.'

Balbus frowned.

'I agree, but we're not the ones who have to live with that decision. From what I hear the general's done as bad or worse before. You must have seen things like that serving with him in Spain. He was tried for crimes after that campaign.'

Fronto shook his head.

'He was more subtle about it in Spain. He knew some of us didn't approve, so it was always done quietly and while many of us were absent. Spain was too well-known to Rome. Stories get back too easily. I figure he thinks out here no one will ever find out. He's got a free hand. I just don't know whether he made it so overt purely to make a point to me, or to demonstrate his resolve and power to the army in general. I don't think he's prey to his emotions enough to have done it for revenge. With him there's *always* an ulterior motive.'

Balbus shrugged. 'And I think you've chosen a bad spot to sit and sulk in. It smells like a dead pig here.'

Fronto gestured to the edge of the clearing.

'That's because their burial pit is just the other side of those trees. Five hundred and seventeen bodies. I counted them. Not to mention the thousands we killed on the field.'

He took a pull at the wine flask, only to discover that it was empty.

'What about Caesar. What's *he* doing?'

Balbus smiled a sympathetic smile.

'The general's a very happy and generous man tonight. He's sat in his tent with most of the officers, drinking and laughing. He honoured

Longinus, Priscus and Galba in front of the other officers, and praised you in your absence.'

Fronto sighed.

'I hate being in a position where I have to smile blandly and celebrate the things I disapprove of. This is what happens when you get mixed up with politicians, Quintus.'

Balbus said nothing; wordlessly passed the jug over to Fronto, who took a swig.

'Nice. From Caesar's personal baggage I suppose.'

The older legate nodded.

'Most of the troops are across the river now, Marcus. There's maybe a thousand still here until the general's ready to move, but that won't be until the morning, and I can't believe there would be any trouble tonight. Your man Velius was wandering around down by the bridge, getting involved in everything. I think he's still a bit confused, and he was ordering the men of the Eleventh around, trying to get them in lines. In the end, I had to get him away myself and order him to stand down and report to the medicus. Head injuries can take months to heal, if they ever do, and that one he took was a fair mess.'

Fronto grinned.

'You underestimate Velius. Sounds like he's quite rational and normal to me. He's got a vested interest in the Eleventh. He helped turn them into a legion. I think he feels responsible for them in a way he doesn't for the Tenth. There's nothing confused about him. A little manic maybe, but not confused.'

Balbus' brow creased.

'But he told me to piss off because he was busy. No centurion in his right mind would say that to a senior officer.'

Fronto laughed for the first time in half a day.

'You'd be surprised what he'd do. Problem is: he's very good at the job, and he knows it. He's got a great respect for authority and senior officers when he agrees with them, but if he thinks they're wrong, he's not shy in telling them. I tend to put up with it, because I'd hate to imagine the Tenth without him, but I do occasionally have to put him in his place. No. Velius is fine, believe you me.'

110

Balbus watched Fronto take another swig from the jar.

'Your head's going to hurt worse than his when we move out tomorrow; you know that, don't you?'

Fronto grinned again.

'I think tonight's your night for underestimating. I have a capacity for good wine unparalleled among my peers. See, I can still form sentences and use long words and everything.'

Balbus laughed out loud.

'Alright. On your head be it. Literally. Now come on... time we went up to Caesar's tent so that you can receive your praise like a good boy. Show them all how noble a good general can be, and try not to fall over.'

He held out an arm. Fronto grasped it and pulled himself to his feet.

'I suppose I'd better put in an appearance, hadn't I.'

Balbus nodded.

'It's been a long day, but it's nearly over.'

CHAPTER 6

(HILLTOP IN AEDUI LAND BEYOND THE SAONE)

'Via Decumana: The main street running east-west in a Roman town or fort.'

The Helvetii spread out like a mass on the plain below the hill. The sun glinted off helmets, armour and spear-tips, and the gentle breeze rippled the patterned Gaulish breeches and tunics. Once they would have seemed like a fearsome sight to the Roman officers but now, after six battles, the legions were stronger than ever, while the Helvetii travelled with perhaps two thirds of their tribe intact. A surprise was the appearance of the Helvetian cavalry unit. There had been horsemen within the tribe during the previous encounters, but spread out and disorganised. Now, they appeared to have taken a leaf out of the Romans' book and formed a central unit of cavalry perhaps five hundred strong.

Fronto glanced over his shoulder at the six legions drawn up in perfect order on the plain behind him; rows and rows of well-trained men ready for anything. Behind them were the baggage wagons and the siege weaponry. To either side were the cavalry, still commanded by Longinus and growing in number daily. Horses had been made available to more of the legionaries, and Longinus now led fifteen hundred regular cavalry drawn from all six legions, and nearly three thousand auxiliary and mercenary levies drawn from the tribes allied to Rome who were now indebted to Caesar for their protection.

And here on the hill in full view of both armies and sandwiched between them sat the leaders, four Romans and three Helvetii, all on horseback. The army had caught up with the barbarian tribe three days after crossing the bridge. The Helvetii had been totally unprepared and were astounded at the speed with which the Romans had chased them down. Two more days had followed with the Helvetii attempting to stay just ahead of the Roman vanguard. Finally, this morning, the barbarians had stopped in their tracks, allowed the pack animals to graze, and turned to face the pursuing army. The three tribal chieftains had ridden to the crest of the hill to wait for the Romans.

As soon as Longinus had reported to Caesar the location and disposition of the Helvetii, the general had given orders for the legions to fall into parade formation. The staff officers had joined the general at the front, and the army had moved into position opposite the Helvetii in perfect order and formation. Fronto could only guess what was about to happen. He presumed it would be face-off and blusters between the two leaders; attempts to threaten and surpass each other.

The Gaul was the first to speak, in good Latin, with barely an accent.

'I am Divico of the Helvetii. I am leader in peace and in war.'

Caesar's face took on a grim demeanour.

'I am familiar with your name, barbarian. However, since it's been fifty years since your people killed Cassius and his army, I will presume it was your father who led at that time. I may be tempted to violence, were it not that Cassius is already avenged. As it is, I will treat with you as though you were a civilised leader.'

Divico nodded and bowed.

'Great Caesar, we have journeyed far from our ancestral land in search of a place where we can settle and rebuild our lives, and where we need not live in constant apprehension of German tribes attacking our villages. We are free from that threat now, and I will defer to Rome on this matter. Tell us where you are content for the Helvetii to settle and we shall do so. The Helvetii will do this in peace and will maintain such peace with the Roman people.'

Fronto blinked. 'They must be worried', he thought. 'They're trying to come to terms with Caesar.'

Divico continued.

'Your army has a made a habit of pursuing and harassing my people. I am willing to put this aside in the name of peace but, should you continue to make war on our people, you would do well to remember a few things.'

Caesar raised an eyebrow, though he did not interrupt.

'Remember, Roman, that the Helvetii have fought and defeated an army of this size before, under this same Cassius that you speak of. Remember that we are a valiant and hardy people. You may have destroyed a part of our tribe by the river, but you achieved that only through devious means and the outcome may have been entirely different had we met on a plain of battle like men. I ask you again to let us settle in peace, and not to turn this plain into the violent and embarrassing defeat of Rome that our last meeting could have been.'

Fronto looked around at the general, half expecting to see him foaming at the mouth over this insolent barbarian's words. He himself seethed over the speech, knowing that it was *his* battle and *his* strategy that this chieftain was inferring had been carried out in an underhanded and cowardly way. Fronto could have lashed out and knocked the man from his horse, had he not been forcing himself to remain motionless and expressionless.

Caesar took a breath and sat high in his saddle.

'Have you finished with your empty threats, barbarian?'

Not pausing long enough to give the chieftain the chance to speak, he continued:

'Your words do not fill me with fear, nor do they justify what you have done. Indeed, it angers me that you could carry out so many acts of brutality in the past against our people, and more recently against my army and the tribes that are allied to Rome, and when you are faced with your accusers you can do little more than beg and threaten. That is the sign of a small and insecure man, Divico.'

The chieftain's mouth fell open in astonishment, and still Caesar gave him no chance to interrupt.

'However, I am not in the habit of genocide in order to achieve a degree of justice.'

For a moment, Fronto glared at his general, images of murdered prisoners flashing into his head.

'I am willing to acquiesce and to find an appropriate and acceptable parcel of land for your people on two conditions.'

This time the general was not fast enough to prevent the chieftain's interruption.

'Roman, I am unused to any man placing conditions upon me.'

Caesar rode over the top of the comment, ignoring the chief's outburst.

'Firstly, you will deliver one hundred of your women and higher-born men to us as hostages for the duration of your journey until you settle.'

Divico's face took on a ruddy cast as the rage rose within him. Caesar continued, quietly and calmly.

'These will be our assurance that you will cause no further trouble. Secondly, you will make restitution out of the wealth and possessions of your people to the Aedui, the Allobroges, and any other tribes against whom you have committed acts of barbarism and destruction. Then we will help you find a place in the world to be comfortable and safe.'

The general sat back on his horse and folded his arms, adding emphasis to his final statement.

'In the name of the senate and the people of Rome, I make you this offer. There will be no other.'

Divico threw his arm out in an angry gesture at Caesar.

'The Helvetii do not give hostages. We take them, as the Roman people are well aware!'

Turning his back on the Roman officers, he rode away down the hill, the other chieftains immediately behind him.

Fronto exchanged glances with Labienus. The other officer shrugged.

'What now? You surely can't let him just ride away after that. Do we mobilise the legions?'

Caesar shook his head.

'I have no intention of launching any sort of battle here and now. The ground is not favourable, the enemy are far too prepared, and we are in the territory of our allies. I have no intention of turning our recently acquired Aedui auxiliaries against us by destroying their lands in battle. We will follow and harry them, making sure they cause no damage to the other tribes, until we can deal with them more surely.'

He turned to Fronto.

'I want you to find Longinus and Balbus. Send Balbus to me. He and the Eighth will lead the vanguard of the army with the colour unit. Also, I want you to deliver these orders to Longinus: I want him and his cavalry forever on the tail of the barbarians to keep them moving and busy. We need to herd them along at this time until they're out of our allies' lands or at least in an acceptable place for battle.'

Fronto bowed as far as his saddle allowed and wheeled his horse to carry out the orders. As he rode back down the slope, he spied Balbus riding up toward the group of officers. As the two approached each other, Balbus reined in and leaned in the saddle to address Fronto.

'What the hell's he up to? It sounds like the Helvetii are leaving.'

Fronto shrugged.

'That's exactly what they're doing. I've no idea what he's playing at, but we're apparently going to be following them. He tossed out some feeble explanations, but he must have some good reason not to grind them into the dirt now. He actually offered to help them settle, but I'd say it was an empty offer. He made demands they were never going to accept. Anyway, the general wants to see you and I've got errands to run. See you at camp tonight?'

Balbus nodded and continued his way up the slope.

Fronto rode off in the opposite direction, making for the Ninth Legion and the massive cavalry contingent out to one side. Scanning the front ranks of the steaming horsemen, he finally spotted their commander in deep conversation with an auxiliary horseman in Gaulish dress.

'Longinus!'

He made his way across the front of the army, aware that a shouted name was unlikely to be heard over the cumulative noise of six legions and several thousand horse. Longinus smiled as he saw Fronto approaching.

'Fronto, have you met Dumnorix, the head of our auxiliaries?'

Fronto nodded a brief greeting at the Gaul and then turned back to the legate.

'Longinus, I need to have a word with you briefly.'

The tired-looking officer glanced briefly at the Gaulish officer and rode forward to join Fronto away from the throng.

'What's up?'

117

Fronto tried to think how best to phrase this. Caesar had given him the most perfunctory of orders, and had assumed that *he* would fill in the necessary blanks. The general had been doing this a lot recently, trying, Fronto supposed, to train him into thinking like a senior staff officer and into taking command decisions at a strategic level.

'You're going to be moving out ahead of the column again. Not as a scout this time, but with your entire cavalry. The army's going to stay on the back of the Helvetii throughout their 'march' at a distance of a few miles. You get the fun, though. You get to stay less than a mile behind, always in sight and keep an eye on them. Stay just far enough back so as to not get entangled with them, but to still be a constant nag and reminder to the bastards. I've no idea why Caesar's delaying this fight, but we're not going to be the ones to cock up his plans, eh?'

Longinus nodded and, turning, trotted back toward his cavalry.

Fronto and Balbus walked along the Via Decumana of the temporary camp. For three days now the army had been shadowing the Helvetii, marching at a peculiar three quarter pace so as to stay far enough back from the stragglers of the tribe. Longinus had been having immense trouble manoeuvring his cavalry without either running into the Helvetii or getting in the way of the Roman vanguard. Every night after an exhausting day of what Velius had named 'midget marching', the legions had to build a series of fortified temporary camps and set picket lines, scouts and guards.

Whispered complaints had become the norm among the soldiers. Constant campaigning was one thing; being ever watchful and ready though not allowed to actually engage the enemy in battle was another. Also, the quartermasters were beginning to be quite vocal concerning the diminishing grain stores and the increasing distance from the supply line at the Saone. Fronto could quite understand their mood even if he could not condone it. Every day since the meeting of the armies, Fronto had tried to persuade Caesar to bring the barbarians to battle, and always he refused.

Ahead, the command tents of the Tenth stood at the centre of the camp. Fronto had quarters with the staff officers in the camp of the Eighth, but had made sure Priscus had put up his tent with the Tenth as well, and he had spent as much time as possible among his own legion. Priscus had, after the first night, actually followed Fronto's orders and had a tent erected for himself at the command centre next to the legate's.

Tonight, Balbus had suggested that they meet at his tent among the Eighth, but Fronto had declined due to the proximity to the general. If they were near the staff officers, Fronto would get given jobs. And so they had made their way across the picket lines, giving the appropriate passwords, and into the camp of the Tenth.

Fronto smiled at the other legate.

'Shall I ask Priscus to join us?'

Balbus smiled.

'Why not? The more you get dragged into high-level strategy, the more he's having to act as a legate anyway.'

The two officers stepped toward the second command tent and then stopped as Fronto caught his arm.

Sounds of laughter issued from the primus pilus' tent. As they listened further there was the 'clonk' of an amphora tipping against the side of a metal drinking vessel, followed by the gurgle of liquid refreshment. More laughter and the sound of rolling dice.

Fronto grinned at Balbus.

'Looks like the drinks are on him.'

As Fronto made to enter the tent, Balbus held up his hand and stopped him.

'Let's have some fun.'

As Fronto stepped back, Balbus drew himself up to his full height next to the tent flap and took a deep breath.

'Centurion Gnaeus Vinicius Priscus, this is the camp prefect and the provost. May we come in?'

A clatter within suggested that Balbus' announcement had had the desired effect. A table was heard overturned and there was the slosh of a spilt drink. At least five voices swore in hushed tones. Balbus and Fronto grinned at each other and then hauled the flap of the tent back. Fronto was first inside.

As Balbus ducked in behind him, he laughed out loud. In much the same way as rats flee into dark corners when suddenly illuminated, eight men were caught mid-flight. A small gaming circle with dice and piles of denarii sat in the centre, surrounded by cushions. Of three tables that had supported oil lamps, drinking vessels and wine jugs, only one remained upright. Two men were already halfway under the leather at the back of the tent. Priscus and Velius stood at attention in the wreckage of a table. The four other men were caught like rabbits in bright light in the act of rescuing fallen wine jugs and putting out the fire on a cushion caused by a falling oil lamp.

'Precious!'

Fronto collapsed onto a small pile of cushions next to the door. Balbus stood in the doorway directing a broad, beaming smile at Priscus.

The primus pilus stayed at attention, as did Velius. The other four officers stood, surreptitiously stamping out the singed cushions with one foot.

'Sir?'

Fronto waved an arm expansively.

'Oh for crying out loud, at ease. Sit down and pass me some of that wine; we're off duty and looking for somewhere to relax. What stakes are we playing for, lads?'

Velius gratefully sank once more to a cushion, as did a number of other men. Two centurions Fronto recognised from the Second Cohort scrambled back under the wall and into the tent, smiling nervously. Priscus continued to stand, trembling slightly and with a purple hue to his face.

'Permission to speak plainly, sirs?'

Balbus nodded as he unfolded a seat next to the door.

'That was a bloody miserable prank, and not worthy of a shit-ditch digger! If you was a centurion and not an officer, I'd...'

He ground to a halt as he realised that he was starting to look foolish in front of the others in the tent. The high colour slowly draining from his face, he sank into a pile of cushions.

'As it goes, I'll just have to strip you both of a month's wages to even up the score, eh? Do you two both know how to play 'Kill the King'?'

The two legates shook their heads.

'Good. Then we'll start with that.'

The ten men sat in their circle around the dice pit, Balbus taking the only campaign chair in the tent to ease the pain he occasionally felt in his knee.

The dice game began in earnest. Fronto fished his purse out and emptied the pile of coins onto the floor in front of him. Balbus, likewise, emptied his coins, ready to place his bet. Cominius, the chief centurion of the Second Cohort, took the dice and shook them, blowing on his hands for luck. Raising his eyes heavenward, he muttered a brief prayer to Nemesis, the Goddess of Retribution. Priscus clicked his tongue.

'We'll have no time to win anything tonight if you don't hurry up and throw the bloody dice!'

Cominius grinned at Priscus, winking slyly at the others.

'Come on Nemesis, Cominius needs a new pair of boots.'

Raising his cupped hands to his ear, he put on an expression of confused surprise.

'Did anyone else hear that? They said Priscus is going home broke! Looks like the Gods have already decided *for* you Gnaeus. Might as well give us your cash now and piss off.'

Priscus gave a throaty cough and nudged Cominius so hard in the arm that the dice left his hand and bounced across the floor and under a cushion.

One of the minor centurions, Fronto could not remember his name, cried 'Out of play! Cominius is out this round. Cough up man!'

Cominius leaned toward the junior centurion as though he were going to whisper in his ear. As soon as the younger man leant in, Cominius punched him mid-upper arm, deadening the muscles.

'Now let's see you throw, you prat.'

'Get your hands off him.'

'Get him, Priscus.'

Fronto smiled at Balbus as a small melee developed on the other side of the tent.

'Think we'd best break this up. Caesar'll have a real go at the Tenth if half the officers turn up with a black eye.'

As Fronto grabbed Priscus, pinning the primus pilus' arms to his sides, Balbus, with a speed belying his age, lunged for Cominius. The two legates dragged the principal brawlers apart. Fears that there might be bad feeling were soon assuaged as Priscus and Cominius collapsed onto the cushions laughing.

'You fight like a girl.'

'Yeah? Well you punch like a chicken.'

Fronto stood between them. The two glanced at him apprehensively, aware that this was their senior officer and that he had every right to discipline them. The look on his face, however, told them Fronto had taken the whole thing in good spirits.

'Alright you two. You want to mess around? This is why the camp prefect doesn't allow gambling on camp. Fights! You lot can't resist kicking the crap out of each other over a couple of denarii, can you?'

'You.' He pointed at Priscus. 'Make it up to everyone. Go and get two jugs of wine out of storage. You're paying for them too.'

Grins split the faces of the watching officers. Cominius smiled smugly at Priscus.

Fronto wheeled on Cominius.

'And *you* can go to my tent and get *my* dice. *They* haven't been weighted. And while you're there you can pick up the tablets on my desk. Casualty reports for the general that need to be in tomorrow night and you're running the figures, lad.'

Muttering, Cominius left the tent, hot on the heels of Priscus. Fronto looked around at the self-satisfied faces of the others. 'I don't know what you lot are smiling about. Get this tent cleared up and ready. We've some serious dice playing to get on with.'

As the various centurions went about clearing up spilled wine and charred cushions, Fronto and Balbus sat sharing the remaining wine and smiling benignly at their juniors. Balbus leaned forward.

'I sometimes wonder if Caesar hasn't got more than he bargained for. He could have selected any legates he wanted to control these legions, but he stuck with us. Don't think he realised how many old-school commanders he was taking on.'

Fronto looked around in surprise.

'Caesar doesn't like new men. In the political climate of Rome these days, the only people you can trust are old-school. Anyone else has political motives for everything. He should know; he has to be the worst of them.'

Balbus frowned.

'I thought you two were old friends. You've campaigned with him before. Why so hostile?'

Fronto took a huge tug straight from the neck of the wine jar.

'He was different back then. Another politician trying to climb the ladder, but he seemed to care more than most. A man the army felt at home with. He's changed. I don't know what's happened in the few years since Spain, but he's become cold. I don't know quite how to put it. Nasty, I suppose. He's still a great general, don't get me wrong, but I'm not sure I trust him anymore.'

Fronto suddenly became aware that the various centurions had stopped their cleaning and were listening intently to what he was saying.

'I don't hear much cleaning. And incidentally, if any of you are bootlicking sons of bitches, this conversation is off the record. I will categorically deny anything that has been repeated and anyone I suspect of passing opinions on will be emptying latrines as an excused-duty legionary within a day. Do I make myself clear?'

The others all nodded humbly and in silence.

'Remember why you're here. Anyway, here comes Priscus with the wine.'

The primus pilus threw open the tent flap and staggered in carrying not two, but four jugs of wine.

'Hell with it sir, we'll be packed and ready to go an hour before the other legions anyway.'

Fronto smiled.

'Dish it out, Gnaeus. Dish it out.'

Balbus nudged Fronto.

'That other centurion of yours has been gone a long time considering he's only in the next tent.'

A young centurion from the Sixth Cohort stood to attention, a cushion in his hand.

'I'll fetch him sir!'

Fronto smiled in a friendly manner.

'Sit down son and have a drink. It's my tent and my orders. I'll fetch him myself.'

Staggering slightly and rubbing his hip, Fronto stood and made his way out of the tent.

The grass was yielding and light beneath his feet as he crossed between the two tents. He was enjoying the sensation of the springy turf so much that he was tremendously surprised when he slipped and came crashing down on his back. His head hit a flat stone with an unpleasant 'crack'. Momentarily, his eyes glazed and his mind filled with an explosion of white light and roaring sounds.

'Too much wine already, I must be getting old' he thought through the mire and blur.

It was at that moment that his groping hand came across something hard and edged. He lifted it into the glow of the guttering torches and saw the finely carved dots staring back at him. Squinting to focus his eyes and to concentrate his swimming head, he glared at the object. The colour of the bone cube was all wrong.

All wrong.

Cube.

Red.

Slipping while trying urgently to pull himself up, he lifted his hand to his face and sniffed the sticky liquid he had been lying in. Smelled of tin. Warm. His or someone else's? Couldn't be his. He had not been lying there long enough to lose all that. As he swayed, eyes continually focusing and defocusing, he saw the rest of the blood, trickling down the slope from the entrance of his tent.

In a panic now, he staggered forward and wrenched open the flap of his tent. There lay Cominius, a cavalry spear through his chest pinning him to the grass. The slick, tin-scented blood ran in a small rivulet down the grass just inside the tent flaps. Frantically moving, he slipped once more and came down next to the body. He became aware that he was shouting. Shouting wildly. Nothing had prepared him for this.

The next thing he knew, he was being helped into a seated position by Priscus, the cloaked figure of Balbus leaning over the body.

'Should've been me. Meant to be me.' It was all he could find to say.

Balbus leaned down over Fronto.

'Did you see anyone?'

Fronto shook his head woozily as visions of imagined assassins swam through it.

Balbus stood once more and addressed the primus pilus.

'Centurion Priscus, call the Tenth to attention.'

He looked around for anyone else he knew.

'You!'

Velius staggered where he was crouched over the body, the bandages still wrapped round his head.

'Velius sir!'

'Get to the Eighth. Call them to attention. Then get to Longinus and send him to me. Don't tell him anything; just tell him Fronto needs him. When you see the Tenth's camp guards on the way past, send them here too.'

The detachment of camp guards were first to arrive. To avoid embarrassment in front of the rank and file, Balbus had sent Priscus into one of the rear rooms, supporting the visibly shaken Fronto.

The guards were understandably surprised to see the legate of the Eighth standing in their commander's tent and two of them had levelled pila at Balbus before he spoke.

'In the absence of legate Fronto and centurion Priscus, I am temporarily assuming command of this unit. There has been an incident involving your commander, and he has been removed to his private rooms for the time being. I want that body searched, and a perimeter set up around this tent. Absolutely no one comes in or goes out without the permission of myself or your commanders.'

The guards slammed their sword-hilts against their chest armour in salute and ran outside to relay orders to the other soldiers. 'Probably relieved to have something to do and not have to make decisions', thought Balbus.

A moment later, Fronto stormed out of the back room, red faced and angry, his hair matted at the back with his own blood, and covered with the smears of Cominius'.

'I'm gonna find the bastard!'

Drawing his sword from its sheath on the table, he made for the entrance. Priscus appeared from the back room and ran over, grasping his legate by the shoulder.

Balbus gently plucked the sword from Fronto's hand and passed it back to Priscus.

'What you are going to do, Marcus, is go to my headquarters under guard. I'm not losing the only other legate in this army that I truly trust just because he's suffering a concussion. Anyway, the culprit will be long gone by now, so we'll have to identify him somehow.'

Fronto struggled a moment longer against Priscus' grip.

Balbus smiled reassuringly at the primus pilus.

'I know it's your legion when he's not here, but I think you need to go with him. Do your trust me to run things for an hour or so?'

Priscus gave him a hard glance, still maintaining his grip on Fronto.

He nodded.

'Come on sir. It'll do none of us any good if they get a second try.'

Fronto gave up and allowed Priscus to help him from the tent.

A few moments later the tent flap opened with no knock. Longinus came in at high speed, Velius hot on his heels. Glancing down as he entered, Longinus gestured to the trickle of blood on the floor.

'What's the silly old sod got himself involved in now?'

Balbus stood over the body that lay draped with a red military cloak.

'Velius. Get out there and make sure the guard has been replaced. Take command, but stay close. I want to see you afterwards.'

Velius saluted and stepped outside.

Once he was sure they were truly alone, Balbus removed the cloak from the body.

Longinus whistled through his teeth.

'I can see why you sent for me.'

He crouched down and examined the spear.

'Problem is that we've had literally thousands of recruits since Caesar requested them from our allies. They all give one word names and half of them are the same or so close as to make no odds. Equipment's a shambles. Even if I run a complete roll call, I can't be sure I'll know whose spear is missing.'

Balbus grimaced at his opposite number.

'These Gauls are supposed to be our allies. How the hell did one of them get in here, and particularly armed?'

Longinus shrugged.

'A matter to discuss with the gate guard, I'd say.'

He looked down at the spear.

'Fronto led the attack against the Helvetii by the river. I saw the way they looked at him. He's at least as much a figure of hatred among them at the moment as Caesar is. There are more of them out there than of us. You know as well as I do that with this number of men in the field, all serving in different units, keeping track of individuals becomes a nightmare. Hell, with all the auxiliaries here, it's hard enough to keep track of a unit!'

Balbus scratched his head and Longinus continued.

'There are hundreds of ways someone could pull this off. We may find the culprit, but I wouldn't pin your hopes on it.'

Longinus stood and pulled himself up straight.

'We'll have to tell the general.'

'Not yet.'

'What?' Longinus wheeled on the older legate. 'He *has* to know if something like this is going on.'

Balbus grabbed Longinus by the arm.

'I don't think Fronto would want it brought to his attention yet, and if we want a chance to catch our assassin, we don't want to make this public. Maybe we can make this work to our advantage.'

For a few long moments Longinus tried to pull away. Finally he stopped pulling and gently prised open the older man's hand.

'Fronto may be a bit of a smarmy bastard, but I'd hate to see him get skewered. The Ninth would never get over it. They still think of him as theirs. What do you want me to do?'

Balbus smiled gently.

'I'll deal with matters here, and I'll meet you at your HQ afterwards.'

Again Longinus hesitated, but finally nodded.

'Then we'll all meet for breakfast in my tent. Fronto and Priscus included, agreed?'

Balbus returned the nod.

As Longinus left, Balbus leaned out of the tent flap. Glancing around, he could see Velius giving commands to a group of guards.

'Centurion Velius, if you please.'

The grizzled man turned and made his way to the tent.

Once he was inside and alone with the legate, the older man dropped the leather flap into place. Beckoning Velius to the rear of the tent, he bade him sit.

'Centurion. You are in the Second Cohort, are you not?'

Velius nodded.

'I thought so. I want you to take the chief centurionate for your cohort. It's a field commission, but I feel fairly sure that Fronto will make it official when he's back in the morning. Do you accept?'

Velius nodded curtly.

'Good. No false humility. Just what I expect. You *do* realise what you've let yourself in for, yes?'

Velius' face took on a look of puzzlement.

'Not sure I understand what you mean, sir?'

Balbus smiled a humourless smile.

'That puts you third in line. Fronto's more and more busy with staff duties, and I think your primus pilus is getting used to commanding the legion. That makes you second in command rather often. It's not a nice duty, but I think you can handle it. Still want it?'

Velius nodded. 'I can do it sir, and I want to get this sorted.'

'I know you can do it. First job's a little unpleasant though. You need to staunch any hint of a rumour about what happened tonight. I mean *every* hint. Understand?'

Again, Velius nodded.

'You need to get to the legion's chief surgeon as soon as I leave. Get some of his orderlies to collect the body and keep it out of sight in the hospital. Circulate the word that Cominius died tonight of a seizure. Get the surgeon to support you. We don't want word of assassins leaking out.'

Another nod.

'Finally, when I leave here, I'll send Fronto and Priscus back. You need to make sure they're seen in the camp in full control. I would suggest you get a few of the officers together and have a small drink before retiring. Fronto will need it and we need to staunch any rumours of his demise. In the morning the two of them are to join us in Longinus' tent, and you are in charge of the Tenth. Understood?'

'Sir.' Velius nodded a final time and pulled himself rigidly to attention.

'Alright. Get someone to deal with this man's effects. You'll have to arrange a cremation in the morning.'

Balbus removed the spear gently from the still shape of Cominius and turned to leave. As he walked briskly down the Via Decumana toward the gate, cavalry spear held in hand, he could hear Velius behind him, bellowing out orders from the command tent.

He heaved a sigh and glanced at the spear. A Roman spear, meant for a Roman officer. There could be all sorts of reasons a member of a Gaulish tribe serving with the cavalry might want to kill a successful general. It *was* war after all, but it did not make it right or acceptable. It had been many years since the civil war and Balbus had no wish to live through another time like that. War should be up-front and above board, not sneaking and murdering.

He found Longinus in the camp of the Ninth and persuaded the man to join him for a walk down by the stream. As the two officers strolled along the bank, moonlight flashing off the rippling water and the constant rush and babbling filling the air, Balbus felt himself relax for the first time in over an hour.

'We need to talk about this.'

Longinus turned his head and nodded, almost imperceptibly in the darkness. Balbus went on.

'I've had word circulated that Cominius died of a seizure. I know that won't fool the assassin, but I don't want to set panic or suspicion among the legions. We don't want any word of assassination going out, or the killer will go to ground. One thing's sure: by morning he'll know he failed to kill Fronto.'

'He probably already knows that.'

Balbus shook his head.

'I don't think so. If he's a recently recruited Gaul, he won't know one officer from another apart from his own unit. He wouldn't be able to tell the difference between Cominius and Fronto at speed in the dark. No. He'll be feeling self-satisfied tonight.'

Longinus nodded.

'I suppose so. There's not much we can do right now, but I'll have a think on the matter and see what I can come up with.'

'Plenty of time tomorrow, while we move. You're going to have to keep those Gaulish cavalry under a watchful eye, though.'

CHAPTER 7

(DEEP IN AEDUI LAND)

'Burial Club: A fund looked after by the standard bearer that each legionary pays into to cover costs of funerals and monuments to fallen colleagues.'

'Signifer: A century's standard bearer, also responsible for dealing with pay, burial club and much of a unit's bureaucracy.'

'Magna Mater: The Goddess Cybele, patron of nature in its most raw form'

The funeral of Cominius took place the next day not long after sunrise. The signifer had doled out appropriate funds, men of Cominius' century under the supervision of Velius had cut plenty of timber and erected a funeral pyre and the unit's stonemasons had hastily cut and chiselled a tombstone in memory of the fallen man. Cominius had been a popular officer, and only a small amount had to be drawn from the burial club, the stonemasons labouring several hours for free. His worldly goods remained packed in his tent, ready to be distributed as his will attested.

The smoke from the burning pyre drifted across the ranks, the acrid yet sweet smell of burning meat filling the nostrils of the watching soldiers. Red dress uniform crests were being worn atop every helm in the watching crowd, with the exceptions of Velius and Fronto, both of whose skulls remained too tender to allow the press of metal.

Fronto had been the one to light the pyre, and had stepped forward from the Tenth, where he stood as their legate, the torch extended in his hand. Unhooking one of the medals from his dress harness, he had attached it to the flaming mass, extended the burning tip the kindling and watched it spring into life, the flames quickly spreading around the wooden bier.

Now, a quarter of an hour later, the pyre was starting to collapse. Most of the legionaries in the surrounding circle had a tear in their eye, though more from the stinging cloud than from emotion.

Fronto was itching to move. The legions were packed and ready and after the funeral they would move on, leaving a burial detail to finish off. The fact that a colleague had been taken, not in the heat of battle but by the blade of a murderer, irked Fronto, but the thing that made him fume most was the almost imperceptible way that his friends and colleagues were tiptoeing around him. Since last night, he had had only a few hours alone while he slept and even then he had heard Priscus, Velius, Balbus and Longinus at different times during the night, never more than a few feet from his tent. Against his wishes, the legate's guard had been assigned to watch his tent (a traditional honour for senior officers that Fronto had long since dispensed with.)

His eyes continually strayed across the pyre to Longinus and his cavalry officers. The legionary cavalry were here out of respect for Cominius, though the auxiliary cavalry, under a few trusted officers, were maintaining their pursuit of the Helvetii. Balbus and Longinus had had a long argument about the necessity of keeping the auxiliary cavalry under the watchful eye of the mounted legionaries. Fronto had listened in on the conversation from the other side of the leather tent wall and could appreciate both points of view. Yes it was necessary, particularly after the attack last night, to keep the auxiliaries under close scrutiny, but Fronto could also, surprisingly, see Longinus' point of view. He had specific orders from Caesar to follow the Helvetii, yet wanted the legionaries to honour the death of one of their own, so splitting them was necessary.

As the flames turned to embers and the mound of burning timber fell in on itself like a collapsing building, Fronto realised that Caesar was looking pointedly in his direction. He stepped out in front of the Tenth and called the legion to attention. They had, theoretically, been at attention for the duration of the previous hour and a half but had, over time, slipped into a more relaxed pose. At times of personal reflection, some leeway was afforded the troops, and Fronto was more sympathetic than most.

As soon as the legion had fallen in properly, Fronto turned to face them.

'Centurions, give the order.'

Around the field, commands rang out, letting the units know they were dismissed. The Tenth was first to fall out, though the other legions were close behind.

As Priscus turned once again to face his commander, Fronto indicated with an inclined head that he wanted a word.

Priscus watched a moment longer to make sure the legion had fallen out properly and then walked alongside his commander, who had already made his way toward the pyre.

'Sir?'

Fronto continued to face the pyre, his primus pilus behind him.

'Gnaeus, what do you think of the general.' He cast the other man a sidelong glance.

'Off the record, I mean.'

Priscus hesitated a moment, not because of whom he was with, but watchful for anyone else within earshot.

'You're only asking me that because you've already made your mind up about something and you want me to confirm it for you. Are you sure you really want me to answer?'

Fronto nodded, still not facing his second in command.

'Well, sir, I think he's a political weasel. Vicious, heartless and cold. He'll use any resource he can find to in order to achieve his goals.'

'Much my thoughts on the subject. He's trying to groom me into the position of some kind of senior strategist for the staff, which will mean removing me from the command of the Tenth.' He growled. 'And I've had it up to here with senior staff.'

Fronto made a throat-cutting motion.

'I don't trust him and, if I remain on his staff, he'll stop trusting *me* pretty soon too. Once that happens, I'll be in serious trouble, and the Tenth could suffer too. I'm not good at this political game. If I was, I'd have made more of a try for the cursus honorum. I actually *do* need your advice, not just confirmation.'

Priscus coughed gently, as the smoke of the pyre had shifted in their direction. They began to walk, side by side and hands clasped behind their backs, away from the smoke.

'You may be right. You could be in trouble. *We* could be in trouble. Frankly, I wouldn't worry about that. We're deep in hostile territory, chasing a pretty nasty enemy with unsure allies around us, possibly with years of blood and guts campaigning ahead of us and you're worrying about political squabbles?'

Priscus took a deep breath, a look of concentration on his face and Fronto knew what that meant: his primus pilus was about to say something offensive, ignoring any proprieties of rank.

'Don't be bloody stupid, Marcus! You can't go running away from responsibility every damn time. You've backed out of everything you've ever done that could secure your future. Unless you want to end up like us in the centurionate: dead at forty, or lying in a ditch in Rome with one leg begging for a coin, or living out your last years as a farmer on a soldier's pension, you damn well take everything Caesar offers you.'

Fronto stopped, turned on his primus pilus and raised a warning finger. Priscus gave him no opportunity to interrupt.

'No, Marcus. You wanted a straight opinion, and you'll get it. I'd jump at the chance to make such a position in the world. One day my kids might inherit a shop or an inn. If I had what you're being offered, they might inherit an estate in Umbria. They might even have been a Consul for Gods' sake. If Caesar asks you to be his personal arse-wiper, you do it. You owe it to those of us who'll never get the chance.'

Fronto frowned.

'But I disagree with him. I think he's wrong more than half the time.'

'All the more reason! As one of his senior officers you're in the position to at least have a say in what happens, and the higher up you get, the more say you'll have. If you hadn't been where you are, d'you think we'd have found and beaten the Helvetii last time? No. 'No' is the answer you're too wrapped up in your own uncertainty to see. The problem is: you're one of *us*. Maybe too much one of us for your own good. You'll never be a proper commander, because you think too much like your men. It means you'll never be comfortable and happy, but it serves us well. Our lives get better, safer and more comfortable with people like you tempering Caesar's decisions. I can't understand how a high-ranking noble family managed to bear someone like you. You'd have been more at home with my family, baking bread in Nola. Now go and see the general and wipe his arse!'

Fronto smiled at Priscus.

'You have a strange way, Gnaeus. You can be deferential when you need to, but you could make a King feel like an irresponsible child when you chastise him.'

The smile was returned. Priscus patted his superior officer on the shoulder as if mollifying a minor.

'Never mind sir, one day you'll look back on this and *sob* like a small boy.'

Priscus stopped in his tracks and saluted Fronto before turning and making his way back to the Tenth, who were assembling on one side of the grassy depression that had been chosen for the funeral. The legion gathered around the packs and wagons, securing ropes and tightening the straps on their equipment.

Fronto wandered off in the direction of the command unit. Caesar and his staff officers stood upwind of the smoke on the bank, watching the legions making their preparations. Already the burial detachment was formed up next to the pyre; the tombstone, urn and tools at the ready, waiting for the mass to finish its slow collapse.

As Fronto approached the colour party, Balbus came jogging toward him, carrying the cavalry spear from the night before. Stopping in his tracks, Fronto turned to face the older legate. Balbus was fighting for breath and, as he came to a halt, he thrust the spear into the ground and bent over forward with his hands on his knees, breathing heavily.

Fronto smiled. Balbus complained often about the restrictions his age placed on his physical involvement with the army, but Fronto could only hope that he were as fit and active when he reached that age. There were a number of legionaries and lesser officers in the Tenth that Fronto knew would have trouble making that distance across the field in the time the Eighth's legate had made it.

'Out of breath? Why didn't you send a runner? That *is* what they're there for.'

Balbus straightened up, still puffing heavily.

'I ... I don't think this is a ... messenger job.'

He indicated the spear.

'Have a look.'

Fronto looked in puzzlement.

'I've seen it Quintus. Quite close, remember?'

The older man nodded impatiently.

'Yes, yes. But did you really have a proper look at it?'

Fronto shook his head.

'It's a cavalry spear. If you've seen one, you've seen a thousand.'

Balbus shook his head and wrenched the spear from the turf, slamming it back in a hand-width from Fronto's foot.

'Use your eyes man.'

Fronto leaned forward, making a close examination of the spear. It was a normal, ordinary, dull cavalry spear.

Except for the marks.

The marks.

He bent his head closer.

'What the hell *are* they?'

Balbus shrugged.

'My guess is some kind of Gaulish markings, maybe religious, or political, or even just a curse or something. I didn't want to take it to one of Longinus' Gaulish men; after all, we don't want to alert the man that we're on to him. I have a couple of men in the Eighth that can speak their language with reasonable skill; the result of being stationed in Transalpine Gaul for so long. I do remember seeing marks similar to that though, carved or painted in various places like graffiti.'

Fronto smiled.

'So we want to find out what it says, and maybe see if we can find the matching one of the pair among Longinus' men.'

Balbus nodded and once more, pulled the spear from the ground.

136

'I'll speak to a couple of people about it tonight while things are quieter.'

Fronto smiled.

'Thanks, Quintus. We've got to get this psychopath. Can't have Gaulish assassins hiding in the legions.'

The two clasped hands and then went their separate ways.

Aulus Ingenuus was a lesser cavalry officer, a decurion, who had volunteered for this duty because it got him out in the open. Who could have preferred to be back in that hollow with the choking smoke of burning flesh filling his throat and making him gag? Better by far to be out here, even if it meant the danger of meeting the Helvetii, and the constant smell of Gaulish auxiliaries who seemed unable to grasp the most rudimentary concepts of bathing.

Six regular legionary cavalry decurions had been chosen to keep the auxiliaries in line during this morning's pursuit and reconnaissance mission. Obviously, most of the regulars, including the true cavalry prefects, were back in the dip, respectfully choking in the smoke of that centurion from the Tenth. The auxilia had no such restraints placed on them and had been assigned this morning's duties. It was Ingenuus' first chance at an independent command. Six alae of cavalry, numbering five hundred men apiece, commanded each by a regular officer, temporarily filling in as a prefect.

With the way Caesar's cavalry contingent was expanding on a weekly basis, Ingenuus was looking forward to speedy promotion, and taking every opportunity to command and to shoulder responsibility would be a helpful step in that direction.

The day was bright and clear, and the yellow globe hanging mildly over the horizon promised a warm afternoon. The smell of flowers, grass and all the Magna Mater's bounteous gifts assailed him. Today was a good day to be alive.

He had drawn the Fourth Ala that rode along the eastern side of the valley floor, heading toward a crest where the ground fell away and beyond which would be the Helvetii. The Fifth, slightly further east, rode parallel with them along the ridge and somewhere out of sight beyond them would be the Sixth. The First, Second and Third mirrored their positions off to the west.

The auxiliary units had already had Gaulish officers assigned earlier by the high command, to aid the cavalry prefects, and Ingenuus suspected they resented young Roman junior officers being placed in such supervisory roles. On the other hand, he thought, eyeing the well-bred and well-dressed Aedui officer of whom he had taken control, the man had reacted well and had followed his orders swiftly and efficiently ever since. Perhaps these Gaulish allies were not the barbarous monkeys the regular officers seemed to regard them as.

He glanced over to the west, where the Second Ala rode in relatively good formation along the ridge at the other side of the valley. They seemed to be moving quite fast. Scanning around and behind him, suddenly alarmed that the cavalry may be under pursuit by enemy forces, he could see nothing untoward. The Third Ala was ahead; further ahead than anyone should be. They should be on the valley floor, keeping pace with Ingenuus' men. In fact, the Third was far enough ahead they were at the crest and must be clearly within sight of the Helvetii. What in the name of Jupiter were they doing? Motioning the Fourth to pick up the pace, he began to race after the stray unit.

This was not what he had wanted; not what he had expected. He had taken command this morning because it had promised to be a nice easy reconnaissance mission. Now there were units breaking formation. The Third seemed to be determined to reach and engage the enemy on their own. They had disappeared over the crest of the hill moments ago, and the closest pursuing unit, the Second, had almost reached the saddleback now.

Swallowing his fear, Ingenuus began giving orders to the auxiliaries. The unit moved into a spearhead formation, the best tactic he could think of, not knowing what he was facing.

Moments later, the Second were wheeling their horses and turning. Had the Third found the trouble they were so obviously looking for? Faced with his first critical command decision, Ingenuus dithered. What to do? Should he form up with the rest of the cavalry in the valley? But if he did and the Third had run into trouble out of sight ahead, then they would be abandoning half a thousand men to their fate. Whatever else the young cavalry commander could be accused of, including foolhardiness, he would never be accused of leaving fellow soldiers to die for the sake of his own skin.

With a sigh of resignation, he gave the order to charge. Breaking into a gallop, he heard the hooves of the entire unit keeping pace with him. He daren't turn round for fear of losing his nerve. He had no idea what awaited them over the ridge, and charged on blindly.

The Fourth had crossed the ridge and hit the enemy square on before they were aware of what was happening. With an efficiency that surprised Ingenuus and would have made his commander proud, he had begun swinging with his sword and manoeuvring his horse automatically, his mind still trying to comprehend what had happened. Signalling his unit to rally round him, he made for a small raised mound in the valley and surveyed the battlefield.

The Third Ala had obviously launched straight into the Helvetian cavalry with some force. They were now surrounded by the enemy and were being systematically driven back and cut down. Ingenuus could see around half of the unit making its way as best it could toward the edge, making a break for freedom and the Roman force a few miles away.

There were not that many of the Helvetian cavalry, but the terrain was definitely with them, and the rest of the tribe stood patiently, waiting behind them to mop up anything their cavalry could not finish. Time was running short. As he glanced around, he could see that the tribe were slowly whittling down the numbers around him. The auxiliary cavalry were fighting as hard as they could, but without the discipline of the regular legionary cavalry beside them, they were far too disorganised.

As he watched one of his unit accidentally speared another, mistaking him for the enemy in the press. There was no hope here; they had to pull out. He glanced up the slope to the crest of the saddle. The other four officers in charge of the alae had drawn them up in a line on the hill. While Ingenuus had committed himself to saving as many of the Third Ala as he could, his peers had decided to maintain distance as per Longinus' orders and would not risk getting tangled in the melee. He was on his own, like that poor bastard who had led the Third in. Damn his choice of duties! Today was no day to be in command of a cavalry ala. With a shout, he called his second in command, a warrior of the Aedui tribe with a good grasp of Latin, to him.

'Take the Fourth back out as fast as you can and join up with the other alae on the hill. There's a couple of hundred survivors from the Third that got out safely. Hook up with them and get back to the army as soon as you can. Report to the legate.'

The Aedui warrior frowned.

'What will you do, sir?'

Ingenuus pushed the fear and dread deep down inside and locked it in behind a manic grin.

'I'm going to take a dozen or so men and try to get to the rest of the Third over there.'

He pointed deep into the Helvetian melee.

'With any luck it'll distract them enough to give you time to get away and up the hill.'

The warrior nodded and called a retreat in Latin to the Fourth. The auxiliaries surged toward the rear, catching the Helvetii by surprise though still losing men as they ploughed their way toward freedom.

Signalling to a few of the troopers around him, Ingenuus pushed on deep into the throng. Eleven men followed him, madly battering the Helvetii with swords and spears, trying, not for kills, but to create enough room to manoeuvre.

A moment later he and the eight surviving auxiliaries who had made it through, burst out of the mass of Helvetian cavalry, and into the open space separating them from the waiting infantry. Not far off to his left, he could see a Roman cavalry banner waving defiantly above the press of horsemen. Wheeling his mount, he began to gallop along the clear ground, his eight companions staying close.

As soon as he judged they were level with the entrapped Third, he turned and began to plough his way back into the enemy cavalry, swinging in wild figure-eights with his long cavalry blade. Five of his companions made it back in to the melee, the others being brought down with long spears or vicious Celtic swords while they turned.

Looking ahead, he could see the Third, such as it now was, only ten paces ahead of him. There were little more than a dozen of them. He could see the Roman officer, bathed in blood, swinging his sword madly with his left hand, his right clenched tightly to his side where Ingenuus could make out, even at this distance, a number of wounds in the blood-drenched tunic.

Shouting a defiant cry in the face of the Helvetii and invoking the protection of Jupiter and of Mars, he pushed forward, painfully aware of wounds he was now receiving and the loss of another of his companions. Moments before he was unhorsed and disappeared under the press of the enemy, he saw the commander of the Third also disappear from sight.

On the crest of the hill, the senior of the four officers shook his head sadly, watching perhaps three hundred men make their painful way up the hill, leaving near seven hundred dead and dying in the valley. With the briefest of signals, he led the entire cavalry contingent back toward the legions.

News of the cavalry's return had spread among the senior officers before the first ala appeared over the distant hills. Longinus had ridden out to the highest point close to the marching legions, and Fronto, Balbus and Crispus had joined him. Caesar had remained in the vanguard, leaving cavalry matters to Longinus.

Fronto reined his horse in next to Balbus.

'What the hell d'you think's happened? They've only been out for a couple of hours.'

Balbus shrugged.

'I really don't know, but they had no senior officers out there, and only six regular soldiers altogether. Perhaps the auxiliaries panicked and fled. It's been known to happen.'

As the four remaining cavalry alae formed up on the slope below their commander, the remnants of the Third and Fourth formed under their Gaulish officers, neither of the regulars having made it back. The two

Aedui rode out proudly alongside the four Roman regulars to report to Longinus.

As a mark of respect, the other three legates sat astride their horses a few paces behind Longinus as he received the commanders.

The senior of the cavalry decurions stepped his horse slightly forward and saluted Longinus.

'I beg to report the loss of a number of cavalrymen, sir.'

Longinus frowned, his displeasure plastered across his face.

'You had strict orders to follow and watch and not to become involved, and yet you bring our forces back with the best part of a thousand men missing? This is not a 'loss', decurion. This is a debacle. Who is responsible?'

The Aedui officer in charge of the Third Ala stepped forward.

'Sir, the commander assigned to our unit came across the enemy and ordered a charge. The other units were not close enough to support us. By the time we were deep among the enemy, the commander ordered as many of us as possible to pull out and regroup with the others.'

A moment later the Aedui officer of the Fourth joined them.

'Sir, our commander ordered a charge to try and rescue the Third. When he realised it wouldn't work, he tried to get us clear while he and a dozen others went on to try and reach the survivors.'

Longinus glared at the two Gauls for long moments while he mulled over the information.

'You are all dismissed. Fall in alongside the Ninth in your assigned positions. You.'

He pointed at the remains of the Third and Fourth Alae.

'You are now all assigned to the Fourth. Report to the prefect of the Fourth and form up with him. Find the prefect of the Third and send him to me.'

He turned to face the other legates as soon as the cavalry moved off.

'I'm going to have to send the regulars out under the circumstances. Could I prevail on you three for your opinions of that?' He stressed the last word with distaste and gestured in the direction of the disappearing cavalry alae.

The three looked at each other and, after several shrugs, Fronto sighed.

'I don't like to think that one of our regulars would take such a stupid action in the face of the enemy, but they were all juniors, and juniors are capable of the most surprising strokes of genius and stupidity alike. You sort the cavalry out, Longinus. I'll go and figure out how to report this to Caesar with the best possible angle. Don't be too hard on the Fourth. Sounds like they tried to pull off a hell of a heroic rescue to me. It's just a shame it didn't work.'

Longinus sighed.

'There's often a fine line between heroic and insane, Fronto, but I see your point.'

It was around an hour after sunset when Fronto was shaken awake by Priscus.

'Come on sir, get up.'

Blearily, Fronto grasped the scarf around the primus pilus' neck by the knot and pulled the man down to within a finger-width of his face.

'This had better be important, Gnaeus.'

Priscus pulled his head back, wrenching the scarf out of Fronto's grip.

'Oh, important like you wouldn't believe, sir.'

As Fronto rose and struggled into his tunic and breeches, he rubbed his eyes and wearily questioned Priscus.

'What is it, then?'

'Let's keep that as a surprise, sir. I've taken the liberty of having legate Balbus awakened too.'

Fronto stopped for a moment and frowned quizzically at his senior centurion.

'Alright then. Let's go.'

Priscus led the two of them away from the command quarters of the Tenth and down the slope to the freshly-dug trenches that formed the outer ramparts of the marching camp.

A small knot of people stood near the corner of the ramp and ditch. As they got closer, Fronto identified Balbus. Others he did not know, but he spotted a couple of medical personnel there.

Arriving at the corner, he could see that the two medical officers and two tired-looking capsarii were tending five wounded cavalrymen. The men were under the guard of several of the Tenth's legionaries who had been posted at the ditch.

Balbus hurried to join Fronto as he approached.

'What on Earth is going on? My adjutant woke me at this unreasonable hour on the authority of the legate of the Tenth.'

Fronto glanced at Priscus, who grinned back, smugly.

It irritated Fronto to see that Balbus was immaculately turned out in his full dress and armour, whereas he himself looked like an off duty legionary who had been hauled out of a trench. One of the guards approached the two legates and saluted.

'These five came through the picket line about a quarter of an hour ago, sir. They were creeping around and bumped into us. When we challenged them, they gave the correct password and asked for the legate of the Ninth before the leader passed out in the ditch.'

Balbus cupped his hand around his mouth and whispered to Fronto.

'That's a cavalry officer's uniform. Looks like one of the regulars got back from that attack alive after all.'

Priscus, standing close enough to listen in, said

'Look again, sir. Two cavalry officers.'

Sure enough, the second officer was there, lying drenched in blood and blessedly unconscious in the hole.

Fronto stepped to the edge of the ditch, gesturing at the officer who was on his feet.

'You! Name and unit.'

The officer staggered, trying to pull himself to attention, despite a number of wounds that obviously hampered his movement.

'Sir. I beg leave to report to legate Longinus.'

'You can speak to legate Longinus when you've finished here. As a staff officer, I represent Caesar himself. Now report.'

The officer sighed a weary sigh.

'Aulus Ingenuus, sir: decurion of the Ninth Legion, acting prefect of the Fourth Ala of auxiliary cavalry.'

Fronto barely blinked.

'And your fellow officer?'

'I don't know his name sir, but he's the acting prefect of the Third Ala sir.'

Fronto relaxed his shoulders and dropped to a crouch.

'Alright soldier, at ease. I think you'd better tell me everything.'

As the medical staff worked quietly and efficiently, Ingenuus retold the sad tale of the events of earlier that day. By the time he had reached the end of the engagement, the medical staff had finished with the criss-cross of vicious wounds he had received, and taken the mammoth task of saving the other officer out of the hands of the capsarius.

'Anyway, sir, there were little more than a dozen of us. Once we'd been unhorsed, there was little chance of fighting back, so we stayed down and played dead. I realise that's not very honourable sir, but we thought it would be more important that we get back than taking down maybe a couple more. Unfortunately half of us died when the Helvetian cavalry moved out. Trampled beneath the horses. Since then we've been trying to get back to the legions without bumping into the Helvetii again.'

Fronto smiled a little

'I've heard what you did on the battlefield from the other commanders. Perhaps not the most prudent course of action, but commendable nonetheless. Going to the aid of a trapped unit is the sort of thing that gets one decorated, soldier. You can be sure that Longinus is already aware of your heroism.'

He pointed at the other, unconscious officer. 'Nice job, though you should have left him there. Man who leads recklessly like that's a liability.'

Ingenuus' face took on a sombre cast.

'I think you need to hear the rest sir.'

Fronto frowned once again and motioned to the guards.

'You lot help the medics take these others to the hospital. Don't let anyone else near them.'

He looked at Balbus and Priscus.

'This has the feel of an important and possibly confidential conversation. It'd be better in my tent. Can we help this man there?'

The cavalryman stood.

'I can walk sir.'

'Splendid.'

The four of them made their way across the camp to the officer's tent, where Priscus made himself busy lighting oil lamps and ordering the guards to patrol outside the tent. Fronto retrieved a flask of wine from a corner while Balbus helped the young man get settled on a seat.

Fronto poured a wine for them all, watering all but one, which he handed to Ingenuus.

'You'd best go on.'

The young man took a deep, appreciative swig of the wine.

'When the Helvetii'd gone, sir, we crawled out from under the bodies. The other officer was already in pretty bad shape, but he made sure he told me something before he passed out. Wanted it to get back, y'see.'

Fronto nodded encouragingly.

'Well, he said it was his second in command, a Gaul, who drove the ala to attack first. He was taken by surprise and had to charge in after his unit to try and break it up, sir. He said he was doing alright rallying the men until the *bastard*, meaning his Gaulish deputy begging your pardon sir, stuck him in the back with a spear.'

Fronto looked up sharply at Balbus, who nodded gently.

'You mean this Gaulish auxiliary officer led a fatal charge, attempted to murder his own officer, and then escaped to lay the blame at his *feet*?'

He shared a glance with Balbus again. The older man spoke first.

'I hope that other young officer lives through the night. We may need his evidence when we bring the Gaul to trial.'

Fronto smiled grimly.

'If this is who I think it is, he'll not get a trial. I'll gut the bastard myself. Balbus, do you think we've got enough legal grounds to detain that particular cavalryman in the stockade?'

'More than enough. I'll have a word with Longinus and ask him to arrange it. He and I can go through the man's gear too. Look for some evidence to link our two incidents together?'

'If it *is* him, Quintus, I want him. I want him myself.'

Balbus nodded sombrely. 'I know. You'll have to talk to Caesar as soon as we have enough evidence. In the meantime, are you finished here?'

'Yes.'

'Then, decurion Ingenuus, I think we should go and see your legate.'

The two stood and left the tent, Ingenuus giving a last salute to Fronto as he left.

Priscus made to leave, but Fronto waved him to a chair.

'You sleepy?'

'Me? No, not really. Why?'

'I'm a bit keyed up now. Not much chance of sleep tonight. Think I'll drink for a while, then go see what Balbus and Longinus have turned up. Want to join me?'

Priscus fixed Fronto with a hard glare.

'So long as you're not going to get all fired up and go do something stupid. I know you, Marcus. You're going to go find that cavalryman after a skin full of wine and beat the man to within an inch of his life.'

Fronto grinned at him. 'It's a possibility.'

Priscus sighed.

'I suppose I'll have to stay, then. Someone's got to keep you out of trouble. A primus pilus' work is never done. As if it's not enough having to look after five thousand men for my superiors, I have to look after my bloody superiors too. Give me that!'

He snatched the jar of wine from Fronto's hand and drank deeply from it.

CHAPTER 8

(TEMPORARY CAMP IN AEDUI TERRITORY)

'Decimation: the worst (and rarest) form of Roman military punishment, saved generally for insurrection or cowardice of a whole unit. The entire unit would be lined up; the officer would walk down the line and mark every tenth man, who would then be beaten to death by his comrades.'

'Gladius: the Roman army's standard short, stabbing sword, originally based on a Spanish sword design.
Pilum (pl: pila): the army's standard javelin, with a wooden stock, a lead weight and a long, heavy, iron point.'

Fronto slammed his fist down on the table so hard that he wondered if he had broken his hand. Caesar sat in his campaign chair fuming, his face red and strained.

The guards standing by the tent doorway did their best to blend in with the leather. Balbus and Longinus had long since slipped out; the argument had been going for nearly a quarter of an hour now.

Caesar took a deep breath, ready to begin the next round of verbal pummelling.

'The evidence you have provided, *legate* Fronto, will be laid before my chief provost. He will advise me on the appropriate legal courses and *I* will decide the case myself. I absolutely forbid...'

Fronto once more rose from his seat and slapped his hands flat on the table.

'General, I will deal with this *myself!* That bastard killed one of the senior centurions of the Tenth, and the attack was meant for *me*. You risk losing the respect and support of the whole legion if you take this out of our hands.'

Standing back, he took a deep breath.

'I don't want to fight about this sir, but it really *is* that important.'

Caesar lowered his head.

'I will not allow one of my senior officers to put himself in harm's way for the sake of a grudge. If you want the Tenth involved, I can arrange that. Any punishment, and I'm sure it'll be execution, can be administered by your men.'

'That's no good, sir. You know I'm going to kill him, with or without official sanction. If I don't, one of the others will; maybe even Priscus. Don't make me disobey orders, sir.'

Caesar sighed and cradled his fingers.

'The prisoner can be held a while yet. We'll keep him under the guard of the provosts for a few days. You need time to calm down and see this from an objective point of view, rather than a victim's angle. We'll discuss the matter again then. Maybe you'll have seen sense.'

Fronto said nothing; trusted himself to say nothing. He merely stood, hands flat on the table, glowering at his commander.

Caesar sighed again.

'In the meantime, the matter is closed. I would advise you to make it *very* clear to your men that no attempts on the life of the prisoner will be tolerated. I have no wish to hand out punishments for disobedience. If you fear that the whole Tenth will take the decision badly, I will have to take measures. I will not allow my legions to take matters into their own hands. Decimation has been rare as a punishment for a long time, and I have no wish to resurrect the practice for one legion who goes against their general's wishes. Just remember who pays you all.'

Fronto ground his teeth noisily, his jaw clamped shut to hold back the hundred vicious retorts flowing through his mind.

'I will need you in an hour when the representatives of the Aedui arrive. In the meantime, you are dismissed, legate.'

Without a further glance at the officer, Caesar turned and picked up a pile of reports.

Fronto straightened with a stiff manner, gave an exaggerated salute and, turning on his heel, left the tent.

Not far from the headquarters tent Balbus, Longinus and Priscus stood in deep conversation with Crispus and Galba. Still fuming in his ill humour, Fronto stormed down to the group and pointed an accusing finger at Priscus.

'If the entire command system is standing here blabbing, who the hell's looking after the Tenth?'

Priscus blithely ignored the idiotic remark.

'Things didn't go according to plan, then?'

Fronto's brow lowered until it joined at the centre.

'He won't even listen to anything I say. Bloody politicians! Command of the army should be given to a soldier, not a social climber.'

Balbus and Longinus grabbed Fronto by the shoulders and hustled him down the Via Decumana and away from the headquarters.

'You can't go shouting things like that within earshot of the headquarters. You know that man has the senses of a hawk.'

Longinus nodded.

'None of this is our doing, so don't take it out on your friends. Now are you going to calm down or are we going to have to throw you in the river?'

Fronto stood for long moments, wagging his finger in the air and opening and closing his mouth before he pulled himself away from the grip of the other officers. His shoulders slumped in dejection.

'He *did* agree to discuss it again in a few days. In the meantime no one from the Tenth goes near the arsehole except you and me, Priscus.'

The officers tensed as Fronto drew his gladius from its sheath though in the end he hefted it for but a moment, looking down the blade before upending it and slinging it point first into the turf.

'He threatened the entire Tenth if anything happens to the Gaul. He even uttered the word 'decimation', the arrogant bastard. If he tried that, he'd have a general mutiny on his hands, so no one mentions that, alright?'

He looked around at the solemn faces and waited for the acknowledging nods.

'I'm not having him dealt with by trial. No way. I'm going to gut the son of a bitch myself. I'll wait 'til I'm a little fresher and calmer and talk to the general again.'

Balbus held up a restraining hand.

'You damn well won't, you idiot. You'll just get angry again, then Caesar will throw the book at you. Hard! I'll have a quiet word with him this evening.'

Longinus nodded his agreement, but Crispus scratched his head reflectively.

'I think the muse of deviousness is toying with my brain. I have an idea.'

The others looked at him. Crispus rarely spoke in their company. He and Galba were still fairly new to command and tended to treat the other legates with deference and respect, despite Balbus' regular urging to consider them as equals. Crispus had the look more of one of Rome's young, educated rhetoricians rather than a soldier.

'I imagine it would be easy for influential, intelligent gentlemen like us to sow seeds of dissent among the men.'

He raised his eyebrows meaningfully. Fronto regarded him doubtfully.

'I'm not about to rebel against my general over one man.'

Crispus shook his head quickly.

'You misunderstand me sir.'

'Don't call me sir, Aulus.'

'Anyway, should Caesar hear soldiers throughout the legions discussing the matter and advocating a fitting punishment for him, he may rethink his position.'

Balbus grinned.

'He could have something, Marcus. Caesar's regarding this plan as your ravings, no offence intended. He might not realise how far across the army this might ripple. If we nudge things a little, we could make it plain to him. Good idea, Crispus.'

Priscus turned and saluted Fronto, a grin on his face.

'Permission to return to the Tenth and spread malicious and devious gossip, sir?'

Fronto smiled indulgently at his second in command.

'I can think of no better way of spending a lazy afternoon, Priscus. Get Velius in on the matter too. That man's a born complainer, so everyone'll take it seriously.'

He turned to the others.

'I've got to be back at the headquarters in less than an hour in full dress uniform, but I could spare half an hour to go and hate the prisoner in person. Care to join me, gentlemen?'

Among the shaking heads, Longinus stepped forward and patted Fronto on the shoulder.

'Someone'll have to go with you, or you'll end up stringing the man up in his cell.'

The various commanders went their separate ways, leaving Fronto and Longinus walking alone toward the hastily-erected stockade in the camp of the Ninth.

It struck Fronto once more that he was walking among men he had once commanded, and that he and Longinus had antagonised each other for so long that he had never considered the possibility that they could actually get along. The relationship was still nothing like that he already shared with Balbus, but every day he came to respect and like the legate of the Ninth a little more. He had not noticed when he had become comfortable in his company, and they had not slung even joke insults at each other for some time now. Perhaps it was the pressure of campaigning. Both of them had much more on their minds these days than the exchanging of petty abuse.

Smiling at Longinus with genuine warmth, he passed through the gate of the Ninth's temporary camp as the other legate gave the daily password to the guard.

The stockade was a solid affair. Ten feet along each side, formed of sharpened stakes twelve feet high that had been retrieved from storage in the baggage train. Various materials were carried for just such emergencies. The one gate in the stockade was formed of the same stakes, bound together with heavy rope and barred with a six foot branch fed through two rope loops. A guard drawn from the Ninth stood at each corner of the stockade, and two of Caesar's provosts stood by the gate, stiffly at attention, their eyes straight forward.

Fronto had never much cared for provosts. They were always rules-lawyers with an obsessive nature and no sense of camaraderie toward the rest of the regulars. Velius regularly joked that they stood as though they 'had a pilum stuck up their arse.' Fronto looked at the posture of the provost guards and raised his hand to his mouth, coughing to cover a smirk. Velius had an eye for detail, it seemed.

Longinus threw a questioning glance at Fronto and ordered the guard to open the door. Moving with mindless precision, the provost turned and withdrew the heavy beam, his counterpart levelling a pilum at the gate.

Fronto, still trying to stifle a smile, could see how unnecessary the precaution was as the door was pulled open. The prisoner, disarmed and unequipped, stood at the rear of the stockade, clad only in Gaulish breeches, shoeless. He was chained to the wall and could reach no more than five feet toward the gate.

Longinus regarded the prisoner for long moments and then turned and gestured meaningfully at the provost.

'Get this man a tunic and some boots. I don't care whether he's comfortable, but if he dies of a chill before he can be brought to trial, you might be punished instead.'

The provost stood still and emotionless, answering with only the curtest of nods.

Longinus and Fronto stepped inside and the legate of the Ninth motioned to the provost to shut the gate.

Once they were inside alone, the two approached the prisoner, staying out of reach of his restrained arms, though the Gaul stood still and relaxed at the rear, with no tension on the chains. Fronto regarded him coldly and the Gaul met his gaze defiantly and with head high and back straight.

'There are plenty of men in my legion and probably in the others that would like nothing more than to personally unravel your guts in front of the whole army and I have to admit to being one of them myself. Longinus is here to make sure I don't disembowel you at a moment's notice.'

He stood silently for a moment, waiting for a response that never came. He almost wished the Gaul would say something to goad him. For all Caesar's words, Fronto was fairly sure he could get away with it. Still, killing a chained man was beneath him; even a traitorous dog like this.

'Make no mistake. There's only one direction from here. Death is inevitable. However, I might be persuaded to make it quick and easy for you if you cooperate a little with us?'

Once more he waited for a response, but the prisoner merely stood stiff and straight-backed, glaring at the two officers.

'What the hell did I ever do to you? I assume you're Helvetii, not Aedui? If that's the case, then yes, I did attack your army and I did fight them. I'm not the only one, and I daresay that your generals would do the same to us if the situations were reversed. We would *never* stoop so low as to murder them in cold blood, though.'

As soon as the words were out, he regretted them, visions of Caesar's execution of the Helvetii prisoners swimming once more through his head. How could he hold the moral high ground when senior Romans were capable of such barbarism? The obvious response did not come. The prisoner merely continued to glare at him.

'For Gods' sake, say something.'

The Gaul leaned back against the stockade.

'What would you have me say, Roman? That I hate you? Of course I hate you; all of you. Why did I do it? What did I hope to achieve? Meaningless questions, all. What matters is that I tried and failed. For that, I'm prepared to die. Now leave me be. It's time I made peace with *my* Gods.'

Longinus shrugged as they turned.

'We'll get nothing from him. Arrogant race, the lot of them.'

Behind them the Gaul began to laugh. He muttered something in his own language, but the word 'arrogant' was clearly audible in Latin.

As the two officers reached the gate and Longinus knocked, the Gaul called out.

'I will offer you one scrap of information, Roman, to keep you warm and cosy at night: I am not alone. There are others. Many others, and not all of them Gaulish. I failed, true, but *someone* will succeed.'

Fronto turned, ready to bear down on the Gaul and question him further, but Longinus held his shoulder fast.

'He'll tell you no more Marcus. Look at him. Personally, I want to know how the hell he managed to get into our cavalry. Surely the Aedui auxiliaries must have known he wasn't one of them. I've got several men questioning them, but I doubt we'll find anything out.'

They stepped out and the provost closed and barred the gate behind them.

'I'll head back to my men now. Have fun with Caesar.'

Fronto grunted and walked off in the direction of the Tenth and his own tent.

Caesar's headquarters tent had been decked out in all its finery when Fronto arrived. The standards and flags of the legions were present, along with a huge map of the whole empire painted on animal hide that hung behind Caesar. The staff officers had been directed to various seats around the rear of the tent to either side of the general.

Fronto had been the last to arrive, slightly late, and Caesar had given him a disapproving glance that he currently felt disinclined to care about. He had taken his seat to the far right. A spare chair sat between him and the others, and he wondered why until Balbus entered the tent, bowing slightly. It made sense, really. Balbus had been dealing with Gauls and had been stationed among them for a long time now. Consequently, he was by far the most conversant with their ways among the Roman command.

Much as Fronto did not want to be here, in a political conference with their Gaulish allies and among the staff, he reminded himself that he had a vested interest in the proceedings. The quartermasters had warned all of the most senior officers of impending supply problems. The shipments of grain that Caesar had arranged up the River Saone were now very much out of the legions' reach, since the army had followed the Helvetii far from the course of the river. The supplies in the baggage train had therefore fallen low and were being stretched already. With weeks at least of campaigning ahead of the army, this could prove a serious problem.

The weather had picked up a great deal recently, but the climate here was not the same as home, and the grain in the fields of Gaul would not be ripe for a long time yet, so there was little hope of commandeering supplies on their march. Forage was keeping meat and fruit supplies above the bare minimum, but if supplies of grain were not forthcoming soon, the army would slowly begin to starve and would be forced to abandon the campaign. To this end, Caesar had prevailed upon the Aedui, as allies of Rome, to supply the army with grain.

The Aedui, eager to sustain their alliance, and mindful of the large army campaigning in their territory, had readily agreed. However, it had been several days since the promise, and nothing had yet been produced. In around a week's time, the legions were due their next rations, and there would not be enough grain to meet the demand. It was a worrying situation looming in the minds of all the officers. Fronto had had enough on his mind recently without thinking of such matters and had left it in the hands of Priscus, but could not shirk the responsibility any more.

Daily, scouts had been sent out to the larger Aedui settlements, asking what was happening with the promised grain, and daily the scouts came back bearing the same message: It would take more time. The Aedui were collecting it, but it was a huge task and required more time.

Thus the staff were here, waiting for the representatives of their allies.

A legionary approached the tent's open doorway, bowing deeply.

'The Aedui are here, general. Shall I allow them to approach?'

Caesar nodded and the collective officers shuffled apprehensively in their seats. A great deal depended upon this meeting.

The seven tribal leaders were ushered in, each handing their weapons to the waiting servants by the doorway. The weapons were taken to a cupboard in one corner, where they were stored carefully. Other servants produced seven seats, placing them opposite the officers, lowered the leather tent flaps and tied them together before leaving. The Aedui bowed to the Romans and then took their seats.

Fronto recognised only two of the chieftains. They had both spent some time in camp. Divitiacus had, in fact, been with them now for a while, in charge of the Aedui military contingent. Fronto made a mental note to have a quiet word with him afterwards concerning the assassin among his men. The other chieftain that he knew, a giant with long red hair and a thick beard, was named Liscus. He remembered being told in some previous briefing that Liscus was the top man among the Aedui, akin to the Consuls of Rome.

Caesar waited a moment for one of the few remaining servants to pour wine for all present. Fronto lifted his cup and inhaled the heady aroma. A quick sip confirmed his suspicion. This was a very high quality wine from Latium. He doubted most soldiers could afford even the smallest jar on a week's wages. Caesar was not only reminding them of the benefit of Roman culture, but also of how much Rome valued its allies.

'Where is my grain, gentlemen?'

Short. Curt. Not even particularly polite.

The Aedui sat in silence for a moment. Fronto noticed several of them exchanging worried glances, among them Divitiacus and Liscus.

Pausing only long enough for shamefaced looks to creep across the ambassadors, Caesar jabbed a finger at the map of the local terrain that lay on the campaign table in front of him.

'We cannot gather unripe grain from around us, particularly in the face of our enemy. We cannot reach our own supplies of it. Our *one small request* from our staunchest of allies was help in producing supplies. We *know* that the Aedui have plenty of grain in storage. You can be sure that if we were unsure of your ability to survive on it yourself, we would not have requested it. However, we are here, shedding Roman blood in copious quantities to ensure the safety of your lands and your people from the marauding Helvetii. Why, in the act of defending the Aedui, are we forsaken by them?'

Caesar sat a moment longer, waiting as the chiefs glanced at each other. Suddenly Fronto realised that he felt sorry for them. His general may have qualities that worried him, but the man had power and presence aplenty.

'*Answer me!*'

Liscus stood, sharply. He bowed slightly to Caesar, and spoke in perfect Latin.

'Great Caesar, my companions and I deeply regret any trouble that we have caused your army. We have no wish to anger our allies. We are delayed, not through our own desire, but due to other matters occurring among the Aedui.'

Caesar frowned and glared at Liscus.

'Explain.'

Swallowing nervously, Liscus continued.

'Caesar, there is sedition among my people. We are chieftains, and yet there are private men with more influence over our people. These men are persuading the people of our tribe to delay or halt their gathering of grain.'

Caesar's frown deepened and a thin film of sweat began to form on Liscus' brow. The general motioned with only a finger for the chief to go on.

'These men are unsure of the value of our alliance with Rome; some even favour the Helvetii. They are disheartened by such a great Roman presence in Gaul and fear for our future freedom. They feel that at least with the Helvetii they would be free.'

Balbus motioned to Caesar and the general nodded.

The older legate stood.

'Liscus, I have known the Helvetii for a long time. They are not a people to trust or to bargain with lightly. You put the case very eloquently. I am unsure whether you are relaying the words of these rebels or perhaps declaring your own views?'

Sitting back, he watched the chieftain intently.

Liscus raised his hands in supplication.

'I assure you, all of you, that I and these others remain loyal to our alliance. Should you wish we will take the oath again in order to allay your fears?'

Caesar glanced at Balbus and then shook his head.

'That is unnecessary. Your word is enough. Tell us more of this problem.'

Liscus staggered slightly and sank into his chair once more.

'Some of our people fear that you are not intent on disempowering the Helvetii; that you delay too long. They also worry that when you *do* deal with the Helvetii you will then turn upon the Aedui and the whole of Gaul. They fear that Rome intends us to be another of its provinces like Spain or Africa.'

Caesar nodded, and Fronto could quite understand their fears. Indeed, they were well-founded fears. Fronto could not imagine the general settling for anything less than total domination.

Caesar addressed the Aedui again.

'Rome will always deal with those who quarrel with her. We will also always protect those who call themselves allies. You need have no fear of Roman aggression unless your tribe chooses to bear arms against us.'

Yes, Fronto thought, but how long would it be before Caesar engineered an argument with the Aedui that would cause the alliance to break down?

Liscus cleared his throat and continued.

'I place my trust, as always, in Rome. These men in our tribe, however, go beyond blocking our attempts to supply you with grain. They spread rumour and lies and report everything they hear to the Helvetii. We have all tried to pin these men down and deal with them, but they are elusive. We had hoped to deal with the problem before it ever became large enough to cause you distress. We have failed in that and we must apologise.'

Fronto gestured to Caesar and was given permission to speak. Sipping his wine quickly, he stood.

'Liscus, this problem is much larger than you may be aware. A Gaul, serving with the cavalry as Aedui, has already turned traitor and killed a senior officer. He seems to be a Helvetian, but it remains to be seen how such a man managed to join our cavalry without being given away by your tribesmen. He is in our custody and faces judgement soon. If what you say is true, then there may be more. This puts our trust in any of our allied cavalry at risk.'

Liscus nodded and spoke with a dry mouth.

'I was not aware of such an incident, but it does not greatly surprise me. I would have brought the matter to your attention long before this, but I have put my neck beneath the sword merely by speaking of it. I will now be in considerable danger myself; even in my own town; my own house.'

Fronto had not been paying attention to Liscus for a moment and became aware, as silence fell on the group, that Caesar was watching him. The legate had, in fact, been watching Divitiacus quite closely. Something about this had seemed wrong, and he was trying to piece it together. As he had watched Divitiacus, the man had started to look increasingly nervous, developing an unbidden twitch.

'Is something wrong, legate?'

Fronto stood and stared a moment longer at the nerve-ridden chieftain.

'If you'll permit me sir?'

Caesar nodded.

Fronto singled out Divitiacus and gestured him to rise; a demeaning treatment for a man who was, theoretically, at least an equal.

Divitiacus rose instantly, shaking slightly.

'You are in overall command of all our allied auxiliaries, yes?'

The chieftain nodded at Fronto.

'And you should, by rights, pay very careful attention to whom you enlist into our service. Particularly in view of the dissent in your tribe.'

The man nodded again, his Adam's apple bobbing up and down in his throat like a float on a fisherman's line.

'And yet your rebels manage to infiltrate the cavalry. You are a well-placed and wealthy man, are you not?'

Divitiacus nodded again. He was sweating profusely now.

'Are you prepared to swear an oath of loyalty to Rome again?'

Divitiacus nodded hurriedly. He opened his mouth to speak, but his voice came out an incoherent croak.

Liscus was now looking agog at his fellow chieftain.

He rounded on Divitiacus and said something very quickly in their own language. Two other chieftains stood, their hands dropping unbidden to where their weapons should have been.

Liscus turned once more, addressing Caesar directly.

'General, may I request a private audience?'

Caesar frowned, but Liscus added 'Please. Myself and Divitiacus; you and this officer.'

He gestured at Fronto.

Fronto looked at Caesar and nodded encouragingly.

The general sat back and sighed.

'Very well. Gentlemen, you are dismissed for the time being. Procillus?'

One of the staff officers stood to attention.

'Take our allies and your fellow officers to the staff mess and entertain them for a short while.'

'Yes general.'

Once the chieftains had collected their arms, they and the staff officers trooped out of the tent, one of the servants holding the flap open for them. As soon as they had gone, the tent flap was tied back in place and the four remaining men eyed each other warily.

Liscus spoke first, addressing Fronto.

'Legate, your fears may be well-founded, but a little misplaced. Divitiacus is as loyal to our alliance as any man I know.'

The other chieftain nodded vigorously, sweat still pouring from his face.

'It is his brother that is now in doubt. Dumnorix has long been a wealthy man and coveted power among the Aedui. His purse has grown fat from taxes gathered and contracts won by the fear that he instils in the lowest people. Not only this, but he has won the heart and mind of many a well-placed man through gifts and flattery. I had not realised how far his ambitions reached, but now it is all too clear.'

Fronto frowned.

'Dumnorix. I know that name.' He cradled his chin in one hand as his mind stretched back over the last few weeks, trying to picture Dumnorix and where they had met.

Divitiacus spoke for the first time, his voice still croaky and scratched; his Latin shaky at best.

'General, I not want to tell this. Dumnorix my brother. Family. I am in shame for him, but he still my brother.'

Caesar nodded gravely.

'Go on. Tell me about your brother.'

'He wealthy and people like him. He have horsemen. His own horsemen. Plenty horsemen. He influence more than Aedui. Other tribes like him. Bituriges like him. He related to them now because of mother. His wife from Helvetii so he like them. He hate Romans for getting in way, and for making me more powerful than him. He think if Romans leave,

162

Helvetii help him be lord of all Aedui. He think if Romans win, he become nothing.'

Liscus stared at him.

'How long were you thinking of keeping this from me? This man wants to replace me!'

Divitiacus lowered his head in shame.

Caesar looked at Fronto.

'Legate, you've heard of this Dumnorix?'

Fronto looked up from his reflection. Understanding dawned on him, and he looked at Liscus for confirmation.

'Dumnorix is the man in charge of our allied cavalry contingent, isn't he?'

Liscus nodded.

Fronto turned back to Caesar.

'I think that the mystery of our overeager cavalry has been solved. Dumnorix must be the man who gave the orders for both the suicidal charge and for the assassination.'

Caesar nodded sadly.

'I think, gentlemen, that this Dumnorix had better present himself unarmed to the camp provosts for investigation and possible trial. See to it, Fronto.'

Fronto smiled a cold and vicious smile.

'Yes *sir!*'

Liscus stood hurriedly, holding out both his hands in a placating gesture.

'Please. Dumnorix has wronged you, yes, but he has also wronged us and the whole of the Aedui people. If you will allow us to prosecute him, I will immediately arrange for the grain supplies to be delivered to your men.'

Caesar frowned at the chieftain.

'You think to bargain by promising again what was already promised? Dumnorix should stand trial under Roman law.'

'I meant no insult, Caesar. We would not ask to try one of your men. We trust enough in your justice for that. Please trust in the Aedui to try our own.'

Caesar sat for long moments. He looked at Fronto, who nodded reluctantly.

'Very well. You may take Dumnorix and try him, but when judgement is called for, Romans, including myself and the legate here, will make up half of the jury in redress for the wrongs he has done us. I trust that is acceptable?'

Liscus nodded.

'That is fair, Caesar.'

Divitiacus once more stood and approached Caesar.

'Caesar. I long respect Rome. Want to be friend of Rome. But want brother to live. Romans often kill in punishment. Please not kill Dumnorix.'

Fronto suddenly straightened up and approached Caesar's chair. Leaning down, he whispered in the general's ear.

'Sir, if we can arrange to let him go with suitable lesser punishments, we can have him watched. There's bound to be more of them than just him, and this could be our perfect chance to sniff them out. If he dies, any information he has dies with him.'

Caesar nodded.

'Divitiacus, I am not predisposed to be generous or even lenient to a man who has wronged us as your brother has. However, it *is* important that you control and be seen to control your own people. Very well. We will not ask for the death penalty at the trial.'

Liscus bowed.

'Very well Caesar. We will apprehend Dumnorix and arrange everything. As soon as it is organised, we will send a messenger to you.'

Divitiacus also bowed, and the pair of them collected their weapons and waited for the servant to lift the tent flap before exiting.

As soon as they were alone, Caesar smiled at his legate.

'Very good, Marcus. We can both win on this. Rome gets a trial for treason that will help us root out any other dissenters and bind the Aedui ever closer to our cause. In return I feel I can safely grant you your request to deal with the assassin personally.'

Fronto grinned and made to rise as Caesar continued.

'I will, however, impose a couple of restrictions myself. I will not, as I said, countenance any of my senior staff officers endangering themselves needlessly. Should you entertain a one-on-one fight with the man, I will have archers stationed discretely. He will not leave the field alive, and you will not be allowed to die.'

Fronto opened his mouth to object, but Caesar gave him no time.

'I absolutely refuse any alternative. I am not unmanning you Marcus. If you beat him, it will be legitimately, but if he gets the best of you, I will *not* lose you.'

After a moment, Fronto nodded.

'Also, this has to be a major exercise in morale-boosting. Despite what Liscus said, I suspect the grain will be a few days late for the troops, and we will need them to be in high morale to deal with a couple of days of relative hunger. Let the officers know that the grain is imminent, and make sure they inform the men.'

Fronto grinned again.

'Yes indeed sir. What do you mean by 'major exercise in morale-boosting', though? Am I to be preceded by acrobats and dancing girls, sir?'

'Don't be needlessly facetious, Fronto. I mean that this is to be a *real* show. Detail your engineers to raise an arena in one of the hollows around here. It needs to be as close to a true amphitheatre as we can manage with the meagre supplies available to us. I want it to be able to seat up to fifty thousand, so it's a big job.'

Fronto staggered back into his chair.

'Fifty thousand? That's three times as big as the one back home! You actually want to seat the whole army to watch us?'

Caesar smiled a warming smile.

'I think it's absolutely essential, don't you? The whole army will be talking about it for months anyway. Let's make sure they've all seen it. And I want as many of our Aedui allies as we can manage watching it too. Might do a lot of good to put a bit more fear and respect in them. See to it.'

Fronto sat staring blankly at the tent wall, repeatedly muttering 'Fifty thousand' and 'three times bigger'.

Caesar watched him a moment longer and finally spoke.

'Legate, are you alright?'

Fronto snapped out of his mental reverie.

'Sir? Oh, yes sir. It's just a bit of a tall order. And a bit of pressure on me, sir.'

Caesar smiled again.

'This is what you wanted, Marcus, isn't it?'

Fronto grinned.

'Oh yes. Don't worry sir. I'll turn him into joints of meat. I'm just not looking forward to what young Pomponius is going to say when I tell him what he's got to do.'

Caesar nodded.

'I understand, but you don't have to rush particularly.'

'Sir?'

'We've stopped chasing the Helvetii for a moment. One of Longinus' scouts reported to me this morning that the Helvetii have stopped moving and are making camp about eight miles from here. The time might now have come to scratch our collective itch. We'll be here for a few days. Tell your engineer he can draw labour from all six legions, so long as he has the arena ready the day after tomorrow. With our current supplies and manpower he should be able to work reasonably at leisure in that time.'

Fronto could not help but grin once more. The possibility of putting an end to the Helvetii was like a balm. And Caesar was right. Pomponius should be able to build an arena in over a day.

After a fairly bad start, today was looking up.

CHAPTER 9

(TEMPORARY CAMP IN AEDUI TERRITORY, NEAR THE TOWN OF BIBRACTE)

'Caligae: the standard Roman military boot. A sandal-style of leather strips laced to above the ankle with a hard sole, driven through with hob-nails.'

'Vexillum (Pl. Vexilli): The standard or flag of a legion.'

T he sun shone bright above the makeshift arena. The twittering of birds, the humming of bees and the babbling of the river nearby were drowned out by the collective noise of more than forty thousand eager and expectant observers. To mark the occasion, the troops had been permitted to attend in their tunics and breeches, leaving their hot armour and kit in guarded compounds in the camps. Almost everyone was here, barring the various units that had opted to remain on guard duty on the promise of double pay for their efforts.

The sea of white and red tunics was broken up here and there by small knots of Aedui observers who wore their traditional Gaulish tunics and breeches of patterned wool. The staff officers and higher level commanders sat in prime position just above the arena to one side, lounging in comfortable campaign chairs. The rest sat on the terraced banks of the hollow.

Fronto, staring out through a narrow slit in the wooden door behind which he waited, marvelled at the work of his engineers. Pomponius had really excelled himself. Not only had the engineers levelled out the grassy banks so that they were even all around, they had dug concentric terraces just over a foot apart around the entire oval floor. On the lower of these terraces, they had laid wooden planks to serve as benches. The higher ones retained the cut turf. The effect was staggering. There was actual seating for over forty thousand people. The base of the hollow they had dug down five feet and erected a wooden palisade around the edge to protect viewers and prevent escape from the arena. At each end, a wooden hut had been built into the slope for the two combatants. Fronto stood in one such hut with the Gaul opposite him, some distance away, though just visible through the crack in the wood.

Fronto adjusted the helmet strap. He felt strange in this equipment. He had served in the military for most of his adult life, but had never ranked below tribune, and had never borne the standard kit of a legionary. The helmet padding itched. His own padding had been hand-stitched by some high-class tradesman or other in Rome. This was itchy and uncomfortable and, he was convinced, smelled slightly of urine.

The sword and the shield he was used to. The shield - rectangular but with a slight curve and displaying Caesar's 'Taurus' emblem - was that of Cominius, borne by Fronto partially as a mark of respect for the dead centurion, and partially to claim vengeance for the man. The Tenth would appreciate the gesture. The sword, on the other hand, was his. Since the day he had been given it on a battlefield in Spain, he had never used another, and it had served him well.

He wore the standard tunic and breeches of the legion, but had opted for his own enclosed boots rather than the caligae that normally went with the uniform these days. More protective and definitely more comfortable.

On top of these, he wore a heavy tunic of fur and leather, to protect his skin from the pinch and rub of the armour. The armour itself was of overlapping scales sewn onto leather, a form that was currently very much in fashion among centurions and signifers.

All in all, he was ready. Not decked out like a Myrmidon gladiator in the arenas of the capital, but very much like a soldier of Rome. He would have felt uncomfortable any other way.

Balbus had told him that the organiser of the contest, Sabinus of the general staff, had given the Gaul the option of exactly the same equipment in the spirit of equality. The Gaul had refused, choosing only a bronze breastplate and horned helmet over his Gaulish clothes, along with a midsized, round shield and a heavy, long Gaulish sword.

The heat in the small, wooden shed was becoming unbearable, and his breath steamed. Fronto stood and waited, unable even to give his sword a practice swing in the confined space. He listened intently to the sounds of thousands of expectant and excited people.

After a few more uncomfortable and sweaty heartbeats, a horn rang out clear in the arena. The melody was disjointed and very military, such as a musician for the legions might produce if asked to play something other than a standard call.

The crowd fell silent. Finally, for a few moments, Fronto could hear the birds and the river.

Then the roar began.

Rising and falling like waves of a tide, the sounds rippled round the arena. Sabinus, standing next to the musician, held up his hands for silence and the roar diminished to a background rumble.

Sabinus, his vine staff held high above his head, cleared his throat.

'The combat this morning, for any of you who are unaware, will be between Marcus Falerius Fronto, legate of the Tenth Legion, representing the interests of Rome, and one Domiticus of the Aedui. Should the legate win, the death blow will be delivered without consultation of the crowd, as his opponent will be proved traitor. Should the Gaul win, he will be returned to the Aedui for trial, alive.'

A series of cheers, boos and hisses accompanied the announcements. Sabinus waited long enough for the enthusiasm to wind down, and then raised his vine staff again.

'Legate Fronto has elected to bear the arms of a legionary for this combat. He will be limited to helm, armour, shield and gladius. Domiticus of the Aedui has chosen his own Gaulish equipment. He will be limited to his helm and armour, a shield, and his sword.'

The cheering began once more. Fronto knew that appearing in the equipment of a common soldier would earn him a great deal of respect from the watching legionaries. He would have to be careful, though. He kept reminding himself not to underestimate the Gaul. It was far too easy to view him as an assassin who could only stab backs in the dark. The defiance in his eyes at the stockade, though, spoke of fatalism and a quiet confidence – a deadly combination in close combat such as this. Fronto would definitely have to watch his step.

Once more the cheering died down, and Sabinus' voice rang out.

'When the horn is sounded, the bars will be withdrawn from the cages and the two combatants will be free to enter the arena. From that point there will be no further breaks, announcements or interference. After a thousand count, if both contestants still live, pila and daggers will be dropped into the arena, two of each.'

Provosts that stood around the arena, next to the wooden wall, held pila and daggers aloft for the crowd to see clearly. The cheering began again.

Not waiting this time for the noise to die away, Sabinus waved an arm and the horn sounded out over the crowd. Burly provosts at each end of the arena heaved the great wooden beams to one side and the doors swung open.

The Gaul, Domiticus as he had been named, stepped out of the shadow into the glare of the dirt-floored arena. His eyes were locked on Fronto and he spared not even a glance for the watching thousands. Pieces of half-eaten fruit and salted meat bounced off the Gaul's helmet and breastplate, as the assembled Romans vented their rage on the assassin.

Fronto stepped out of the other end and into the light. He was aware of Galba' words a little over an hour ago, as he was ushered into the shed. Galba had been a keen visitor to the arenas in Rome and had become something of a semi-professional gambler on the gladiatorial games. He knew what he called 'form' and how the crowd would react. Fronto had listened intently to everything the other man had said, nodding blankly, and had promptly forgotten most of it. Three comments remained with him, though.

Firstly, crowd-pleasing. He had to be a showman. It was less important here, obviously, where the fight was to the death and the fickle crowd had no say, but the morale of his opponent would be affected by even the noise of the crowd around him. Plus the officers were looking forward to days of good spirits after this.

Secondly, the man was tall. Galba had advised Fronto how to use that against him.

'Thirdly', Galba had wagged a finger in front of his face, 'everything in the arena is a weapon. Every part of your body, every item you carry, the walls themselves and the dirt you walk on. Use everything you can. It increases your chance of success and makes it much more exciting for the crowd.'

And here he was, standing in front of that crowd, not knowing what the hell to do other than attack. He glanced around the spectators, trying to pick out his friends. Finally, he spied Priscus in the front row, other centurions of the Tenth around and behind him. Priscus extended both arms, palms upwards, in a gesture imploring Fronto to do something. As he looked left and right, he became aware that he was standing like a statue and that the noise of the crowd was gradually fading away.

He thrust his shield and gladius in the air.

'For Rome!'

Suddenly the cheers were back and increased tenfold. Fronto grinned. He could get the hang of this showmanship crap.

'For Cominius!'

Word of the realities of Cominius' death and the true culprit had now been released, and every man present would have known that the Gaul had killed a senior officer of the Tenth Legion. Although few outside the Tenth would even have known Cominius by sight, every legionary resented such an ignominious death for a high-ranking Roman officer at the hands of a barbarian. As he invoked the name of the man most wronged by this Gaul, the crowd went mad.

The barbarian had walked perhaps a third of the way across the arena and had stopped, his long, broad bladed sword hanging at his side, and the small, round buckler shield strapped to his arm.

Fronto realised that he could not stand there and shout clichés at the crowd for long before he would begin to look like a coward. Gritting his teeth, he adjusted the large, squared-oval red shield bearing the bull image and the 'X' numeral of his legion on his arm and hefted the shiny, pointed stabbing weapon. With a deliberate exaggerated slowness, he began to plod toward the Gaul.

Domiticus looked confused at the speed and manner of his opponent, and readied himself to defend against a possible charge. But the charge never came. The Gaul watched in astonishment as Fronto reached a standard marching pace and tramped toward him, shield high and sword held out just next to the rim. The Romans in the audience, of course, knew exactly what he was doing. It was what Marius' Mules had been doing for centuries. A determined attack with the shield covering as much of the body as possible. A pace that would not leave Fronto breathless.

The Gaul, to his credit, did not launch the obvious charge, nor did he take the opportunity to taunt his opponent. Instead he stood his ground, arms at the ready, his grey eyes silently sizing up the Roman.

Fronto reached the centre of the arena at his steady pace. The crowd had gone quiet again; this time not through lack of excitement, but rather with anticipation, as they waited the tense moments that seemed like hours for the two to meet. Fronto was playing the role of legionary down to the soles of his boots and the troops loved it. They could respect an officer fighting hand to hand for the honour of Rome, but this was something else. Not just respect, but love. He was one of them.

As Fronto came within the Gaul's reach, the tall warrior finally gave release to the tension that had been building for what felt like hours as the damned Roman had played to the crowd. He swung the great Celtic sword in a wide arc that could have smashed or removed a man's leg. Fronto, however, was prepared. He swung the shield to the side and dropped down on one knee. The edge of the shield rammed into the dirt, and the Gaul's sword hit the domed boss in its centre with such force that the shudder rattled every bone up from Fronto's arm and to his jaw.

It had been a heavy blow, but Fronto was a step ahead. While the Gaul wrenched the sword back, his own arm also ringing with the blow, Fronto sliced out with his gladius. The Gaul's shield covered the more vital areas of the lower torso and upper thighs. Dropping his sword hand slightly, the pointed tip cut through the calf of the Gaul; not a muscle shearing blow, but one which would cause discomfort and blood loss. Fronto could not allow the man to die too quickly. The legions needed a show, and so did the general. The Gaul gasped, but did not scream. If Fronto did not hate the bastard so much, he might have admired him.

The barbarian had to pull his arm back a long way to make another swing like that, and Fronto took advantage, using the speed of his short, stabbing sword in close quarters. Another thrust brought a blossom of red in the thigh of the Gaul's breeches. A third scraped along the man's ribs with a sound that made Fronto wince. Again, the Gaul gasped. As the legate began to pull himself back to stand up, the tall warrior lashed out with a foot, catching Fronto's shield and hurling him bodily backwards.

The Gaul grinned as Fronto, stunned by the blow and lying on his back, tried to drag himself to his feet. Domiticus issued a smile of the sort more usually seen on the muzzle of a hunting animal.

'My turn, Roman.'

Fronto was stunned. Two wounds to the same leg and the man was walking relatively straight and steady, and picking up speed! The blow to the man's ribs was off-target, but must still be incredibly painful. The blood the man was losing would kill him eventually, but Fronto wondered how long he would have to hold him off for that to happen.

Struggling up, he came to his feet just in time to raise the large, oval shield and block the overhead swing of the Gaul's sword. The blow splintered the shield and sheared a whole arc of wood from it, leaving just over two thirds of the shape intact. The bronze edging strip where it had been ripped apart protruded like the lightning bolts of Jupiter. It took Fronto a moment to realise that the sword had actually grazed his arm. Very lucky he had held it where he did or he would have been fighting the rest of this with a stump.

He attempted to get his sword into a position for stabbing, but the inevitable swing of that huge sword brought Fronto's attention back to the shield again. The blow hit the boss at the centre again, severely denting it. The bones in Fronto's arm felt like they had jumped about and jumbled up. He was sure at least one of the bones in his hand was broken.

He stepped backwards, giving ground to avoid contact with that blade again. He was aware that this would look terrible from the stands, but he was past caring. There was more to worry about than the crowd. He had to avoid those blows long enough to think, and for the feeling to come back into his arm.

Perhaps ten steps back and he stumbled, righting himself quickly, but not quick enough to avoid the Gaul's next swing. He hurriedly threw the shield into the way, not paying attention to its most correct usage, and the huge sword cleaved a large portion off the top. The tip of the sword scraped along the brow of Fronto's helmet and he could actually see down the length of the blade. That was too close for comfort. One more blow and his shield would be kindling. Nothing he could do then. He needed to fight for just a little more time. An idea was forming. If only he could just...

Priscus watched from his place at the head of the Tenth, though he was wondering how much longer he could watch. This was getting embarrassing. The Roman tactics had been fine to begin with, but they needed a unit of men following them, not an individual. The inevitable had happened. The Gaul had turned the edge and had discarded his own shield, subsequently pursuing Fronto most of the way across the arena, chopping chunks out of his shield as he went. Now things were looking a little desperate.

Fronto raised his shield and gladius in the face of a huge sweep from the Gaul's weapon. The broadsword sheared another small shard from the oval and hit the gladius just below the hilt, missing Fronto's wrist by only a hand-width. The strength of the blow ripped the sword from Fronto's grasp and hurled it twenty feet across the dirt. Several of Fronto's fingers had been broken by the strike, and maybe his wrist. Priscus, from his vantage point that was now quite close to his legate, had heard the bones crack above the silence the crowd now sat in. The Gaul grinned.

Priscus looked up and around to the three vantage points where Caesar had had archers positioned 'just in case'. Fronto had immediately rescinded those orders, without deferring to Caesar, and there were now no archers in reserve. Priscus now wished fervently he had not done that.

He turned back and looked down, dreading what he would see, but knowing he had to keep calm in front of the men. Fronto had reached the stockade at the edge of the arena and his back rubbed up against the rough timber. His sword was hopelessly out of reach and the remnants of his shield were so shoddy it could hardly be used to stop another sword blow. His right arm hung limp where it had been broken by the sword.

The Gaul raised the broadsword high above his head, laughing like a hyena, and brought it back over in an arc toward Fronto; a blow that would split the legate in half or at least crush his head. As the sword reached its apex, Fronto delivered a left-handed punch with a force Priscus could not believe he was still capable of. The hand still tight on the grip of the shattered shield, he rammed it into the Gaul's face, the bronze dome of the boss breaking bones as he drove it home.

The Gauls cheekbones went, along with his jaw and his nose. His eyes were probably a mess, but Priscus could not see through the large quantities of blood that streamed from the man's forehead across them.

Domiticus faltered, his sword high in the air, as his nerves told his brain that his face was ruined. Priscus doubted the Gaul could hear or see a thing, and had perhaps even lost track of where he was.

As the Gaul staggered this way and that, the sword still held perfectly aloft, Fronto pulled himself upright, using the stockade for support. He tottered three steps forward and reached up with his good hand. Gently, he plucked the heavy sword from the Gaul's hands, swung it in a wide arc, and drove it through the warrior, falling as he did, knocking the Gaul to the ground, where the sword pinned him to the dirt as the legate collapsed on top of him.

'Now we're even, you bastard.'

Everything went black but, as consciousness slipped away, he heard the gurgle that announced the passing of the Gaul, and the day suddenly felt like a victory.

'The medicus tells me he thinks you'll be able to use your arm again.'

Fronto turned his head painfully and gave Priscus the sourest look he could muster.

'Eleven fractures and breaks from one bloody hit. It's a damn good job they're *not* all like him, or we might as well pack up and go back to Rome. He had a blow like Vulcan's hammer.'

Priscus smiled at his commander. The man had taken a pounding, but had triumphed, despite the primus pilus' fears. When Fronto had been carried from the arena, the crowd had gone insane. The legionaries had cheered so loud that Priscus had suffered a headache for hours. The body of the Gaul had been left lying where it had fallen on the dirt. Priscus had stopped by it long enough to wrench the Celtic sword free from the body, but presumed some of the Aedui had come and taken the rest away after the Romans had all left. Frankly, he didn't much care. Let the murderer rot in the hollow. The sword, on the other hand, was quite a fine one and he had taken it to the best blacksmith in the Tenth, who had given it a sharper edge and cleaned and tidied the blade for him. Now the sword lay next to Fronto's bed, on the silk sheet in which it had been wrapped; Priscus' victory gift to his commander.

An orderly entered the tent and placed a fresh bowl of water and a plate of fruit on the side.

Fronto gave another bitter look and called out.

'This is supposed to be a bloody private tent. You lot walk in and out of here like it's the Via Appia.'

The orderly's face retained perfect composure. He looked seriously at Fronto and said, as he turned to leave, 'Calm down commander. You need rest.'

The young man left the tent just as the pottery cup bounced off the door frame.

Priscus smiled. 'I see you've maintained your charm and good humour throughout this. And your left arm seems good, anyway.'

There was a large dressing along the legate's left forearm, where the blade had caught him, but the majority of the damage Fronto had suffered had been his right arm. His right was fully wrapped and splinted and bound to his torso. Priscus had watched as they had done it and had marvelled at the glorious yellow and purple colours that blotched his commander's arm from fingertips to upper arm.

Fronto sighed.

'I am actually left-handed Gnaeus. I could probably function just as well now as I did before this.'

He gestured at his dressings with the good arm.

Priscus nodded. He knew a number of people in the legions that were left-handed, but due to the tactics, equipment and rules of the Roman military, the shield was carried with the left and the sword hung from, and was wielded with, the right. Otherwise the shield wall tactic so favoured by the legions would become a shambles. Consequently, many had had to retrain using their offhand. Priscus had never realised that his commander was one of them.

'The medicus also said you'd be staying in his care for at least a week before he'd let you go out and about on your own. He wanted me to stress that to you. Everyone knows you have a habit of doing whatever the hell you like.'

Fronto smirked.

'In that case, he probably expects me to stay cooped up in this mobile latrine pit for three or four days in reality.'

'Anyway,' Priscus continued 'we're all probably staying put at the moment. We're waiting for the grain deliveries from the Aedui, and Caesar's not moving on the Helvetii until he's very sure of the terrain. The information our allies gave him is inadequate. He asked where they were camped, and the Aedui said: a mountain. He asked them to describe the mountain, and the man just said: it's a mountain. I think the general gave up then and sent his own scouts out to have a look. They should be back any time now.'

Fronto grimaced as he pulled himself further upright. In addition to his two main wounds, his body was a criss-cross of scars and scratches, and the discolouration of bruises left no large expanse of skin clear.

Priscus hurried to help the legate up, but Fronto pushed him away.

'I'll stay here until Caesar decides to make a move. I don't care how infirm I am, I'm not missing that fight. Anyway, it's more comfortable walking or riding than lying in one of the wounded carts. Rickety bloody things, I'm surprised any of the wounded survive a journey on one.'

Priscus sighed.

'Don't go running around causing trouble, sir. I'll let you know well before anything important happens. In the meantime, the sawbones said you need rest and so, if you don't rest, I shall have to ask him to recommend that you spend the next month in a wagon.'

Fronto glared at Priscus.

'Alright. I'll not make waves, but *you* make sure I don't miss anything.'

'Agreed.'

Priscus turned to leave, but stopped as he reached the doorway.

'The rest of your beloved fans are here to see you. They're heading this way like a herd of cattle.'

He looked out of the tent again and grinned.

'Well... like a herd of *drunken* cattle, anyway.'

He stepped out of the tent and to one side as Balbus, Longinus, Crispus, Galba and Sabinus came barrelling through the open doorway. Each of them was laden. Balbus, Longinus and Galba carried jars of wine and bowls of pastries, Crispus carried dice and a game board, and Sabinus a small wooden box.

'Hail the conquering hero.'

Balbus slumped gratefully into a chair next to the bed.

'I see Priscus has been keeping the seat warm for me.'

He turned to face the door again.

'You're not going are you, centurion? The fun's only just starting. We've food and wine and games to entertain the invalid.'

Priscus looked in through the tent flaps.

'Much as I'd love to join you, gentlemen, I've got to go see the general.'

Balbus shrugged. The others had taken various places around the bed.

'What's *he* going to see Caesar about?'

Galba prodded Fronto in the leg from his seated position on a cushion on the floor.

'Never mind. Time for you to relax.'

Fronto looked around. He was surprised to find Sabinus in the company of the legates. In the short time Fronto had been serving with the general staff, Sabinus had rarely exchanged a word with Fronto, and had not spoken at all to the other legates.

'Sabinus. What brings *you* here with this motley bunch? Doesn't Caesar need you at headquarters?'

The staff officer smiled at him.

'Just making a delivery and renewing an acquaintance Fronto.'

He reached out with the small wooden box and dropped it gently in Fronto's lap.

Fronto stared at the box. It was heavy.

'Well, open it.'

Fronto looked up, suspiciously.

'You don't know this lot, Sabinus. This could contain a scorpion or a turd for all I know.'

Sabinus grinned.

'This hasn't been anywhere near any of them. Open it.'

Fronto released the catch and swung the lid up. A pile of coins of different denominations glinted within. He looked up questioningly at Sabinus, who nodded at the box.

'Winnings. In actual fact, a share of winnings. A number of soldiers throughout the legions made an awful lot of money out of our Aedui guests by betting on you. The soldiers in the Tenth all chipped in and sent a quarter of the winnings to you.'

Fronto boggled at the box.

'There's a hell of a lot in there. It's about a year's wages for a legionary.'

'Yes. Spend it wisely.' Sabinus and Galba shared a glance. 'I would suggest wine, women and song.'

'Well,' Fronto gestured with his good arm, 'you've brought the wine, I can provide the song. Who's going to bring me women?'

Priscus jogged down the slope from the headquarters tent to the makeshift hospital. Fronto was sitting, as usual, outside the tent in the warm, late afternoon air, scratching irritably at the dressing on his arm. A large jug of wine and a cup sat on the grass next to him. Occasionally an orderly would walk past and 'tut' meaningfully at him.

He looked up as a shadow fell across his knees.

'Nice day, Gnaeus. I could get used to this.'

Priscus stopped and leaned on the tent frame for a moment, regaining his breath.

'Don't... don't get too used to it. Things are happening.'

Fronto raised an eyebrow.

'The Helvetii?'

Priscus nodded.

'Caesar's scouts told him that the ascent on the hill should be easy, so Caesar's decided we'll go deal with them.'

Fronto smiled and took a swig from the wine.

'Sounds good. I'll have to have a little word with the doc.'

Priscus shook his head.

'No need. Caesar's sent your orders.' He gestured with a scroll in his hand. 'I'm to give these to the medicus. You're to dress formally, but without armour, and report to the general staff as soon as you can.'

'What's the situation, Gnaeus? I can't go lumbering in without a clue.'

Priscus waved the scroll at a medicus and beckoned him as he spoke.

'Caesar's sent Labienus in command of the Eighth and the Eleventh to take the high ground above the Helvetii. We're following up a few hours behind them. This entire hospital unit's going to be mobilised with the army. The whole camp's being emptied.'

Fronto smiled.

'It's been nice being in camp for a few days again, but I suppose we had to move on sometime. At least we might get to deal with the Helvetii for good this time.'

As Priscus went through Caesar's orders with the medicus, Fronto began gathering up the meagre possessions he had brought to the medical tent. As he left the tent with a single armful of gear, he motioned back inside.

'Gnaeus, could you grab the rest of my stuff for me?'

Priscus nodded, entering the tent and returning with the rest of the legate's gear in his arms.

'Now let's go and get you ready so that you can present yourself to Caesar.'

A quarter of an hour later the two officers left Fronto's tent, Fronto wearing a standard red military tunic and breeches, a cloak thrown over the back to add a little official weight to the ensemble.

Caesar's command tent was busy. Sabinus stood by the door, deep in conversation with Crassus. He waved a greeting to Fronto as he approached.

Fronto smiled a fixed smile. Sabinus was turning out to be a good man, against all expectations. He still was not sure he liked Crassus though, and he was beginning to form a suspicion that the young man coveted the command of the Tenth. He had begun making noises about the lack of a full-time legate recently, and Priscus had complained about the close attention the young legate had paid the Tenth on their march from Vienna. He would be one to watch, but not to cross lightly, with his father being one of Caesar's sponsors and one of the more powerful men in Rome. He forced himself to continue smiling.

'Afternoon lads. How's tricks?'

Crassus made a gesture to indicate that he was bored. Sabinus just sighed.

'Busy as always. We're all being run ragged to prepare for the off. How's the arm?'

Fronto shrugged, and winced at the pain the ill-thought out manoeuvre produced.

'I'll live.'

'Good,' replied Caesar as he stepped through the tent doorway.

'Fronto. I want you with us on the staff in an advisory role for now. I can't have you charging off and trying to conquer Gaul single handed. You're convalescing, and I had to argue very hard with the surgeons to get you permission to ride a horse. On no account are you to leave the colour party.'

Fronto nodded to the general.

'Yes sir. Have the cavalry been mobilised yet?'

Caesar raised a hand to shelter his eyes as he gazed into the distance.

'You can still see Longinus and his men on the ridge over there if you strain your eyes. They'll be moving a little ahead of us as we march.'

Fronto thought for a moment.

'We are presuming here that Labienus has been successful. If not, the cavalry will be unable to deal with anything they might find. Have you given thought to scouts?'

Caesar sighed.

'I want you here in an advisory role, but you don't need to mother me quite this much, Marcus. Yes, I've sent out Publius Considius with the scouting party.'

Fronto frowned.

The general drew himself up to his full height and placed his hands crossly on his hips.

181

'What now?'

'I know that Considius is a member of the staff, Caesar, but I rather thought that was more as a reward for past deeds than for his active military usefulness.'

Caesar bridled.

'Be careful what you say, Fronto. He has considerable seniority over you.'

Fronto shook his head.

'I'm intending no insult Caesar, but I'm a plain speaking man, and if I can foresee a problem, I have to question it. Considius served well under Sulla and Crassus, but that was twenty years ago. He's seen no active duty since then, and he's had precious little involvement so far with any of this Gaulish campaign. He's going to be very rusty and out of touch with tactics. I would very much have advised against that choice sir.'

Caesar put his hands to his forehead in deep thought.

'You can be a trifle inelegant at times, Marcus, but you do talk some sense. However, what's done is done, and we'll have to hope he doesn't get himself into any trouble. At least he should have Labienus ahead to look after him, and Longinus supporting him from the rear.'

Fronto nodded unhappily.

'Is there anything else, sir, or should I find my horse and get ready to ride.'

'You do that Fronto. Be here in a quarter of an hour. And warn your officers: we march through the night'

Fronto reached out with his good arm, steering the horse with his thighs, and tapped Sabinus on the arm.

'Yes?'

'I presume that's where we're headed?'

He pointed into the distance where about a mile and a half away a large peak stood high above the surrounding hills, glowing in the dawn light.

Sabinus nodded and grunted an affirmative.

'Labienus is up there somewhere. Let's hope he's managed to avoid any major confrontation with the Helvetii. Otherwise we could be in a world of trouble. What's that?'

A column of dust rose up from the hillside a little ahead.

'Horsemen,' replied Fronto, shading his eyes from the glare on the white peak ahead. 'Looks like irregular cavalry.'

Caesar pulled the vanguard to a halt. The legions ceased their steady tramping as they came to a stop in perfect unison. The staff officers pulled forward into a horseshoe, waiting for the half dozen riders.

A number of cavalry officers reined their horses in, raising a cloud of dust, with Publius Considius between them. Beyond them, in the distance, Fronto could see the rest of the cavalry heading for the column, Longinus among them.

Considius bowed to Caesar as deeply as his saddle would allow. Caesar brushed the formalities aside with a wave of his hand. Out of breath and sweating, Considius made his report.

'Caesar, I've recalled the cavalry and made my way back here. I beg to report that the high ground is in the hands of the Gauls. I can see no sign of Labienus and his legions.'

Fronto's eyes opened wide.

'How in the name of all the Gods did he fail to take the peak?'

Caesar nodded.

'How indeed.'

Considius, breathing deeply, gestured in the direction of the mountain.

'I don't know sir. All I know is that there are Gaulish standards flying above the peak and no sign of a Roman force.'

Caesar pondered a moment.

'Longinus. Get your cavalry back here. Have them patrol at a distance of half a mile from the column. Considius, unless you've anything else to report, go and change your horse; you've ridden that one into the ground and it needs to rest. Gentlemen?'

The staff who had to a man been watching the distant hill, turned to look expectantly at Caesar as Considius and the scouts rode away, meeting up with Longinus on the slope.

183

'I need ideas and plans now. I hate to think that Labienus might have lost me ten thousand men, but we need to plan accounting for only the four remaining legions. Suggestions?'

Fronto, still astounded by the turn of events, worked through their goals and their resources in his head, and then turned to Caesar to put forward his proposal.

'The highest hill around here is the one to the right and ahead. That'll put us around a mile from the objective peak. It's a nice defensive position, in case Labienus really *has* lost us a third of the army. While we maintain that ground, we can send out scouts to find out what has really happened. We can't move on while we're blind, sir.'

Caesar nodded.

'Very well. Pass the orders down to the column. I want a score of the best individual scouts we have sent to me. I have no intention of sending out a full scouting unit. They're far too obvious. Each man will ride independently, giving them better range and making them less visible. I don't want anyone blundering into anything.'

Gradually, the column moved into position on the side of the hill, creating a defensive line. The scouts requested by Caesar were sent out with specific orders to find Labienus and his two legions, or at least a trace of their remains to tell what had happened; also to locate and examine the Helvetii with a view to removing them from their position of control, and to look at all surrounding countryside for any escape routes that the army could take if things went badly.

While the scouts were out, Caesar gave orders that the four remaining legions should fortify the position on the hill with ditch and mound, the auxiliaries maintaining a defensive cordon while they worked.

Fronto found himself a quiet patch of turf high above the fortification work and relaxed, lying back. He had not realised just how weary and weak he was; the day's ride had taken a great deal out of him. He had been travelling for more than twelve hours, and yet it was still only lunchtime. Reaching out to his pack, he retrieved some salted pork, bread, apples and a small flask of watered wine.

Some of the tension slipped away from his limbs, but an oppressive weight remained in his chest. Balbus was part of Labienus' missing contingent. In this whole army there were maybe half a dozen people Fronto could really talk to, and only two with whom he felt he could really share anything: Priscus and Balbus. It was odd how much his friendship with the ageing legate of the Eighth had blossomed over the short time they had known each other. He had never had the time or inclination to make that kind of friend when he had been in Spain. Then again, he had been a lot younger then and intent climbing the ladder of the cursus honorum. He had not had time for friends. He had treated the Ninth Legion well and led them to victory a number of times, but had never had the kind of relationship with its officers that he did with the centurions of the Tenth. It would be a shame if Balbus had vanished ignominiously in the middle of Gaul.

The crack of a twig sounded behind him and he started. Longinus took another step and then slumped to the turf beside him. Wordlessly Fronto proffered the wine flask and, gratefully, Longinus took it.

'It's a bright, hot day. Makes you glad you outrank the poor buggers who have to do all that digging.'

Nod.

Longinus regarded Fronto with a slightly worried expression.

'Marcus, don't take this the wrong way, but you don't look well. You're still recovering from some fairly nasty wounds and will be for weeks yet; maybe months. Caesar only invited you to re-join them at the moment because your primus pilus badgered him repeatedly until he agreed. You should by all rights still be with the medics. I know it and you know it.'

Fronto waved a hand dismissively.

'Nah. I can ride, drink and think. Nothing else required of me at the moment.'

Longinus reached around and grabbed a handful of tunic at Fronto's shoulder.

'Don't be so bloody stupid. None of your friends will say a word to you at the moment. They're all too proud of you and too frightened of hurting your feelings to tell you what's what. They just pussyfoot around you like you're a teething babe.'

Fronto stared blankly at the cavalry commander.

'*You've* taken your nasty medicine today, haven't you?'

Longinus released the handful of tunic.

'I'm just talking straight, same as you would to me. We have no pretence at being caring friends, and sometimes that's useful. You need to rest; to stay completely out of things for now. If you 'ride, drink and think' as you put it, you'll slow your recovery down interminably. If you don't have yourself relieved and go back to the medici, I may be tempted to break your other arm just to save you from yourself.'

Fronto continued to stare. 'You can be really nasty,' he told Longinus, 'when you're right.'

He sighed and lay back on the grass.

'Gaius, I'm weary and I'm worried. What the hell happens if Labienus has got Balbus and Crispus killed? We can't hope to maintain a campaign if we lose a third of the army at one stroke.' Longinus stood and brushed the grass from his breeches.

'You know as well as I do that Labienus is a good man; a good officer and a good tactician. Unless the whole of Gaul has united to attack him, he's out there somewhere with the Eighth and the Eleventh, pulling some kind of clever manoeuvre. And Balbus is too bright to get himself pulled into that kind of trouble without sending a messenger to the commanders.'

Fronto nodded. Longinus reached down, offering to help the injured legate to his feet.

'Anyway,' he said, looking out over the fortifications and down the hill, 'I think we're about to be given the whole story. Some of those scouts are coming in already. I think you'd better go see Caesar before you go off duty.'

Fronto nodded once more.

'You wouldn't care to help a poor wounded soldier back down the hill, would you?'

Longinus looked at the outstretched hand and the smile on Fronto's face. He grinned back.

'Piss off. You can walk, you lazy animal.'

The two of them sauntered down to the command unit, laughing as they went.

By the time they had reached the rest of the staff officers, the riders were dismounting, handing the reins of their steaming horses to servants.

The three scouts who had returned initially had escorted a fourth rider, who stepped forward from the group and bowed to Caesar.

'Labienus?'

Caesar stared. Fronto and Longinus started. What had happened to his men? Evidently the same thought had immediately occurred to Caesar. The general walked forward to the weary-looking man.

'Labienus, what happened to your legions?'

Fronto noticed that the three scouts had shrunk back into the edge of the circle. Labienus raised his face. What Fronto had assumed was tiredness was, in fact, anger. Labienus' face was red.

'My army is *fine* sir, if a little bored. We've been in position at the top of the peak now for around ten hours. We watched the Helvetii break camp and march away hours ago, but we had to let them go. My orders were to launch no attack until you were there. Where were *you* sir?'

Caesar's eyes opened wide.

'You had the hill?'

'Of course we did. We walked up it and stopped. Not even a hint of a problem. The Helvetii never saw us; didn't even know we were there. We've been waiting for the rest of the army to launch the attack. I'd still be waiting now if your scouts hadn't come to us.'

Caesar threw the cup he was holding to the turf and ground it in with his boot. Fronto stepped back. The general was shaking violently.

'Considius was wrong. Those weren't Gaulish standards the lunatic saw, they were legion Vexilli. How can the imbecile not know his own flags?'

The circle around the irate general was widening as the moments passed. No one dared speak for fear of directing the blast of the anger toward them.

'That's it. No more dancing around. We're going to go and get the grain from the Aedui ourselves and then move on fast and finish these Helvetii. The time has come to break them.'

Turning, red faced, to Sabinus and Fronto, he shook a finger at them.

'Get me Considius. Get him now.'

CHAPTER 10

(THE AEDUI TOWN OF BIBRACTE)

'Amphora (pl. Amphorae): A large pottery storage container, generally used for wine or olive oil.'

'Oppidum: The standard Gaulish hill town of the pre-Roman period. A walled settlement, sometimes quite large.'

Fronto was surprised at the size and complexity of the Aedui Oppidum. He was not the sort of man to label every non-Roman he came across 'barbarian' without cause, but he had met these Aedui leaders, and had expected perhaps a collection of huts and a well. In fact, Bibracte covered the top of an entire hill, the best part of a mile across, surrounded by a wide and high wall formed of shaped stones and heavy timber. The city inside, for Fronto could think of it as nothing less than a city, was complex and large, with a patchwork of crossing streets and houses jammed together in close proximity. The city rang with the sounds of blacksmiths, market traders and the chattering public.

Fronto had stopped at a wine store and had been astonished to find high quality Roman wine from Campania on sale. He had bought an amphora of the best product and had been surprised at the price, which was at most what he would have expected to pay in Rome, and perhaps even cheaper. The storekeeper had accepted Roman coinage and had given Fronto his change in coins of the same intrinsic value as Roman ones, minted in Bibracte and showing Aedui designs. He was beginning to understand why Caesar supported these people and why the Roman government nurtured this alliance. These were no more barbarians than the people of Pompeii or Puteoli.

Sitting in a small and shady garden outside a local tavern, with green trees and creeping plants growing overhead, Fronto, Balbus and Longinus drank heartily from the choice of wines they had picked up around the main street of the town.

It had only been two and a half days since the debacle on the hill, but it seemed like a lifetime while they sat in the sun, officially off duty and relaxed. The army had followed the Helvetii for a day, less than three miles behind them, but had veered off early yesterday morning and made for this place, the largest and wealthiest of the Aedui towns and, by chance, the home of Liscus, the Aeduan who had made the promises of grain to Caesar.

All six legions were now officially off duty. The Aedui had welcomed the Romans to their city, and Caesar had magnanimously given the order for the soldiers to take time off, though to keep their wits about them and to remain armed. The tents of the legions had been erected below the city walls. Today the grain would be gathered and distributed, and the legions would rest. Fronto had asked Caesar whether the army would be moving on the next morning, concerned as to why no defensive systems had been erected, but the general had merely smiled and tapped his finger to the side of his large nose.

In fact, the only people who had not been excused duties were the non-legion based staff officers, who had been given the task of liaising with the Aedui leaders and merchants in the gathering of the grain. Fronto would probably have been with them had not his wounds given him reason to stay off duty. As Longinus related a long a lurid tale of a lady of debatable virtue, punctuated regularly by Balbus' laughter, Fronto watched the sacks of grain being moved continually down the main street toward the supply section of the Roman camp outside. A group of labourers went past with two merchants arguing, accompanied by Sabinus, who turned and frowned irritably at the legates drinking and sunning themselves. Fronto gave him a happy wave and smiled.

Only tomorrow were the troops due to be given their rations of grain, so Caesar had timed the visit perfectly. Liscus had lived up to his promise, though with a little delay. When the Romans had arrived, they had found the merchants of the city already piling the grain in carts. The army would have received its rations only a day or two late, but now, and with the organisational aid of the staff officers, the grain would be distributed a day early. By nightfall tonight, all personnel would have their allotted quantities.

Fronto suddenly became aware that a cavalry soldier was standing by the entrance to the tavern garden, looking nervous and clearing his throat. Longinus and Balbus, exchanging wild tales, had not noticed the arrival of the man.

'Longinus, I think you're wanted.'

Longinus turned to look at Fronto and noticed the cavalry trooper. He swung around on the bench to face the young man.

'Soldier, you can stand at ease. The entire army is off duty, and that includes you.'

The soldier gave a nervous nod but made no move to relax. He cleared his throat again anxiously.

'Sir, I beg your indulgence, but I have bad news to report. The duty stable hand in our ala didn't show up for his stretch this afternoon, sir. Prefect Aemilius ran a head count to see if he was missing, and the count came up eight men short. It looks like we've had deserters, sir. When we checked, their horses and all their pack and equipment had disappeared.'

Fronto looked at Balbus and Longinus.

'Sounds serious.'

Longinus shot a warning glance at Fronto before turning back to the cavalry trooper.

'Very well, soldier. Send Aemilius to me. I want a word with him.'

'Sir!' The trooper pulled himself even further to attention and, turning smartly, jogged off down the main street toward the city gate.

Fronto narrowed his eyes at Longinus.

'Alright. What's going on?'

'I beg your pardon?'

Longinus met his gaze with eyes full of innocence.

Fronto slapped his palm on the table, then winced as the shockwave coursed through his still tender arm.

'You showed absolutely *no* surprise when that soldier warned you of deserters. You may be a fair officer, but you're a terrible liar. Now, *what's going on?*'

Longinus glared at Fronto a moment longer, and then gestured with his thumb to a table in a rear corner of the garden beneath a huge oak tree.

'If we're going to have this discussion, let's go over there.'

As Fronto, grumbling, moved to the other seat carrying his cup and a jug of wine, Balbus followed suit. Longinus instead made his way inside. Fronto heard a short, hushed conversation with the innkeeper and a moment later the staff of the tavern were standing by the gate, out of earshot and blocking the entrance.

Longinus collected his drink and joined them at the rear table.

'Thanks a lot Marcus, you just cost me a packet to buy us a little privacy.'

Fronto shrugged, wincing with the pain of the movement.

'Learn to be a better liar. It'll cost you less.'

The cavalry commander frowned at him and lowered his voice to a hushed whisper.

'I'm well aware of the deserters, yes. In fact I sent them off myself, early this morning on the orders of Caesar.'

Balbus perked up a little at this.

'Why is Caesar having you fake desertions?'

Fronto grinned.

'I think I can answer that, Quintus. And I think if you work it through yourself, you can too.'

Balbus closed his eyes for a moment.

'Misinformation you think?'

Fronto smiled again.

'That's why we're off duty and we haven't made a fortified camp. That's why Caesar won't tell me when we're moving again. He has no intention of moving from Bibracte at all.'

Longinus nodded.

'We'd have had to move at a hell of a pace to catch up with the Helvetii after our detour here to collect the grain. We can't catch them, so the general's arranging for them to come to us. We'll only have to move to one of the surrounding hills for favourable ground.'

Balbus slowly began to grin now.

'These 'deserters' then must be telling the Helvetii that we've left off the pursuit and turned round; that we're running. Why would we do that? What possible cause?'

Longinus clicked his tongue.

'Think, lads. We're cut off from our supply line now, the grain from the Aedui hasn't been forthcoming, and the Helvetii don't know we've found the traitors among our allies. They have every reason to believe we're heading back to the Saone.'

Fronto banged his fist on the table again, wincing once more. He seemed totally unable to consider the consequences of any course of action on his wounds. His voice was getting louder as the excitement grew in him.

'I'll bet Caesar has scouts out over at least a five mile radius, waiting for the Helvetii to turn up. That's why we're not fortified. Caesar wants the entire army to be easy to manoeuvre when the enemy appear. It all makes sense.'

He became aware that Longinus and Balbus were waving their hands, gesturing Fronto to lower his voice, and shushing him.

Fronto was grinning like a maniac. In a lower voice, he continued.

'We'll be here for a few days, then. The army'll be on standby from tomorrow, but we'll still be here. Boys, I think we can relax for a bit. No more chasing the buggers. Now we just have to wait for them.'

Balbus smiled and nodded. Longinus rose from the seat and went to the gate to thank the innkeeper for his discretion. When he returned, he spoke to the others again.

'Needless to say, you can't breathe a word of this. Caesar doesn't want any cock-ups, and it'll be at least tomorrow morning before we'll have confirmation that it's worked. Until then, this is top secret.'

The two legates nodded seriously, though the smiles continued to creep across them when they lowered their faces to drink again.

As Fronto glanced toward the street, he saw Sabinus travelling back up, with a labourer carrying four empty sacks. The staff officer looked over at the legates. Fronto waved happily again, and Sabinus muttered something under his breath, flicking an uncivil gesture at the lounging officers.

Fronto smiled.

'I quite like that Sabinus, you know. For a senior staff officer, he's not altogether a pointless upper class twit.'

Longinus smirked.

'Unlike you, of course.'

Balbus roared with laughter as the smile fell from Fronto's face. He picked up his drinking mug, examined it, and dropped it quite heavily on Longinus' knuckles where they lay flat on the table.

'Oops.'

Longinus muttered something unflattering concerning Fronto's lineage and blew on his knuckles.

'Bastard.'

Fronto smiled.

'That's right; I'm a humourless bastard, not an upper class twit.'

Balbus picked up the fallen mug and set it upright, examining it briefly for cracks. Satisfied it was unbroken, he filled it to the brim, emptying the last few drops into Longinus' mug before he set it down. Leaning round the corner, he called the innkeeper for more wine.

'I know we've not been in the field long since I was stationed more-or-less permanently at Massilia and Geneva but, for some reason, I'm enjoying this off duty more than I ever enjoyed it in either of those places.'

Fronto lifted his mug and toasted Balbus.

'I'll say.'

For a moment, a sad look crossed the older legate's face. 'Apart from Corvinia. I do miss her.'

'Ah, but think of what'll be waiting the conquering hero when you next see her, eh?'

Fronto winked lewdly at Balbus.

Longinus smiled. The sun rained down in shafts between the leaves. Birdsong filled the air above the ringing of blacksmith's tools across the street, and all was right with the world for a short time.

Fronto awoke from his comfortable, warm sleep with a start. Someone was shaking him.

'Mwahhh?'

'I said wake up, sir. You'll want to see this.'

Fronto opened his eyes, blearily. The face of Priscus swam into view.

'Piss off Gnaeus, there's a good chap.'

Priscus continued to shake him.

'Honestly sir, you're really going to want to see this.'

Finally, way beyond hope of sleep, Fronto used his good arm to grasp Priscus' elbow and pull himself upright.

'Alright. Find my tunic and let's go and see what the hoo-hah's about.'

Moments later, the pair appeared at the doorway of the tent. Sometime during the night a gentle shower had begun and, though the rain was still light and fine, several hours of precipitation had turned the ground into a mire. Picking their way around the edge of the tent on the drier, more solid ground, Fronto and Priscus trudged through drizzle to the edge of the slope. Only ten paces behind the tent, the walls of Bibracte rose high and powerful and ahead down the slope lay the arrayed tents of the Tenth Legion.

Fronto looked at Priscus and shrugged.

'Now what?'

Priscus pointed off through the murk and into the distance beyond the legion's camp.

Fronto followed the primus pilus' pointing finger and shaded his eyes from the fine rain. Around half a mile away from the edge of the encamped army, a column of men approached. Fronto strained to see a Vexillum or identify the soldiers.

'Can't quite make it out. Can you see?'

Priscus grinned at him.

'Don't need to, sir. I know who they are. We saw them about a quarter of an hour ago, and scouts were sent out. It's the auxiliary units from Geneva sir.'

'Geneva? What the hell are they doing *here*? I thought they were stationed there for good.'

Priscus nodded.

'I thought so too, but they're here now.'

Fronto stretched and the insistent rain trickled down his arm and into his tunic.

'I'd best get dressed properly and head over to the headquarters. I need to find out what's going on.'

A quarter of an hour later, Fronto made his way out of his tent again, stepping round the steadily growing pool outside the doorway. Moving at a quick pace, with his red military cloak pulled tightly around him and rain running down his face, Fronto picked his way through the tents to the headquarters.

By the time he reached Caesar's tent, the late dawn sun was making a shoddy attempt to pierce the veil of rain. Stepping round the quagmire in front of the doorway, Fronto reached the entrance and was confronted by one of Caesar's attendants.

'Could you ask Caesar if I may see him?'

The attendant smiled beatifically at him.

'You are expected legate Fronto. Please enter.'

Bedraggled and cold, Fronto stepped inside. Caesar sat in his campaign chair at the back of the main room, with several of the staff officers nearby, including Sabinus and Labienus. The legates of the other legions were here too. Standing in the centre, very wet and travel-worn, stood Tetricus, the tribune from the Seventh. He looked thin and slightly frail but very much alive. He turned to the new arrival and his face, slightly pale and hollow cheeked, broke into a smile.

'Fronto.'

A simple greeting. Nothing more. Fronto stepped forward and the two locked arms in the age-old fashion. Behind them, Crassus cleared his throat.

'That will do tribune. This man is a superior officer.'

As Tetricus obediently withdrew his hand, Fronto wheeled on the other legate.

'This man is a hero and a friend. You can stick your superiority where the sun doesn't shine, if it isn't too tight!'

Ignoring the blustering noises from Crassus, he turned back to Tetricus.

'I ... We all feared you were dead.'

Before Tetricus could answer and before Crassus finally found a gap in his rage long enough to speak, Caesar leaned forward in his chair, his hands on his knees.

'Gentlemen. I shall be calling a full staff briefing later this morning, but I think the time has come, particularly with the arrival of the Geneva units, to clear up a few matters. Their presence here has no doubt raised questions among you.'

Caesar took a deep breath.

'I requested the presence of the auxiliaries once I was sure that Geneva was no longer in danger from the Helvetii. Tetricus has brought most of them with him, leaving only four units under the command of Geneva's decurions to defend the town from any possible incursion by the German peoples. When we next meet the Helvetii, I want the battle to be decisive.'

He looked around at the gathered officers and gestured at Tetricus as he addressed them.

'The tribune here has proved not only his worth as an officer, but also his value as a commander of fortification engineers and his valour on the field of combat. While there is still a need for him at the rank of tribune and no available higher command, I have requested that he take on the full-time responsibility of all major works of fortification for the army.'

Caesar smiled and was about to continue when Fronto held up his hand.

'General, I have had some experience dealing with the tribune in his work, and I feel that I value him higher than some.'

He glanced over his shoulder at Crassus.

'I would like, if the tribune gives his consent, to request his transfer to the Tenth.'

Crassus began to bluster again, his face turning a vaguely purple colour. Fronto sighed. He was just destined to make political enemies.

Tetricus grinned at Fronto.

'I would like that very much sir.'

Caesar smiled at the young officer, then at the gently steaming form of Crassus.

'Crassus, I would not transfer one of your men without your consent. Do I have it?'

Crassus nodded, his face grim.

'I wouldn't have the man in my legion, Caesar, bearing in mind his appalling manners and his disturbing failures of loyalty.'

The general leaned forward in his seat and jabbed a finger at the young legate.

'You may be a legate, Crassus, but that is at *my* whim. Your lineage has put you in a strong position, but it does not excuse rudeness and accusations. Tetricus has served with nothing but loyalty and courage, and if *Fronto* values him, then *I* value him, it's as simple as that. I have known and trusted Fronto for longer than you have lived. See to your legion and get out of my sight.'

As Crassus left hurriedly and with a look of distress, Caesar turned back to the room.

'Very well, once this meeting is over, Tetricus will report to Fronto and take his position with the Tenth. Now, onto other matters.'

Caesar gestured at the map.

'There may have been rumours circulating in the last day or so about deserters among the auxiliary cavalry. These were carefully staged incidents that have allowed us to infiltrate the Helvetii and to feed them false information. These 'deserters' will join the column again shortly, once their task is complete.'

Fronto registered the looks of surprise on the faces of his fellow officers with some satisfaction.

'Their task, as you might now guess, was to convince the Helvetii that our army is in retreat due to lack of supplies, and to bring them back toward us and force them to join battle with us. This they have achieved. My outlying scouts report the Helvetii just less than a day's travel away from us, giving us today to prepare and tonight to relax. The army should be fully positioned and rested when the Helvetii actually arrive.'

Fronto smiled quietly to himself. The excited muttering among the officers spoke volumes for the army's morale.

The general sat back in his chair and cradled his hands.

'I have given much thought to the end of this particular chase. I have always intended to destroy the Helvetii as a body, keeping survivors for the slave market in Rome. However, we are in Gaulish territory and may stay within it for some time yet. We have shown them, and will again, the might of Rome on the field of combat. Perhaps it is now time to show them why we call ourselves civilised.'

A number of the officers stared at Caesar, wide-eyed and surprised. Longinus was the only one to speak out.

'Caesar, the Helvetii cannot be trusted. They have wronged the Roman people, and they continue to wrong the rest of the tribes of this benighted land. They should be wiped out for the benefit of *all* mankind.'

Caesar smiled a weary smile.

'I understand your position, Longinus, but my mind is set. We have revenged the wrong they have done Rome. Fronto saw to that by the banks of the Saone. They must be broken for the good of our allies, but by no means am I expecting, or even desirous of, genocide. To eliminate all vestiges of the tribe would be to leave no one to rule, and no one to act as a buffer against the Germans. No, we need to *break* the Helvetii for good and put them back where they belong.'

Caesar looked around the tent at the gathered officers. Attendants and servants went about their various tasks, almost invisible to the commanders. The general regarded the servants and made a gesture toward the doorway.

'Out. All of you.'

The officers dithered for a moment, unsure as to whether the general was referring to the servants or themselves. As the various attendants left the tent, Caesar leaned through the doorway and addressed the guards.

'You two, move the guard line ten paces down the hill and keep everyone away from this tent.'

The soldiers saluted and made their way down the slippery bank. Once they were well and truly alone, Caesar took his seat again.

'Gentlemen, I would have preferred to have kept some of this under wraps as yet, but I suppose you'll piece things together soon enough, probably wrongly, and I'd rather you had all the information than filled in the gaps with guesses. With the likelihood of a final encounter with the Helvetii looming, I need all of my officers to be prepared for subsequent action.'

As the officers looked at each other questioningly, Fronto paid particular attention to Tetricus. The man looked tired, but he certainly did not look surprised. Whatever was afoot, Tetricus was already in the know. He looked round as he realised the general was talking again.

'Once we have defeated the Helvetii, I intend to send them back to their lands near Geneva. That does not, however, herald the end of the campaign. The following information goes no further at this time, of course.'

Nods and affirmative noises filled the tent. A redundant phrase, Fronto thought. Caesar had enough presence and power over these legions that the officers would betray the confidence of their own family before they would betray the general, whether that be through respect or fear. He looked back across at his commander as the man continued.

'There has been a great deal of movement on the German border over the past few months, while we have been campaigning against the Helvetii. In much the same way as the Helvetii have invaded lower Gaul and moved west, a number of German tribes under a man named Ariovistus have crossed the Rhine and settled in the lands of the Sequani to the west.'

Caesar leaned forward and unfurled the larger campaign map on the table once more.

'These German tribes have been used as mercenaries by the Gauls for many years now, fighting for the Sequani and the Arverni against our allies the Aedui. That they have turned on their former employers and settled on their land is no concern of ours, but we cannot ignore the threat that they constitute to the stability of our alliances in Gaul. I anticipate a request for aid from certain quarters very soon.'

The general paused a moment to allow all this fresh information to settle in.

'Just as we will not allow the Helvetii to threaten our allies, nor will we give the Germans free rein. They must be kept on their own side of the Rhine. So, gentlemen, barring a miraculous turnaround by Ariovistus, we will be continuing our campaign in the field for the foreseeable future.'

The muttering began once more. Caesar waited a moment longer, and then stood.

'Gentlemen, I shall require your presence in two hours when we shall prepare our strategy for tomorrow and attend to the disposition of troops. In the meantime, find your legions and go about your duties. I want the entire army ready to manoeuvre into position by the time we have finished our next briefing. Dismissed.'

As the officers made their way respectfully out of the tent, Caesar sat back once more.

'Fronto? Stay a moment if you would.'

The legate waited until the last of the staff had left and then closed the tent flaps for the general. As he turned, Caesar gestured to a chair.

'Marcus, I need your advice.'

'Sir?'

Caesar shifted uncomfortably in his seat.

'I am concerned over Geneva, Crassus, and the wisdom of long-term troop command and I want your honest thoughts.'

Fronto sighed. It was going to be one of *those* conversations. He had not had this kind of talk with Caesar for some time now.

'Firstly, sir, if you really want my honest advice, I'm going to have to speak quite plainly and openly with no fear of reprimand. Are you happy with that?'

Caesar nodded.

'You know I've always allowed you a measure of independence that I don't extend to the rest of my staff.'

Fronto shuffled in his seat and unhooked his cloak, letting it fall to the ground. He reached out and took the jug of wine from Caesar's table and filled two glasses, offering one to the general, who accepted it readily.

'As far as Geneva is concerned, how many units are stationed there again?'

Caesar rubbed his chin, deep in thought.

'There should still be four auxiliary units, two infantry, one cavalry and one mixed. They're commanded by individual prefects under the general auspices of the decurions of Geneva.'

Fronto furrowed his eyebrows.

'Unless there's a full-scale German invasion, that should be sufficient. I don't think the Germans will come across the Helvetian territory any time soon. They're too busy crossing the Rhine to the north. Besides, if the Germans launched any kind of large scale operation, even ten times that number would be unlikely to stop them.'

He sighed.

'Just in case, however, I would be tempted to send a message to Aquileia and raise the same number of troops again. I'd have a proper military officer assigned to them from the base at Aquileia and send them all to Geneva. That way you'd have a sizeable force under a proper commander that won't cost too much to raise and won't dig in to your reserves of regular soldiers. I'm intrigued to know why Tetricus is here with most of the force?'

Caesar sighed.

'A courier arrived a while back during our time by the Saone, when you were off trying to defeat the Helvetii on your own. Tetricus had received word of Ariovistus' crossing of the Rhine and thought I would need to know. He also believed that Geneva was in absolutely no danger with the absence of the Helvetii and with the German tribes pushing northwest, away from there. He requested permission to re-join the army, so I sent him a message telling him to join us with all speed and to set the auxiliaries off on the way. It was his idea to leave a small defensive force at Geneva. I didn't think we particularly needed Tetricus there in command, so I brought him here. I gather that during his short stay in Geneva he was healing very quickly from his wound, but I see now that such a long journey has perhaps set his recovery back again. Perhaps in retrospect I should have told him not to come.'

Fronto shook his head.

'Now he's here he'll be fine. It's a long and gruelling journey from Geneva, particularly for someone who isn't fully healed.' He looked down at his arm. 'Believe me. Tetricus will be fine now. You're probably right about Geneva being secure, but I'd prefer to play it safe.'

Caesar frowned and put his hand to his temple, a sign Fronto recognised that heralded one of the general's numbing headaches.

'Then my big problem is probably Crassus. Do I even need to ask what you make of him?'

Fronto grimaced.

'Disregarding my personal dislike for him, I think he's a jumped up, arrogant, nasty little politician riding on the back of his father's fame.'

The general rubbed his temples again and continued.

'*Disregarding* your personal dislike?'

Fronto smiled his least pleasant of smiles.

'Crassus is not well-liked by his peers and that cannot have escaped your notice. I am not alone in my opinions. The Seventh don't like him a great deal. He's unnecessarily hard and officious with them and unless he calms down he could cause trouble. Whole armies have mutinied before now due to that kind of command. I realise that he's young and trying to prove himself among his elders. He may even be a good tactical man, but his attitude is going to have to change if he wants to keep a command. You saw how he treated Tetricus. If I hadn't requested the transfer, he'd have made the tribune's life hell when he re-joined his unit. Is that plain enough?'

The general nodded sadly.

'It pains me to say it, but I do agree with you. I need to speak to him privately and try and adjust his aggressive command technique, but there *is* a problem. I know you're aware of a lot more than you probably should be, but I also know you're discrete. I need you to bear in mind when we talk of Crassus that not only is his father one of the most powerful men in Rome, he's also largely responsible for me being where I am. I owe the man a lot of money and a great deal more besides. I cannot afford to disgrace his son. I need him where he is, but I'll have to calm him down. You see, even I'm not above having to pander to people.'

Fronto nodded. It was an all too familiar story.

'We'll do what we can to help, as always Caesar, but please don't expect me to prostrate myself in front of him. I owe him nothing, and if he needs putting in his place, I damn well intend to do it.'

Caesar smiled.

'Good. If I'm restricted by personal ties, it might be good for him to have someone else doing that. My other thought is connected to this, though. I'm worried about the legions becoming too tied to their commanders. In the case of some officers, notably you and Balbus, I feel safe in the knowledge that you're the right men for the job. Other commanders I don't know as well, though. It occurs to me that they may show more allegiance to their commanders than to me or to Rome. I have given much thought to abandoning my policy of long-term legates and returning power to the tribunes and temporary commanders. What are your thoughts?'

The legate raised his eyes and focused on Caesar.

'Sir, the legions *are* tied closely with their commanders, but that is a *good* thing, and the legions will always become closely linked with a charismatic leader. I would respectfully submit that the benefits of your unusual command policy seriously outweigh the setbacks. I can foresee a day when all the legions have a permanent commander. I think it's the only feasible way forward. To my mind you needn't worry about the troops so long as you have strong and loyal legates. *They're* the ones you need to watch. After all... when it comes down to it, who pays them all? You, Caesar; not us.'

Caesar smiled.

'You always make me feel better Marcus. I feel confident in my decisions once they've had your approval.'

Fronto smiled wearily.

'Caesar, the six legions have marched readily and almost continually for a long time now, and the new auxiliaries haven't rested since their departure from Geneva. I saw the effect that the free off duty day in Bibracte had on the men and I think that, should the battle go our way, we should stay encamped here for perhaps a week. The legions could all do with the rest and it'd give us time to mend, heal and recover. Besides which, we still have the trial of Dumnorix to attend to. We can spend the time strengthening our ties to the Aedui.'

Caesar smiled.

'Agreed. A time of recuperation and political manoeuvring after warfare is done. Thank you, Marcus. As always I find your advice a comfort. Now all we need to do is to win the battle.'

'Bloody Typical.'

Priscus looked over at Velius and raised his eyebrows.

'What?'

'Being at the front. As usual.'

Priscus grinned.

'Gives you a chance to prove yourself, man.'

'Huh.'

The legions were camped on a hill about half a mile from Bibracte. According to the latest intelligence, the Helvetii would arrive a little after dawn. The army had been given its positions and there was no time or need to erect tents and fortifications; no one would be caught unawares tonight. The evening was dry and quite warm, the rain having given way to sunshine well before lunchtime. The ground had dried out thoroughly, and there was a strange atmosphere on the hill. Rather than a pre-battle tension, there was something of a summer camping expedition feel. In the twilight, soldiers from six legions lay wrapped in their cloaks and blankets under the open sky. Those who were still awake munched on the remains of game and salted meat cooked over the small fires dotted around the hill. A few drank to bolster their courage for the next day; others played dice to take their mind off it.

Priscus, Velius and Fronto sat with a flask of well-watered wine halfway up the hill, where the Tenth had been assigned. The legion had been organised (as had the others) in three rows, with four cohorts in the front line, and three in each subsequent one. Thus the crescent formation on the hill stood fifty men deep and, with the four legions side by side, four hundred men long. The Tenth were stationed as one of the two centre legions, alongside the Eighth. The Ninth took the left flank and the Seventh the right, side by side with Fronto's men. The Eleventh and Twelfth Legions, still relatively untried, stayed on the crest of the hill with the auxiliaries, surrounding the baggage and the staff officers. The entire hill was covered with men, such that virtually no ground was visible beneath the resting bodies.

It had been a very long time since an army this size had drawn up lines for engagement anywhere. The cavalry were visible on the plain at the bottom of the hill. They would leave before dawn and engage the Helvetii, drawing them closer and egging them on. The plan was well thought out and would be carefully executed.

The cavalry now controlled the only beasts on the field of battle. Caesar had had his own horse, along with that of every officer and all of the pack animals, removed to a corral at the very crown of the hill, surrounded by baggage carts. No one would be given an easy way to flee this field.

Velius looked up at Fronto, reflected firelight dancing in his eyes and across the metalwork of his uniform and armour. Fronto sat in his tunic and breeches, but without the cuirass. He was still suffering with the damage to his right arm and would be doing, so the medical staff said, probably until the winter and the campaigning season was over. As such, he would take no active part in the battle, but had refused to stay entirely out of the way.

'Sir?'

'Hmm?'

Fronto reeled in his thoughts from afar. Velius shifted his bulk on his blanket, crossing his legs.

'How many men do you reckon they have? The Helvetii I mean.'

Fronto frowned.

'I remember their numbers being estimated in one of the old man's briefings. I think they had about three hundred thousand when they left Geneva, but maybe a third of those were men of fighting age.'

'Whew...'

Priscus whistled.

'I hadn't realised there were that many. They always look like such a disorganised rabble when they're on the move you kind of forget how many there are.'

Velius sniffed.

'Bunch o' rectums the whole lot of 'em.'

Fronto and Priscus turned to look at Velius, who shrugged.

'What?'

He continued to sit, chewing on a piece of salted pork while the other two rolled around in laughter on the floor.

'You do have a way with words, man, have I ever mentioned that?'

Velius grinned.

'Anyway, dunno why we're counting on that many. We know a quarter of 'em disappeared by the river.'

Fronto nodded darkly. He had no wish to revisit the site of that slaughter, though it occasionally haunted his dreams. Trying to lighten the conversation, he turned to Priscus and gestured at Velius with a hooked thumb.

'Have you ever noticed that he talks differently when he's in front of a senior officer?'

Priscus smirked.

'He's in front of a senior officer now, and he sounds like one of the gutter-tramps that sleep under the Pons Aemilius to me.'

Fronto laughed as Velius delivered a nerve-deadening blow to Priscus' upper arm.

'Laugh that one off.'

Priscus' face took on a more serious cast.

'Is this it, now, sir? Are we going to beat them here and go home to Aquileia?'

Fronto frowned.

'You know I can't give you information concerning future campaign planning, Gnaeus, so stop probing for information.'

'I'm not, sir. Honestly, I can't see what else we're up to here after we trash them. Maybe take slaves, collect up booty, and back to Aquileia.'

Fronto gave a non-committal shrug.

'All things are possible, but don't start banking on anything until we've done for the enemy tomorrow. Even with the auxilia we only number thirty five or forty thousand. They've probably still got seventy thousand able men, so we'd best make use of this hill tomorrow. They'll outnumber us two to one. I hope Caesar's worked this through properly.'

Someone behind Fronto cleared his throat. Turning round, he saw a legionary sitting up in his blanket. No veteran, this boy; little more than twenty years old.

'Yes lad?'

'Sorry to interrupt, sir? I don't want you to think I'm eavesdroppin' or anything, but I can't sleep, and I couldn't help overhearing.'

'What's up?'

The young man shuffled forward, into the orange glow of the fire around which the three sat.

'Well, sir, some of the veterans say that you're the best general this army's got, better even than Caesar.'

Priscus grinned at Fronto.

'See, your fame's spreading like wildfire.'

He turned to face the young legionary.

'Better not inflate his ego too much, soldier. He's already got a big head, and he won't be able to fit it into his helmet tomorrow.'

Fronto thought for a moment, looking at his bandages and scars, then delivered a quick rabbit punch with his left fist to the same spot on Priscus' upper arm. The primus pilus fell back on the grass laughing and holding his arm. Fronto turned to the young man once more.

'I've studied my tacticians, and I've had the chance to put a few plans into practice in my time.'

The legionary looked up at him, wide-eyed.

'What would *you* do, sir?

'What do you mean?'

'How would you have planned this battle?'

Fronto looked thoughtfully into the fire.

'I think I'd have left all the baggage in Bibracte for a start. I'd have split the cavalry into three separate units. One to do what Caesar plans with them, one stationed in Bibracte as a reserve, and one hidden behind the hill.'

The young man grinned excitedly.

'And the army itself?'

'Three legions on this hill in the crescent formation; probably the Eleventh in the centre, with the Tenth and the Ninth on either side. The Twelfth on the slopes below the walls of Bibracte, and the Eighth I'd have sent on a forced march with most of the scouts to get in a position behind the Helvetii. The Seventh in reserve around the baggage.'

'And then sir?'

Fronto smiled.

'And then the Helvetii would get here and engage the three legions on the hill. Not long after that started, the Eighth would arrive behind them and we'd have them trapped. As soon as they first engaged, I'd have sent a signal up, and the Twelfth and a third of the cavalry would charge down from Bibracte and slam into their flank. They'd be ground to minced meat between the three fronts. Their only hope would be to break out the other side, and we'd have two remaining cavalry wings to harry them as they broke.'

'Wow.'

The young soldier grinned like a madman.

'Do you think *this* way will work?'

Fronto nodded.

'Oh, it'll work, and we'll beat them. I just hope the enemy don't have any nasty surprises planned. We'll have stationed our entire army in one place, with no reserve force, so casualties could be high if we screw it up.'

He suddenly realised this is not what he should be saying to young, impressionable soldiers on the eve of an important battle. He reached round and gave the boy a comforting pat on the shoulder.

'We'll beat them. We've beaten everyone so far on this campaign, and we're Roman, so it's our destiny to win. What's your name, lad?'

'Florus, sir.'

Fronto smiled benignly.

'Well, Florus, you look me up after the battle tomorrow, and I'll buy you a drink. We'll drink to the glorious destiny of Rome, eh?'

The legionary grinned again.

'Yes, sir!'

Fronto turned back to the other two officers. They were smirking at each other.

'What?'

Priscus put his hands together in a pleading manner, let his lower lip hang pathetically and fluttered his eyelashes.

'Please mister Fronto, you're our *hero!*'

Velius spilled his drink as he fell about laughing.

Fronto sighed.

'Get it out of your system lads. It's going to be a long day tomorrow.'

The four men sat silently, staring into the dancing flames of the dying fire.

CHAPTER 11

(A HILL NEAR BIBRACTE)

'Phalanx: Greek/Macedonian infantry tactic in which rows of men form a veritable hedge of long spears, backed with a shield wall.'

'Cornu: A G-shaped horn-like musical instrument used primarily by the military for relaying signals. A trumpeter was called a cornicen.'

The first the army knew about the arrival of the Helvetii was when the cavalry under Longinus came cantering down the valley in an ordered withdrawal. Moments later, the vanguard of the tribe appeared behind them on horseback. The Roman cavalry remained quiet except for the occasional bellowed order. The Helvetii, on the other hand, shouted, cheered and screamed as they rode, a tactic that Fronto knew was meant to frighten the enemy. He turned to the centurions of the Tenth.

'Let 'em know we've heard 'em lads.'

Under the orders of the centurions, five thousand men began to bang rhythmically on the bronze edging of their shields with their short swords. The act was soon picked up by the surrounding legions, right the way up the hill, where auxiliary troopers banged a variety of weapons on the edge of equally varied shields. The sound was deafening and well and truly drowned out the cries of the Helvetii.

Longinus' cavalry continued to hold the advance units of the Helvetii at bay while the legions formed into closer order. In the distance the main Helvetii force could be seen by the soldiers on the higher elevations, pouring into the valley. The enemy baggage train was brought part way down the valley and left in a dell bordered with trees, by the side of the main track.

Fronto shuffled his feet, wishing he were standing on flat ground. He could see the advantage of a slight incline, but it was making his shins and calves ache unbearably, and with the dull pain still in his arms, he certainly did not need any more discomfort. He silently cursed the Helvetii and wished them on, looking down over the massed heads of the Tenth and trying to see what was happening with the cavalry. Longinus would have to break the enemy horsemen. If he did not, the legions would have to face skirmishing cavalry, and they could be in trouble. Fronto strained to see.

The cavalry were making headway against the mounted tribesmen and, as soon as the beleaguered Helvetii realised this, their horsemen pulled back and around the flanks of the main bulk of the tribe. As they melted away and Longinus' riders reformed into a coherent unit, Fronto saw something happen among the enemy that he would never have expected to see in this barbarous land. The front ranks of the Helvetii formed up into what could only be called a phalanx! He could not believe there had been much contact between these people and the Greek world of the east. Perhaps among them were learned men who had read the military histories? Whatever the reason, there was no other way to describe the manoeuvre.

Longinus and his men were obviously equally struck with disbelief. The unit milled about in confusion as the cavalry troopers stared at the unusually strategic Helvetian advance. Unfortunately, as they dithered too long, the front ranks of enemy spearmen met the cavalry with enough force to remove some of the men from their horses. With a quick shout, Longinus drew the cavalry away from the front of the phalanx. The riders split into two groups that peeled off in opposite directions and cantered around the lowest slope of the hill to take up a reserve position for when they may later be needed to flank the enemy.

As soon as the cavalry had cleared the front of the massed legions, the cornicen began to play at the summit of the hill, relaying commands from the general and his staff. Caesar himself stood on one of the wagons, high and visible, shouting words of encouragement that precious few on the battlefield would be able to hear. Fronto, standing in the back row of the Tenth, listened to the call and gave the order for his men to sheathe swords and heft their pila. Caesar had requested Fronto's presence among the staff on the crest of the hill, but he had fought for his position as commander of a legion. He had after much argument been allowed to take a place with his men, though not to fight, but purely to lead, direct and encourage. To this end, he carried a sword with his left hand and no shield. This was an important fight, and Fronto needed the best possible morale among the Tenth, hence his camping the previous night among the men.

The Gaulish phalanx closed inexorably with the front lines of the legions, thousands of long spears thrust from behind a wall of the Gaulish shields. The legions took a few steps forward on the command of the officers, reaching the lower levels of the slope, where a slight ledge allowed the legionaries to defend at a slightly advantageous though not unfeasible gradient. The Helvetii reached the initial slope just as the order was given for pila to be released.

Each legionary throughout the army on the slope took a firm grip of one of the two pila they carried as standard kit. The whole bulk of men shifted position slightly and, as the final cry went out, twenty thousand pila arced out from the four front legions and into the phalanx moving toward them. The impact was phenomenal. The Helvetian shield wall at the front shattered and disintegrated like painted wall plaster. pila tore through shields, sometimes crippling the bearer but always making the shield useless, the soft metal neck of the missile bending and becoming lodged as it passed through the wood and leather.

As the front lines of the Helvetian offensive collapsed under the hail of missiles, the four legions repositioned, drawing their short swords once more. At the top of the hill, the Eleventh and Twelfth reacted to the signal and released another volley of pila, arcing way over the heads of the lower units and crashing among the mass of Gaulish warriors.

As the Tenth moved forward, the other three legions keeping pace to the sides, Fronto settled into step. The Helvetii ahead of them were disorganised and in something resembling a state of panic. Realising that a wall of Roman steel was closing on them, the non-wounded men in the nearest group of Gauls desperately pulled themselves into as solid a front as they could manage. Few had managed to retain their shields due to the pilum volleys; most had cast them aside as useless. The front ranks of the armies met with a crash that shuddered across the Roman lines, but smashed the Gaulish wall. The order to break ranks came from Caesar's staff cornicen on the summit, and was relayed by each legion's musicians. By the third note, the shield wall of the Tenth had broken and the true melee had begun.

Priscus led the First Cohort from the front of the army, and they spearheaded into the enemy. Once the front line of the Gauls had been broken, the ranks behind were disorganised. Discipline and command passed away from the generals and became the province of the centurions, who controlled their individual groups of eighty men according to a grand plan but with a great deal of individual freedom. Priscus raised his head as high as he could above the men of his century and looked around. The First Cohort was in danger of getting cut off if the enemy managed to organise themselves again. He could see the rest of the Tenth some distance behind, and could hear Fronto's cornicens relaying commands, but there were now pockets of Gauls between the First Cohort and the rest of the legion.

Realising the danger, Priscus called his signifer and gave the command for defensive formation. The entire cohort pulled in as close as possible, forming a solid square, with shield walls facing outwards on all sides. Once the formation was complete, he relayed a second set of signals to the senior centurions of the other cohorts to inform them that the First Cohort would hold where it was.

Suddenly, there was a crashing sound behind him. A number of Helvetian warriors had banded together to try and break through the cohort's outer wall. The first two came hurtling over the shield wall and crashed onto the heads of the men behind, bringing a whole section down in a heap. The two barbarians, who must have been thrown bodily by their fellows, died within moments of landing, but the damage to the formation had been done. Following on in their wake came a dozen burly Gauls. Having dropped their broad bladed swords, they were armed only with a dagger in each hand. They smashed through the collapsed shield wall and cut and shredded their way in among the tightly packed Romans at the centre. The legionaries immediately started their work with the short thrusting swords, but the lack of manoeuvring room left them unable to put up an effective fight. While those few barbarians cut at and stabbed whatever they touched in the press of men, other Helvetii were attacking the hole in the shield wall, trying to widen it.

Priscus bellowed at the top of his voice

'Close the damn gap, you arseholes.'

Other centurions within the First Cohort delivered orders and the various centuries on that side of the wall pushed to close the gap. Meanwhile, the centre of the formation was gradually regaining control of the situation and the barbarians were being whittled down until the threat disappeared. Unfortunately, due to the large number of dead in the centre of the square there was now a considerable open space, littered with prostrate bodies, and the few remaining Gaulish warriors were making good use of it.

Priscus raised his head to make out what was happening and saw one of the three remaining warriors, who had rescued shields from among the dead Romans, making straight for him in the press. It was always a dangerous situation; centurions led from the front, and their high visibility made them an obvious target. The centurionate bore a ridiculously high mortality rate, and Priscus was determined not to become just another statistic in the legion's records. He eyed the wounded, blood-stained warrior who clutched a dagger in one hand, a large Roman shield in the other.

Reaching out, he gripped the shaft of a standard that one of his signifers held.

'Give me that.'

The signifer relinquished the tall, heavy and unwieldy standard reluctantly. It was an honour, though a dangerous one, to carry the standard.

Swinging the weighted pole above the heads of the men, he brought it down and angled it like a spear. Indeed, there was a spear head on the very tip, above the golden laurel wreath. Bracing himself, he pulled it back. The barbarian sneered and held the large shield over his torso, looking over the top in the manner of a legionary, and picked up pace into a charge. The legionaries held back. Though they could probably have tackled the barbarian, none of his men would dare dishonour the primus pilus like that. The barbarian pushed the shield out forward to ward off the spear head and laughed.

At the last moment, Priscus braced himself and dropped the point of the standard toward the ground. The spear point jammed deep into the lower leg of the barbarian, who stumbled and tripped, shredding his shin. As the point tore out of the side of his leg, his momentum carried him forward, pitching him into the air. He landed some several feet from Priscus, and struggled to get to his feet. His right leg was useless, but Priscus had to give him credit as he managed to pull himself upright with his left, leaving the shield on the floor. He turned to face the Roman, snarling, and failed to see the swinging standard in the arms of the primus pilus in time. The heavy bronze and steel weight at the top of the standard smashed into the side of his head with a crunch. Priscus hauled the thing upright and held it out for the signifer to take. The man took one look at the blood-soaked spear tip and the bent and dented decoration.

'I hope you're not going to try and take that out of my pay, sir.'

Priscus snorted. He turned to look at the Gaul, lying on the disturbed turf with a broken face and a shredded leg.

'If he's not dead, you can finish him off and strip him of goods to pay for any damage.'

He turned to survey the situation. He had lost maybe forty or fifty men in the one brawl, probably nearly a hundred all told. Messy and stupid.

'Everyone in the second and third lines, get those pila angled upward. I don't want anyone else coming through, or over, the front rank.'

He became aware of shouting in Latin, and scanned the battlefield for the voice. He saw Velius leading the Second Cohort into the depths of the Helvetian force. They drew level with the First Cohort and formed a solid block. Behind them, in the distance, he could see men from other legions manoeuvring in among the barbarians. They would not get to try a trick like that again.

A second voice from behind them made him turn. Fronto was visible on the lowest slope, with the rest of the Tenth pushing onwards. Priscus knew his commander well enough to realise that Fronto felt his rank demanded he keep a rear position. He knew also that the officer was pushing the Tenth further forward than the other legions in order to get himself involved.

'Alright lads. We've made our inroads. Now it's time to form up and carve ourselves some Helvetii.'

He grinned and waved the signifer forward.

The mid-afternoon sun beat down on the battlefield as Roman and Gaul alike sweated and fought both the enemy and exhaustion. The main force of the Helvetii had broken around half an hour ago after long hours of butchery, and had beaten an ordered, if hasty, retreat toward a hill perhaps half a mile distant. The Romans had given the Gauls little time to disengage, but had been forced to take a few moments to reform the legions again for the next regimented push. The Helvetii had raced only moments ahead of the Roman front line toward the slopes of a second hill. Now the six legions marched along the valley, intent on ending the deprivations of the marauding Gauls.

In the same basic formation that they had held on the hill, the legions marched three cohorts deep, with the Eleventh and Twelfth forming a rearguard. On the crest of the hill, the baggage remained under guard of the auxiliary units. Now that the Helvetii had drawn themselves into a tight unit rather than a great wide sprawl of men, there did not look to be half as many of them. There must, of course, be a great number of their dead strewn across the plain between here and the hill that Caesar had made his own, and the Romans began to heave a collective sigh of relief at the whittling down of the enemy.

Aulus Crispus, commander of the Eleventh Legion and relatively new to the rank of legate, raised his voice above the jingle, clatter and rumble of a legion on the move.

'Come on men. We need to maintain close proximity to the Ninth, or we shall see no action at all.'

He still felt uncomfortable giving commands to so many men, including a number who were considerably older than he was. It was easy, he reflected, for Fronto, Balbus and Longinus. They had all had long and often distinguished careers in the military. The men looked up to that, and it had given them the experience to deal with command.

And, of course, young Crassus had the benefit of family. His father was one of Rome's most notable generals, and a man that even Caesar respected. Command came naturally to him.

Crispus had been in the military since Caesar had taken over Cisalpine Gaul. Before that, he had been in Rome serving in a lower administrative role of the grain dole. His mother had insisted that he was too old now to be stuck in such a low position and that he should join the army to get himself a little further up the ladder. She was right, of course. If he survived this campaign with no serious harm, he could expect a high administrative post in the city at the very least. And so he had signed on into Caesar's patronage (his family had been clients of the Julian family for some time) and accepted the position of a military tribune in Cisalpine Gaul.

The military tribunes were almost always men of little military experience and great ambition. They were far removed from those staff officers that were given command of legions, who were generally older, wiser and more self-assured. Crispus had had barely enough time to become accustomed to his post as tribune before Caesar had summoned both he and Galba and placed them in the position of legates.

In a way, there was more to be said for the position in this army than elsewhere. It was rare for a legate to be identified with a specific legion. When his father had served in the east, he had been made a legate and commanded three different legions in a fluid role. That was what the position was. The legate was expected to move freely between legions, taking command wherever he was needed at a time. Few generals had taken to the idea of assigning a specific legate to a legion, but Caesar, like Crassus and Pompey on occasion, had adopted the practice. In fact, Crispus had gathered, Caesar had been doing this since his earliest commands. Fronto had served with the general before, and had always had a specific legion of his own.

Galba, on the other hand, was born to this. Crispus had watched his colleague since they were both promoted and had noticed that the dark, stocky and quiet Galba had already gained much the same respect of his men that could be seen in Fronto or Balbus' legions. The man was obviously meant to command. Crispus just could not see why Caesar had put *him* in charge of a legion. He was pretty sure that the men made jokes behind his back; 'mummy's boy' or 'pretty boy' or some such. He could not really blame them. He knew he was far too young and unassuming to command the Eleventh. An educated poet and rhetorician, he had read much of the tactics of the great generals, and had found himself fascinated with the stories of Alexander the Macedonian, but had never considered that he might make a leader of men himself.

In front of him, the entire Eleventh spread out over half the field, with the Twelfth on the other side. Somewhere ahead were the Ninth and the Eighth, though he could barely make out the standards. Glancing around, he could see Caesar's colour party riding behind the legions, some of the cavalry protecting them, and covering the flank and over to the left...

Over to the left...

That could not be right.

Crispus felt the panic flood through him. He had been relieved to discover that he would be held in reserve at the rear, where he would not need to make any kind of decision or try to impose his will on the legion. From his position, he could continue to observe the tactics and abilities of the experienced legates.

But now he had been dropped in it. So far in it he could not see daylight. The Eleventh were the flank and all the Helvetii had been driven before them, so who in the Gods' name were *they*? He scanned the low ridge near the road once more, and saw the shapes again, moving mostly hidden behind the ridge. What on Earth should he do?

He tried to calm down; get a grip. What would Fronto do? Forcing himself to a decision, for good or ill, he called to his cornicen.

'Sound the alarm and have the entire legion halt and configure a shield wall facing left. We have company.'

The cornicen furrowed his brow and followed the pointing finger of the young, fair haired officer.

'Shit.' The cornicen, his horn still hanging on his shoulder, put his hand over his eyes and squinted toward the road.

In the grip now of a concern for the whole army, Crispus said sharply '*Soldier!*'

The cornicen pulled himself into an attention stance and saluted.

'Apologies. I meant 'Shit, *Sir*?''

Crispus rapped emphatically on the cornicen's helmet with his knuckles.

'Let's forego the formalities, soldier. Just issue the signals *now!*'

Nodding, the cornicen unslung his cornu and began to blare out signals. The Eleventh halted in their tracks and obeyed with practised ease. By the time they had faced left, the second enemy were above the ridge and making their presence known. The flanking Gauls, members of the Boii and Tulingi tribes that travelled as part of the Helvetii, outnumbered the Eleventh Legion by more than two to one. Crispus would need to pull off an impressive manoeuvre to hold this together. He wondered if the Ninth would stop their pursuit and join in the protection of the flank. Other signals were being relayed across the army.

Straining to hear, he could make out just enough to understand what was happening. The Helvetii had halted and drawn up into a formation mirroring that with which Caesar had initially held the other hill. The Ninth would be no help to Crispus; they would be engaging the front lines of the Helvetii by now. He wondered briefly whether to send a runner to Galba and the Twelfth, but then realised that the Twelfth would already be swinging out the other way to try and flank the Helvetii.

Crispus scratched his brow, trying desperately to think. He would have perhaps fifty heartbeats before the new threat closed on the flank and the Romans would be hemmed in. The Eleventh had no pila left after the volleys at the hill. Any tactics he could come up with would have to be brutally hand to hand. Grinding his teeth, his mind flipped back through ethereal pages of the great battles of the Scipios, Alexander and others.

He suddenly became aware that although his legion stood alert, tense and awaiting the crash of the charging Gauls, the officers were looking at him expectantly.

'Maintain the shield wall.'

It was weak and they knew it. Longinus or Fronto would have come up with a brilliant last-moment manoeuvre that unmanned the Gauls. He was not experienced enough; did not have the instinctive flair for strategy. He averted his eyes from the glares of the centurions. They might well hold the shield wall, but for how long? How long would they need to protect the flank? Would the Eleventh even exist afterwards? Crispus offered a fervent prayer to Nemesis.

A moment later, the second front of the Gaulish force smashed into the Eleventh, and the pyrrhic butchering began. There were more than twice as many of the enemy, but the legionaries were better equipped. Both sides would wear down at roughly the same rate, Crispus estimated, and that was unacceptable to his centurions.

He made his way along the rear ranks of the legion to the highest piece of the ground on this irritatingly flat plain. Desperately casting around for ideas, he glanced once more at the hill and could see the fight going hard on the other legions too. The outcome was far too unsure with the Helvetii now holding the high ground and fighting with renewed vigour, knowing that the Romans were engaged on two fronts and fighting for their life. The only solution would be to break their spirit. There would be precious chance of that at the front, so the Eleventh would have to do something. If the flanking Gauls got through the shield wall, they could attack the army from the rear and the legions would be massacred.

He spotted another ala of Longinus' cavalry making their way across the centre of the plain. Perhaps they could help in some way. He waved and bellowed until one of them finally noticed him and the unit turned and made their way toward him. The prefect in charge of the unit leaned down over his horse's neck to address Crispus.

'Sir?'

Crispus, still flustered and visibly so, tried hard to pull his hoarse voice under control and to appear in full command of his faculties.

'Prefect, are you riding to engage the enemy?'

The cavalry officer looked momentarily taken aback.

'Sir, we *did* our job at the start. We're undermanned and tired now and...'

Crispus waved the talk aside with his arm.

'I'm not asking you to make a stand or fight to the death, man; I would just like you to perform a small service for me, unless you're otherwise engaged.'

The prefect was visibly relieved. He had missed a full night's sleep before the battle and then lost nearly half his ala in the first quarter of an hour.

'So what do you want us to do, Sir?'

A slow smile spread across the legate's face. The bare bones of an idea were forming in his head.

'I need you to skirt round these Gauls, giving them a wide berth, and remaining out of sight. Make your way around behind them to that ridge by the road; do you see it?'

The prefect nodded as he followed Crispus' gesture.

'I need to know how many troops can be concealed behind the ridge, whether there is sufficient cover to get them there without being observed, and how long this would take. Can you do that for me?'

The cavalry officer nodded.

'I think we can manage that, Sir.'

Crispus smiled again.

'Good fellow. Return with all possible alacrity.'

He scanned the horizon for a moment, before becoming aware that the prefect remained where he was.

'Is something amiss, prefect?'

'What's alacrity, sir?'

Crispus sighed. This was not going to be easy.

'Speed, man, speed!'

The cavalry rode off and Crispus, suddenly full of energy, turned back to his legion. Finding the rearmost of the centurions, he caught his attention.

'Pass the word along to the other centurions. Necessity demands that we maintain the line as long as possible. There cannot be a single break, though we are in no way going to press the enemy. I do *not* want to see any heroics; just hold and maintain a defensive posture for as long as we can.'

The centurion looked at Crispus, one eyebrow raised questioningly.

'Just do it, centurion.'

'Yes sir.'

Crispus shielded his eyes with his hand and looked up at the sun. It would be around three or four in the afternoon now. With the high hills around them, the sun would set a lot earlier than it should at this time of the year, and the light would begin to fail at around seven. No general, or soldier for that matter, wanted to fight in the dark, so the officers would be pushing to finish this in a few hours. He doubted Caesar would let the legions pull out without finishing the enemy for good, but would the Helvetii want to stay after dark? Either way, it would need concluding soon.

He glanced around the horizon to see if he could spot the cavalry prefect and his ala, but they were not to be seen.

A series of shouts drew his attention to the front line of the Eleventh, where something was happening. This was no good. He would have to get himself a little involved. Fronto was always in the thick of it with his men, hacking and cutting and that was part of what made his legion respect him. Crispus would have to be seen to be involved.

Drawing his sword, he pulled one of the rear rank cornicens aside.

'I'm not sure what the correct signal is, but I'm coming through to the front and I need a corridor clearing.'

The cornicen stared at him, shrugged, and began to blow on the mouthpiece of the instrument.

As the men of the Eleventh pulled to either side, Crispus grabbed the cornicen's shoulder.

'Remain in position here. The moment that cavalry prefect returns, signal me immediately.'

The cornicen nodded.

'Sir.'

Rolling his shoulders and flexing the muscles in his sword arm, Crispus began to make his way between the soldiers toward the front. As he reached the front cohorts he immediately identified a problem. The Gauls were pulling back at several places along the front, opening up a gap between the two lines. Despite the desperate urgings of the centurions, the legionaries of the shield wall were bowing out, filling the space vacated by the Gauls. In their desire to reach the withdrawing Helvetii, the legionaries were stretching the shield wall to breaking point. If the Gauls managed a solid push back from where they were, they would punch through the line with hardly any resistance.

223

The Eleventh were still a green legion, unused to field warfare. Caesar had kept them back as a reserve unit on a number of occasions and, being suddenly in a frontline combat situation, the troops were eager to push and gain ground. The centurions, veterans drawn from other legions, were experienced enough to know that the line must hold together. They shouted their commands, and the optios at the back echoed the orders, but the troops were too enthusiastic and inexperienced to pay a great deal of attention.

Crispus was unused to command and relatively untried himself, but he had the advantage of a decent education and the access to military histories that came with it. Something would have to be done, and he would have to do it.

Swallowing nervously, he made his way through to the front ranks, the path that had opened up narrowing as he reached the front. Close enough to the enemy, he spied one of the gaps that had opened up and the bulge in the shield wall. Shouting orders for them to step aside, he pushed and manhandled his way to the shield wall. Another nervous gulp and a fervent prayer to Mars and he pushed through the shield wall from the rear, bursting out into the no-man's land between the lines.

Turning his back on the Gauls, he faced the advancing bulge in the lines of the Eleventh and shouted at the top of his voice.

'If *I alone* can shatter your formation, how effortlessly do you think the Gauls will manage?'

Gesturing over his shoulder with a thumb, he dived at the shield wall, where the arc was at its most stretched. Slamming into a legionary's shield, he punched a hole in the shield wall and fell inside. Moments later the line closed up again, but the point had been made. The advancing arc began to pull itself back into a straight line. A centurion helped Crispus to his feet.

'Nice one, sir.'

Crispus brushed down his tunic and stood straight, addressing the legionaries in general.

'Now secure the line with all swiftness and the next man who disobeys his centurion will answer with his head.'

As he began to push his way back through the crowd, he heard the renewed shouts of the centurions to hold the line. Breathing a sigh of relief, he reached the open ground at the rear and nodded briefly to the cornicen.

'Alright, I'm back. Do I presume that there has been no sign of the cavalry?'

The cornicen shook his head.

Crispus looked around at the horizon and up at the sun. There was indeed no hint of the cavalry ala returning. They had only a couple of hours of light remaining on the battlefield, and he could not wait for the cavalry any longer. The Eleventh were already under great strain. Once more, he gestured for the cornicen to join him.

'To which cohort do you belong?'

The cornicen nodded toward the rear line of the soldiers.

'The Ninth Cohort, sir.'

Crispus looked over the heads of the troops.

'In your opinion, are the four rear cohorts capable of useful action at this juncture?'

The cornicen shook his head.

'Unless the front breaks, we're all in reserve sir.'

Crispus nodded. It was a gamble.

'In that case, have the senior centurions of the four rear cohorts report to me immediately.'

'Yes sir.'

As the cornicen made his way back across the line, Crispus offered up yet another prayer. To relieve the legion of almost half its number in the current circumstances was dangerous. If this worked, he would save the Eleventh, and possibly the whole army, but if he took four cohorts away and then the front line broke, there would not be enough support to stop the Gauls from getting through and behind the army.

Four centurions made their way gradually out of the rear ranks and hurried over to the legate.

Crispus cleared his throat.

'I have new orders for you, gentlemen. I appreciate that what I am about to attempt is a gamble and that you may not approve, but the orders stand regardless.'

225

The four centurions looked at each other and back to Crispus, nodding assent.

'The way should be clear for the Ninth and Tenth Cohort to make their way around the perimeter of the field, keeping out of sight of the Gauls, and to achieve the ridge that the Gauls initially used for cover. I would estimate that you could reach your objective in a little less than one hour. You will need to remain completely hidden, however. If the Gauls are alerted to your presence before you are in position, you will not stand a chance.'

He waited for the inevitable complaints and comments, but such were not forthcoming. Glancing around the senior centurions, he saw speculative smiles playing across their faces.

'Once you are in position, you must remain out of sight and hold until you hear the call for a general advance. I will have that call put out in a little over an hour, so that is all the time you have. Can you do it?'

Two of the centurions saluted.

'It'll be a pleasure sir.'

'Then get them moving immediately. Oh, and should you come across an errant cavalry ala on your journey, tell them that they are no longer needed here. In fact, you might prefer to commandeer them yourself. A few cavalry might prove useful to you.'

As the two centurions hurried off beck to their units, the other two shrugged.

'Then what do you intend for our cohorts, sir?'

Crispus smiled.

'We need to instil some confusion in the enemy, and to distract them for a time so that they do not see the other two cohorts leaving the main force. I want your units to pull out to the end of our line and perform a sweeping advance on the Gauls, pushing in on them in the fashion of a closing gate. Keep them occupied for the next half hour or so.'

'Sir.'

As the others rushed off and left Crispus alone on the slight rise, he felt a thrill. The earlier trepidation he had felt had all but dissipated in the knowledge that he was doing everything an officer could do in the situation, and understanding that they were now in the hands of the fates.

Balbus had been aware for some time that the army had been flanked. He could only hope that Crispus was up to the task. As soon as the report had come in that the Eleventh had been forced to deploy alone and protect the army against a large reserve force, Balbus had tried to manoeuvre the Eighth to give him some support. Unfortunately, the Gauls had timed their attacks perfectly. By the time the enemy reserve had attacked the Eleventh, the front lines were well and truly mired down with the Helvetian main force.

Things were going slowly at the front. After making good initial headway, the Helvetii had taken up a very defensive position on the hill, echoing the earlier formation of Caesar's army.

Now the fighting had come down to a brutal pushing back and forth of the lines. The casualties on both sides were terrible, and no one could gain the upper hand. If the Eleventh broke and the Gaulish reserves got behind the main force, they would all be butchered where they stood.

His heart had fluttered a little around an hour ago when he saw almost half of Crispus' force separate off and split itself into two further groups. Half of them had left the battlefield by a long, circuitous route, while the other half had engaged the enemy in a hopeless attempt at a pincer movement. Balbus desperately hoped that Crispus had something up his sleeve. The force defending the flank was weakening as he watched.

A shout from one of the staff officers made him turn. From his position on the lower slopes of the hill, Balbus had a good view of the rear ranks and the events unfolding on the periphery of the field. Leaving the Eighth in the hands of its capable centurions, he stood and watched the Eleventh with a growing sense of excitement. Something *was* happening there.

A general advance call had been given, despite the fact that the Eleventh had absolutely no room to manoeuvre. His mouth hanging open, Balbus watched as a full fifth of a legion, around a thousand men, appeared over the crest of a ridge behind the enemy reserves. He laughed. The Gauls had outflanked the Romans, so Crispus had outflanked them in return. It was almost too perfect. As he watched, the newly-positioned Roman force closed on the rear of the Helvetii, reaching them almost before the Gauls were even aware the Romans were there. With a crash, the two cohorts hit the Gauls, crushing them now between two shield walls. The pincer units that Crispus had set off now came round the end of the line and fell in with the new attacking force, bolstering their numbers. Balbus grinned. The man was a genius. He had even managed to find some cavalry from somewhere to harry the few Gauls who managed to flee the crushing pincers. It was like poetry.

Aware that the main Gaulish force on the hill would have had an even better view than he, Balbus realised that this was it; *now* they could be broken. Turning back to his own legion, he raised his voice to spur his men on.

It had been fully dark now for almost an hour. There had been a period of dusk where the legions had still been able to manoeuvre properly, but command had now fully passed to the level of the centurionate, each century acting almost entirely independently. It was not the way any of the officers would have had it, given the choice, but the battle had gone on so much longer than any of them had expected and could not be stopped now.

After the rather risky manoeuvre that Crispus had pulled with the Eleventh, the reserve force of the Gauls had broken. Little more than a quarter of that force had escaped the jaws of Crispus' trap alive, and they had fled back to the Helvetian baggage train. Crispus had set off on their heels and had been joined by Balbus and the Eighth.

The main force on the hill had broken shortly afterwards, fleeing higher and higher up the slope, turning to fight a desperate rearguard action every few hundred paces. Fronto's Tenth, Crassus' Seventh, and primus pilus Grattius leading the Ninth had continued a slow, deliberate push up the hill. Galba had long since taken the Twelfth round to the other side of the peak, and had brought the Roman attack in from another side. Unfortunately, much of the bulk of the Helvetian force had fled down the other side of the hill before Galba had arrived and made escape for the rest impossible. In response, Longinus had sent a scouting party to follow the escaping Gauls and track their movements.

Now, under a thick covering of cloud, illuminated only by the burning torches that many of the Roman units carried, the four legions encircled the hill, almost at the summit. They had perhaps three thousand of the enemy trapped on the hill. Initially the legates had sent the legions forward at speed to finish them. That had been a mistake that had been paid for in large numbers of Roman dead. From their position on the hill, the Helvetii had showered the advancing force with arrows, spears, rocks and anything else that came readily to hand, including the dead. The angle of the hill prevented the Roman forces from casting enough missiles up at the Helvetii to cause any real threat, and the large boulders at the summit provided adequate protection for the Gauls in any case.

Velius and his Second Cohort were now pinned down on the side of the hill. He had given the order a quarter of an hour ago for the various centuries under his command to form tortoises, a square formation that allowed the legionaries to create a shield wall on all four fronts with a roof of shields above them all. Unfortunately, every time they moved, the tortoise came apart due to the terrain, and they had barely made an advance. From the little he could see, the other cohorts around him were taking the same steps and suffering the same problems.

He clicked his tongue in irritation. There was no way they could stay here. They would probably still be in the same position in the morning, with considerably fewer troops from the odd missiles that managed to penetrate the shields. He briefly considered calling out to the Gauls and demanding they surrender, but he knew that would do little good. There would have to be a charge, but that would involve the loss of a number of men and the legionaries would not be favourable after the last few attempts. One thing was sure, if *he* did not do something, no one else was going to.

He glanced around at the men closest to him.

'Nonus, Albius & Curtius, come here.'

Three legionaries made their way through the throng and reported to the centurion.

'You three are dangerous lunatics, aren't you?'

The three looked at each other, confused.

'Nonus, you won that inter-century wrestling match all but naked in the snow! Albius, I was told you once broke your nose just to see how it felt! Curtius, well you're just plain deranged!'

A number of grins issued around the nearest troops. Albius furrowed his fairly impressive and low brow.

'Alright, point taken sir. I don't much like the sound o' this. What d'you want us to do?'

Velius set his jaw firm and looked at the three. Nonus was small and wiry but with incredible endurance and at the peak of physical fitness. Albius was at least a foot taller than Velius, and much broader in the shoulders, with an impressive physique and a Neanderthal look. Curtius barely stood out from a crowd with the exception of his beard, very unfashionable among all civilised circles.

'We're going to break this party up. The four of us are going to get to the top of the hill and keep them busy while the rest of the troops come up.'

Nonus choked.

'*Four* of us? There's hundreds of them just on *this* side of the hill. We'll get killed.'

Curtius grinned and rounded on Nonus.

'I dunno, Nonus. It's only a few moments' run from 'ere to the rocks. Once we're there, we can cause a bit o' trouble. All we've to do is stay alive for a hundred heartbeats.' He turned to Velius. 'I'm up for it sir.'

Velius called to the signifer and cornicen of his century.

'As soon as we move to the front, give it a count of fifty and call a single blast to time our breakout together. The moment we get to the top of the hill, you get the whole mass moving as quick as possible. Forget the formation, just run. Break ranks and move in for the kill. Formations are worth shit in this kind of terrain, anyway.'

The two nodded.

'We'll get 'em going sir.'

Velius gritted his teeth and drew his sword, setting his shield straight on his arm.

'Alright lads, we're going to break out of the front of the tortoise in four different places and give 'em several targets. I'm relying on you. If you get hit, ignore it and keep running. Our job is to keep them busy long enough for the Tenth to move up the hill. Got it?'

The others nodded and, saluting briefly, pushed their way through the mass of people to the front ranks. A few moments later the horn sounded, and the four Romans burst from the front shield wall at a fast run, shields held high and directly in front.

Velius ran as fast as he could, and with years of outrunning the fittest recruits the military could provide, that was a fair turn of speed. He blindly ignored the sounds of heavy items bouncing off the front of his shield and concentrated instead upon where his run took him, zigzagging as much as possible and avoiding obstacles that could trip him and leave him open to the enemy. In his mad dash, he could not spare time to consider the others. He just hoped they were the fearless lunatics he thought they were.

Something whizzed past his sword arm, grazing the flesh and drawing blood. Cursing, he stumbled as the incline suddenly became a great deal steeper. As he regained his balance, the point of an arrow pierced his shield and came within a hand-width of his face. Risking a look above his shield, he could see two huge rocks, not more than ten paces away. Gritting his teeth once more, he sprinted diagonally up the slope and then, turning on his heel, came back across and dropped in front of the rock.

For the first time, he spared a glance to see where the others were. Nonus was little more than ten paces behind him, floundering on the slope which had almost tripped him. Curtius was at around the same elevation, but twenty paces to the left. Of Albius he could see no sign.

In order to give Nonus as much cover as possible, he grabbed a handful of pebbles from below the rock face and, clambering round the side of the boulder, hurled the pebbles at head height among the Gauls. The shouts suggested his aim had been accurate, and the missiles aimed at Nonus slackened for a moment.

Velius held the shield up to ward off a number of blows and, moments later, Nonus was by his side. As he made a few tentative strikes with his sword, Nonus grabbed a handful of pebbles and repeated the earlier gesture. The two continued to harass the Helvetii as much as they could, and finally Curtius arrived at the rock, his sword arm hanging limp at his side, clearly broken. Jamming his shield into the gap with his good arm, he leaned toward Velius.

'Anyone seen Albius?'

'No. He can't have made it. Are the troops moving yet?'

Curtius glanced around and over his shoulder.

'They're on their way.'

Velius breathed deeply. This was it. The legions surged up the slope like locusts over a lush field, bearing down on the beleaguered and now doomed Helvetii.

Balbus, who had been at the rear of the legion, jogged forward to reach the primus pilus. Balventius led, as all the centurionate did, from the front. The Eighth was closing in, slowly but surely, on the Helvetian baggage. On the other side of the baggage train, Crispus' Eleventh was closing the trap. There was no escaping the encircling Romans, but the Helvetii had formed a makeshift rampart from their wagons and were fighting with spears from beneath and behind the vehicles.

Balbus knew as he felt Crispus must, that one quick rush would overwhelm the survivors, but would cost the legions dearly. Instead, both legates were maintaining a careful attitude to the assault. The wagons were surrounded by a Roman shield wall, and every cycle of the horns a different century or two were sent forward to push at one of the wagons. The tactics were working. The Roman losses had been negligible, but the Gauls were gradually being thinned out, and the defences of their makeshift wall were becoming dangerously stretched.

Balventius stood dangerously close to the enemy, in front of the Eighth, wielding only his vine staff and with his shield propped against his leg. One well-aimed shot from the Gauls could kill him outright.

The man would never learn. Balbus sighed. He had now known some of the Tenth for a few months, and their primus pilus, Priscus, reminded him strongly of Balventius. It must be something about the position. To become a centurion took a certain fearlessness and strength of character; indeed to *want* to become a centurion indicated a certain audacity. To survive as long in the centurionate as Balventius had suggested invulnerability. Balventius was due his honesta missio at the end of this year, and would probably leave the legion to go farm somewhere in Cisalpine Gaul. Good for him; bad for the Eighth. They would have to promote a new primus pilus, and change was never that good. Balbus reached the front of the Eighth, legionaries respectfully making way for him, and motioned Balventius aside.

'Titus, you sent for me. What's up?'

Balventius smiled at his commander. His face was a patchwork of scars, and one of his eyes was filmed over with a milky white, the result of an action against bandits near Geneva early last year. The smile was disturbing in such a face. Balbus wondered what the enemy felt when they saw him, as the sight made even him shiver occasionally.

'Sir, it's nothing vital, but I would think we're going to break through in the next couple of pushes, and I thought you'd want to see.'

Balbus nodded.

'Absolutely. I can see how thin their defences have become. Well done. A marvellous job. I shall say so to Caesar when I see him.'

Balventius turned his evil features toward the Eighth again.

'Fabius! Petreius! Your turns. Get your centuries moving and see if we can break them this time.'

Two sets of horns blared and the signifers signalled the advance with their standards. A hundred and fifty men moved out of the shield wall at a steady pace, keeping formation. The two centuries, side by side, moved in toward a wagon that had been turned on its side. Five bodies in the kit of the Eighth lay before the wagon, but dozens of Celtic bodies littered the ground around and behind it. The wagon was defended by little more than two dozen men now.

Balbus, his hearing sharp as he carried his helmet under his arm, could hear the two centurions speaking to each other and to their men as they moved forward.

'Alright lads, we're not making a bit of a push. We're not stopping until we're in the centre of the baggage, you got that?'

The rumbling affirmative noise from the troops radiated enthusiasm. The men of the Eighth were itching for a fight after being held back for so long.

As Balbus watched, the two centuries picked up speed on their assault, finally hitting the wagon at a run. After his earlier discussions with Balventius they had decided on a slow and steady advance each time, gradually wearing the enemy down. Nowhere in their discussions had there been mention of a mad charge.

The front wave of legionaries leapt and climbed, surging over the wagon and into the Gauls, heedless of the blows they received from the defenders. Among them the two centurions were in the first few men over the barricade. Once they were clear and fighting in open ground, the second wave hit, putting their shoulders to the wagon and heaving it back onto its wheels. As they trundled the wagon aside to leave a gap in the wall, the rest of the centuries swept past and into the defenders.

Balbus turned to Balventius.

'I think you might as well sound the general advance.'

Balventius cupped his hand round his ear as the signal to break formation blared out.

'Way ahead of you sir. Now if you'll excuse me, I've got some Gauls to disembowel. Can't let the rest of the lads get there first, or they won't leave me any.'

With a quick salute and without waiting for a reply, Balventius turned and ran toward the defences, his sword in one hand, vine staff in the other and shield left forgotten, lying in the dirt. Balbus shook his head again. The man *should* be given his honesta missio for his own good, before he got himself killed.

Glancing at the rest of the Eighth as they moved in, he realised that Balventius was not alone. The legion screamed and roared like the crowd at an amphitheatre as they hurtled in an unruly mass toward the wagons. Even the signifers were running, bloodlust contorting their faces.

It struck him again how much good the campaign was doing his legion after their long sojourn in Massilia. He sighed, flicked the point of his sword with his thumbnail, and placed his helmet on his head. Ah well. If he was going to go today, nothing he could do about it. Time to join the lunatics.

As he turned and charged, his shouts were lost among those of his men.

CHAPTER 12

(THE AEDUI TOWN OF BIBRACTE)

'Praetorium: The area in the centre of a temporary camp reserved for the tent of the commander and where the legion's eagle and the signifers' standards were grounded.'

'Immunes: Soldiers excused from routine legionary duties as they possessed specialised skills that qualified them for other duties.'

The staff officers, legates and military tribunes sat in the command tent facing the general. Caesar wore the same self-righteous smile that had graced his visage since the middle of the night, when the last of the Helvetii on the field had surrendered, and the legions had stood down from battle status. Fronto kept having to avert his eyes, watching the other legates. Every time he saw that smug look it made him angry. Caesar had seriously underestimated the enemy, planned the attack badly and turned what should have been a foregone conclusion into a desperate and dangerous battle. If it had not been for the tactical knowledge and the quick thinking of young Crispus, the army might have been entirely destroyed.

Word had quickly passed round the officers of what had happened yesterday, though most of the troops had been either dealing with their wounds, attending to the dead, or collapsed through exhaustion. No official account had been taken, and now the officers had been called together for just that purpose.

Longinus was wrapping up his account as Fronto turned his attention once more toward his colleagues.

'...so I sent two alae of cavalry after them. It seems that the rest of the tribe were waiting about a mile away from the hill, staying out of the way of the battle. There must have been about ten or fifteen thousand survivors from the battle, and they hooked up with the women and children and headed away up north. One of the Aedui cavalry commanders informs me that they're probably headed for the land of a tribe called the Lingones, as they're likely to be sympathetic. All in all, we can estimate somewhere from a hundred to a hundred and fifty thousand of the tribe have got away, but we'll keep them tracked. They can't get away. Most of their warriors are gone.'

Longinus stood for a moment longer and then took his seat. Caesar nodded at Balbus, who struggled to his feet.

'Sir, the Eighth and the Eleventh acquitted themselves well at the Helvetian baggage camp. I'm sure you're aware, as all the officers are, of the part legate Crispus played in this victory, so I'll not go into detail. Suffice it to say that we had to kill most of the defenders before the remaining few would consider surrender. We took just over a thousand captives and they are currently being held under guard in a specially constructed stockade within Bibracte. Perhaps more importantly, I am informed that among the survivors are two of the children of Orgetorix, the man who tried to pull off a coup early this year, before the Helvetii left. We have all the Helvetii goods and baggage. In all, we suffered grievous losses during the mid-phases of the battle, numbering...'

Caesar raised his hand.

'Don't bother with the statistics, legate. I have had Sabinus collect all the figures, so we'll hear from him afterwards. It is enough that we know how the legions acquitted themselves.'

As Balbus sat, Caesar motioned to Fronto, who sighed and stood.

'As you're probably already aware Caesar, we lost a number of men in the assault on the hill. It was Velius and some of his more idiotic men who broke the stalemate. Not how I would have preferred it, but he *did* get it done. We captured a little over a thousand ourselves, and they're in the stockade with Balbus and Crispus' captives. Nothing more to say, I think.'

He sat down and smiled. He knew his offhand manner would irritate Caesar, and the thought that he might get on the general's nerves soothed him. Someone had to be a thorn in the great man's side, and it often fell to Fronto.

Caesar cleared his throat in annoyance and gestured to Sabinus. The officer got to his feet and opened a series of wax tablets.

'I've received the totals from each legion and totted them up. We suffered a loss of a little over five thousand men, and another six thousand wounded, walking or otherwise.'

Fronto whistled through his teeth. An entire legion's worth of dead and a legion's worth of wounded. That *was* critical.

'Taking into account the losses we had already suffered before yesterday, I felt it prudent to have a headcount made for each legion. The results are a little disturbing. Counting the walking wounded toward the surviving totals, the Seventh Legion are currently operating nearly a thousand below strength, the Eighth: one and a half thousand, the Ninth: a thousand, the Tenth: one and a half, the Eleventh: two thousand, and the Twelfth: five hundred. All in all, the army is currently down seven and a half thousand regulars, including the drastically injured, with a further four and a half thousand currently unavailable due to injury.'

Sabinus sat back.

Fronto and Balbus exchanged perturbed glances.

Caesar tapped his chin, deep in thought for several long moments, before he spoke.

'We cannot move from this location at the current time. It's going to take a few days to stabilise all the wounded and to bury the dead. Longinus, I would like you to arrange a courier for me. I want a message taking to these Lingones. Tell them that if they give any sort of help at all to the refugees, we will do to them what we did to the Helvetii. I refuse to play around any longer. The Helvetii are to be given two choices. Either they come back to Bibracte immediately and surrender, or we will follow them and bring war to them again, killing the two thousand survivors we have here in the meantime. Make sure they understand, Longinus. I *will* not pursue them any more. If I have to chase down the rest of them, I will kill them all, sparing no one.'

Longinus stood, saluting.

'I will take care of this myself, sir. I'll take an honour guard and deliver your terms.'

Caesar nodded.

'Very well. In the meantime, we must tend to the wounded and the dead and deal with the trial of Dumnorix. I will not call this campaign short, and I won't return to the province to resupply or bolster the legions. I will have a dispatch rider sent to Aquileia, telling the garrison commander to begin recruiting and training men ready to join us during the winter break in campaigning. In the meantime, we press on with the numbers we have.'

He looked around once more at the officers.

'I want volunteers to sit at the trial of Dumnorix. Fronto and I are attending, but we will need another eight volunteers. Anyone from the rank of tribune up will be acceptable. I realise this is none of your idea of a relaxing time, but I will be personally grateful for your attendance. If you are interested in attending the trial in three days, come to my tent between now and the evening watch. Other than that, I believe we're done here. Dismissed, gentlemen.'

As the officers poured out of the tent, Fronto collared the other five legates.

'Unless you have anything serious to attend to, I suggest we go into the town and find that nice little tavern with the shady garden. I don't know about you, but it's been a long night, and I need a drink.'

Balbus and Longinus nodded wearily. Crispus smiled.

'Perhaps a couple before I turn in.'

Balbus grinned at him.

'I think you earned it, Aulus.'

Galba declined, claiming exhaustion, and Crassus shook his head.

'I have more important matters to attend to. Thank you.'

Balbus stretched and grasped Fronto's shoulder, noticing the blazing irritation in his eyes as he glared at Crassus.

'If we're going to do any kind of celebrating, we need to get a few others here. Priscus and Velius, Balventius and Sabinus... and Tetricus?'

Fronto nodded.

'Why not, and there's someone else, too, but I'll find him. I'll see you at the tavern in about half an hour.'

As the others went their own ways Fronto wandered wearily, stretching as he walked, to the camp of the Tenth. Spotting Velius shouting at a couple of legionaries in the praetorium, Fronto stood patiently behind him and waited for the ranting to subside. As the two legionaries went off shamefaced, Velius turned, inhaling, on the man standing behind him, ready for a second outburst until he realised who it was.

'Sir.'

Fronto smiled at him.

'Yes. Sorry to disappoint you but I want you to go and wake Priscus. You're both going off duty with me, coz there's drinking to be done.'

Velius beamed at his commander.

'If you say so, sir.'

'I'll meet you back here in a hundred beats.'

As Velius headed off toward Priscus' tent, rubbing his hands gleefully, Fronto wandered up to the signifers who stood in a small knot, talking among themselves.

He motioned to Petrosidius, the senior signifer, and took him to one side.

'You organised the head count after the battle, didn't you?'

The signifer shrugged.

'I combined and correlated the figures, sir, yes.'

Fronto frowned.

'Can you find out if a young recruit called Florus from the First Cohort is still alive? He might be in the Second Century, but I'm not sure. If he's still breathing, I owe him a drink.'

Petrosidius smiled.

'Florus? Yes, I know him. He's still alive. He took a bit of a battering on one shoulder, but he's been asking the staff every few moments if it's possible to see you. I think the doc's about to put him to sleep!'

Fronto returned the smile.

'Thanks. I think I'll go and rescue him.'

Wandering off in the direction of the medical tents, Fronto's mood began to darken again. Littering the grass to either side of the path were men clutching an assortment of severed or damaged limbs. In a number of places the grass was slippery and red, and amputated limbs lay in a heap not far from the main surgical tent, awaiting burning. Sickened, Fronto tried to put on a sympathetic face as he passed the wounded, wondering how many would be sent back to Rome pensionless. He was prepared for losses in battle and a variety of horrifying wounds but had rarely seen anything on this scale, even during the most brutal battles in Spain. Caesar's lack of strategy had certainly left its mark on the legions.

As Fronto made for the tent flap, a medical orderly barred his way.

'I'm sorry legate, but the medical staff has enough to contend with right now. Please be good enough to call back tomorrow, when the worst cases are dealt with.'

Fronto scowled.

'I just want to find a legionary called Florus.'

The orderly narrowed his eyes.

'Are you legate Fronto?'

Fronto nodded.

'In the name of Fortuna, yes. I know Florus. He's been asking for you ever since he came in. You'll find him just up the hill behind the tent, mixing up some poultices for us. We had to put him to some use to shut him up.'

A smile crept back across the legate's face. This was why he was in the army: the down sides may be horrifying, but the entire army was one big family. Edging round the tent, keeping as far away as he could from the stinking pile of limbs, he made his way up the slope.

Florus was not easy to spot. Fronto had only met him that one night. Asking around the preparation area he was eventually directed to a corner where Florus stood, naked from the waist up, mixing a large tub of something evil-smelling with one hand. His other shoulder was bandaged and a flower of red blossomed in the centre, the result of some wound from the battle. Around the bandage, a huge black and blue bruise was coming slowly to the surface.

Fronto wandered over to him.

'Florus, what's for lunch?'

Florus turned.

'Lunch? This is...'

Realising who had addressed him, Florus blushed.

'I'm ever so sorry, sir, I...'

Fronto grinned at the young man.

'Knock it off, lad. I'm not in the mood for a great deal of formality. I offered you a drink, and I'm here to collect you. A few of the legates and I are meeting up at a nice little tavern in the town. I presume you'll join us, since the drinks are on me?'

Florus smiled again.

'Oh yes, sir. Is it right though, sir? I mean, me drinking with the officers?'

Fronto returned the smile.

'Only if you relax a little. If you don't stop tensing you'll snap something!'

Florus slumped a little.

'I'd best get my kit, sir.'

Fronto smiled benignly.

'Just sling a tunic on. None of us are particularly bathed or manicured today.'

They reached the praetorium a few moments later, Florus still trying to pull his tunic over the bandaged shoulder as he walked. Priscus and Velius awaited him. As the two approached, Priscus pointed at Florus.

'He joining us, sir?'

Fronto nodded.

'Yes he's joining us. Remember? I offered to buy him one a couple of nights ago.'

Priscus smiled.

'Indeed. In fact, I was going to talk to you about this young man later. He's still on 'new-boy' fatigues in the Sixth Century, but I think the way he acted last night, we should put him on immune status. His centurion lauded his activities to me, and I gather he's even made himself useful to the medics during his convalescence.'

Fronto nodded.

'Fair enough. On your recommendation, I think we should attach him to the medical section.'

He turned to Florus.

'You'll be excused normal duties from now on. You're attached to the Tenth's medics as an assistant. Who knows, you might make it to being a capsarius one day.'

Florus beamed with pride as Fronto squared his shoulders.

'Anyway, now there's drinks to be had, and a number of senior officers sat impatiently waiting for me to arrive and buy a round. Shall we go?'

Dumnorix was fat. Fat and ostentatious, no less. He stood at one end of the square, dressed well in high quality local Gaulish garments and bedecked with gold and silver jewellery. He was being treated, as Fronto had expected, with the deference and respect that would be due a citizen of Rome. The man did not look worried. In fact, he looked arrogantly unconcerned. Fronto took an immediate dislike to him and began to regret having suggested that he would be more use alive.

Fronto sat to one side of the square on a long log seat with a flattened surface that was draped with cloths and padded with cushions. To his left sat Caesar and to his right Sabinus, with Balbus, Crassus, Cita and Labienus seated around and behind them. Along with them sat Decimus Brutus, a young staff officer favoured by Caesar's wife, the vapid and easily impressed Plancus, and a staff officer Fronto did not know well called Pedius who had an air of competency, completing the Roman element of the jury.

On the other side of the square, ten of the Aedui sat facing them. Fronto recognised Liscus and Divitiacus, but the other eight were unknown to him. None of them looked particularly content, but there was a grim and determined appearance to them, in particular to Liscus.

Fronto found his eyes straying across behind them to the tip of a tree, standing high above a nearby building, that he knew grew in the corner of a nice, shady tavern. What wouldn't he give to be there right now rather than here? He frowned and nodded reflexively, trying to put forth the impression that he was paying some kind of attention to proceedings.

The Aeduan magistrate, or whatever these people called them, strolled around the square, his hands clasped together behind his back. He had been annunciating at the top of his deep, resonant voice for the last quarter of an hour, though Fronto had heard barely a word. Caesar had been listening intently but had not interrupted. Balbus had begun to snore gently a few moments ago, until Longinus had nudged him.

The whole thing was something of a charade anyway, put together to enhance Liscus' standing among his people. Caesar had discussed the matter with the Aeduan leader the previous night and planned every detail. Dumnorix would be stripped of any titles and rights he held among the tribe, fined to within the borderline of poverty, and his personal cavalry would be disbanded. Dumnorix would be left no better off than the lowliest fishmonger in the tribe and would be under a restricted movement policy. He would be unable to leave the confines of the town, and must report to the magistrates at dawn and dusk. He would be effectively disempowered and imprisoned. In addition, Liscus would have him under surveillance, noting any contact he had with others and reporting appropriately to the Roman command.

In order to build Liscus' reputation among the tribe the Roman officers, when asked, should demand execution as a penalty. Liscus would then make a very nice and persuasive speech in defence of Dumnorix and the Romans would relent, accepting whatever punishment Liscus and his companions cared to lay upon the accused. A charade. A scene from a playwright to be performed in front of the Aedui.

Fronto's mind wandered, as it was prone to do on occasions like this. When *was* the last time he had been to see a play? Oh, he had seen the gladiatorial shows a number of times in Rome, Puteoli and Pompeii over the last few years. He had seen the quadriga racing at Rome. He had even once been persuaded to go to a music recital by some of the Greek slaves in Rome; an outing he would rather not repeat.

No, the last time he had seen a play would probably be in Spain. In fact, he could remember where it was precisely. Tarraco was the place, in the wooden theatre down near the river. He and the other officers had been drunk by the time they arrived, having spent a good few hours around the taverns of the city before they had made their way to the theatre. He had the sneaking suspicion that Longinus had been there. He had been expecting a good old-fashioned play from the pen of one of the famous Roman playwrights, and had been pleasantly surprised to discover that Tarraco had its own flourishing artists. The play he had seen had been little more than a sarcastic and slapstick attack on the morals of the upper class in Rome. A number of the higher ranking citizens and some of the officers attending had left in an outrage. Fronto however had laughed until his eyes watered and his sides hurt. He had noticed when he left that he was the only soldier of any standing left in the theatre. Everyone else was a low-ranker.

Suddenly, his attention was pulled back to the present. Sabinus was nudging him as unobtrusively as possible. Glancing left and right quickly, he realised that Caesar was glaring at him. There was silence from the centre of the square. Fronto's mind raced. He suddenly felt like an eight year old boy again, caught gazing out of the window toward Vesuvius when his tutor was trying to teach him Thucydides. Sabinus gave him a sharp, painful nudge and whispered under his breath 'say something!'

Clearing his throat, he realised that the Aedui were all staring at him. He took a deep breath and prayed to Minerva that he knew what was going on.

'Death.'

Trying to look calm and unconcerned, he glanced surreptitiously at Balbus for confirmation, but was relieved a moment later to hear Sabinus call out 'Death!'

He smiled and whispered under his breath. 'Thank you, Minerva. I'll pour you a libation next time I see an altar.'

Shuffling in his seat, he realised that Caesar was still glaring at him. Oh well. It was Caesar who wanted him here. He turned and smiled warmly at the general, who turned a nice shade of purple.

He should not be required to say anything else for the duration of the trial, but he had best stay relatively alert this time.

He focused on Liscus, who was making an eloquent speech, his hands raised imploringly toward the Romans, his face contorted with concern for his countryman. The man, like all politicians, was a consummate actor.

Fronto turned once more to stare at the prisoner. For all that he could see the sense and the reasoning behind leniency, he wished he could offer a more permanent solution. Leaving an enemy, or even a potential enemy, of Rome free went against the grain. Once more the words of Domiticus the Gaul, standing naked and bound in the temporary stockade, came flooding back into Fronto's memory. 'There are others. Many others, and not all of them Gaulish.' And so this man *must* be used to identify any more of these conspirators.

He sat in silence, working through lists of potential enemies. The Helvetii should still be considered enemies until they were found and dealt with. The Aedui were generally allies of Rome but, as Domiticus had proved, not all of them were content with the tribe's alliance and some may be eager for Celtic power. Then there were the innumerable Gaulish units serving as auxiliary troops in Caesar's army. Some of them were Aedui, but others had been drawn from any number of smaller tribes on or near the border with the empire. Then there was always the possibility of disaffected Romans; officers who disagreed with the campaign and, most importantly, those who resented Caesar or were allied with his political opponents. Theoretically such men would have been weeded out by now but, with an army this size on continually mobile campaign, such control was tough.

He became aware that Liscus had finished speaking. Rebuking himself for having drifted off again despite his best intentions, Fronto glanced around the assembly. This time no one was staring at him. He relaxed a little as Caesar stood.

'Friend Liscus, I would request a short recess in order to confer with my officers.'

Liscus turned and bowed. 'By all means, general. Shall we reconvene in, say half an hour?'

Caesar nodded confirmation and the Roman contingent rose from their seats, knees creaking from the extended period of rest. Fronto shuffled out of the square with the rest. As they entered the main street Caesar stretched, raising his arms above his head.

'Gentlemen. Since there is, in fact, very little to discuss, I would suggest we retire to the officers' mess tent for quarter of an hour.'

Balbus cleared his throat.

'General, I think we would be better served staying close to the square. There is a rather pleasant tavern that we found just a little further along the street. Perhaps we should stop there instead?' Turning his head, he winked at Fronto.

Caesar smiled.

'Very well Quintus, we'll try your tavern.'

The tavern keeper nodded in friendly recognition to Fronto and Balbus as they approached, then breathed in sharply and performed a deep bow as Caesar rounded the corner, surrounded by staff officers. Fronto smiled and patted him on the shoulder.

'Can I suggest your very best wine, innkeeper.'

The Gaul nodded nervously, swallowed and scurried off inside.

By the time the group of Romans had seated themselves around the two rearmost tables under the cover of the trees, the Gaul had returned carrying a tray of fine goblets. He was followed by two servants heaving a large amphora of wine. Once at the table, they began to decant the wine into several smaller jugs, which Balbus and Fronto used to fill the goblets. Caesar craned his head and looked around the yard.

'A pleasant establishment this, Balbus. Very nice indeed. Shame I hadn't heard of it earlier.'

Balbus grinned.

'Needless to say, general, it was actually Fronto that found it.'

A number of the officers laughed as Fronto shrugged. 'What can I say? It's hard to find good wine when you're on campaign. We've been in here most days when we've had free time.'

Balbus glanced toward the door whence the tavern keeper had returned and smiled.

'I expect he's raking in the money. He'll probably want to put a sign over the door saying 'By appointment to the Roman army'.'

Fronto frowned and spoke darkly.

'I don't think that would be a very safe thing to do at the moment. Sentiment is not a hundred per cent pro-Roman among these people.'

A cavalry trooper appeared at the gate of the inn and bowed. Sabinus, nearest to the entrance, raised a hand and beckoned him in. The young man was visibly nervous in the presence of the high command.

'Sir... Sirs...'

Caesar sighed.

'Yes trooper?'

'Legate Longinus sent me to warn you that he's escorting ambassadors from the Helvetii and'll be here in an hour or so.'

Caesar smiled and his shoulders slumped a little as he relaxed.

'Thank you, trooper. What of the rest of their tribe?'

'The cavalry's escorting them all back here. They should be here tomorrow.'

Caesar's smile widened.

'Excellent. Well done, man.'

The staff quartermaster, Cita, gestured at the trooper.

'Report to my adjutant in camp and draw yourself some extra rations and wine. You may take the rest of the day off.'

'Thank you, sir.'

The trooper stood to attention and saluted. Turning, he left the tavern, reached up to the reins of his horse and walked it off down the street.

Fronto relaxed, leaning back and stretching his feet out under the table. Today was really rather nice. The sun-dappled yard hummed with the sound of bees. Barely a cloud marred the sky where it could be seen between the trees. Even Caesar appeared happy and relaxed now.

'They'll be panicking when they get back here and have to wait for you to finish the trial before you deal with them. Should give them a bit more time to live on their nerves.'

Caesar grinned, though only with his mouth. His eyes stayed hard and cold. The effect was thoroughly disconcerting.

'That would no doubt be the case Fronto, but they won't have to wait. I shan't be dealing with them myself. The rest of us will be occupied with the Aedui, and I cannot afford to offend them. Moreover I intend to demean the Helvetii as much as I can. To that end, none of the general staff will be dealing with them. *You* will be dealing with them Marcus.'

Fronto coughed, spilling wine on the table.

'*Me*, sir?'

Caesar grinned that distressing grin once more.

'I can't think of anyone better, can you? You're a legionary legate with, and no insult intended here, little of the rigid bearing of a regular staff officer, which means that their surrender will be accepted by a ranking officer, not the high command. Not only that but, apart from myself, you are the man they hate most; the man who destroyed a quarter of their tribe. That will vex them further. Oh, and you seem incapable of even staying awake in court, and so, frankly, I'd rather not have you back with us after the recess. Good luck in your new role, Marcus. I think you'd best get going. You'll want to tidy your tent no doubt, and gather an appropriate retinue of officers.'

Fronto sat, his head turning and mouth open, trying to think of an excuse, but failing to find one.

'Fronto, you're getting shorter on time.'

Grumbling, Fronto refilled his goblet and threw the wine down his throat before he left the table. As an afterthought, he reached back and swiped one of the smaller jugs of wine.

'I daresay you won't need *all* of this if you have to go soon.'

———————

Fronto felt stupid. He always did when he was dressed in full ceremonial uniform. He was fairly sure that Caesar had meant him to deal with the Helvetii looking as he normally did; scruffy and dirty and wearing the trappings of a veteran soldier. That would be the most insulting. Instead, Fronto had sent his cuirass and helmet to the legion's smithy for a quarter of an hour, and they had come back burnished and bright. His red plume had been brushed out and washed and now adorned his helm proudly. He had the red ribbon tied in the military knot around the shiny breastplate, clean boots, and clean red cloak. All in all he looked every inch the Roman general.

Sitting on a campaign chair in the centre of his command tent, he was backed by a number of officers. Wagering that the Helvetii would not know the uniform of one rank from another, Fronto had filled his tent with tribunes, centurions and optios, a dozen in all. Tetricus, Velius and Priscus stood behind him, all wearing the best clothing and armour available. Everyone below tribune rank had been forbidden from wearing helmets, so that the crests would not give away their ranks. Fronto held his own helm on his lap, with his officer's vine staff laid across behind it.

In the last few moments the camp had been manic as Fronto had given the order for the whole legion to stand to and clear away all the loose equipment. Legionaries had brought all the standards, eagles, flags and maps they could find and arranged them in an honour display at the rear of the tent. As an afterthought, Fronto had ordered the other officers to stand throughout the meeting. It would be uncomfortable, but imposing. With Fronto seated in a campaign chair, the effect would be impressive. He had arranged for one of the low log benches to be brought in for the Helvetii ambassadors. They must be made to feel as small as possible.

Now it was a matter of waiting. He nervously reached out to the goblet by his side and took a swig of the wine. Behind him Priscus cleared his throat and whispered.

'Sir, lay off the drink. It won't look good if you slur at them.'

Muttering under his breath, Fronto put the goblet back.

Longinus had been spotted with a number of riders by a lookout a few moments earlier and would be here any time now. The sentries at the camps' perimeters had all been given the instructions as to what Longinus should do with the ambassadors.

A sentry arrived at the door of the tent and bowed.

'Sir, Commander Longinus is here with a number of Gauls. Shall I admit them?'

Fronto nodded. 'Yes soldier, show them in.'

Speaking out of the corner of his mouth, he addressed the assembled officers behind him.

'Stand straight and tall and keep quiet. I want to you interrupt only if I start drivelling and lose the thread entirely.'

Just as he closed his mouth, a weary and dirty Longinus entered the tent, a cavalry tribune at each shoulder. Behind him came three Gauls in a similar state. Finally, four more cavalry troopers brought up the rear. As they entered the tent, Longinus seemed to have immediately grasped the situation. He bowed deeply to Fronto and then stood to attention.

'Permission to dismiss guard, sir?'

Fronto raised two fingers in the gesture he had watched Caesar use time and time again to show consent.

Longinus turned to face the four troopers.

'Dismissed. Report to your camp.'

Addressing the Gauls, his voice took on a sharper tone.

'You three! Sit there.'

He gestured at the low log.

The three men hurriedly took a seat on the uncomfortable makeshift bench. They looked tired and frightened. Fronto could not help but feel sorry for them. They were beaten and they knew it. The middle of the three had sat astride a horse on a hill not too far from here defiantly threatening the commanders of the army. He must feel broken now. Hardening his heart and steeling himself, Fronto pressed on, maintaining his façade of cold-hearted command.

'Very well. We shall now hear what you have to say.'

One of the Gauls looked up at Fronto. He mumbled something to the man in the middle in their native tongue. The chieftain translated into clear Latin.

'You win. There's not enough of us left to fight. We have more wounded than healthy and more dead than both of those. We'll go wherever you want us to go; do whatever you want us to do. Just don't persecute the women and children. They are all there is now.'

Fronto waited to make sure they had finished and then scratched his chin reflectively.

'Very well. Here are our demands. You, along with your allies the Tulingi and the Latobrigi, will return to your ancestral lands near Geneva. Once you return, you will deliver five thousand young men of fighting age and spirit to the garrison commander at Geneva, to form the bulk of the new Geneva garrison. This unit will protect the city and all Roman interests but will also protect your lands from marauding Germans. You will rebuild your settlements and you will live in peace with the Roman people. You will, before you exit this camp, take the same oath that the Aedui have taken. In addition, you will supply a ten per cent tithe of all goods and food you produce for five years to the decurions of Geneva, beginning one year after your return. You will take a further oath never to ally with the German tribes or any other tribe that defies Rome.'

He sat back and took a deep breath. That was quite a lot to take in. The chieftain in the centre narrowed his eyes and looked up at Fronto, a glint of his former pride beginning to show once more.

'General, we will submit to any course of action you deem fit. However, we cannot hope to reach our lands from here without carrying out raids on farmland. It is a long way back to Geneva, and we have no food. We will be moving slower than ever with all our wounded. Even when we return our people will starve as there is no farmland cultivated. Also, you have named only two of our allies. What of the Boii?'

He gestured at the man on his right, obviously one of that tribe.

Fronto sat forward once more. Sabinus had walked with him down to the camp from the tavern before returning to the trial. The senior staff officer had given Fronto a few pointers and suggestions since the general had left things entirely in his hands. Thank all the Gods for Sabinus. He had predicted almost everything and armed Fronto with a response.

He smiled benignly at the Gauls.

'I have arranged for a supply of food to be drawn for you from both the legions and the Aedui, who are not unmindful to your needs. Once you reach the borders of your own land, you may approach the Allobroges, who are allied to Rome. They will supply you with enough food and resources to rebuild your homes and restart your economy. A vexillation of the Eleventh and Twelfth Legions will escort you on your return and smooth over matters with Geneva and the Allobroges. They will also help you transport your wounded and your gear back to your lands.'

He smiled again.

'As for the Boii, we have other plans. I take it you are of the Boii?' He gestured in the direction of the third man, who nodded.

'The Boii are reputed to be loyal and fierce and extremely valorous. As such, the Aedui have invited you to settle in their lands. You would be bound by the same oath as they, but would come under their jurisdiction, and not ours. The high command is inclined to agree to this. Your tribe will separate when they arrive tomorrow and you will need to see Liscus of the Aedui in the morning. I think that covers everything. Agreed?'

For the first time the Boii leader to the right addressed Fronto. He stood wearily and stooped. For the first time Fronto realised that he was wounded. From the matted bloody hair and the bloodstains around wounds on his torso and arms, Fronto would easily have pronounced the wounds mortal. How the man had managed was unfathomable. A grudging respect crept into Fronto and he began to understand why the Aedui had such faith in the tribe. The chieftain looked up at the Romans, meeting Fronto's gaze levelly.

'Your words are just, Roman. You speak for the benefit of our tribes despite our differences. I doubt your general would offer such consolations as enthusiastically, and so I presume you have been left to deal with all arrangements accordingly. May I speak to you in private?'

Fronto was taken aback. Not only had he not anticipated any spirit left in these people, he had certainly not expected eloquent speeches in perfectly balanced Latin. Deep in thought for a moment, he focused on the Boii leader.

'Your Latin is impeccable and you speak with the rhetoric of a politician. How is this?'

The man shrugged.

'We are not animals. I am Boii, but I have also been a citizen of Ocelum. Will you speak to me in private?'

Fronto stared for a while and finally nodded, rising and beckoning the Gaul outside. The two of them exited, leaving the Roman officers and the two remaining Gauls frowning and regarding each other suspiciously.

Outside, the Gaul staggered slightly and fell against the tent support. Fronto had been finding it harder and harder to maintain the tough façade, and finally he cracked.

'Sit down man, for Elysium's sake. If you stand any longer, you'll fall over.'

The Boii leader gratefully sank to the grass.

Making sure that there was no one but the guards in view, Fronto sank to the floor too. With one word he dismissed the guards and the two of them were alone.

'Alright. I can see you're an intelligent and educated man. You can probably see through the façade that I'm a soldier, not a politician or high commander, so let's speak man to man.'

The Gaul nodded.

'Indeed, though I think you put yourself down legate Fronto. We all know who you are. You are an able commander and I have the feeling you're a just man.'

Fronto nodded.

'I would like to think so.'

The Gaul shrugged wearily.

'Our tribe has staked our future on the plans of the Helvetii. I think it would have paid well had not your general chosen them as his scapegoat for a campaign.'

Fronto raised his hand to stop the Gaul, but the man continued.

'No need to deny it, legate. I am well aware of how Roman politics work. Caesar is hungry for war because war fuels careers. We had legitimate cause and concerns. In the end we lost because we were convenient. This is in the past. Rome is the future of this land, whether we like it or not. I know, as I'm sure you do, that Caesar will not stop with the Helvetii. In the end this will become a province and only those of us who do not capitulate will suffer. We have had our fight and made our stand. Now we will sit and await the inevitable.'

Fronto nodded again. There was a lot of sense and a lot of truth in what the Gaul was saying. It did not matter how long it took; this land would be Roman. The Boii recognising and accepting this would be a first step to peaceful domination.

'What did you want to speak about in private?'

The Gaul shifted on the grass.

'There are several thousand of the Helvetii that have not surrendered in the group. They escaped well ahead of your cavalry and will be making for the German border. I will accept the Aedui proposal, and I believe my

253

tribe will support me. There is no future for the Helvetii without Roman support. Whether you can catch these fleeing tribesmen I do not know, but even if you don't I cannot imagine them remaining a threat. There are not enough of them to create any kind of force, and they are unlikely to be treated kindly by the Germans. I thought you should hear this in private. If I speak of it in there, it may cause further trouble.'

Fronto nodded. He would have to inform Caesar, but he already knew exactly what Caesar would do. Messages would be sent out threatening all the tribes until the remaining Helvetii were found and either returned to Geneva or made an example of. No point in causing trouble among the ambassadors when things were going so well.

'Very well. It will be dealt with in time but, for the moment, we have enough to worry about. Let's get back inside. I want to get this finished and go for the drink I've been thirsting for over the last hour. I'd like to thank you for your candour and your honesty.'

As they walked back inside, Fronto did not even bother retaking his seat. Instead, he addressed the Gauls directly from next to the door.

'Unless any of you has something to add, I believe we are finished. Anyone?'

The Gauls remained steadfastly silent.

'Very well, leave now and settle for tonight within this camp. Your tribes will be joining you tomorrow, and arrangements will then be made.'

Turning to the other officers, he said 'Velius and Gallus, show these men to an area they can make camp and have a guard assigned to them.'

The two saluted and escorted the Gauls out.

As soon as the other tribunes and centurions had left, Fronto slumped into the chair and motioned Priscus to the other seat in the corner.

'Well Gnaeus, looks like we've finished with the Helvetii at last. I kind of wish it was us going with them back to Geneva rather than that vexillation. We're all tired and undermanned, and Caesar's got something up his sleeve. We've not seen the last of Gaul or of blood yet.'

Speechless, Priscus merely nodded wearily and reached for the wine jar.

PART TWO

ARIOVISTUS

CHAPTER 13

(BIBRACTE CENTRAL SQUARE)

'Pteruges: leather straps that hang from the shoulders and waist of the garment worn under a cuirass. From the Greek for 'feather'

'Aquilifer: a specialised standard bearer that carried a legion's eagle standard.'

The morning sun beat down on the baked earth of the square. The gentle sounds of summer surrounded the staff as they sat on comfortably draped benches to one end of the square. Even in his summer uniform, with the linen tunic rather than the wool, Fronto was aware of the spreading patches of damp accumulating around his armpits and the pools of salty sweat collecting beneath the bronzed cuirass and leather pteruges he wore. He could only imagine what the various signifers and cornicens felt like, wearing much the same but having to stand constantly at attention, carrying their heavy trappings of office.

Next to him, Sabinus wiped his brow for the umpteenth time. Away to the right beyond the career officers sat Caesar in his campaign chair on a hastily-constructed wooden dais. Beside the general, Liscus sat on the same dais, seated in his own throne. The Aeduan leader had, over the past few weeks, taken to wearing a very Roman style tunic. He still wore the trappings of his people, including the golden torc around his neck, but had adopted much of the civilised Roman style. Fronto had noted how, over the following week, many of the better-off members of the tribe had taken to sporting these tunics. Somewhere in Bibracte there must by a tailor laughing and counting coins.

Fronto shuffled uneasily and felt his bare leg peel away from the wood where it had stuck with the heat. He fervently wished he could stand and

257

air himself out a little, but the entire command had to be both present *and* presentable for the arrival of the chieftains. Word had reached them a couple of weeks ago that an assembly of the Gaulish chiefs had been called and that they would be congregating here. Most of the lower ranks continued to relax during their month-long respite after the battle, looking forward to seeing such a grand assembly of barbarians. Fronto and a few of the others knew better. There was no way that the assembly being called here was an accident of timing and, recalling Caesar's words, he wondered whether the chieftains had come to ask for Caesar's help against Ariovistus or whether Caesar had, indeed, engineered the whole thing.

Glancing at Sabinus, he smiled. A good thing the man was here. He was the only member of the staff that Fronto felt remotely comfortable around socially, and the legates and senior officers of the six legions were seated along one side of the square, opposite the various higher-born Aedui. Priscus, taking his place as commander of the Tenth, sat between Balbus and Longinus shuffling uncomfortably in the legate's uniform he had been allocated by the staff. The ranks of the Roman command glittered in the sunlight and Fronto could not help but wonder what the troops were getting up to without a single senior officer in sight.

A braying of horns became audible at a distance. That would be the various chieftains arriving at the city gate. They had elected to stay outside the walls in their own camps until the last of their number had arrived and now they were making for the assembly at the square. The discordant blaring of the strange wolf-head-shaped horns grew slowly louder, birds taking to flight from the trees in flocks. Of a sudden, the sound of Roman cornicens echoed round the city, drowning out the native horns. Tetricus was carrying out his duty to the letter. Fronto had assigned him as the senior prefect at the city gate, waiting to greet the Gauls. He had been told to leave the natives in no uncertainty as to who held the power here. Consequently, Tetricus was determined to assert Roman superiority even in the blared fanfares of the arrival. Fronto nodded approvingly. The cornicens were in perfect tune.

Around the square, the officers straightened in anticipation. The sound of the horns from both armies faded and, a few moments later, the sound of tramping feet and creaking wheels announced the approach of the tribal envoys. A Roman honour guard of cavalry entered the square first, fanning out and taking positions around the empty end of the square. Moments later, Tetricus rode in, his plumed helmet under his arm and his weapon sheathed. The Aquilifer of the Tenth rode at his side, a Roman eagle leading the way for the Gauls. The whole event had been well choreographed in advance by Longinus. Once the honour guard were in place, the first of the chieftains arrived, riding in a chariot pulled by two large black horses, with a ceremonial spear bearer by his side. He glittered in gold finery and wore a very well made cloak of deepest blue over his native tunic and breeches. A small group of his horsemen accompanied him. As the chariot ground to a halt, raising more dust than all of the cavalry had managed, the chieftain stepped down and alighted. The horsemen and the chariot pulled off to one side and exited the square by the other road, where they would be taken care of by one of Longinus' cavalry alae.

As the second chieftain arrived in his chariot, the first walked to the centre of the square, gave a deep bow to Liscus, a curt half-bow to Caesar, and strode over to one of the campaign chairs that had been set aside and covered with fine silks to accommodate the guests. The second leader stepped from his chariot and followed suit as further natives entered. Fronto watched with interest as the chieftains arrived by the dozen. He found himself wondering how many tribes there were in this land and how many the army would have to put down before this land could be called a province, for he was under absolutely no illusions now that this was the future of Gaul. The tribes that already held an alliance with Rome or that could be considered pro-Roman were self-evident. Here and there Roman style tunics or jewellery caught his eye. Some had gone so far as to wear purple after the fashion of Senators or some of the Eastern client Kings.

Finally all of the guests had arrived. With a salute to Caesar and a bow to Liscus, Tetricus turned and trotted from the square, the cavalry escort following him in precisely-drilled motion. Four of the chieftains stood and faced each other. Without a word being spoken, some kind of agreement was reached, and three of them sat. The fourth turned to face the two leaders. He wore a long white tunic and robe over his Gaulish breeches, his beard was whitish grey and braided at the sides, and his hair was held back from his forehead with a band of interwoven flax. Although he bore the traditional Celtic broadsword at his waist, he leaned on a long, knotted oak staff. Fronto squinted, trying to take in as much detail as possible. This must be one of the Druids of whom he had heard many tales since his first stationing in Spain. Most of those tales, told by Romans, had been variations on a horror theme, though he had never seen a Druid in all those years of campaigning. If they were all like this specimen, Fronto could see why they held such a position of influence in Celtic society. The man was imposing in the extreme. His long hair and beard, the white robes and the staff were partially responsible for that, though much of his arresting appearance came from the fact that the man stood head and shoulders above anyone else in the square. He must have been close to seven feet tall, ox shouldered and with fists like hams. As he opened his mouth to speak, his voice proved every inch the match of his physique, deep and booming.

Though he spoke in his local tongue, a member of the Aedui stood on hand as an interpreter and translated the Druid's words for the benefit of the Romans.

'Liscus of the Aedui, the tribal council brings you greeting. As it is not your duty to host the gathering this year, we are not ungrateful for your cooperation in this matter. After the day's discussion, we will provide fitting tribute for your hospitality. However, our business must come first. Not all of the tribes have chosen to attend today.'

For emphasis, the Druid turned and gestured to around a dozen empty seats with his staff. The absences had apparently not gone unnoticed, from the rumble of agreement among the chieftains. Fronto had paid no attention to that particular detail.

'With a powerful Roman army making waves in the centre of our land, and strong tribes both supporting and opposing this man,' a quick gesture toward Caesar, 'some chieftains disapprove and feel they cannot in good conscience attend this meeting.'

Liscus nodded gravely.

'I understand, Aforix.'

The Druid nodded in return, his face still bearing a grave expression. He then turned to face Caesar. The interpreter was a little slower with his translation this time.

260

'Roman, I will state outright that I do not like you. I disapprove of your people in our lands. I think you bring us nothing and that you will take away our future. I do not think that you truly believe in your Gods. For me, this is unthinkable. However, I am not here today to defy you, nor to bring opposition. I come to represent that element that refuses to be here. I am not your enemy, but nor can I cannot consider myself your ally.'

Caesar waved his hand dismissively.

'I thank you for your candour. I have experienced Druidic welcome before, and I cannot say that I would expect anything else. We shall agree to disagree at this time.'

The Druid nodded once more.

'Despite my feelings, I have agreed to speak for all of the tribes in the first and most important matter.'

He gestured toward the Aeduan interpreter and gabbled off a long sentence in his own language. The interpreter turned to the Romans

'I have been forbidden from translating until I am given the signal to begin again.'

With the barest glance at Liscus the man nodded hurriedly. Fronto was impressed once again at the respect and awe these Druids carried among the Celts.

The man turned once more toward the chieftains and rattled off a long speech in his own language. A few chieftains quizzed him and he replied calmly in his deep voice. After a long pause, with a word, the chieftains all stood and slowly drew their swords. Next to Fronto, Plancus jolted to his feet, his hand reaching for the pommel of his sword. Fronto's hand closed round his wrist and jerked him back into his seat and he whispered in the young officer's ear.

'Don't be stupid boy. If they were going to cause trouble, they'd hardly do it slowly and packed into a tight group. What the hell could they hope to achieve? Sit down and be still.'

As Plancus slowly turned a beetroot red, Fronto faced the gathering again, interested in what this ritual could mean.

At a further word, the chieftains plunged the swords into the dirt. Liscus rose and took a step forward, plunging his own sword into the ground in front of the dais.

261

Fronto leaned slightly closer to Sabinus.

'What the hell do you think that was all about?'

Sabinus smiled.

'I think it was some kind of vote. I noticed that a number of them changed hands with their swords. If you look, they've all grounded their swords either to the left or the right.'

The Druid turned once more to face Caesar and slammed the butt of his staff into the hard earth with a loud 'crack' that raised a small cloud of dust. Behind him, the chieftains all sat. With a quick nod to the interpreter, the old man once again addressed the Romans.

'It appears to me that you brought war to the Helvetii for your own personal reasons involving both hatred and ambition and few of those behind me differ in their opinion. However, we are not unmindful of the fact that the Helvetii are a warlike people, and had brought violence to the rest of Gaul. However unintentionally, you have aided the tribes of Gaul in your quest for vengeance. For that you have our thanks.'

Caesar directed a humourless smile at the Druid.

'Flattery indeed from one of the opponents of Roman involvement. Flattery, I feel, that is about to come with a price. Am I wrong?'

The tall Druid grimaced at the general. He clearly disliked the position he found himself in, and Caesar was determined to make the Gauls plead. The man once more addressed the general.

'As you are no doubt already aware the Germanic tribes have, for many years, been employed as mercenaries by Gaulish tribes when extra force was needed. In particular, during power struggles between those supporting the Sequani and Arverni and the Aedui.'

Caesar nodded.

'I have made it my business to know some of your history, yes.'

'It appears too much freedom has been given to these Germans in the past. In recent months they have not returned to their own lands across the Rhine. Indeed their leader, a man called Ariovistus, has brought more and more of them across the river. Where these Germans had once all but destroyed Aeduan power in Gaul, they now cause grief to the Sequani, for it is in their land that Ariovistus has settled.'

The Druid gestured to one of the empty seats.

'Despite all his power and authority, the chieftain of the Sequani is not here today. He is busy in his own lands protecting his people from these marauding Germans. They already occupy a third of his land and are making demands of more every day. Many of the tribes of Gaul feel that the time has come to request the aid of Roman forces. The Germans are a powerful people. They crushed the Sequani at Magetobria and took hostages. If they can defeat one of the most powerful tribes in Gaul so easily, we cannot do other than look for help from the victor over the Helvetii. The Aedui are diminished after many years of war, as are the Arverni. The Sequani have been smashed by the Germans, and the Helvetii by you. The four greatest powers upon whom we might rely: all gone.'

The mumbling among the chieftains behind him spoke volumes of how the Gauls felt at finding themselves forced to seek Roman aid.

'If you know anything of the Germans, Roman, and I think you do, then you know they will not be satisfied with the land they have taken. They will continue to conquer until all Gaul is their land and all the Gauls their slaves. Ariovistus is a cruel and vicious man, and once he has everything he needs, other German leaders will follow in his footsteps.'

The Druid gritted his teeth as he prepared to make the request he so hated to make.

'Caesar, in the name of the tribal council, and for the good of all Gaul, we seek your assistance in driving Ariovistus from our lands. Some hope that merely the threat of Rome will be enough to make him release his hostages and return to his own lands, but I fear that force is the only solution. We are a proud people and will ask you this only once. Should you refuse us we will not beg. What is your answer?'

Caesar smiled, though Fronto could not understand why. They damn well *should* beg. They needed Rome and everyone knew it. He could only believe that Caesar was already prepared for this and that the Gaul was trying to manoeuvre him. If he was, he would be in for a shock. The general knew a thing or two about rhetoric.

Caesar cleared his throat.

'Whatever your fears and whatever your opinion of me, Aforix, I support the pride of the Gauls. Pride *is* what makes a people great, and Rome's allies *should* be proud. I say allies, for that is what you are, regardless of what you believe. Very well, we will march on this Ariovistus for you, and drive him from Gaul. However, the war with the Helvetii has seriously depleted our numbers, and to march against a large Germanic force without sufficient manpower would give us no better chance than the Sequani. I will require two agreements from your chieftains in return for our aid.'

The Druid paused a moment as the interpreter relayed the words to him. He frowned and nodded reluctantly at the general. Fronto realised that he was holding his breath. A lot rode on the outcome of this meeting and the general had something up his sleeve. He was being far too deferential and supportive of the Gauls, and Fronto had seen that before. He knew he had them over a barrel and was playing them. Caesar cleared his throat and spoke in a loud, clear voice.

'I will require each tribe to adopt the oath that the Aedui and our other allies have already taken. I do not expect you to submit to Rome, but I do demand peace and an alliance.'

As the interpreter passed this on, the murmuring grew among the chieftains.

'Furthermore, we will require a commitment of military support. There is no time for us to reinforce the legions with troops raised within the empire. Instead, I will allocate one of my staff officers to speak to each chief and arrange a number of levies to join us as auxiliary troops and bolster the numbers.'

The muttering grew to a deep grumble. Fronto wondered how far Caesar could push them before they rejected him. Caesar, on the other hand, seemed to be prepared.

'You can view this in a negative light if you so desire. I urge you all, however, to think on two things. Firstly, in return for this you will receive not only our aid against Ariovistus, but also Roman support in future troubles, as well as trade agreements. Secondly, by delivering auxiliary levies into the army, you yourselves will share in the victory and the destruction of the Germans. What price your pride if you refuse? Once you have made your decisions, your spokesman can find my staff and I at my command tent outside the walls. I have no doubt that there is much that you need to discuss.'

With that Caesar stood and, gesturing to the other officers, turned and strode from the square.

———————————

'I just don't understand why you want to go and deal with him now!'

Fronto sat back, his left hand still gripping the arm of his campaign chair. His right was still too weak for him to even remotely consider clenching his fist. Caesar sighed patiently and replied.

'I know that we need more men and that waiting for the next campaigning season would give us those troops but, regardless of whether the Gauls had even asked me, we'd still need to deal with this for our own benefit. If the Germanic tribes are allowed to settle on this side of the Rhine, how long will it be before they oust the Aedui, d'you think? And after that? How long before they cross the Rhone and threaten our own border? No, they need to be dealt with soon.'

Fronto grimaced.

'But we're not ready, Caesar. Even if they agree to supply us with extra auxiliary troops, we'll still be a considerably smaller army than the one that set out after the Helvetii, and this enemy is reputedly much more dangerous. The new auxilia will be untrained and unruly. Even Scipio wouldn't have launched a campaign early if a difference of a few months would bring the army back up to full strength.'

Caesar tapped the arm of his chair.

'Fronto, I *do* know what I'm doing. We cannot wait until next spring. However, I'm also aware of the dangers of untrained cavalry. I shall be having a word with Longinus once the rest get here. I'm bringing him back into the senior staff. Publius Sulpicius Rufus will be assigned as legate of the Ninth. I want Longinus to devote all of his considerable talent as a cavalry commander to the army's mounted contingent. I'm making Longinus 'commander of the cavalry' with authority to completely overhaul the entire division.'

Fronto thought for a moment.

'I suppose that makes sense. He *is* good with cavalry. What's Rufus like, I don't think I know him?'

Caesar smiled.

'You'll have seen him at staff briefings. He's quite competent. Commanded men out in Greece. I think it's time he had a chance with us. Any thoughts?'

Fronto's brow creased.

'There's a couple of things I'd like you to consider, Caesar. Firstly, my position on the strategic staff. I don't mind being one of your senior circle, and I don't mind being a legate, but by doing both, I'm forgetting how to do either of them well. I think you should either put me back in permanent command of the Tenth or make me permanent staff and promote Priscus to command of the Tenth.'

Caesar shook his head.

'I will *consider* assigning you back to the legion, though I may still occasionally need to haul you out. I will not consider Priscus for senior officer, though. He is a centurion. A good one, but low-born. He is at the top of the ladder as far as he is concerned. The only place he might go from here is camp prefect. He's most use where he is.'

Fronto frowned again.

'The second thing I'd like you to think on is command of the Eighth. Balbus is a very good officer and a personal friend. I can think of no one I'd trust more, but he should be back in Massilia, or even Italy, with his wife and daughters. I'd like you to consider giving him release at the end of this campaign to return to his family. You've got lots of desperately ambitious little magpies in the staff that would love to fill his boots.'

Once more Caesar shook his head.

'Marcus, quite apart from the fact that I prize Balbus as one of my top officers, could you see him laying down his command and walking away? I won't ask it of him. If he should ever ask to be released, I would do so gratefully, but I'll not ask it of him. You should appreciate that; you're more like him than you might care to guess.'

Fronto grunted and stretched his arms.

'Shall I shout the others in now?'

The general nodded and Fronto climbed from the seat and threw open the tent flaps. To his surprise not only were the staff officers gathered just down the slope, but the Druid and several of the Gaulish chieftains stood in a knot next to them.

'Sir, I think your answer's waiting outside.'

Caesar straightened in his chair.

'Best show the whole parade in then.'

At a gesture from Fronto, Sabinus called together the staff and exchanged brief words with one of the chieftains. The Gauls made their way into the command tent, with the staff close on their heels. The officers filed off to either side as they entered, taking positions around the edge of the tent, while the Gauls stood just inside the tent flap. The tall and imposing Druid glanced around at the Romans, waiting for the movement to cease and, once they were all in position, stepped a little closer to Caesar.

Once again, the interpreter among the retinue of Gaulish chiefs translated the huge man's words.

'Roman, the chieftains of almost all of the tribes of Gaul have agreed to take an oath, though they want me to examine the oath before they take it to be sure they are not selling themselves and their lands. They also each agree to provide a small number of warriors to help you in this war.'

Caesar smiled at the Druid, who had not broken his impressive frown throughout the day so far. Fronto wondered if the man had even heard of humour.

'Very well. Sabinus, I would like you to speak with each of the tribes and work out roughly what numbers of men, both mounted and infantry, they can spare, totting up the amounts of each, and then come back to us with the figures. I'll leave the details in your hands.'

Sabinus nodded and stepped toward the Gauls.

'Labienus, I want you to draft up a copy of the standard oath of allegiance that the Aedui took and speak to this man about it. Agree everything with him. I don't mind a few alterations, so long as you deem them acceptable and appropriate.'

Labienus saluted and joined the knot in the centre of the tent.

Relaxing back in his chair, Caesar scratched his prominent nose reflectively.

'Thank you, gentlemen. I see no reason to protract this meeting any further. I realise that some of you feel bitter about this, but I would like to think of this whole situation as the start of a long and peaceful Gallo-Roman coalition. I want to ensure you all that my fight is with the enemies of Rome, and not with non-Romans. You are our allies and thus we will always protect you.'

The general sat back in his chair, looking far too smug for Fronto's liking. His thoughts were echoed a moment later by a familiar voice speaking in relatively good Latin. He looked up in surprise to see the immense and impressive Druid addressing Caesar directly.

'Caesar. I must say one thing and then stop. I am, as Greeks say, barbaroi, that you Roman call barbarian. How can you say you distinguish between enemy of Rome and non-Roman, when to Rome we are all barbaroi?'

The interpreter seemed as surprised as Fronto had been. Glancing at his superior he realised, though only because he knew the man so well, that Caesar was equally surprised. He doubted the man had flinched as far as any other observer was concerned. Caesar cleared his throat.

'I am unused to dealing with so wily a political adversary. If I had known you spoke not only my language, but that of the Greeks, I would have rather addressed you directly as a spokesman. Still, I would answer you this way. The word we use, barbarian, is used to describe those who do not follow our ways. If you have heard the word from someone, then I am not surprised that you'd interpret it this way. If you truly have a knowledge of the Greek language and their history, you may realise that this is not a derogatory term. It is merely a catch-all term for non-Romans. I would welcome the chance to speak to you alone, if you would favour me, after this meeting.'

The Druid glared at Caesar.

'You are clever, and very quick. No. I will not meet with you. I do not believe we need you and I do not like you. I speak here only as spokesman for the tribes. I do not speak Greek or Latin not because I speak it badly, but because I dislike speaking the language of deception and wickedness. I speak my mother tongue, because that is true. We have made our deal, so we do not need to speak more. This is over. Goodbye.'

Turning, he made for the tent flap, the other Gauls following him as he went. Caesar glowered after him, and for moments after the Gauls left,

Sabinus and Labienus stood tensely, expectantly, waiting for an outburst. Instead, the general cleared his throat and turned his thunderous expression on the two staff officers.

'Still here?'

Sabinus and Labienus saluted hurriedly and rushed from the tent to catch up with the Druid and his entourage. Fronto glanced sideways at the general, wondering whether the general would manage to contain himself until later. A dreadful feeling of foreboding stole over him.

Caesar shifted slightly in his seat.

'Longinus!'

The man jumped at the sound of his name and sidled into the centre of the tent.

'Yes, general.'

The red hue was slowly draining from the general's face and his breathing had subsided a little. When he spoke, his voice had returned to its even, politician's tone.

'Longinus, you've served well so far in this campaign, and your talents as a cavalry commander have not gone unnoticed.'

The legate bowed respectfully.

'It has been my privilege to have served in such a capacity, Caesar.'

Caesar smiled at him and gestured to one of the staff officers' seats.

'Gaius...'

Longinus looked up in surprise at the use of his first name - an honour few men received from the general.

'I have made a decision regarding your place in this army. I would like you to step down as legate of the Ninth. I'm sure you're aware, as are we all, that the legion needs a more readily accessible commander. You simply do not have the time to devote to the duties of both a legate and a cavalry commander.'

Longinus nodded. He was, Fronto noticed, starting to look a little older; a little more worn. Indeed, he had lost a considerable amount of weight over the last few months, dividing all his waking hours between the legion and the cavalry. Fronto could sympathise to an extent, sharing his own time between the general and the Tenth. He shook his head and looked up once more as the general continued.

'Longinus, there are going to be an increasing number of cavalry units in this army as we progress through our campaign. I want you to take the position of Master of the Horse, commander of all cavalry, both legionary and auxiliary. You may take a couple of the staff officers with you to help you organise what I'm sure will be a fairly massive undertaking, if you wish. However, from the moment you agree to step down from the Ninth, you will be placed on the staff in that role. Have you any objections or comments?'

Longinus stood, his finger pressed to his lip deep in thought.

'I don't think so at this time, Caesar. I'm quite happy with the idea, but I'll have to run through the whole thing with a few of my fellow officers and iron out some problems. Then I'll come and see you sir, after we've found out what the issues are. Can I ask who you're considering as a replacement with the Ninth? Grattius has served well in the interim. You could do a lot worse than promoting him...'

Caesar waved a hand to one side to indicate a small knot of staff officers standing near the fabric wall of the tent.

'I'm afraid that won't be possible, Longinus. Grattius will continue to serve in his current position. Publius Sulpicius Rufus will be taking the position.'

He turned to the staff.

'Rufus, I presume you'd be happy to take the command?'

Rufus stepped out from the side of the tent. He was an average height, with pale, sandy blond hair and, very unfashionably, a neatly trimmed beard. Despite being visibly quite young, he put forth the impression of a hardened veteran in the way he moved. As his arm came out from under his military cloak to salute the general, Fronto noticed an old but livid scar running along his inner arm from the wrist to the elbow. He decided he would probably like the man.

Rufus bowed his head before Caesar.

'I'd be glad to take any command, general. My sword arm's atrophying!'

Balbus laughed.

'I know how that feels. I nearly wasted away in Massilia. Think I was actually getting old.'

Caesar smiled at the two of them. This was why he tried to keep officers with units for as long as possible. They built up a rapport with their men and became hardened veterans. Political weasels were far too common in military command, and few politicians who took such a position had any tactical ability. Caesar liked to think that he followed an illustrious line of those with tried and tested ability, but he would sooner trust a career veteran to lead his men than another politician. Too many agendas and not enough talent. Things would change in time, when Caesar reached his long-sought after goals. He pulled himself from ambitious reverie and looked across at the two officers again, then back at Longinus.

'Very well. Longinus, you are hereby promoted to the staff as Master of Horse. You've got two days to put together your plan and apprise me of it. Rufus, report to the Ninth and find their primus pilus, Grattius. He should be able to fill you in on anything specific you need to know and sort out your accommodation for you. Balbus, you may want to accompany Rufus and give him a hand.'

Balbus nodded.

'Very well,' the general went on, 'we'll be staying here for about a week, while the army is marshalled and the initial process of pre-war negotiation is carried out. Now that these damn Gauls are out of earshot, I presume you all realise that this campaign cannot be avoided and, even if diplomacy with this German were possible, I have no intention of carrying it through. We *must* have military supremacy here if we are to achieve anything.'

He turned to his other staff officers.

'Brutus. Go into Bibracte and speak to Liscus. Find out exactly where this Ariovistus is currently based, somewhere in the lands of the Sequani.'

He then turned to Longinus again.

'I want a small party of heavily armed cavalry dressed in full regalia. I'm going to send an ambassador to speak with this German. That's your job, Brutus.'

Brutus nodded and squared his shoulders.

'I take it you're going to give me the details, general?'

Caesar smiled viciously.

'Oh yes. When you've found out where he is, come back here and we'll go through the conditions. I fully intend to make them unacceptable, even unbearable, for him. I won't let him deal with this quietly.'

He squared his shoulders and stood.

'Alright gentlemen, you've got your orders. Let's start a war.'

He strode from the room, through the curtain-covered doorway and into his personal chambers. At this cue, the other officers exited the tent. Fronto stood by the entrance, waiting as the staff and senior officers exited. Balbus and Rufus left together, heading for the ranks of the Ninth. Longinus and Brutus left in the direction of the cavalry enclosure and Bibracte. Fronto sighed. It was a rarity when one of Caesar's meetings ended and he did not have some task to attend to.

Wandering down the hill, he caught sight of Priscus and a couple of the junior centurions from the Tenth. As he approached, he broke into a smile as his ears caught the familiar sound of a dressing-down. The two juniors stood, red faced, their helmets and vine staves under their arms. Fronto waited respectfully until Priscus had finished shouting and the two men had left, sheepishly but in a great hurry.

'Gnaeus, I do believe you were born with a centurion's crest. Have you finished shouting? I'm looking for someone to join me for a quiet drink, or possibly even a raucous one.'

Priscus smiled.

'I think I'm about done here. Are you thinking of that nice little tavern in town, 'cos I just saw Crispus and Galba heading that way too.'

'Good. Let's go see them and get drunk. We've got nothing to do, and we might never see the place again after this week.'

Fronto tagged along with the small party of officers striding to the main gate of the camp. At a word from Sabinus, the soldiers that had gathered at the gate pulled themselves out of the way of the officers, coming to attention with a snap. Fronto stood next to the others, watching the slight rise on the other side of the valley. The sun hung pale and watery over the grass, casting an eerie half-light over the early morning landscape.

It all looked slightly unreal to Fronto's tired eyes. After a moment, he caught the distant jingle of armour and equestrian equipment and then, over the saddle he saw the standards appear and sagged with relief. Though the scouts had reported Brutus and his escort returning when they were still two miles distant, they had not been close enough to give too many details.

Fronto had worried. It was not unknown for Roman ambassadors to be ill-treated by barbarians, and the sight of legionary standards protected by only a few cavalry could have proved too tempting for them. Fortunately, despite the fearsome reputation of the Germans, Ariovistus had apparently dealt with them in the manner of a civilised leader. The cavalry looked tired and travel-worn but intact and fully equipped, with all standards accounted for.

Brutus was clearly exhausted. Though still in good health he looked weary, pale and drawn as the party reined in outside the gate. He slid with little grace and decorum from the saddle to the grass, his cloak billowing slightly in the breeze.

The common soldiery saluted smartly, while Sabinus reached forward to grasp the reins of Brutus' horse. Brutus barely acknowledged the salutes of the men, waving a hand dismissively. He turned his pale face and watery eyes on Sabinus and Fronto.

'Let's get to the command tent, so I can get this over with and get some rest.'

Nodding, the staff officers fell into step alongside Brutus as he wearily trudged up the Via Decumana toward Caesar's command post. They passed through the guard at the praetorium without a word and made straight for Caesar's tent. The general would have been informed of the ambassador's arrival by now. The guard by the entrance of the command tent took one look at Brutus and wisely decided that, since Caesar was expecting them, challenging the travel-beaten officer would hardly be a positive career move. He stepped to the side of the doorway and snapped to attention, the horsehair crest on his helmet brushing the leather flap of the tent. Again, Brutus barely noticed him as he shuffled inside. Sabinus followed and Fronto gave the poor soldier a sympathetic look. He could imagine how hard it must be for the common soldiery to deal with the irrational actions of the staff.

Caesar stood to one side of the tent, pouring his own goblet of watered wine. He turned and gestured to the half dozen campaign chairs in the room.

'Brutus, do sit down please before you fall down.'

Brutus sank gratefully into a chair. The other officers remained standing until Caesar noticed and irritably waved them to the other chairs before taking his own seat and nodding at his ambassador.

'A quick report, Decius, and then you can go and catch up on sleep.'

Brutus sighed.

'As you commanded, Caesar, we rode hard and met with Ariovistus. I demanded, fairly imperiously, that he name some patch of neutral ground where he could meet with you and discuss affairs of state.'

Caesar frowned.

'And? You're back so fast. Don't tell me he agreed? You went armed with the most unreasonable and insulting terms. Don't tell me he just rolled over and said yes?'

Brutus shook his head wearily.

'No, Caesar. I didn't get time to dig into him and get him fired up. He all but threw us out of their camp. As soon as I'd got the first sentence out, his guards were around us and shoving us toward the gate.'

Caesar's eyes widened.

'Who in the name of Minerva *is* this man? Does he have any idea who he's dealing with? Is that it, they just threw you out?'

'Not quite Caesar. He gave me a few words for you. He said that if he'd wanted anything, he'd have come to you, and if you want anything, you should go to him. He said that he wouldn't come into the lands you occupy without his army, and asks what you're doing in *his* Gaul anyway, since he's the one conquering it, not you.'

Fronto winced. Caesar was unlikely to take this kind of answer well, not being noted for his patience. Gritting his teeth, waiting for the outburst, he turned and looked at the general.

Much of the colour had drained from Caesar's face, a sign well-known to Fronto that the man was reaching the end of his tether.

Caesar gripped the arms of his campaign chair so tightly his knuckles went white.

'Brutus, go and get some rest.'

The officer nodded and, standing slowly and painfully, turned to leave.

Caesar drummed his fingers on the chair arms irritably. Fronto tried to shuffle out of the general's line of sight. A number of times he had seen Caesar planning something like this and had been in the wrong place at the wrong time, resulting in his being landed with an unpleasant or arduous task. He was determined this time not to be Caesar's victim.

In the event, when Caesar did look up, his eyes locked only momentarily on Fronto before slipping sideways to Labienus.

'Very well. Labienus, you've represented Rome in general and me in particular on a number of occasions. You've a good command of rhetoric and are not easily fazed.'

Labienus bowed, respectfully, though hesitantly.

'Thank you, general.'

Caesar smiled his most predatory smile.

'Don't thank me, Titus. You've just volunteered to be my next ambassador. I haven't the time to develop diplomatic frippery with you, so I want you to go and keep him busy. Improvise. Just be rhetorical and act the part of the ambassador, but do *not* play humble to him. I need you to buy us time.'

Fronto raised himself a little from the chair and gestured to Caesar.

'That's a little dangerous, general. You heard how he reacted to Brutus. If we keep pushing him, he might break. You're talking about a very warlike and proud man here.'

Instant regret. Caesar's eyes alighted upon him.

'You are, of course, absolutely correct, Marcus. Take an entire cohort of the Tenth. Speak to Longinus to arrange cavalry support. Go in force, and make sure the entire unit is in full ceremonial uniform, including crests. Don't take the First Cohort though, as I'll need your primus pilus here.'

Fronto nodded miserably. There was no point in arguing. He had done this to himself.

'What will Priscus be required for, Caesar?'

The general smiled the same, tight, wolfish smile as before.

'Obviously Fronto, while you're keeping this arrogant German occupied, we'll be marshalling our forces and preparing for war. After you've spoken to him, have Longinus sent to me. He's going to need to put his auxilia in order sharply. You can all go about your business now. I need to think for a while.'

The officer rose and made to leave, but Fronto stood and confronted the general.

'Caesar, how long do you need? When are we to come back? Will there be a signal? We'll need to know these things.'

Caesar shook his head irritably.

'You'll stay there until I send a dispatch rider to you. Then you'll know we're ready. Now go and get things underway.'

As the officers piled out of the tent, Labienus caught Fronto, grumbling audibly, by the elbow.

'Marcus, feel free to go back in and persuade Caesar otherwise. I can get by with a small ceremonial guard.'

Fronto shook his head resignedly.

'No point. There's no way he's going to change his mind now, and I was right anyway. This could go very wrong and you could need support. Can I suggest we meet at my tent in around an hour? I have to see a few people beforehand.'

Labienus nodded.

'I've got some planning to do myself.'

As the other staff officer strode off in the direction of his own quarters, Fronto made for the praetorium of the Tenth and found one of the duty centurions overseeing the polishing of the standards.

'Centurion. Leave those for now. Find Lucius Velius and get him to come to my tent as fast as you can.'

The centurion saluted and jogged off in the direction of the temporary mess tent.

He looked down at the two soldiers polishing the standards.

'You two. Get into kit as fast as is humanly possible. Go to the staff quarters and find Gaius Longinus and Decius Brutus. I don't care whether they're sleeping, just wake them and tell them I need to see them urgently.'

Fronto smiled. Whatever happened, he was always proud of the Tenth. He reached his tent and had just managed to remove his cloak and unstrap his cuirass before a familiar cough outside announced the presence of Velius. He smiled again. He imagined he was something of a novelty among the command. His was the only tent of a senior officer with no guards outside and no servants within. There were better uses for the men of the Tenth than challenging visitors to their commanding officer, and servants meant clutter and constant company. Fronto preferred a little peace and quiet and was quite happy to pour his own drinks and don his own armour. Velius would cough three times and then make a suitably sarcastic remark just loud enough for him to hear.

Tempted though he was to wait and see what Velius would call him, time was getting a little short.

'Come in Lucius. Don't stand on ceremony.'

Velius entered with his customary scowl.

'Sir, I've got a lot to do. Without wanting to sound insulting, why don't you get Gnaeus to drink with you? He's only wandering around finding people to shout at anyway.'

Fronto smiled again.

'It's not a social matter, Lucius, though you might want to pour yourself a drink anyway.'

Velius' eyes narrowed and one eyebrow rose in an inquiring manner.

'Why are you being agreeable with me? What are you planning?'

Fronto finished removing his armour and sank onto a couch, reaching out for the wine.

'I sort of accidentally volunteered myself for something stupid. And I can't think of anyone better to go on a stupid mission with.'

He grinned a mad grin and he handed a mug of wine to the centurion and poured another for himself.

Velius sighed.

'What's the job?'

'We're going to see the Germans, Lucius. We're going to be the military escort and guard for Labienus as he spins out enough bullshit to keep Ariovistus busy while Caesar prepares for war.'

Again, the grin.

Velius slung the wine down his throat and banged the goblet down on the table emphatically.

'Have you any idea how much trouble we could land ourselves in? How many men are you taking, and why not Priscus? He's just being a miserable lazy fart and making our lives difficult anyway.'

'We're taking the Second Cohort and a cavalry contingent. I don't know how big that'll be until Longinus gets here. I've asked for him and Brutus to join us. Labienus will be here in about three quarters of an hour too. You're going to command the infantry while we're there.'

Velius nodded.

'Do we know how long we're to play hostage?'

Fronto's' brows knitted together.

'Until Caesar says otherwise. I get the feeling I just said the wrong thing at the wrong time and Caesar's venting his irritation on me.'

'Nothing new then. I'll get the Second Cohort formed up.'

'Wait a bit. I need you to be fully aware of what's going on, so you'd better speak to the others too.'

The two sat and drank in silence for a few moments until there was a tentative knock on the doorframe and, without waiting for an invitation, Longinus walked in. Fronto smiled.

'Lucky I'm not naked, eh?'

Longinus nodded.

'Yes, but who for?'

He took a seat opposite Fronto and nodded at the centurion.

'Velius.'

'Sir.'

'Sir? It's a preciously rare moment I hear you call someone that!'

Velius smiled.

'Ah, but you're a big nob now sir.'

Longinus sighed and raised his eyes skywards.

'What's all this about then? I'm a little busy at the moment. I've had over a thousand cavalry turn up over the last few days, and they're only from the *local* tribes. It's a nightmare of organisation.'

Fronto smiled again.

'Well now you've got another job, Gaius. I'm accompanying Labienus on the next diplomatic mission to the Germans. Well, Velius and I and the Second Cohort. Caesar wants you to supply a cavalry contingent. He didn't tell me how many, but I'd imagine an ala would fit nicely with a legionary cohort. What d'you think?'

Longinus frowned.

'One ala shouldn't be a problem. You'll want good men if you're going into that kind of situation. If you're taking a cohort, you're expecting trouble, yes?'

'Yes.'

'Well my time's taken up quite seriously with the auxilia, so I can spare some regulars. D'you remember Ingenuus?'

Fronto chewed a moment on his lower lip and then brightened up.

'That was the cavalry decurion who charged in against the Helvetii to save his compatriots, wasn't he. The one who went above and beyond? I haven't thought about him for months.'

Longinus smiled.

'Then you've not been paying attention to the cavalry, Marcus. Aulus Ingenuus is now a full cavalry prefect, with a squadron of his own. He's itching for action, and I think you could do worse. I'll send him; he should do nicely.'

Fronto leaned forward and refilled his cup.

'Sounds good. I'll feel better knowing I've got good men by my side. Labienus is a fair old talker, but I'm not sure about his ability to keep Ariovistus spinning until the general's ready.'

The cavalry commander sighed and stood.

'Good. Well, I'd better be heading off. I'll have Ingenuus drop by in the next hour to work things out with you.'

Fronto caught him as he turned.

'Hang on, Gaius. Caesar wants to see you straight away. He's getting onto a war footing and wants to be ready for campaign as soon as possible.

Due warning: I don't think you're going to get the time you need to organise things properly.'

Longinus smiled.

'When did the general ever give people what they wanted? We'll be ready, don't you worry. You just keep your mind on your own problem. I'd rather be in my shoes than yours!'

Fronto frowned as he let go of the commander.

'One more thing Gaius. Caesar's planning to send a messenger to us when he's ready to go. Could you arrange a little private cavalry messenger service on top of that? I'd like to have a lot more warning than the general's likely to give us. I don't want Caesar to suddenly hove into view over the hill while we're surrounded by thousands of startled Germans.'

Longinus chuckled.

'I think we can set something up. We'll have a lot of semi-local auxiliaries who know the area. They'd be perfect. I'll organise it.'

'Thanks Gaius.'

The cavalry commander turned and left the tent whistling a happy-sounding tune. Fronto was once again struck by the enormous change the last half-year had wrought on Longinus. He was brought back to the present by a further knock on the tent frame. Brutus walked in, still looking dreadful, without his armour, but still wearing the same worn and stained clothing he had returned in.

'Alright Fronto. What do you want? I haven't slept in three days of riding.'

Fronto nodded toward a spare seat.

'Sorry Brutus, but this really couldn't wait. In a few hours, we're going out to bridge the gap between embassy and war with the Germans, and I need to know everything you can tell me about their land, tribe and stronghold.'

CHAPTER 14

(ARIOVISTUS' FORTRESS IN SEQUANI LANDS CLOSE TO THE RHINE)

'Subarmalis: a leather garment worn under armour to prevent chafing and rust, to which the pteruges are attached.'

'Carnarium: a wooden frame covered in hooks for hanging sides of meat.'

Fronto sat sullenly in the doorway of the hut. After such a protracted stay at Bibracte, he had become far too used to a civilised town and the soft life. Even under the rule of the Sequani, this place would have been dour, dull and backwards. Under the rule of the German invaders, it was the nadir of culture to Fronto. He sighed and spat out into the muddy street. It had not rained in these parts for many weeks and yet due to the lack of hygiene facilities the entire settlement swam in murky slurry and stank like a latrine.

The Sequani inhabitants of the settlement went about their business with a perpetual frown, trudging through the slick with their shoulders hunched and exchanging few, if any, words. The feeling of dejection and oppression in the town was tangible. The stockade gates stood permanently open. The Germans could not care less if anything happened to their Sequani subjects, so long as they themselves were safe. Beyond the revolting huddle of huts stood the temporary camp of the German leader, Ariovistus.

On the rise beyond the far gate a new stockade had been erected, surrounding an area of greater size than the original town. Within, the German warriors lived in squalid leather tents that still stank of the tanning process.

Almost two weeks the Romans had been here now with no sign of a word from Caesar or Longinus. Things had been strained from the beginning, but Labienus had truly excelled in his task. He had managed to be offhand, insulting and outrageous enough to keep getting ejected from the chieftain's enclosure for days at a time, but never quite insulting enough to get them into serious trouble. The balance was perfect. If Labienus kept playing it this way, they could spend months teetering on the edge of talking with Ariovistus, but never quite achieving anything. It would have made Fronto laugh had he not spent those two weeks living in squalor here in the backside of Gaul. He and Labienus had each been given a hut, as had the cavalry prefect. The troops themselves were quartered in their tents outside the walls of the settlement. Fronto rather wished he was camped with them, away from the smell.

Rising from the doorway, he determined to get away again. Stretching and touching the lintel above the doorway with his good arm, he glanced around the hut and shuddered. His locked travel chest sat in the corner. He had not taken it from the baggage train since early in the campaign, but now he had decided it would be wise to keep things under lock and key. So close to a large, hostile force, he would have to keep his armour and gear stored in the hut, but away from prying eyes and thieving fingers. Labienus, having not been concerned with such matters, had left his armour and weapons with the Second Cohort outside the walls. As an afterthought, Fronto tried to reach up and grip the lintel with his right arm. The strain was painful and it felt like his arm was tearing to pieces, but for the first time in two and a half months, he could reach as high with both arms. Wincing, he gripped the wood and tried to pull his weight off the ground. A sudden pain like liquid fire ran the length of his arm several times and, letting go of the lintel, he collapsed in a heap inside the hut. Oh well, it was still improving faster than the medics had told him.

Fronto trudged and sloshed out into the street, grateful once again that he had brought two pairs of comfortable, enclosed leather boots with him from Aquileia. Trying not to meet the unhappy stares of the people, he made for the open gate and the legionary encampment beyond. Two German warriors stood guard (though Fronto could only apply the term loosely) at the gap. They looked a great deal like the Helvetii in Fronto's opinion, though their speech was considerably harsher and their personal habits made him cringe. There was no denying their courage, on the other hand. Fronto had seen a crowd amassing in the square one night and had gone to investigate. He had been impressed to see a German warrior, unarmed and clad only in his trousers, fighting off three savage dogs. He had walked away before it reached serious unpleasantness, but had heard the snaps and squeals as the man had dispatched all three.

One of the guards pointed at Fronto and said something guttural. The other laughed. He wondered for a moment whether breaking arms or legs would cause an incident and, coming to the conclusion that Labienus would disapprove, smiled sweetly at the two guards while he told them in Latin to piss off.

The camp of the accompanying Roman force was guarded by members of the Second Cohort. Ariovistus had forbidden them from fortifying the location, so Velius had, in his usual efficient way, set up a rota that kept an extremely strong and alert guard around the camp. He had also refused to allow the cavalry to take their turn. He considered the cavalry to be 'faeries' as he had put it the other night. They 'needed looking after' and 'couldn't tie their bootstraps without the help of the infantry'. Fronto smiled. Nothing made him laugh like Velius.

He was gratified to note that despite his close ties with the Tenth, he was stopped and the password requested by the guard. Velius would probably be in line for a position as primus pilus before too long. Fronto suspected one of the other legions would require a primus pilus in the near future, and he could see Caesar allocating Velius in the place.

Nodding in recognition and giving the password, the legate passed by the guards and made for the praetorium where Velius would be camped.

The centurion stood in full armour by the standards in front of his tent. His vine staff jammed tightly beneath his arm, he surveyed the soldiers wandering around the camp with a professional eye. Velius took his job very seriously.

Smiling with relief and breathing deeply to sample the fresher air of the Roman encampment, Fronto nodded to Velius, who saluted smartly and then took up his position again.

'Morning, sir.'

Fronto wandered up to the centurion and stood at ease beside him, rubbing his sore arm.

'What in the Gods are you watching so intently?'

Velius smiled.

'We're not allowed to fortify, but this position makes me very nervous, so I'm hedging my bets. Arm bothering you again?'

Fronto raised his eyebrows enquiringly.

'Tried to exercise it and I think I've torn something again. What do you mean hedging your bets?'

The centurion sighed and gestured around him.

'I've had weapons and shields stashed at appropriate positions around the camp, out of sight of the town. No soldier has been allowed out of his armour except during sleep, and you see that large tent nearest the town gate?'

Fronto nodded.

'That's a rather large tent.'

'Yes, I got it from the cavalry. I've been sneaking timber in there now for about four days. We've got a lot of defensive stakes ready, faggots of brushwood and twigs ready to light with flint and tinder. If we get more than a couple of moments' notice, we can be on a defensive footing.'

Fronto grinned.

'Nice thinking. I don't like this much either. I wish Longinus would send us some kind of word. The army *must* be ready to move by now. I might have a quiet word with Ingenuus and send a courier back to Bibracte. I need to know the full picture.'

The centurion nodded unhappily.

'I just hate being so tied up with arse-wipe bureaucracy that I can't carry out a professional action. By now we should be settled into a well-fortified marching camp, not pissing about like children. Hello, here comes Labienus.'

The staff officer strode through the camp in just his tunic and subarmalis. He wore only his dagger, hanging from his belt, his sword kept in the camp armoury with the rest of his gear. The look on his face spoke of an anger and a frustration that Fronto was sure would be shared by every Roman here.

'Morning Titus. Nothing changed then, I take it?'

Labienus grimaced.

'I think we're going backwards. Ariovistus is running out of patience. I swear I hadn't even finished speaking this morning when his guards hustled me out. I'd love to give the man a sound thrashing. I'm not used to being treated like that.'

Fronto frowned.

'That German irritates me beyond compare. I'm seriously tempted to give the order to fortify just to spite him. I've had trouble at times dealing with war against the Gauls, as some of them seem so civilised and, after all, we're in their land carrying out campaigns, so you can see it from their side. These Germans though, they're invaders. They deserve everything we can throw at them. Look what they've done to the Sequani.'

Velius nodded emphatically and tapped his vine staff on his leg.

'They're only barbarians. With a full cohort, we could probably rush that camp and take them before they knew we were there.'

'Don't be stupid, centurion.'

Labienus turned angrily to face Velius.

'You haven't been up there; you've just seen it from a distance. There's around a thousand of us down here. There are at least ten times as many up there, maybe more. And don't forget how many other smaller forces that madman's got stashed in other locations around the Sequani land. They don't need to equip before battle. If you attack them, they're already prepared. They live for it. Think before you open your mouth!'

Fronto stared at Velius, who was beginning to turn a faint purple colour. He knew that look, and dragged Labienus to one side before Velius could get himself into deep trouble.

'Titus, that was a little harsh and unfair. He only said what we're all thinking. He's not that stupid; he's just venting his anger and frustration. I know the man and, believe me, if he thinks you're insulting him, he'll flatten you no matter what rank you hold.'

Labienus sighed and glanced sideways at Velius. He could swear the man was actually steaming.

'I'm sorry centurion. I'm just so bloody frustrated with all the shit I'm having to wade through and I can't take it out on the Germans, which is what I'd really like to do.'

Velius cleared his throat.

'Permission to do my rounds, sir?'

Fronto nodded.

Labienus watched the centurion make his way toward the barracks with a slightly relieved look.

'I hear such great things about that man, but I'd not realised he was such a hothead. I'm surprised he's made it that high in the legion.'

Fronto grinned.

'Maybe, but he's one of the best centurions I've ever met, and I've known quite a few. He trained some of the others too. Just think. If he scares our troops like that, what kind of fear does he put in the enemy?'

He turned quickly, becoming aware that someone was shouting his name. Labienus followed his lead and they saw a cavalry officer running up the path from the town toward them. Fronto shaded his eyes from the sun and could make out the features of Ingenuus, the cavalry prefect. Labienus shook his head in disapproval.

As Ingenuus came to a stop, panting heavily and red faced, Fronto glared at him.

'Prefect, in front of the men you call me sir or legate, and you certainly don't shout it across the camp like a fishwife.'

Ingenuus tried to catch his breath.

'I... I know sir... But I had... I had to get your attention as quickly as... I could.'

Alert suddenly, Fronto reached and supported the weary prefect.

'What is it, prefect?'

After a couple of deep breaths, the officer straightened.

'I was over near their military stockade sir.'

Labienus reached for his other shoulder.

'Why? I thought I'd made it clear the army should stay away from there.'

'Yes sir, but I went off duty and I've been going to see their stables. They've got some lovely horses.'

Fronto tutted.

'Never mind that. What's up?'

'They're on the move sir.'

Labienus interrupted as Fronto opened his mouth to speak.

'What do you mean?'

Ingenuus pointed over his shoulder toward the town.

'All of them. They're gathering in the centre of their camp. They've got all their travelling gear there and someone came to take the horses. I think we're in the shit, begging your pardon, sir.'

Labienus looked at Fronto.

'You're the commander here. What's the best course of action?'

Fronto frowned in frustration.

'We can't stand and hold. We'd be swamped. I'm pretty sure Caesar would want us to re-join the army, especially if he doesn't know they're moving. Ingenuus: have a small party of riders head straight back to the army at full speed and apprise Caesar of the situation. We're going to get out of here as fast as possible, then follow them and see where they're headed. Titus, you'd best head back with the riders. Caesar'll want to speak to you. Let's move!'

The Second Cohort backed across the deserted camp in good order, moving quickly but with their formation intact and presenting the cohort's fighting front to the town. Velius walked alongside, shouting orders. In the distance, far above the abandoned camp, Fronto could see Labienus and the riders making with all haste for Bibracte and Caesar's army. The six men with Fronto moved from wall to wall like thieves in the poorer districts of Rome, the legate glancing back over his shoulder constantly to make sure the cohort was still in sight. Velius had disapproved of his commander heading back into the settlement, but Fronto had insisted. Not only was all his best armour and uniform packed in the chest, but his sword lay there and he was damned if he would leave a fine sword like that in the hands of this German rabble.

They reached the corner of the hut in which he had been staying and the optio leaned round the corner while the legionaries protected Fronto.

'They're by the gates to the compound, and the gates are open. Velius is going to have to start moving fast soon or there'll be a hell of an engagement here. Give me the key to the chest sir, and I'll go get your stuff.'

Fronto glared at the optio.

'I'll get it myself. I need to throw on my kit though. You'd best help me, quick as you can, while these five keep watch.'

The optio nodded and slipped round the corner of the hut and into the street. Aware of the dangerous situation he had put them all in, Fronto followed. Glancing nervously at the gathering crowd by the gates, he stole as quickly as he could into the hut. The optio had already dragged the chest to the centre. Fronto ran in, fumbling for the key.

As he flung the chest lid back, the optio hauled out the cuirass and subarmalis. Fronto slung the rest to one side, wondering momentarily whether it would be feasible to carry his spare boots with him. With a sigh he gave up and flung them into the corner of the room. He looked up as the optio reached out with the subarmalis and hurriedly pulled it round his commander. As he tied it at the back, Fronto took up his helmet and buckled it into place. The optio picked up the heavy cuirass and Fronto tried, even with his weak arm, to hold the front and back plates in place while the junior buckled them together for him. Finally strapping the sword at his side, he noticed in the bottom of the trunk his two cloaks. Wearing a flowing cloak in the current emergency would risk entanglement and was asking for trouble, but he considered it for a moment. Sighing sadly, he slammed down the lid and the ornate, decorated cloak that meant so much to his sister vanished from sight.

'Optio, let's get out of here as fast as we can.'

The optio nodded and moved quietly to the door. With a glance out to one side he pulled his head back in and stood straight against the wall.

'The street's full of Germans. They're on their way now. We're trapped.'

Fronto looked round the hut. The windows were far too small to climb through. While the structure of the hut was poorly put together, and they could probably break through the walls in moments, the noise and mess would draw a great deal of attention and almost certainly get them all killed.

'Optio, get under the bed. Hide and keep damn quiet.'

The optio hesitated, nodded uncertainly and dropped to the floor. Aware of time running short, Fronto leaned to the window and whistled quietly.

'Sir?'

The face of one of the legionaries appeared in the gap.

'All five of you need to go hide, now.'

'Yes sir.'

The legionaries moved away from the hut as stealthily as they could manage and disappeared into a back street. Fronto glanced round the hut. With the optio under the bed, there were no other convenient hiding places. He could clearly hear the stomping feet and guttural voices of the German warriors out in the street. Drawing a deep breath, he reached up for the beams of the roof. Wincing with anticipation and hoping that the roof would not collapse under his weight, he hauled himself up among the smelly, dirty, cobwebbed eaves of the hut's roof. His right arm burned with a wrenching pain and, in his need to keep from crying out, he bit his lip so hard that blood ran down his chin.

Hooking his legs over a beam, he grasped the top of the door lintel tightly with his left arm, his right resting on his torso. One slip and he would come down with a crash. He tried to breathe as quietly and shallowly as possible. Dust motes drifted to the ground below as he turned his head at the sight of trousered legs tramping past the hut door. Briefly he cast a silent prayer to Fortuna and hoped that Velius had taken the initiative, moving the troops out as fast as possible. He should have taken an oblique angle as soon as he was out of sight of the town, and all but doubled back on himself. The Germans could search for hours, but would be unlikely to find them. It would only work if he had moved out before the Germans reached the encampment, though.

Over and over the Germans stomped past the hut in small knots, disorganised and shouting. Fronto could feel the muscles in his arm beginning to burn unbearably with the constant strain of holding up his entire bodyweight. He glanced the other way and was satisfied to see that the optio was well and truly out of sight.

More and more Germans passed and Fronto began to wonder truly how large this army actually was. Gritting his teeth and closing his eyes for a moment, he shifted his grip on the lintel, almost losing it altogether. Dust drifted down to the floor. Breathing heavily but slowly, he relaxed a little.

With a sudden flurry of activity and a guttural shout, several warriors broke off the column and made for the hut. Fronto tightened his lips and tried very hard to become invisible. The mass of Germans in the main street was diminishing. Most of the army had gone past and there had been no cavalry, so they must have gone out a different way. That could, of course, spell trouble for Velius and the cohort, but he would worry about that later.

Half a dozen Germans reached the door of the hut. Two hung around outside, laughing jovially in their indecipherable tongue and then wandered off. The other four walked into the hut, their matted hair and horned bronze helmets coming within a few finger-widths of Fronto's chest as he clung, suspended, above them. The warriors looked around the hut and two of them made for the chest. Another went for the bed, while the last strode over to the corner to investigate the abandoned pair of boots.

Gripping the lintel tighter than ever, Fronto glanced out of the window. The mass of warriors had passed, and only a few stragglers moved in the street. He knew that this would not hold much longer. Should any one of the warriors look up, they would be found. He ran through the scene in his head, planning what moves he could make should there be trouble.

Trouble, however, came to the optio first. The warrior investigating the bed pulled back the sheet and prodded around inside. As he rummaged in the linen of the bed, he became aware of something beneath it. He turned and gave an angry cry in his harsh language. The optio must have been prepared, though perhaps not enough. A moment later the point of the soldier's sword thrust out from under the bed, shearing the muscle of the German's calf. With a brief scream the barbarian collapsed to the ground, blood spraying from the wound. The other three turned to face the bed, hands going to their swords.

Fronto in one fluid motion turned over and let go of the lintel with his fingers. He held his good arm out to the side, bent at the elbows as he swung downwards in an arc. The jarring as his helmet met with the shoulder of the tallest warrior was intense, but the warrior lost his footing from the blow and, falling on the wounded man, his head struck the floor with a sickening noise. The third German, standing by the chest, was caught full in the face by the legate's elbow and collapsed with a bone-crunching sound.

Reaching out and grabbing the downed German, Fronto unhooked his knees from the beam and landed rather gracelessly on the floor. The optio had pulled himself to the edge of the bed, where Fronto could see him, and was frantically thrusting and swiping with his sword, causing lacerations and wounds to the two men on the floor in front of him.

Climbing to his feet, Fronto drew his sword and advanced on the warrior in the corner, who had drawn a large Celtic-style sword. Feinting with his own blade, he moved closer carefully, keenly aware of the range of the large, sweeping blade in the German's hands. Without looking away, he addressed his junior.

'Optio, finish those three quickly.'

Aware vaguely of the wet sounds and the sighs and whimpers as the optio slit the throats of the three men on the floor, Fronto concentrated on the remaining warrior. He looked nervous; as well he might be facing two Roman officers now on his own. Surprisingly, he was quiet. In his position, Fronto would be shouting at the top of his voice, trying to get the attention of the warriors not far down the street. There was no way he was going to be able to gut the warrior with that massive blade swinging between them. He just did not have the reach. Shame he was not carrying the Celtic blade that Priscus had saved for him. He could not wait for the optio to stand and join him, or the man would have long enough to come to his senses and start shouting. Only a distraction could work.

The optio watched in astonishment as Fronto stopped stabbing with the blade and held it vertically in front of him with his left hand. He smiled warmly at the German and pointed at the blade with his damaged hand.

Confused and intrigued, the sweeping motion of the Celtic blade slowed, its wielder watching the blade in Fronto's hand. With an elaborate gesture, the legate threw his sword away, into the corner of the room. The German's eyes followed the arc of the gleaming sword as it fell and pulled themselves back toward his adversary, just in time to see Fronto's fist hurtling toward him.

The German slid down the wall at the side of the hut, unconscious and with a broken nose. Fronto bit his already lacerated lip to prevent the unbidden cry escaping, rubbed his fist and made a face. Muttering, sure he had re-broken several bones, he went to retrieve his sword and stopped in the centre of the room.

'To hell with them.'

He picked up his ornate cloak and tucked it beneath his arm. Slipping the sword back into its scabbard, he straightened.

'Right, optio. Let's go and find your men.'

The optio nodded, and the two officers moved toward the hut door. Fronto peered gingerly round the corner and could see the stragglers near the settlement's gate. The mass of the German force was visible on the hill, moving rapidly away from the town. The German cavalry were with them, so the cohort had apparently made it to safety. Fronto and the optio left the hut and dashed around the side into the back streets of the town. He looked at the optio and made motions suggesting a search. The optio shrugged. They stood for a moment, and the legate smiled. Leaning back against the wall, he began to whistle the call to arms of the Tenth Legion. Grinning, the optio joined in, and the two regaled the empty street with two full blasts of the call.

A couple of moments later, a legionary's head peered gingerly around the street corner.

'Sir? Thank Fortuna. I thought it was more of those bastards. We had a couple of run-ins and they chased us half way round the town.'

Fronto gestured to him to come out from behind the wall.

'Is everyone alright?'

The legionary shook his head.

'We lost two sir, and Mannius is looking quite bad.'

Fronto grimaced and sighed. They had done better than they had any right to.

'Well we should be alright now. Take us to the others. We'd best collect the dead and get them back to the cohort. Don't want to leave them at the mercy of these barbarians.'

With a nod, the legionary turned.

The relief on Velius' face was evident at the sight of his commander. Fronto and his small party came down the embankment on a horse and cart stolen from the all but deserted Sequani town, the two corpses lying in the back between their more fortunate fellows. The small group passed by the scouts and through the picket line without being challenged.

As Fronto dismounted, the optio clambered down the other side and came to attention in front of his centurion. As the other legionaries saluted, Fronto turned to the small party.

'Dismissed. Get those two buried and get some food. We'll be moving very soon.'

Gratefully, the men of his patrol fell out, taking the bodies and the horse and cart with them. Fronto turned to Velius.

'As you can see, we had varying degrees of success. I take it things went without a hitch for you?'

Velius nodded and opened his mouth to speak when he was interrupted by the clatter of hooves and shouting.

'What's all that bloody noise? If you don't shut up, I'll string you up and leave you here for the next lot of bloody Germans!'

As Velius spoke he turned toward the clamour in time to see three cavalry men dismounting. One was Ingenuus, the prefect. He turned back to Fronto, raising his eyes skywards.

'See what I mean. A waste of good flesh, the cavalry. We should put the troopers to work on ditches and eat the damn horses.'

Fronto's smile went as fast as it appeared when he became aware of the look on the cavalry prefect's face. Ingenuus was pale and looked sickened and the other two cavalrymen appeared equally unhappy.

293

'Ingenuus. What's happened?'

The prefect pointed down the valley.

'We've just been scouting on ahead and we've found... something. I think you ought to see this, sir.'

Fronto nodded. He would have liked to sit down for a while but, from the look on the prefect's face, he felt this would have to take precedence. Indeed, Ingenuus had proven himself to be as astute and brave as Fronto remembered, and if what he had seen had taken him that badly, it would need investigating.

'Velius, get your second in command running things here. You and I are going with the prefect.'

The centurion nodded and shouted his orders to the optio before turning back to the prefect.

'How far are we going? Do we need a horse?'

Ingenuus shook his head, swallowing hard.

'You can take these two horses. Their riders are reporting back to the ala. The ... it's about a mile and a half away, I'd say.'

Fronto and Velius took the reins from the two cavalrymen and clambered onto the horses, kicking their heels and following Ingenuus as he trotted down the hill. The valley was long and shallow, with lush green grass and a great deal more vegetation besides. If it were not for the purpose of the ride, Fronto could rather have enjoyed it. The journey was short enough on horseback however, and after only a short while Ingenuus reined in ahead of them on a low rise. As the other two came up next to him, he pointed down into the dip.

'That's just as we found them.'

Fronto and Velius swayed in the saddle for a moment before moving slowly down the low slope and into the grisly scene. The smell was torture and the buzzing of flies was loud enough to make it hard to think.

Half a dozen large wooden stakes, branches even, had been driven into the ground. Tied to each were men; Romans and judging by their tunics, cavalrymen. Their armour and weapons were gone, as were their faces and their arms below the elbows. Their heads had been stripped of flesh, not by animals, but by a rough, knifelike tool. Their torsos had been opened up, and the contents allowed to fall out to the ground in front of them in heaps that, despite the several days they had hung there, still glistened. Fronto felt himself growing light-headed and imagined he was probably now as pale as Ingenuus. Velius did not look too good either.

'Did you know them? Are they from your ala?'

The prefect shook his head.

'None of ours are missing. Besides, how would we identify them even if they were mine? That's not all though...'

Ingenuus pointed across the dell, behind the bodies. A fire pit of considerable size lay there, though the blaze had long since burned out and the residue was cold. As he gazed across at the pit, Fronto began to make out shapes in the ash. It took him a long moment to realise that they were horses.

'Minerva save us, they gutted and maimed the riders and then burned the horses? What kind of animals *are* these people? Is this some kind of German carnarium?'

Ingenuus' face had taken on a particularly hard look.

'Germans, sir. And bastards. We're going to make them pay, yes?'

Velius nodded.

'Oh yes. We'll get them for this. But who are they if they're not ours?'

Fronto tapped his temple with an index finger.

'Who do you *think* they are? Who *could* they be but the messengers Longinus and Caesar have been sending us? No wonder we've never heard anything. They must have kept them imprisoned until they were ready to move, then done this to them.'

Ingenuus swallowed again.

'I'll have some of my lads come and clean the place up and perform the proper burials.'

Velius shook his head.

'I don't think that's a good idea. Let the infantry handle it. These are cavalrymen and I think my boys are a bit more detached. Don't want them getting stupid ideas of revenge.'

Fronto nodded.

'He's right. I don't think we want to let your men know just yet. Remember what happened with the Helvetii. We don't want to get them so tightly wound that they'll get themselves into trouble. I do want the three of us to search the place first, though. We'll take back anything military or personal we can find before anyone clears up.'

The three began to move among the mess, scouring the ground for anything of value or importance. After a few moments of searching, Velius shouted them over to the fire pit.

There, along with the remains of the animals and the charred effects of the troopers, was a pile of charred scrolls, the wax seals melted onto the carbonised parchment. Velius was about to reach down and pick one up, when Ingenuus grasped his wrist.

'You can't pick them up. They'll just turn to dust in your fingers. Try to make out what you can where they are. We should be able to make something of them.'

The three moved around the pile of charred parchments, squinting at the mess and trying to decipher words that were defined only as a darker patch on the charcoal grey.

'It says something here about the Suevi. Aren't they a German tribe?'

Fronto nodded, grateful that he had read up so carefully on the tribes in the command tent over the last few months.

'The Suevi are a sizeable tribe, but they're not with Ariovistus.'

Velius shook his head pointing to a parchment roll.

'They will be soon. They're crossing the Rhine. I think Caesar's set off with the army to meet them. That's what this looks like to me.'

Ingenuus nodded.

'Here's the orders for you, sir, telling you to get the hell out of there and meet the army somewhere. I can't tell where. The rest of it's too far gone. What do you want to do, sir?'

Fronto frowned.

'If the Suevi are coming to join the party, Caesar'll have his hands full. Ingenuus, you've scouted this area a lot. What's that way?'

He gestured in the direction that Ariovistus' army had taken.

The cavalry prefect thought for long moments.

'Nothing immediate. Certainly nothing for at least ten miles. Although there *is* a big town out that way, quite a long way. I think it's the Sequani's capital.'

Fronto slapped his forehead.

'Vesontio!'

He turned and grasped Ingenuus' shoulder plate.

'Vesontio's huge and very easily defended and it's probably better supplied than Bibracte. If Ariovistus takes Vesontio and the Suevi join him, it'll take every man Rome can supply to remove him. Shit! Caesar's marching the wrong way. He'll beat the Suevi, but by then Ariovistus will be in the best position to be found in eastern Gaul! We've got to...'

A neighing noise stopped him in midsentence. Two German warriors on horseback had just crested the ridge. They surveyed the scene for a moment, then spotted the Romans and wheeled their mounts. Fronto shouted at the others.

'They can't get away. Velius, get back to the cohort and send scouts off to Caesar with this news. Prefect, we're on!'

As Velius galloped off in the direction of the unit, Ingenuus jumped onto his horse in a swift move, quickly overtaking Fronto, who was less practised in the saddle. The two raced up the hill after the Germans. It struck Fronto as they rode, that this might be a bad idea. What if they followed to the two straight into the waiting arms of a thousand German cavalry?

Cresting the hill, they could see the two ahead of them. Willing his horse on, Fronto tried to keep up with the prefect. Slowly they began to gain ground on the Germans when suddenly the one on the left veered away from his companion. Fronto swore and then shouted to Ingenuus.

'Keep on the other. I'll take this one.'

Leaning in the saddle, Fronto drove his mount as hard as he could. Again, slowly he began to gain distance. The German kept turning to look over his shoulder at his pursuer and, failing to notice an incline while he was doing so, almost became unhorsed. His steed bucked and whinnied as it tried to keep steady on the treacherous slope and Fronto knew that he had his man now.

Coaxing the horse on, he ploughed down the slope at a pace the animal could handle, mere feet behind his quarry. Realising that there was no way he could reach the man with his short infantry blade, he pulled alongside the man as best he could, judged the distance and, pulling up his knees so that his feet rested on the saddle, hurled himself at the surprised German.

The two tumbled to the ground, Fronto landing on top of the man. Hurriedly he drew his blade, ready to cut the German before he could properly fight back but noticed as he raised the sword the unpleasant angle at which the man's head lay and the trickle of dark blood running from the corner of his mouth.

He stood and with only a little work, retrieved both horses. Heaving the body of the German onto one, he tied its reins to his own saddle horn and began to ride back up the slope.

After around a quarter of a mile he saw Ingenuus, leading a spare horse.

'What happened to him?'

'He went in the river sir. A few sharp rocks and a sword blow. He washed far downstream before I could even dismount. I think we can count him as gone sir.'

Fronto smiled without a trace of humour.

'Good. Let's get back to the men and get on the trail of Ariovistus. We should meet up with Caesar at Vesontio or at least this side of it if the general gets our message and detours. So long as we get there before the Germans.'

'And if we don't?'

'If we don't, we're walking into one hell of a problem.'

CHAPTER 15

(FOREST CLEARING TWENTY MILES FROM ARIOVISTUS' FORTRESS)

'Turma: A small detachment of a cavalry ala consisting of thirty two men led by a decurion.'

'Ludus: 1) a game, 2) a Gladiatorial School.'

'German scouts!'

The cavalryman rode out of the late afternoon sunlight and into the column at high speed. Fronto and Velius came running from the vanguard and met Ingenuus as he arrived on the scene. The cavalry trooper had slid from his horse and stood to a close approximation of attention. Fronto thought he looked a little unsteady until the man turned slightly and he saw the shaft of a rough arrow protruding from his back.

'Capsarius!'

Fronto jogged forward to the wounded trooper.

'For Gods' sake sit down man before you fall.'

'Sir, I need to report...'

Fronto waved the words away.

'You can report while the capsarius looks at you.'

The trooper, dropping painfully and carefully to his knees, shook his head.

'No sir. Won't wait. There's around twenty German scouts less than a mile away. I would estimate Ariovistus' entire army can't be more than two or three miles. If their scouts know we're here now sir, we'd best either get out of here fast or get set for battle.'

Fronto sighed.

'You leave that to me.'

A capsarius appeared and knelt next to the trooper. He reached round behind him and gingerly touched the shaft of the arrow. A small trickle of blood came out from below the entry wound. Ingenuus frowned.

'How many in your scouting party?'

'Three sir.'

'And you're the only one who made it?'

The trooper nodded and then winced at the pain the movement caused.

'Am I going to die?'

The capsarius looked up at the officers from where he knelt behind the man and made 'unlikely' motions at them.

'I don't think so lad. These Gaulish arrows are fairly narrow-bladed, without barbs. There's not a massive blood flow and your complexion's good, so I don't think it pierced an organ. You're going to be out of action for a while though.'

He turned to the nearest legionary.

'Help me get him in a cart.'

Another soldier brought the nearest baggage cart around and halted the horses near the wounded man. Velius whacked his vine staff on the side of the cart in anger.

'We've got too close to them. We should've given them a wider berth. Now they know we're here they might just consider it worth the delay to turn round and do for us.'

Fronto sighed.

'It was my decision, Lucius; my fault. I didn't think we could spare any more time. We've got to get to Vesontio. If we don't get past the Germans soon, we'll end up with them between us and the rest of the army. We'll just have to pick up speed again.'

Velius growled.

'We can't pick up any more speed. The troops are moving as fast as they can. They're exhausted. It's late afternoon and by rights we'd normally be making camp shortly. We can't do with weeks of three hours rest a night.'

'Lucius, they're going to *have* to move faster. Exhausted is better than dead. Ingenuus.'

The cavalry prefect turned to face him.

'Sir?'

'Have one of your decurions take a turma and ride like the wind for Vesontio. See if the rest of the army has reached there yet. If they have, detail our situation to Caesar, Longinus and Priscus, the primus pilus of the Tenth.'

'Yes sir.'

'Oh, and have the scouts pull back in to a visible radius. I don't want any more losses like that.'

As Ingenuus ran off to take care of the task, Velius turned to his commander.

'Sir, the troops would be able to move faster if they could dispose of their tools and entrenching gear. It's not like we're going to have time to build marching camps between here and Vesontio.'

Fronto nodded.

'Have them put the gear in the carts with the rest of the baggage. How far is Vesontio d'you reckon?'

Velius tapped his chin.

'I really don't know. Too far?'

Fronto looked back at the cavalry scout who was being loaded onto the cart by the capsarius and another soldier.

'How much faster do you think the cavalry are capable of moving than the cohort?'

The trooper winced as he bumped down into the cart.

'At least twice as fast, maybe three times. A lot more if we can change horses, but we don't have fresh horses here.'

The legate smiled.

'Late afternoon. Making camp.'

Velius raised an eyebrow. He knew that smile all too well.

'What are you thinking?'

'The Germans are only moving as fast as us because they travel very light and don't have a lot of baggage with them. They're all warriors, not a tribe like the Helvetii with their women, children, the old and all the baggage. They don't know there's Romans ahead of them, so they're in no hurry, are they? They presumably camp down properly every night.'

Velius shrugged.

'I would have thought so, yes. You've got a plan, haven't you?'

Nodding, Fronto grinned at Velius.

'Is it insane by any chance?'

Another nod.

Velius started to grin back.

'Tell me.'

'The Germans have a fairly strong cavalry arm. They must corral their horses at night. We just have to work out a way to get around three hundred horses out and back to the cohort without getting the whole German nation on our heels.'

Velius nodded.

'Then we might as well let the column rest here for now. No use us getting the horses if we can't find the cohort afterwards.'

'Agreed. Give the orders and then meet me over by that copse of trees off to the left.'

As Velius walked off to the signifer to give the orders for making camp, Fronto scanned the line for Ingenuus. The prefect was briefing one of his decurions a few paces away.

'Ingenuus!'

The prefect looked round at his name being called and saw Fronto walking toward him.

'Sir?'

'Belay that order.'

He turned to the decurion who was arranging the riders.

'No message needs to be sent right now. Instead I just want a small unit sent out, giving the Germans a suitably wide berth, to ride to Vesontio and see if the army's there yet. If they are, inform the commanders that we're on the way, but the Germans will be close behind us, yes?'

The decurion mounted his horse again.

'Yes sir. I'll do it right away.'

Fronto turned back to Ingenuus.

'I want you to join me and Velius in a touch of planning.'

By the time the two had walked over to the copse, the grizzled centurion was already there, making marks in the earth at the foot of the tree with his vine staff.

'I've been giving some thought to the problem. Removing the guards quietly might be a bit of a problem, but the big trouble comes when we try and shift three hundred horses quietly.'

Ingenuus stared at the centurion.

'*What?*'

Fronto grinned.

'We're going to get the whole cohort mounted. Put them on German horses and then try to reach Vesontio in less than half the time.'

He smiled at Ingenuus, who continued to stare in stunned amazement at the centurion.

'What we need *you* to do is figure that problem out. Three hundred horses, quietly and quickly.'

He turned to Velius.

'We're obviously going to have to be sneaky. No armour or shields. I think the only weapon we should take is a pugio. We can't afford to get drawn into a proper fight anyway, so just something for a quick, quiet kill.'

Velius nodded.

'We've got a few auxiliary archers with us, but they'd make too much noise. I think there's some Balearic slingers too, though. They'd be useful.'

'Indeed. We don't want a large group to go in though. I reckon about a dozen. The sneakiest bastards you can find. Sneaky, mind you, not mad. We don't need the lunatics you like to hang around with; those mad bastards who charged the rocks when the Helvetii were entrenched.'

He was greeted with a warm smile.

'We don't need Nonus and Curtius, sir. We've got plenty of prize sneaky bastards in our cohort. Just give me an hour and I'll bring 'em back here dressed just right. You'll think you're looking at a bunch of burglars and bandits from the backstreets of the Aventine back in Rome.'

Fronto looked up at the sky.

'Light's starting to fade. We'll set off in about an hour and a half. Ingenuus, what d'you think?'

The cavalry prefect shook his head, his eyes still wide with disbelief every time he looked at the others.

'Commander Longinus said he thought I'd be good for this assignment, but he did ask me if *I* thought I would. He said, and I quote here sir so no offence intended, that 'the leaders of the Tenth are dangerous, idiotic and possibly insane'. I think I'm beginning to see what he means.'

The other two grinned wildly at him. Velius snorted.

'Don't have a problem with that. To the Tenth, that's probably a compliment!'

Fronto laughed.

'Anyway, true confessions aside, have you any ideas?'

Ingenuus shrugged.

'To move three hundred horses quietly and quickly, the only really feasible way is to have three hundred riders standing by. My only suggestion is that the cohort looks after our horses here and the entire ala follows you in on foot, keeping far enough back to prevent discovery. As soon as it's clear for them, they mount up and ride the horses back here.'

Fronto smiled.

'It's a plan. More people than I'd usually like to take on a quiet bit of subterfuge, but if it's the only way, then it's the only way. Talk to your decurions and arrange it. Have them muster here in an hour dressed the same way as we will be.'

Ingenuus frowned.

'You mean all three of us are going on this loopy adventure, sir? Begging your pardon, but shouldn't you stay and command the cohort. What happens if you get hurt?'

Fronto grinned wolfishly.

'If you think I'm missing out on a bit of fun like this, you've got another thing coming. Anyway, I'm not essential to the daily running of the cohort. That's what centurions are for.'

As Ingenuus jogged off in the direction of the milling cavalry, Fronto smiled at Velius.

'I know your opinion of the cavalry in general Lucius, but what do you think of the man?'

Velius shrugged.

'He seems to be good at the job. Pleasant in a kind of wet way. He charged in to save his colleagues despite stupid odds, which means he's brave. Oh, he's alright. Bit of a prat, but better than most of the mind-blowingly stupid cavalry officers who couldn't find their own arse with both hands and a map.'

The legate smiled.

'Don't pull blows Lucius, speak your mind man.'

'I tell it like I see it.'

Fronto tapped his chin.

'I'm thinking of requesting that he be transferred to the Tenth. We don't have any good cavalry officers. Think I'll have a word with Longinus when we get back and ask him if he's happy with that.'

Another shrug.

'One day you'll find him trying to wear his own arse like a hat, mark my words.'

'Ow!'

Velius turned and whispered 'Shut the hell up!'

Fronto, hobbling on the foot he had just stubbed against the heavy bole of a tree, swore very quietly and whispered back to the centurion.

'What kind of way is that to speak to your commanding officer? Anyway, we can't be near them yet. I can't hear the horses.'

'Begging the legate's bloody pardon, but *I* could hear them until you started all that muttering!'

Fronto winced at the temporary pain and clamped his mouth shut. He glanced around and felt, once again, how truly clumsy he was in comparison with some people. He never really considered legionaries agile; they were the heavy infantry that hit the enemy line like a rolling boulder. It was a surprise, then, to see the dozen men that Velius had picked out. They had stained their white tunics with soot that had turned them charcoal grey, and had wiped the blades of their daggers with wet carbon to dull the gleaming. With the same applied to their faces and arms, they were barely visible in the darkness of the woods. They moved with a catlike grace and made virtually no sound. To his own ears Fronto, on the other hand, sounded like Hannibal's Elephant parade crossing the Alps. He had cut himself no less than six times since entering the woodland and had stubbed his toe twice. He was beginning to wonder why he had come after all. He should have stayed at the column with the slingers. Velius had looked them over briefly and then decided that they would be too noisy and visible.

Velius stopped dead. Fronto was equally surprised at the dexterity and quiet with which the veteran centurion moved. As he watched, the man made a number of mysterious motions at the legionaries, who dropped low and spread out, moving forward very slowly. Fronto shrugged at him and could see the irritated look on the man's face even under these conditions. He would have to buy the centurion some good wine after all this was over. Velius repeated his arcane gesture and Fronto shrugged again.

Moments later, a crackly voice next to his ear whispered 'The centurion's asking you to drop low and move forward to his position slowly sir.'

He turned, startled, to see a short, wiry, blackened man crouched next to him.

'Oh. Alright.'

With a minimum of grunting, Fronto picked his way forward to Velius. When he arrived next to the man, he dropped down and whispered to him.

'Who the hell is the really short one? He moves like lightning and I didn't even see him coming.'

Velius' face still wore its annoyed look.

'He worked in a Gladiatorial Ludus before he joined the army; now will you kindly be quiet and let me think.'

Fronto followed his gaze and saw the horse enclosure not far away. Now that he actually listened, he *could* hear the horses. He could see four warriors from here, but assumed there would be others. The four were near the wicker gate by a flickering fire. The corral itself was a temporary structure formed from woven branches and vines. It was not anywhere near as big as he had expected. Certainly could not hold more than a hundred horses.

'Velius, there's nowhere near enough horses there. This must just be the scouts' enclosure.'

Velius turned, the annoyed look back on his face.

'That's exactly what it is and yes, there's probably only a hundred horses there, but if you open your eyes you'll probably see the three other fires that I've already spotted. If you focus around them for a while, you'll start to spot the other horse corrals. Stay here with the men. I need to creep back and have a word with Ingenuus.'

Fronto considered arguing, but only for a moment and the look on the centurion's face suggested how bad an idea that might be. He sighed quietly and settled into another position on the knobbly tree root. No way he sat was remotely comfortable. His heart skipped a beat when something tapped him on the shoulder. The short legionary was next to him again.

'Wotcher sir.'

Fronto smiled uneasily.

'Evening. What's our next move?'

The legionary grinned.

'We're going to have to take the guards out; probably one group at a time. We can't move any of these horses while there's a single guard left in visible range.'

Fronto nodded. It made sense to him, though he would have split them up and done it all in one go.

'What happens if one group sees us silencing another?'

The legionary smiled again and flicked the point of his dagger with his thumbnail.

'We'd best make sure they don't, eh sir?'

Velius' voice piped up very quietly from behind the legate. It must be difficult, Fronto decided, to maintain a whisper when your natural vocal state is bellowing at people.

'Right. We're all in position. There are seven guards as far as I can make out. Four standing by the fire and one sat close by, one off to the right next to the corral's fence and one to the far left sat down, possibly asleep. Ingenuus is waiting for an owl hoot I'm going to give when we've dealt with them, then he's going to bring all the cavalry to this position as quietly as possible. By then we'll have split into two groups of seven and gone for the next two fires. Sir, can you lead one group over to the fire on the left and sort them out? I'll lead the other group and we'll deal with the two fires on the right. I'm then going to give another hooting and Ingenuus will send a third of the cavalry to your position, a third to mine and the rest will mount up at this corral. Then we just have to move as quickly and quietly as possible.'

Fronto nodded a lot through the briefing, aware of how much the central command relied on the tactical ability of the centurionate. As Velius finished, his legate frowned.

'Velius, how are we going to get the horses back out? We can't go the way the Germans have cleared, or we'll run into the rest of their army, and *I* could barely get through the way *we* came *myself.* I can't see a squadron of horsemen getting through there.'

Velius sighed.

'Have all those command briefings late into the night destroyed your senses? Did you not hear Ingenuus' men behind us?'

Fronto's frown deepened.

'No. I didn't hear a thing, and I thought that was the point.'

Velius had to stop himself shouting, and the irritated look was back.

'The cavalry has been widening a path behind us as quietly as they could, but I've been quite worried about the volume. If you couldn't hear it I think you need to see the legion's doc about your hearing when we get back.'

Fronto harrumphed and then looked guilty for the sudden noise.

'Alright. How do you propose we go about this?'

Velius gestured at the corral.

'I've selected six men to deal with the ones by the fire. They should be over the other side by now and ready for the signal. In a moment we're going to split into two groups of four. I'm taking three off to the right to deal with the one there. You're going to go left with the other three. Once they're down I'll hoot and the other group will move in on the fire and Ingenuus will start to bring the cavalry up.'

Fronto raised his eyebrows.

'Did you plan all this earlier, or is it all spur-of-the-moment thinking?'

Velius grinned.

'You should know me well enough by now to know that I try and keep planning as basic as possible until I see how the land lies. Everyone ready?'

There were a number of low affirmatives.

The centurion made another gesture that Fronto could easily interpret, and the men moved out. The legate suddenly found he had three grey legionaries next to him urging him on.

With a conscious effort to keep his movement quiet and agile, he crept through the forest with the other three close by. Pausing for a moment he made a crude signal, gesturing at himself with his thumb and then drawing it across his throat. The others nodded and Fronto swallowed nervously. He was a senior officer of the Patrician class in Rome, a war-hero and a personal 'friend' of the most powerful man in the Northern Provinces. And yet next to these common legionaries he felt like a blundering imbecile. He would have to take down the first man to prove his worth to even *himself.* Swallowing again, he reached out and touched the woven fence with his fingertips. One of the horses neighed quietly and its warm breath clouded around his fingers. He stood very still, watching ahead for any sign of alert movement. Nothing. He could not even see the seated man and had no idea how Velius had spotted him in the first place.

As quickly as he dared, he made his way along the fence, squinting off into the dark woods ahead as he did so. Every five or six paces he stopped, panicking that he had made too much noise but still there was no reaction from ahead.

He was almost on top of the guard when he finally noticed him. The man, about five feet away, reclined against the bole of a tree. Fronto watched him for a moment, trying to determine whether or not the man was asleep. As he stood, hunched in the shadow of a tree, the man snorted and spat into the woods. So much for that. There was no way he could cross that five foot gap fast enough without the man making noise. Briefly he considered trying to climb a tree and get the drop on the man, but not only would that make so much noise he would be bound to be discovered, just about any move from here would attract attention. He thought for a short while. Well, it was an old trick, but he was fresh out of ideas.

309

Picking up a small twig, he threw it across behind the guard at one of the horses. The twig bounced off its neck and the horse reacted predictably, neighing and shaking its head. The guard looked up over his shoulder at the horse and, groaning at stiff muscles, pulled himself to his feet. Fronto waited for a moment until the man was standing, slightly hunched. Stepping forward, his movement covered by the sounds of the guard, he reached out as the man stretched and, putting one arm round the man's neck, covered his mouth. As the man struggled to breathe, trying to fight back, Fronto's other arm came round holding his dagger. The knife plunged into the man's neck and, wincing at the sounds, Fronto dragged the knife across the man's windpipe. There was a gurgle and the German thrashed for only a moment before falling limp. Fronto gently lowered the blood-soaked body to the ground and into a seated position resembling the one that he had previously occupied.

He stood straight again, looking around him for the other three. It took him a few moments to spot them, but spot them he did, and then scanned the forest on the other side of the corral over the heads and backs of the various horses. He could not see a sign of Velius and his group, but moments later a remarkably convincing owl hoot echoed out across the woods. Turning back toward the fire he was astounded to see the legionaries materialising out of the dark of the forest like the shadows cast by the flickering flames. They fell straight on the guards like a silent wave and within moments the Germans had been disposed of silently and efficiently.

Fronto smiled grimly to himself. The legions were renowned as a frightening force on an open battlefield, but they would never been known for stealth. It said a lot for the army in general and the Tenth in particular that they were capable of such varied military activity, and specifically, he suspected, it said a lot for the Tenth's chief training officer and his methods.

The sounds of activity not far behind him heralded the arrival of Ingenuus and the cavalry. Now that he had stopped muttering and complaining so much, Fronto realised he could hear the cavalry moving quite clearly. He hoped the Germans could not. A cavalry decurion, leading his own turma, approached the legate.

'Sir, prefect Ingenuus is in position now, and the ala is ready to move. We'll await the second signal and then move in.'

Fronto scratched his head.

'How is Velius going to know that we're done when he gives you the signal? He's going to be a long way away.'

The cavalryman grinned.

'Maybe he won't sir. Maybe he thinks you're already on your way.'

Fronto nodded and looked around for his group of three men. He was surprised once again to see that three of the men from the fire had joined them, and his entire unit of six were standing, impatiently waiting for his order to move out.

'Let's go.'

The seven men crept through the woods until they were close enough to the second fire to see how the land lay. The setup was much the same as the central corral, though the guards were a lot more spread out. He gestured for the men to gather round.

'I know I'm the commanding officer, but I realise that you're good at what you do and that centurion Velius has trained and briefed you very well. I assume you're quite capable of dealing with this?'

There were a number of nods.

'In that case, I'll take the guard next to the fence nearby and you can deal with the rest according to your own methods, yes?'

More nods, followed by arcane gestures reminiscent of those Velius had used, as the troops worked out who would do what with not a single word spoken. Fronto moved out toward the guard nearby as the rest of them melted away to deal with their own targets.

The man was considerably more alert than his previous victim. Fronto ducked behind a nearby tree when he thought he had been observed. Peeking out, he realised that the guard was just clearing his throat. He brought his dagger up ready to make a dive on the man when suddenly, not far from where he stood, an owl hooted.

Not wasting any time, Fronto merely broke cover and ran at the man. The German had been scanning the upper branches of the nearby trees looking for the noisy owl and was surprised enough when a senior Roman officer in a grey-stained tunic leapt out of the undergrowth and hit him in the midriff. The wind was knocked out of the man and as he struggled to draw breath and shout a warning the knife blade entered his torso once; twice; thrice. He stared in horror at the Roman nightmare from the trees as the blade arced in toward his neck.

Fronto stood, sickened by the fact that unfortunate necessity drove him to kill like this in cold blood. He would much prefer an open and fair fight. He sighed and wiped his dagger on the man's tunic. He had obviously not been fast enough for Velius, and would have to have words with the centurion when they got back. Moments later there was the sound of broken undergrowth as the cavalry moved in to deal with the horses. A shout of warning in the guttural German language was silenced by a legionary's blade, but too late. The cry had gone up.

Moments later, as Fronto rushed around the edge of the horses' corral to the gate to free the beasts for the cavalry that were now arriving, he heard a distant owl hoot and realised. The Gods had played a horrible trick on the Tenth tonight. Velius was now giving his signal, but the cavalry were already on the move, and there was little chance the cry of alarm had not been picked up by another German somewhere.

A cavalry officer appeared out of the woods not far from Fronto. He turned to face the man.

'Quick. The alarm's out. Get the horses and let's go.'

The cavalry started to pour into the area around the corral and men moved to individual horses. Fronto reached out for a nearby one. Fortunately, not only did the Germans appear to use the same Gaulish-style saddle that was the standard for the Roman cavalry, but they also appeared to have left many of the saddles on the beasts, whether for speed or through laziness he was not sure. He pulled himself up on one of them. These animals were very different from the horses generally used by Rome. By comparison they seemed immense. He hauled himself into the saddle and looked around. Everywhere around him cavalry troopers were climbing onto horses, with or without the saddle. He could see the legionaries struggling onto horses too. There seemed little point now in subterfuge. He called out, still relatively quietly, but loud enough to hear over the rest of the noise.

'Move out. Fast.'

Fronto was having difficulty. He was unused to being in the saddle anyway, but this brute of a huge German horse had been increasingly hard to handle since they had left the confines of the wood. With the unfamiliarity of the terrain and the darkness weighing against him, he considered it a lucky thing that he had made it this far without pitching off the animal or falling into something and ending with the beast lame. Although there was nothing behind them as far as he could see, he felt uneasy. They had made too much noise and commotion in the woods once the signal had gone up. He felt absolutely sure the Germans were following them, even if he could not see them. Once more he pulled the madly charging animal over toward Ingenuus, who had refused to set any speed for the unit other than charge.

'Prefect!'

He had to shout to be heard over the thunder of hundreds of hooves around them. For a moment he wondered how a cavalry unit was ever able to give or respond to orders on the battlefield. Ingenuus turned his face to the legate and Fronto was surprised to find him smiling.

'Sir?'

'Why are you grinning like an idiot?'

Ingenuus laughed.

'I'm enjoying myself sir.'

Fronto shook his head.

'I'm worried about you. You're starting to sound like one of my centurions!'

More laughter.

'Aulus, I'm pretty sure there are German scouts after us.'

Ingenuus nodded vigorously.

'I know.'

'*You know?*'

'Yes. I've seen them a couple of times so far. They're way over to the right. I think they must have come out of a different part of the forest; the track they would have entered on. They're almost certainly trying to cut us off. That's why I'm trying to maintain this speed; I don't want them to reach the cohort before us.'

Fronto nodded emphatically. The legionaries would certainly be able to hold their own against German cavalry, but a lot of good men would be lost if they had little warning.

'Do you have a plan, prefect, or is getting there first your plan?'

Ingenuus raised an eyebrow.

'My plan is to get back fast enough to give the cohort time to get on these horses and head for Vesontio, while we reequip and retrieve our own horses. We'll take on the scouts and protect your back.'

Fronto thought for a moment.

'Even if we have time to do that, it'll be dangerous for you. We don't know how many there are. Better if we all face them together.'

Ingenuus shook his head.

'No sir. We need to get as far ahead of the German army as possible, so you need to get your men mounted. And there's no point your men joining us on horseback. They're not used to fighting a mounted action. They'd just get in the way, begging your pardon sir.'

'Harrumph'.

Fronto did not like the idea of leaving the cavalry behind to face unknown odds even under this man, who seemed to have more of both sense *and* guts than the cavalry officers he was used to in the Tenth. On the other hand, the young officer was absolutely right: any attempt to marshal the cohort into a mounted force would likely end in disaster.

'Alright, but I'm staying with you and I don't want you going fight-mad. We'll just hold them off and when they back down or run, so do we. We'll catch up with them as soon as we can. I don't want to lose the cavalry.'

'Me neither sir. I can see the column.'

Squinting hard, Fronto could just make out in the sparse moonlight the column of men on a hill ahead. They were stationary and a number of them would be asleep. He turned his head to the right and squinted off into the darkness that way too. It took a few moments, but finally he saw a number of horsemen, quite well hidden below a ridge. It would be a close-cut thing and Fronto personally doubted whether there would be time to rearm and change horses.

He turned his attention back to Ingenuus and the cavalry. Peering around him, he could see that not only had the cavalry troopers not been blackened up, but they had also taken their swords with them, though no armour. He grimaced at the thought of unprotected cavalry, but then that was how most of the Germans and Gauls fought anyway. He grinned at the prefect.

'Forget changing your animals, Aulus, there isn't going to be time. You're all armed and you all have horses. Give the order to form up and get one of them to give me a sword.'

As Ingenuus nodded, unhappy at the idea, Fronto looked around for Velius and drove in closer to him.

'Lucius. Take your men back to the column and get them mounted up on the ala's horses. Do it quick and get them moving toward Vesontio. Ingenuus and I are going to deal with our pursuers.'

For a moment, he thought the centurion was going to argue with him. Velius tended to ignore rank at times like this and had his own very set ideas of what a legion's commander should do. Instead, the grizzled veteran nodded once and turned his own horse toward the front of the Roman column, gesturing to the other legionaries as he did so.

Fronto was sure he heard the man say 'Idiot!' as he left.

He looked back at the cavalry, who had formed into a spearhead formation and slowed enough to maintain the line. Ingenuus, at the head of the unit, gestured Fronto to join him. As the legate pulled into his place in the formation, Ingenuus held out a spare cavalry long sword. Fronto took it and gave it a few experimental sweeps. The weight and balance were so different to the standard gladius that he almost lost his grip on the blade. He wished he had had time to retrieve his own sword. Despite the fact that the army was trained to use it in a stabbing motion, the shape and sharpness of the gladius made it reasonably effective in a slicing motion. Ah well.

The Germans were closing on the column. Velius and his men were a little ahead of them, shouting orders. All along the hill there was activity as wagons were set rolling and men climbed onto the unfamiliar steeds of the cavalry, who would have to move right now or the Germans would be among the cohort. Ingenuus let forth a cry and the ala charged at the barbarian riders down the very slight incline.

The ala hit the Germans from the side. The effect could have been devastating had they been correctly armed and armoured and on their own steeds. Equipped as they were, however, and with no element of surprise, the impact on the mass of Germans was soon dealt with. A few of the scouts tried to pull out to the other side and continue after the cohort, but Ingenuus had sent off a third of the ala around the front to head off any such attempt. The Germans ground to a halt, unable to pursue the column, and began to take out their frustration on the Roman cavalry.

A big man wearing a strangely horned bronze helmet and a breast plate of the same material over a rough woven shirt rose up on his steed and held a large Celtic sword above his head, ready to bring it down on Fronto who was looking the other way. One of the troopers shouted a warning and the legate, turning just in time to see the man begin his downward sweep, pulled his horse in close and ducked. The sword, aided by gravity and its weight came down wide; Fronto was too close for the clumsy blade. Instead, the man's balled fists and the hilt of the sword smashed into his shoulder.

An explosion of pain and blinding white light went off in his head. He had had such little experience recently of proper combat that he had almost completely grown used to his delicate arm, desensitised to its steady, constant throb. A heavy blow to it, however, brought back all the pain he had felt all those months ago. His arm felt as though it had been dipped in a vat of hot oil. Fortunately he had, over the intervening period of convalescence, taken to wielding blades with his left arm, so the blow did not disarm him.

The trooper was rushing in to help him against the big German, but he would not get there in time. Grunting with the pain, Fronto looked up to see the German leaning back in the saddle and raising the sword for another downward stroke that would surely cut him in half.

Wincing, Fronto brought up the heavy blade with his left arm, wishing once again that he had his own sword with him. With immense effort, he thrust the sword at the German in a stabbing motion that strained the muscles of his arm. Unable to manage an accurate thrust with such a heavy blade, the blow went awry. Shaving a piece of metal from the side of the breast plate, the blade passed through only the very edge of the man's abdomen, drawing blood but not inhibiting him.

Fortunately, the surprise threw the German's blow off-target again and the heavy sword swept down a mere finger-width from Fronto's head. The blade cut deep into the leather horn at one corner of the legate's saddle and drew blood from both Fronto's leg and the horse's back. Fronto held his breath for what seemed an eternity, expecting the horse to collapse with a broken back or to buck with the pain of the blow. Instead, the beast kept its composure, most of the blow having been absorbed by the saddle. A look of surprise crossed the German's face, and Fronto suddenly realised that the blade had jammed in the saddle and the brawny man was trying to wrench it back out.

The legate tried moving his right arm, gripping his hand into a fist. He could close his fingers though there was precious little strength evident in the grip. His arm moved, so nothing had apparently been re-broken. His shoulder may have been chipped, however. There was immense pain as his arm came anywhere near shoulder height. There was no hope then of using his right hand to take the blade off the German. Instead, he swept the long cavalry blade back and down, and then rolled his shoulder, bringing his left arm over his head in an arc. The sharp, sweeping cavalry blade came down with less force than the German's blows had, but so much sharper. The big man stared in horror as the top half of his arm wrenched free and sprayed his precious lifeblood over the Roman. The lower arm remained attached to the blade jammed in the Roman's saddle.

Fronto had just enough time to register, with satisfaction, the look on the barbarian's face, before the man toppled backwards from his horse, out of sight. Wincing again, he grinned at the cavalry trooper who had come to help him, but had not been in time to interfere.

'Big bastard, wasn't he.'

The trooper grinned back.

'Best have the capsarius have a look at that when we get back to the column.'

Fronto nodded and held out the cavalry blade.

317

'Hold that for me.'

With a working free hand, the legate prised the fingers free from the hilt of the German sword and let the severed arm fall to the grass. He suddenly became aware of how he must look. Soot-blackened and now liberally covered with sticky drying blood he would hardly be recognisable as the commander of the Tenth, which explained why the trooper had not been addressing him as sir. Fine by him. He did not really feel like a legate right now anyway. With a great deal of effort, he levered the Celtic blade from the saddle horn. Below, a thin stripe of red betrayed the minor wound received by the horse. He smiled and, retrieving the cavalry sword, sheathed it at his side, hefting the German's Celtic blade with his left hand. Now *this* was a heavy blade.

He smiled at the trooper again, weighing the sword.

'Looks like I'm starting to collect these!'

It took him a moment to realise that the cavalryman was no longer paying attention. He had turned away from Fronto and was urging his horse on into the fray. The legate glanced around him. There had been perhaps two hundred German scouts; maybe two hundred and fifty. The ala had numbered three hundred, so the results were not entirely predictable. The mass of horsemen were now hard to distinguish from one another. The regular cavalrymen wore red and a light leather colour with no armour so that, in the poor light, it was hard to tell who was fighting who. Fronto squinted into the mass until he spotted a man who was clearly a German hammering blows at a Roman.

The legate made for the attacker, sweeping the Celtic broad sword back and out to one side. He doubted he would have the strength required to deliver an overhead blow with it like the Germans did. Coming within reach, Fronto swept the blade around in a wide arc. The edge caught the unarmoured German in the lower back, smashing through ribs and almost certainly severing the spinal cord. A single, violent spasm wracked the man's body, and his blade toppled from his fingers.

Fronto wrenched the sword out of the man's back and, with a sickening crunching noise, the man's top half fell forward, all but severed, onto the horse's neck. Fronto pulled his gaze away from the horrible sight and looked around. The worst of it was over, with pockets of fighting still going on, but the majority of the cavalry had assembled on the nearby rise. Fronto made for the group.

It took him moments to spot Ingenuus, also drenched in blood; some of it his own. The man was laughing and talking to one of his men. Fronto trotted his horse up to the cavalry prefect.

'Good evening.'

A number of the cavalrymen nodded nonchalantly.

Ingenuus raised his eyebrows.

'Some decorum please, lads. This here's legate Fronto of the Tenth and the general staff.'

The cavalry pulled themselves to attention.

'Don't worry about it lads. *I* wouldn't recognise me right now either.'

Laughter rippled through the ranks as more of the troopers joined the knot on the hill. The fighting was effectively over. Fronto tried to do a rough count but gave up.

'Ingenuus. What's the damage to the unit d'you reckon?'

The prefect made a swift move and jumped up onto the saddle with the practised ease of one of the equine entertainers that occasionally preceded a race at the hippodrome in Rome. Standing on his saddle, he scanned the crowd around him and then dropped back into a seated position in another fluid action.

'I'd estimate about fifty sir; seventy five at the most.'

'Hmm.'

It was more than Fronto liked but considerably less than they deserved. A quarter as many casualties as the enemy.

'Let's catch up with the cohort. We should be able to get ahead of the Germans in no time now.'

Ingenuus nodded.

'I'll have a detachment round up spare horses. We might as well take them with us.'

CHAPTER 16

(THE CITY OF VESONTIO)

'Tribunal: A platform, carefully constructed in forts, or temporarily made from turf or wood, from which a commander would address or review troops.'

'Praetorian Cohort: personal bodyguard of a general.'

Gnaeus Vinicius Priscus pounded up the main street of the town. The street ran from the great bridge through most of the length of the place up to the massive hill that, with the horseshoe of the Dubis River, surrounded the city; the hill that was where the citadel stood and where Caesar had made his headquarters these last few days.

He was starting to understand why Fronto liked to be in among the soldiers and involved in the lower levels of command and activity. Since the legate had been away swanning about impressing German leaders, Priscus had been called to Caesar's headquarters almost every day and often more than once. Where he used to send a subordinate to run messages and errands, now he found himself running everywhere. No wonder Fronto was always either running or drunk. The appeal of a quiet jug of wine was tangible.

Glancing to the sides of the street as he ran, he could see the large piles of goods that Caesar had acquired from the city. Much of it had, in all fairness, been purchased, though more had been seized. A lot of it had been moved into the camps on the other side of the river where the six legions rested. Indeed, the supplies allocated to the Tenth were all stored away in appropriate places. The other legions were an entirely different matter however. The other legions...

Priscus redoubled his pace, panting with effort as the incline of the street became more and more pronounced the closer he got to Caesar's headquarters. Finally he burst through the stockade gate at the top and came to a rest, his hands on his knees, puffing and panting as sweat poured from his forehead and on to the ground. The guards approached him to give the password, though half-heartedly. They all knew Priscus very well by now and they also knew he had to regain his composure before entering the building. He would give the password as soon as he caught his breath.

Priscus waved them away, still bent double, and stuttered out the password. Remaining where he was, he drew a scarf from beneath his harness and wiped his forehead and hair with it, smoothing the damp locks back down with his hands. He nodded at the officer of the guard, who acknowledged the gesture, and then walked across the courtyard and into the building.

As always, the headquarters was full of people, all busy and all irritable. The army had only been at Vesontio for four days. How on Earth the staff had managed to accumulate the clutter and records they had was a mystery to Priscus. He wondered if Fronto knew anything about it. Making his way down the long hall, he knocked on one of the doors and the guard opened it for him. In the large, well-lit room sat Caesar along with a number of his senior staff officers, Balbus, Crassus, Crispus and Longinus, and some of the senior centurions. Balbus nodded at him and he returned the greeting. Caesar smiled at him.

Priscus bowed, hurriedly and not particularly respectfully. Caesar waved the pleasantries aside.

'Priscus. Your report on the Tenth?'

The centurion cleared his throat.

'They're still standing to, general. I've got a full guard and no visible problems from the men, but I *do* hear things. I've not pulled anyone up on it yet, 'cause I'm pretty sure that would just be the spark that sets them off. I've called a meeting of all the officers of the legion as soon as I return, and I'll sort 'em out then.'

Priscus looked around. Not only was Fronto's absence still notable, but this time there were no Rufus or Galba either. Half the legions' commanders being absent was not a good sign. Caesar gestured at Sabinus with a finger.

'You see? *That's* a legion. That's my glorious Tenth. They're understrength by an entire cohort, missing their commander *and* their training centurion and they still maintain order and discipline. The rest of the legions could learn a thing or two from the Tenth, as I've always said.'

Priscus lowered his head. A comment that embarrassing to the other commanders could cause resentment, and Priscus was damned if he was going to look smug in front of them. From his lowered eyes, he could see legionary commanders shuffling uneasily. Crassus was the first of them to speak.

'Caesar, it's not a matter of maintaining order and discipline among the men. The rank and file are frightened of the prospect of facing unreasonable odds. All the reports we've received have given the German army as considerably larger than ours. Word has spread of the unpleasant practices of the Germanic tribes, their sacrifices, the fact that they are driven on by blood drinking Druids eight feet tall. All a fiction, I understand, but a fiction designed to terrify our cowardly lower ranks.'

As Priscus looked up once more, peeved at such comments from a man he already did not like, Balbus beat him to the retort.

'Crassus, these 'cowards' you speak of are your own men, Romans, and the backbone of the army. They've been building and maintaining our empire since all our families were farm owners. If the men are losing courage and morale, strength needs to come down from above. *That's* what the centurionate and the tribunes are for.'

Before Crassus could open his mouth, Balbus turned to face Caesar.

'General, I have noticed among the Eighth that there is an air of despair and worry among the legionary tribunes. Some of the centurions have fallen to the same attitude, but others haven't. Balventius, for instance, stands steadfast in his control and confidence. As a result, the First Cohort is still pulling its weight. In fact, due to the failure in morale with several of the other cohorts, the First is pulling more than its weight, and is moving and storing all the supplies for the entire legion. I firmly believe we have to pull the officers together.'

Crassus snorted.

'Don't be naïve, Balbus. The officers are despairing because they can only do so much with nonresponsive troops. I know *my* officers are trying their best. I've had six men beaten today and their century is back to work as we speak.'

Again, Priscus opened his mouth to speak, but was beaten to it by Crispus, legate of the Eleventh, this time.

'My dear Crassus, brutalising your men is hardly a shortcut to improving morale. Balbus is quite correct in his suggestion that the problem has to come down from the apex of the command structure. It is not to us that the troops look for potency, nor is it to the tribunes. The men look to their own commanders; to the centurions. The two most active and dedicated legions present are those whose primus pilus stands akin to a rock upon which the barbarian tide must break. I refer of course to the terrifying Balventius of the Eighth and the daunting Priscus of the Tenth. The path that we *should* be taking is that of a meeting of the centurions, just as Priscus has organised. If we can re-establish a dedicated chain of command, then the men will fall in readily.'

Several of the officers began to talk at once, and Priscus stood, still near the door, wondering how anything ever got done in command meetings. They just seemed to argue for the sake of it. Caesar's voice cut through the cacophony.

'*Quiet!*'

The racket died down immediately, leaving Crassus and Balbus glaring at each other angrily. Before anyone could speak again, Caesar, red faced and fuming, called a halt to the meeting.

'Get out. All of you. Priscus will let me know how things go with the Tenth this afternoon and *I* will then decide what course of action is to be taken by the rest of you. If any *one* of you dares defy me or open his mouth to object, I will send you back to Rome and replace you. A legate is not a permanent appointment, remember? Now go!'

Priscus turned to exit, and was quickly followed out by the others, mostly wearing a sheepish expression. He was amused to see Balbus and Crispus following Crassus out. The looks on their faces and poise of their bodies suggested that murder might be done soon. He gestured to the two of them.

'Gentlemen.'

Balbus had forbidden him from calling any of them sir over a week ago, since he was the effective commander of a legion. The two legates stepped out of the line of departing officers and joined Priscus in the courtyard.

'Gnaeus, what can we do for you?'

Priscus pointed down the street.

'There's a tavern in a side street about half way down the hill that's very used to me dropping in on my way back from these meetings. Care to join me?'

The other two looked doubtful, so Priscus waggled his eyebrows suggestively. Balbus laughed, a smile cracking his lined and weary face for the first time that day.

'Priscus, you have been too close to Fronto for too long. You're both mad as breeding-season hares. Alright, I'll leave Balventius sorting the Eighth and we'll discuss your eyebrows.'

The three of them wandered down the main street between rows of houses and shops built in the local style, with a ground floor of stone and a timber upper. The street was dry and reasonably clean in the warm weather of late Sextilis and early Septembris, but they could easily imagine how unpleasant it would be in adverse weather, with muddy water flowing down the incline. Halfway down the hill, they turned a corner and made for a small tavern with an inviting open doorway. The inside was fairly dim and of dark oak. A heavy, roughly-hewn trestle served as a bar, behind which stood a fat man in a leather apron leaning on one of three huge casks.

Balbus and Crispus sauntered over to a table near a window, while Priscus approached the bar and purchased three jugs of the local ale. These Gaulish taverns were nothing like the ones within the empire's borders or even the ones among the Aedui. Here there was no Roman wine, just local beer, and, although Roman coinage was thoroughly acceptable, the change was given in low grade coins of strange denominations.

He carried the drinks to the table and sat. As he took a healthy swig, Balbus and Crispus stared at their jug, Balbus with a look of mistrust and Crispus with open nausea.

Priscus grinned.

'Bottoms up!'

Balbus took another look at the jug's contents, a glance at Priscus and shrugged, upending the container and taking a large swig. His eye twitched slightly as he put the jug back down and said in a whispery, cracked voice 'nice!'

Priscus and Balbus laughed again and both turned to look expectantly at Crispus. The young officer had been told before about barbarian drinking habits and his mother had made him promise to stay clear or any such indulgence. He smiled uneasily.

'I really ought not to. I do have a chest full of jars of excellent wine from southern Italy that my father had sent to me when we rested at Bibracte for a short time. Perhaps we...'

Priscus almost spat his beer across the table.

'Your father shipped a *chest* of wine outside the empire's borders for you? That must have cost a small fortune!'

Crispus smiled again.

'My family would not approve of my sampling barbarian brews.'

Balbus looked at the centurion who was trying very hard not to laugh and turned back to Crispus with a broad, beaming smile.

'Your family are a *long* way away at the moment, lad.'

Crispus nodded once more, gingerly. Leaning forward and holding his breath, he raised the jug and took a small sip.

Balbus and Priscus watched with bated breath, waiting for the young man to turn green or purple. Instead, Crispus swished the liquid around his mouth and gums with a speculative look on his face. He stopped swishing, swallowed, and then breathed in sharply.

'Tangy.'

He shrugged and took a much larger pull from the vessel as the other two stared at him.

Recovering his composure, Priscus leaned forward conspiratorially and huddled with the other officers.

'I'm worried about Fronto.'

Balbus smiled reassuringly.

'We're all worried about Fronto, man, but you have to remember that that man has the luck of Fortuna herself. I can't imagine he's fallen foul of those Germans. He's too bright for that. I *do* wonder why he hasn't sent messengers, though.'

Crispus nodded, but Priscus lowered his voice and expressed his concerns.

'I think there's something else going on here; something bigger. You remember that Gaul who tried to kill him. What if there's more conspirators out there and they've actually got to him this time?'

Balbus' brows narrowed.

'That's actually a worrying thought. I hadn't put those two together...' He sighed. 'But I'm not sure that any kind of conspiracy would stretch over the Roman army, the confederation of Gaulish tribes *and* the German army. Fronto's not *that* dangerous. The Germans are heading for this place, and I'm sure Fronto will be either well ahead or well behind them now.'

The other two nodded doubtfully as Balbus continued.

'My other main worry now that you've said that is for the problems we've got *here*. I'd not considered the effects of conspiracy among the army, but it does strike me as odd that some of our best troops and our best officers are falling foul of panic and low morale. I mean, the Eighth I've known for a long time. They've faced the Helvetii and bared their teeth. Same goes for your Tenth, Priscus. I know they're holding together at the moment, but how long before they start to fall apart?'

Priscus frowned.

'You're suggesting that the conspirators are spreading some kind of panic among the men?'

Balbus nodded and Crispus put down his drink.

'I think I agree. This disaffection appears to be descending from the higher levels of command in the legions. If there were perhaps a few tribunes or even centurions who had a grudge against either Fronto or Caesar, or even both of them, it could be ridiculously easy in the face of a threat such as Ariovistus to spread rumour and disaffection among the men.'

Balbus nodded.

'I think that while you two attend to your legions, I'll go back and see Caesar. He needs to be warned about this alarming possibility.'

———————————

Priscus strode into the camp of the Tenth purposefully and with a face like thunder. The camp itself lay on the far side of the river from the town, a few hundred paces from the road and the bridge. At the gate the guards saluted and it soothed the primus pilus a little to notice that order was still being maintained among his legion.

Heading for the praetorium, Priscus noticed one of the centurions from the Fourth Cohort standing leaning on his vine staff and watching two legionaries polishing armour. He marched up to the man and pointed at his command tent. The centurion saluted and, barking one last order at the men, made for the tent. Priscus called one of the legionaries over.

'You. Take your friend and go elsewhere. I don't want anyone in the area of the praetorium for the next half an hour. If I see a soldier here, I shall hold *you* responsible.'

The legionary swallowed nervously.

'Yes sir.'

As he and his companion hurried away from the centre of the camp, Priscus listened carefully. There was a low murmur of conversation from within the command tent. Good; that meant that most of the officers were already there. Wasting no time, the primus pilus threw back the flap of the tent. The murmur faded as daylight fell across the faces of the assembled centurions and optios. Standing at the back in a small knot, separate from the rest of the officers, stood the six tribunes assigned to the Tenth. Of the six, only Tetricus was well turned out and standing easy; the others looked dishevelled and tired. Priscus stepped into the tent and let the flap fall back across the doorway.

'Officers of the Tenth. I could be *proud* of the fact that there are six legions at Vesontio and the Tenth are the only one in fighting readiness; that we have guards, pickets and all duties are being attended to.'

He paused a moment to let that register.

'I could be *worried* that there are rumblings now even in the Tenth; worried that there could be a collapse in order and discipline.'

Another moment for that.

'What I *am*, gentlemen, is disappointed. The Tenth have always been the stalwart. That there is even the *possibility* of a breakdown in discipline in this legion annoys me. I don't blame the legionaries. The men would follow a *good* officer into the jaws of Cerberus himself, but a *bad* officer is worse than *no* officer. The morale problems we have at the moment are not because the Germans are ten feet tall, eat Romans and fart fire!'

A ripple of nervous laughter died as soon as it began. The look on Priscus' face suggested that humour had not been his intention.

'The morale problems we have are because the officers have succumbed to rumour and panic spread by a few illegitimate sons of whores. How are the men *expected* to maintain discipline if the officers are flustered and uncertain?'

He became aware as he scanned the crowd that most of them had their eyes lowered, watching the floor intently, but Tetricus, the tribune they had recently acquired from the Seventh Legion, met his gaze levelly, nodding in agreement with everything he said. He realised that the tribunes theoretically outranked him and that they belonged invariably to the high-born families of Rome that would consider him scum. The Tenth were *his* legion though, and tribunes came and went. He was damned if he would let a pretty boy destroy his men. His eyes still on the tribunes, he continued.

'I *will not* have weak men ruining the Tenth. Order and discipline *will* be maintained, stronger than ever before. I want the guard doubled. All duties doubled. I want training sessions instituted on a daily basis. If you're frightened of the Germans, then I don't want you. Anyone who won't stand next to the men and bare their arse at Ariovistus can piss off right now.'

He looked around the tent again.

'If you stay, it's going to get nasty here. I know some of you here are going to break. I'm not going to let you break right when I need you, though, so get gone.'

No one moved.

'*Now!*'

Priscus stood, breathing heavily, his face red and steaming. A number of centurions and optios shuffled toward the door in an embarrassed silence. Three of the tribunes made for the exit. The primus pilus did not even turn to watch them go. He scanned the men left.

'Anyone else?'

No one moved.

'Good. How many have gone.'

Tetricus, still standing at the back, piped up.

'I counted three tribunes, four centurions and six optios. Not too bad, all things considered.'

Priscus nodded.

'Right. You all need to get back to your units and sort the men out. We'll show the other legions what they should be doing. Two last things, though. Caesar will supply us with our new tribunes, but I want recommendations from all of you for promotions. We'll need to replace those centurions and optios we've just lost, and I need you to find them for me. Secondly, you all need to write a will, and you need to have your men do the same. It's time we got this legion sorted. I don't know where the legate is, but he's still alive and he'll be back. I don't want him to come back and think we've gone soft without him. Dismissed.'

The officers saluted and filed out of the tent, grim, determined expressions on their faces.

As Tetricus approached the door, he stopped.

'Centurion, could you spare me a few moments?'

Priscus nodded. The tribune was polite and appeared to have a surprising amount of sense for a commissioned nobleman. The two men waited for the last of the other officers to leave the tent and then took a seat.

'What can I do for you, tribune?'

Tetricus smiled.

'Nice speech. I daresay Fronto would have approved. Sounded a lot like him, really.'

Priscus sighed.

'I've been around him a long time now. He *is* the best commander we've ever had assigned to us. In fact he's the only commander we've ever had for more than a month or two. Caesar seems to think it's a good thing and I think I agree. He's definitely done the Tenth good.'

Tetricus nodded.

'He's a good man and I'm glad I serve with the Tenth now. I have some thoughts. I don't want to step on your toes when it comes to command, but I thought you might want to hear them?'

Priscus shrugged.

'Always happy to listen.'

'It strikes me that you've got rid of the men who would have caused trouble, but we could do with trying to find out where these damned rumours came from in the first place. It's useful to sort out the Tenth, but if we can staunch the panic at the top, it'll help the other commanders get their legions in line.'

Priscus grinned.

'Bloody good point. Problem is, how do we trace it back now?'

Tetricus gazed out past Priscus' shoulder, through the tent doorway and up at the city of Vesontio.

'I presume you can easily do without me here at the moment?'

Priscus nodded.

'What've you got in mind?'

'I thought I might do some investigation among the other tribunes.'

At the top of the hill, Balbus knocked on Caesar's door and waited politely for an answer. When it came, he pushed the door open and stepped inside. The room was dark, most of the oil lamps having been extinguished. Caesar sat in the darkest corner, his head in his hands.

'Caesar? Are you alright? I can come back later...'

The general looked up at his visitor, squinting in the half-light.

'No, Balbus. It's alright. Just a bad headache. Crassus has been back since the meeting requesting that I put you out to pasture. The arrogance of the man, just because he's the son of the great Crassus. He doesn't like you, or indeed any of the other commanders. I even get the feeling he doesn't like me much, and I had to put him in his place just now. He left very deferentially, but not very happy. I'm going to have trouble with that one.'

Balbus nodded.

'I don't like the man myself. That's not why I'm here though, sir.'

Caesar smiled.

'I realise that. You're not petty enough to come here demanding I get rid of Crassus. What *did* you come for?'

'I was conversing with Priscus of the Tenth, and we've come up with a disturbing thought. He only thought it halfway through, but I've taken it a step further and thought I ought to see you.'

Caesar rubbed his head and sighed.

'You're being needlessly cryptic, Balbus.'

'Alright general, here's what I think: You and your campaign have been endangered by the failure of morale in your army. If things get any worse, you could find that you're facing the entire German army with only a dozen men.'

Caesar nodded.

'I realise the peril, but I won't flee.'

Balbus shook his head, smiling.

'I'm not suggesting you flee, Caesar. The question is, who stands to gain from a collapse in your army here in Gaul?'

A frown.

'Ariovistus. The Gauls in a way, I suppose.'

A thought struck him and he looked up at Balbus sharply.

'My rivals and enemies in Rome!'

'Indeed, sir.'

His headache all but forgotten, Caesar leaned forward.

'Do you really think the conspiracy that Fronto unearthed stretches this far?'

'Far sir? No distance at all. If, as the Gaul said to Fronto, the conspiracy spread through the Roman ranks as well as the Gauls, the conspirators will have come with us. This current situation has come down from the higher ranks, and you realise what that means?'

Caesar nodded again.

'The tribunes. They're all high-born Romans. I've got around fifty tribunes attached to the army, along with other staff officers. How many owe their patronage to me? I wonder if there are clients of my opposition among them. I can't bring myself to suspect any of my more senior officers. They'd have too much to lose.'

Balbus nodded.

'I tend to agree, Caesar. Even Crassus I would think above that. What we need is to watch all the officers who try to get out of here. I'd be pretty sure that any conspirator who tried to leave you high and dry wouldn't stick around to share in the consequences.'

'Hmm. I've already had a number of officers call on me requesting permission to vacate the city. So far I've refused them all. I think I need to speak directly to the centurions of the legions. We'll gather them together and I'll go over the heads of the tribunes and legates. If we can shame the army into fighting, it doesn't matter *what* the officers do. I shan't let any of them flee, but anyone who tries will be noted. Any officer who doesn't feel he can fight in the front line will be assigned temporarily to my staff. They're not getting away that easily.'

Balbus nodded.

'I would suggest that you keep your personal guard close and prepared. Keep an eye on all your officers.'

'I shall, Balbus. I shall. Thank you for bringing this to my attention and I hope we can resolve it. I think you need to get back to the Eighth and have them fall in.'

'Sir.'

Balbus left, wandering out of the building and down the main street. As he passed the corner of the side street with the tavern on, he spotted Tetricus coming the other way.

'Tribune.'

'Sir.'

'Has Priscus finished with the Tenth already?'

Tetricus nodded.

'No nonsense. Cut the deadwood away and promoted a few good men to replace them. I don't think we'll have much of a problem now. If you don't mind me asking sir, what are you planning to do with the Eighth?'

333

Balbus smiled at the tribune.

'I don't really have much choice, do I? I either do the same as Priscus or I watch the Eighth slide into rebellion. I've got to do something before Balventius takes matters into his own hands like your primus pilus did. Priscus dismissed the chaff. Balventius would probably gut them. He's not very subtle.'

Tetricus lowered his voice.

'Could I ask that any tribunes you get rid of be pointed in my direction up on the hill sir?'

'If you like. Why?'

'I'm doing a little investigating to try and find out where these rumours came from.'

Balbus frowned.

'That's good, but be *very* careful. There's something deep and dark afoot here. You'll have been back in Geneva at the time, but there was at least one assassination attempt on Fronto and one insurrection among the cavalry. This goes much deeper than a little rumour mongering. Fronto trusts you, and that's good enough for me, so anything you can find out would be most welcome but don't push anything too much in case it pushes back. As soon as you have anything to go on, call Priscus and myself and we'll all go and see Caesar.'

Tetricus nodded again.

'I'll do that, sir.'

They became slowly aware that someone was running up the street toward them shouting 'Legate Balbus!'

Balbus squinted and saw an optio heading for them. As the man reached the crossroads he pulled himself to attention, exhausted from the climb though he was. Tetricus recognised him as one of the men from the Tenth's command tent earlier.

'Legionary, what's all this row?'

The man straightened and grinned.

'Message from centurion Priscus for you both sir. Riders have just entered the camp carrying news of Fronto and the Second Cohort. They're alive and are on the way here.'

Balbus let out a slow sigh.

'Thank the Gods for that. Best get back to your unit, optio.'

As the man ran off, he turned to Tetricus.

'I'll no doubt see you later, tribune. I'd best get along to the Eighth and talk to them before Caesar does.'

The dell was filled with centurions. Balbus knew, of course, how many centurions a legion actually had, but you never saw them all together. Sixty grizzled veterans from the Eighth stood at ease, watching the tribunal. With the other five legions' centurions, excepting the Tenth's Second Cohort that was still racing the Germans to Vesontio, there would still be nearly three hundred officers here, waiting to hear what the army's commander had to say.

Caesar had initially wanted to organise a private meeting at the citadel or in one of the camps, but Balbus had had to point out that nowhere was the general going to be able to have a 'private' meeting with three hundred centurions. And so here they were, three miles from the city in a clearing with only the centurions, a few senior officers and a small group of Caesar's Praetorians.

Balbus stood on the far left of the temporary tribunal, next to Tetricus and Crispus. More tribunes stood to the other side. Of Crassus or the other commanders there was no sign. Perhaps he had taken Caesar's decision to speak directly to the troops as a personal dig. Balbus hoped so. The thought of it brought a smile to his face.

The centurions of the six legions glittered in the dappled sunlight of the clearing. It would be warm for them, crammed in like this in such hot sun, with the trees around them preventing even the slightest of breezes. Balbus continually wiped his own brow, and *he* was standing high on the podium with room to breathe.

There was, as he had expected, the continual murmur of conversation among the veterans.

A creak on the wooden steps behind Balbus caused him to turn. Caesar, with Sabinus at his shoulder, climbed onto the platform. The general walked to the front rail and held out his arm in an age-old gesture.

In other circumstances, Balbus would expect a roar from the crowd to greet such a gesture. Not now. Caesar leaned on the rail with his left hand and addressed the crowd of centurions.

'The Germans are men. Barbarians, yes. They may be tall and vicious, but they are just men. We've defeated men before. We've even defeated Germans before. Gaius Marius himself fought the Cimbri and the Teutones and brought them to their knees, and his army was less powerful than this one.'

A dramatic pause followed. Caesar turned his head and gave Balbus a knowing half-smile. He probably thought that the silence among the crowd was a good thing: soldiers ashamed, contemplating their own failures. Balbus knew otherwise. He knew the common centurionate. What they were doing was waiting for the general to finish before they made any kind of decision or reaction.

Caesar turned back to the crowd.

'The Helvetii have stood between Rome and the German tribes for a long time. They have fought and defeated the Germans repeatedly for centuries, and we beat the Helvetii. Rome is the master on the battlefield and you must all know this. We have beaten the best, so the Germans hold no fear for me.'

Another pause and another half-smile. Balbus hoped to the Gods that Caesar was not willing to push them too far. The centurionate held far more loyalty to their units than to Caesar right now, and an insurrection by the centurions would be worse by far than anything rumourmongering tribunes could manage.

'Do not panic about being caught like rats. When the time comes for us to fight Ariovistus, we will do it in the field like we were trained to. We have full supplies and a good source for more if we need it. The local Gaulish tribes have all agreed to aid us. We have everything we need. Do not tell me that what we lack is fighting spirit!'

The last line was delivered with a thumping of his fist on the front rail of the tribunal. Again there was silence. This time, as Caesar turned to look at Balbus, his face betrayed the first hint of worry. A voice from deep in the centre of the crowd called out.

'What if we *do* have a good fighting spirit? We can only keep the men in line if there are good examples set from above. Senior officers are trying to leave. How does *that* look to the men? If we *all* stand and march on the Germans with you, can we guarantee that the soldiers will go?'

Caesar leaned forward on the rail.

'Are you suggesting that one of these legions would actually revolt? That's unthinkable! These are the greatest force in the empire. If they lack spirit, we must give them it back. *You* must give them it back, for it's to the centurions that they look, not to tribunes or staff officers. Spirit is what matters. The slaves' revolt ravaged Italy twenty years ago and nearly broke legions in their path. They were *slaves!* How did *slaves* manage such power? Because they had spirit. There is no reason for the troops to fear or cower, or even to have reservations. We will defeat the Germans. Tonight we will ride out to meet Ariovistus. I will break camp and the officers will go with me. We will see how many men cower in their camp then.'

Balbus shook his head gently. Caesar was playing a dangerous game.

The general scanned the crowd for a moment until his eyes fell on Priscus.

'Centurion Priscus. Are the Tenth stood to?'

Priscus moved out of the crowd to the front.

'Aye general, the Tenth is ready.'

He turned to face the crowd.

'Officers of the Tenth to the front!'

In perfect military order, fifty three men stepped out of the crowd and lined up behind Priscus, their backs straight and their vine staves under their arms. Caesar smiled.

'Are your men ready for a fight?'

Priscus grinned.

'The Tenth are *always* ready for a fight, sir!'

'And do you not worry about cowardice or reluctance in your legion, Priscus?'

The grin widened.

'No, general. Got rid of 'em all sir. Won't have cowards in my legion.'

Caesar straightened again and addressed the crowd.

337

'The Tenth have always been stalwart and I have always placed my trust in them. If morale fails among your men, I would go with just the Tenth in place of my Praetorian Cohort, and we would *still* beat the Germans. Can any of you match the Tenth?'

There was a great deal of muttering among the centurions. Again, Balbus wondered whether Caesar had provoked them a little too much. To shame the centurionate was a dangerous move. He became aware of a small knot of centurions moving through the crowd.

Balventius reached the front and turned his one good eye to Priscus. He nodded professionally at him and then stood to attention facing Caesar.

'The Eighth will be ready to move out by nightfall, general.'

Without turning, he called out loudly.

'Officers of the Eighth!'

The half dozen men that had accompanied him through the crowd fell in beside him, and the rest of the Eighth's centurions made their way from the crowd to the front.

Crispus coughed politely behind Caesar, who turned and raised an eyebrow.

'May I, sir?'

Caesar hesitated for a moment and then nodded, stepping aside for the young man. Balbus smiled as the young legate approached the rail. He liked Crispus a great deal.

'Where are the Eleventh? I realise that your soldiers are relatively new to military endeavours but you, their centurions, are all veterans. Can I believe that the legion who defended the flank at Bibracte and saved the army's posterior are unwilling to stand with me now?'

A centurion somewhere at the back began to push his way forward. Once he reached the open space at the front, where the Eighth and Tenth stood, he addressed his commander.

'Legate, I and many others will stand with you as always. I cannot guarantee the men, though. We are a young legion; the officers are drawn from other units and have only worked together for a few months. It is hard to appeal to a unifying spirit in such conditions. We will return to camp and call out the whole legion when we leave here. If you would care to join us, sir, I believe that your presence would help give heart to your men.'

Crispus nodded.

'Very well. I will join you presently.'

As Crispus stepped back, Balbus caught him.

'Well done, lad. He's right about the nature of the Eleventh, but they're rapidly becoming a proper force, and a lot of that's down to you. They'll march out tonight. I think all the legions will apart, maybe, from the Seventh.'

Caesar once more took the rail.

'Go then. Go to your men and prepare them for the off.'

With one last salute, the general turned and climbed back down the steps, followed by Sabinus and the other officers. As they walked back along the forest road, Caesar's Praetorians ahead and behind and along the road verge, Sabinus beckoned to Balbus and Crispus. The two jogged ahead and caught up with the general and Sabinus. The four of them walked in a small knot well ahead of the rest. Caesar turned to Balbus.

'Quintus, I still worry about the men. Perhaps it has gone too deep now?'

Balbus shook his head.

'You heard the Tenth and the Eighth, sir.'

'Yes, but I bluff, Quintus. I couldn't go to face Ariovistus with only the two, no matter how good they are.'

He noticed Crispus.

'Even three. I need them all. Every last son of Rome. What do I do if I can't count on them?'

Balbus shrugged.

'Try. All we can do is try. I don't think the legions will fail you, sir.'

Crispus shook his head.

'Nor I, general. Nonetheless I *do* have a suggestion for you.'

Caesar frowned.

'Go on.'

'Diplomacy. Give the legions the leisure to come to terms with facing the German horde. Let them *behold* the Germans and they will undoubtedly arrive at the conclusion that Ariovistus' forces are merely men after all.'

The general's frown deepened.

'I don't want diplomacy any more. I want that German's head on a pilum standing outside my headquarters.'

Crispus' eyes narrowed.

'You do not desire diplomacy, and yet you do crave a killing mood among your men, yes?'

Caesar nodded in irritation.

'Yes, yes.'

'Then you could use diplomacy to create an incident.'

'What?'

'You could do something to incense Ariovistus. Provoke him into making a move that will inflame the legions. In one fell swoop you would have the homicidal tendency among your men and your excuse for battle.'

Caesar's frown slowly metamorphosed into a smile.

'Balbus, Sabinus? What do you think?'

'It should work, Caesar. The legions hate thinking that barbarians have one up on them. Legions might be with you on the march, but that doesn't mean they'd follow you into battle. If you gave them a reason to hate and resent the Germans, *then* you'd have your army.'

Caesar nodded.

'Very well, I'll have a think on the matter and see if I can come up with anything useful. If any of you have a notion, let me know. For now I intend to head to the citadel and gather everything up. We're moving out tonight.'

Balbus looked around the path, wondering where Tetricus had gone. He finally spotted him way behind the column of Caesar's staff, walking with the front number of centurions. He smiled as he recognised Priscus and Balventius among the number. Bidding good day to the others, he stepped to the side of the track and waited for the centurions to catch up.

Tetricus saw Balbus and nodded to Priscus. The two of them jogged out ahead and met the legate of the Eighth.

'We need to talk, legate.'

Balbus raised his eyebrows.

'Very well, what about?'

Tetricus frowned.

'Let's step aside and let the army pass by. I think we need a little privacy for this.'

The three walked a few paces into the woods and watched as the collective centurionate of six legions walked past. Once they had gone and the only sound was the twittering of birds and the hum of bees, Balbus straightened his back.

'Alright, what's up, tribune?'

'Do you remember a tribune called Salonius from the Ninth?'

'Salonius? No. Should I?'

Tetricus sighed.

'I shouldn't think so. I don't remember him either, but it seems he's been very vocal recently on the subject of Caesar and the Germans. I gather he's also been seen among the other legions at camp. I wanted to get hold of him and ask him a few direct questions, but no one's seen him for two days now. Odd that, isn't it?'

Priscus and Balbus looked at each other and then back at Tetricus.

'Salonius. A tribune from the Ninth. Before we go to Caesar with this, I want to find Longinus. He's going to know a thing or two about this man. I want to be sure and fully armed with details before I accuse a tribune of anything like this. Nice work, Tetricus. Stay with Priscus. Once I've found Longinus I'll come back to you. I don't want to rush into anything.'

Tetricus smiled.

'What should we do in the meantime?'

Balbus grinned back as he walked off through the woods.

'Pack your kit, man. Pack. We're departing at nightfall, remember?'

CHAPTER 17

(AMONG LOW HILLS BETWEEN VESONTIO AND THE RHINE)

'Tabularium: The records office. In Rome the Tabularium is in the Forum, though each fort had its own based in the centre of the camp.'

'Valetudinarium: The military hospital in a camp or fort.'

Caesar leaned forward in his seat and frowned.

'So where is this Salonius now?'

Publius Sulpicius Rufus stood and met the general's gaze with a calm and level look.

'The tribune is one of three that has been missing since before your conference with the centurions, general. I gather a number of tribunes applied for permission to resign their posts and to return to Rome, and I believe Salonius is one of them.'

Caesar gave a low growl.

'I gave no one permission to leave. Everyone who requested it was assigned to my staff.'

Caesar looked at Longinus.

'Is there any chance of us picking those three up somehow?'

Longinus shook his head.

'Only in Rome. Can't see any way to get them in the meantime that doesn't involve the entire cavalry. Do you know who the man actually was?'

Another growl.

'Only that he was recommended by the senate and requested permission to be assigned. I daresay when I get back to Rome and pay a visit to the Tabularium, I'll be able to trace his patron and find out how he got assigned. In the meantime, I think we'll have to work on the assumption that he was the highest this thing went and try and get on with the business of campaigning.'

Rufus nodded.

'It irks me that the man was one of mine.'

Balbus reached out and patted his comrade on the shoulder.

'Not your fault Rufus. Could have been any of us, really. Just lucky to have got rid of him.'

Caesar relaxed a little and opened his mouth to speak as one of the guards outside the tent flap knocked on the frame and entered.

'Caesar, I beg to report the arrival of riders, sir.'

'Riders?'

'Looks like several cavalry alae, sir.'

Caesar's brow creased as he turned to Longinus.

'How many alae have we got out there?'

The cavalry commander shrugged.

'A few scout groups of auxiliary riders, nothing more. Oh, and the ala that was with Fronto.'

Caesar frowned at the guard.

'Any infantry with them?'

'No sir, just looks like several hundred horse.'

Caesar turned back to Longinus.

'Best get out there and see who they are, then.'

The officers in Caesar's command tent made their way out into the late afternoon sun. The grass was light and pleasant and the legions were now resting after having made camp and stored away supplies. The legions' morale seemed to be holding, but the commanders were still aware of rumblings among the men. A number of the senior officers were of the opinion that a good fight would sort out the problem. Caesar, on the other hand, reminded them that a good fight may just have entirely the opposite effect and he was not willing to stake the Roman position in Gaul on a roll of the dice.

Balbus nodded in satisfaction as they passed the billets of the Eighth. Everything was squared away properly and a soldier saluted as the officers passed. As they made their way down the hill toward the turf wall-flanked gateway, Balbus could now see the column of riders coming down the hill opposite. They were indeed all cavalry, though not the lightly-armed and Celtic-attired auxiliaries. These were proper alae of heavy cavalry. Moments later he saw a second, much smaller group of riders around half a mile behind.

As they reached the gate, the camp prefect had called the guard together and a reasonable defensive force now stood at the north rampart in case of any unforeseen trouble.

Balbus watched, poised, ready to spring into action as the cavalry came into close view past some trees.

'It's Fronto.'

He turned to Longinus.

'It's bloody Fronto. And his whole cohort. On horses!'

Longinus grinned.

'Ingenuus is with him. Looks like German riders behind them. Can't be chasing them though. There are only half a dozen of them.'

The Roman column crossed the stream and cantered up the slope to the gate where the officers stood. Every one of the riders was almost grey with dust and travel-worn. Fronto, Ingenuus and Velius rode in the lead and reached the gate at the same time. Ingenuus sprang lightly from his horse and landed with agility, coming straight to attention and saluting the general. Fronto and Velius, on the other hand, brought their leg out of the saddle and over to dismount with a great deal of physical discomfort. The pair slid unceremoniously from the saddle and to the floor. Fronto staggered a little and saluted without any real attention stance. Velius merely collapsed in a heap on the floor, rubbing his posterior and wincing.

Caesar smiled.

'Good to see you again Fronto. No doubt you have adventures to recount to us over wine later.'

He gestured at the various bloodstains on the officer's clothes.

'It'll have to wait for a moment, however, while we deal with these other horsemen.'

Fronto nodded and sank to the floor beside Velius. Ingenuus watched him collapse, shrugged and gave the order for the column to dismount.

'Fall out and find your units to billet with.'

Grinning he sat, crossing his legs, next to the others.

'You'd never make it in the cavalry, Marcus. That was just a nice country ride.'

Fronto growled at him and left it at that. Velius looked across accusingly at the cavalry prefect.

'Both of my buttocks have gone completely numb. And it's a bloody blessing I tell you. Those last few miles I thought somebody was going at my arse with a branding iron!'

The three fell quiet at a gesture from Balbus, as the German riders approached the camp.

Caesar stood resolutely in the gateway.

'Why are you here?'

The six riders reined in before the party of officers, two of them watching with amusement the three men on the floor and the Roman column falling out, many of them stiff and painfully. One of the Germans walked his horse out in front.

'You Caesar?'

The general nodded.

'I am.'

'King Ariovistus say now time for you to talk. You and he talk, yes?'

Caesar squared his shoulders.

'If your King wants to meet with me on equal terms, then I agree. Five days from now, at a place equally distant from both our armies. Honour escorts only, though.'

The German looked confused for a moment, as though he were turning over the words in his head and translating them.

'Yes. Only horses. No legion. Just horse.'

Balbus realised that, as he spoke, the German was looking over the top of them at the array of heavily-armoured infantry lining the walls of the camp. He was surprised to hear Caesar's voice in an affirmative.

'Agreed. Cavalry escort only.'

He turned to Longinus.

'Any appropriate terrain around here your scouts have found?'

346

Longinus smiled. He had been scouting for good battle terrain on the general's orders for a week.

'There's a good plain around ten miles from here, with a small hill. Reminds me very much of that one where you talked to the Helvetii. North east from here.'

Caesar smiled back and then turned to the Germans.

'Did you understand that?'

'Yes. We see hill too. Meet there, five days, only horse.'

The riders wheeled their horses and rode away from the camp, back toward the German army so many miles distant.

Caesar smiled at Fronto. A moment later Longinus broke into a wide grin.

'What?'

Balbus reached down to help Fronto stand.

'I don't think your cavalry days are over, Marcus. I think you're about to become a ceremonial cavalry guard.'

Fronto turned and glared at the general.

'You can't be serious. Longinus has plenty of trained cavalry and we're infantry. Use him.'

Behind him, the officers could hear Velius muttering 'my arse, my arse,' and feeling his rump.

Caesar grinned at Fronto.

'Ah, but I want the Tenth. He doesn't want me to bring infantry, so I presume you've given him good reason for that. If he doesn't want the Tenth there, then I *do*. Longinus: have horses transferred temporarily from the auxilia to the Tenth. I want the whole legion mounted and trained in the next three days to sit a horse like a natural.'

Longinus smiled.

'With pleasure sir. Any particular colour you'd like, Marcus?'

'Bastard.'

'My arse feels like it's been kicked by Jupiter!'

Fronto rounded on Velius.

'Will you *stop* talking about your arse, please?'

Caesar took on a more sober look for a moment.

'Seriously Marcus, I want the Tenth there. You'll have a few days to bathe, relax and recuperate, but I want your entire legion there. To start with, the three of you can join the rest of the command at my headquarters tent for a debrief and then some drinks. Later on, though. Get yourselves cleaned up first.'

Longinus took a lingering look at the two officers of the Tenth and turned to Caesar.

'General, I think it might be a good idea if I and a few of my prefects join the tenth at the conference. Prudent, I'd think, to have a few expert horsemen there.'

Caesar agreed.

'I think it's a good idea. Pick a few good men to join us.'

As the general and most of the officers and men turned and disappeared into the camp, Balbus helped Velius up from the grass, smiling at the colourful collection of words the grizzled centurion knew. The two of them joined Fronto and Ingenuus as they wandered slowly back through the camp gate, Longinus' men having taken care of their horses.

'I take it you've not been here long enough for a bathing area to be set up?'

Balbus smiled.

'No. There's a nice cold stream that you just rode through though. It'll get the dust off you at least. Where on earth did all those bloodstains come from?'

Velius sniggered and moments later Ingenuus joined in.

Fronto growled.

'One or two from a fight, but mostly from prickly undergrowth. I'll tell you all about it later, but suffice it to say I wasn't cut out to be a sneak thief.'

The four of them climbed the hill and Fronto could see the camp of the Tenth. Ingenuus tapped him on the shoulder as politely as he could.

'Have I actually been invited to the general's tent for a drink, sir?'

Fronto smiled.

'Get used to it lad. You've got the makings of a fine officer. You'll be seeing a lot more of us, I expect.'

Ingenuus swallowed.

'What do I do? Do I need to bring anything? How do I act?'

Fronto laughed.

'You don't need to bring anything. Just wash and dress neatly and be polite.'

'And don't make jokes about his nose or his hair' added Velius.

Balbus chuckled.

'Try not to yawn. That's *my* main problem, but then you're a lot younger than me.'

A voice called out from the gates of the camp further up the hill.

'What time d'you call *this*?'

Fronto looked up in surprise to see Priscus standing haughtily on the rampart next to the gate.

'Priscus. Hope you kept the Tenth in good order. I'm afraid we lost a few of them. Not many, but a few.'

The primus pilus smiled at the commander.

'Good to see you sir. You may have lost a few men, but I'd bet you haven't lost as many as we have. I think I'd best bring you up to date on a few little details before you go and see Caesar.'

Balbus and Ingenuus stopped at the gate.

'We'll see you at the headquarters later' the older legate said. 'I'm going to take Ingenuus aside and give him some advice for tonight.'

As Priscus ushered Fronto and Velius into the praetorium of the Tenth and detailed the morale failures, conspiracies and replacement of officers, Balbus took Ingenuus to the camp of the Eighth. Balventius came to attention as his commander approached, but Balbus waved aside the formalities.

'Alright, young man. Don't listen to Priscus, Velius *or* Fronto when it comes to dealing with the high command. Priscus isn't a regular and is unused to this kind of thing anyway. Velius is a rude and outspoken old sod who the command tolerate because he so damned good. Fronto should know how to deal with them, but he has too much of a temper and is far too idealistic. He's definitely in with the command, but he falls out with the staff often.'

Ingenuus nodded and continued to listen.

'Be deferential. Only speak when you're spoken to. If you feel there's something that needs to be said, say it. If you say something profound or useful, it can only improve your standing. If it's not profound or useful, be prepared to be the butt of a few jokes. Caesar's very sharp and so are a number of his senior staff.'

Ingenuus nodded again.

'I'm nervous.'

Balbus smiled.

'Don't be. This is social. In less than a week, we'll be facing the Germans. *That* should make us nervous.'

Even from his position at the front of the Tenth, Fronto could hear Velius at the head of the Second Cohort groaning and shifting uncomfortably in the saddle. He had spent the last few days walking with a curious gait that reminded Fronto of a duck. There had been a number of humorous comments made on the subject and consequently a number of black eyes. The centurion did not take kindly to that kind of joke.

The Tenth had stopped around sixty or seventy paces from the large earth mound on which the two leaders would meet. Straining to observe through the murk and past the small hillock, he could just see the German cavalry roughly the same distance away at the other side of the plain.

Dust blew across the grassy space, kicked up by thousands of horses on both sides. Fronto could barely see Caesar less than ten feet ahead of him. The two leaders had agreed on ten men with which to approach the mound. Caesar had left that with Fronto and so he, Priscus, Velius, Longinus, Ingenuus and Varus, the prefect of the Ninth's cavalry wing, and four of the more impressive riders of the Tenth sat between Caesar and the column, waiting for the order.

'Can you see anything, Fronto?'

Caesar blinked away the dust as he looked over his shoulder at the legate. Fronto shook his head.

'Ingenuus, do that standing in the saddle trick I saw you do and see if you can spot anything above this dust.'

The prefect grinned and hopped up onto his saddle. He put one hand to his brow, shading his eyes and, with the other, pulled his military scarf a little higher over his nose and mouth.

'Looks like a small party of horses moving out front, heading for the hill.'

As he dropped back into the saddle, Caesar gave the order for the honour guard to move forward. The eleven men trotted slowly toward the hill. A lull in the breeze saw the dust die down for a moment and the officers caught a glimpse of the German riders on the other side of the hill. A moment later they trotted up the slope and stopped, facing Ariovistus, who had crested the hill at the same time.

Here on the mound the air was clear and fresh.

Fronto glanced around at the Tenth, gleaming in red and bronze and iron, poised a few hundred feet from them. On the other side, a mass of several thousand German cavalry, dressed individually in the Celtic-style, watched intently and suspiciously.

Caesar initiated the meeting as soon as the horses had stopped moving, giving Ariovistus no time to begin.

'Ariovistus the German. It is not fitting that we should be here at all. You have been labelled both a King and a friend of Rome by our senate. Why now do we find a Roman army facing a German army if you are a friend of Rome?'

The general gave his opposite number no chance to reply, but pressed on with an onslaught of words.

'We have granted you favours in the past, *because* you are a King and a friend of Rome.'

He gestured with a wave of his arm out toward the west in a wide, sweeping gesture.

'But you are not Rome's only friend. The Aedui have been both friend and ally to Rome for a great length of time. We have just fought a long and bloody campaign against the Helvetii, one of your oldest enemies, largely for the benefit of the Aedui. We fight to protect our friends and allies, and we're not frightened to take on a powerful enemy if the general good requires it.'

Fronto had been watching Ariovistus and had expected an inflamed response. He was surprised to realise that the German 'King' just looked bored. Caesar sighed and continued.

'You are our ally. The Aedui are our ally. Many of the Gaulish tribes are either our allies or theirs. Do *not* fight our allies, because for all that you are a friend or Rome, we *will* come to their defence, and the contract between our peoples will be broken.'

Caesar began to gesture in an angry fashion, pointing at Ariovistus.

'Do not fight them! Restore all the hostages you have taken! Go home to your lands in Germany and do not cross the Rhine into Gaul again!'

Ariovistus waited patiently, the slightly bored look still on his face, until Caesar sat back and folded his arms. He then leaned forward over his horse's neck and addressed Caesar.

'I came here... we *all* came here because of the Gauls. They *asked* us. I've been given lands, settlements in Gaul and promised great rewards for my help to the tribes here. You cannot possibly imagine that I will give up those settlements and go home without my rewards?'

He gestured at a gold torc around his neck.

'The loot I *have* was taken legitimately in conquest and is mine by a right that even the Romans cannot deny. The hostages I have were not ripped from their homes by my men. They were *given* to me by their tribes. We have fought these Gaulish tribes, but *they* attacked *us*, not the other way around. We beat them, individually and then together. We defeated the joint tribes of Gaul in one battle and you expect us to quake at *you?*'

He smiled an unsettling smile, for he was missing a number of the more visible teeth.

'Now there is peace. They pay me tribute. If they stop paying me tribute, I will crush them again, but there will be peace as long as *they* allow it. You do not bring peace; you bring war. I do not think that your alliance is for the benefit of the Gaulish tribes, and I think they get nothing from it. They are stupid and weak, though, and will not break your alliance for they fear you too much.'

The German King tapped the hilt of his long sword with his fingertips.

'I am different, Roman. I am *not* afraid. If I begin to think that Rome's friendship is less of a benefit and more of a burden, I will renounce it and may the flames take you. You have *your* Gaul, which lies on the mountains and along the coast to the south. *This* is *my* Gaul. I claimed it before you came anywhere near it. You have never come north from your Gaul before, so I can only assume you mean war regardless of the process.'

He pointed past Caesar at the mounted Tenth Legion and his eyes widened. Fronto had wondered how long it would take him to realise that the Roman troops here were Caesar's veteran legion. Once more he gestured angrily at the general.

'If *I* had come into *your* Gaul, you would attack me. I would *expect* reprisal. Why then do you feel you can walk into *my* Gaul and threaten me without suffering the same?'

The King laughed.

'As for the Aedui, are they so close allies as you claim? If they are, why did they not help you in your recent war with Allobroges? Why did you not aid them against the Sequani in *their* time of need? You care nothing of alliance *or* friendship. You make and break treaties at your whim to your own best advantage. Your army is here to fight *me* and to take my lands off me. Why? Have you not enough lands of your own? If you do not leave *my* lands, I will label you 'enemy' and treat you as such.'

Reaching into his tunic, he pulled out a small purse and threw it to the ground in front of Caesar. Roman coins spilled out onto the ground.

'I have assurances from some of the great men of Rome that I'd have their friendship and their support should the great Caesar die. If you go home, I'll count you friend and give you gifts to take back to Rome, and we'll have peace. If not, I may make a gift of your body to your enemies in Rome. It's *your* choice Caesar. Are you my friend or my enemy?'

Close behind Caesar, Fronto waited for the outburst he had felt building. Balbus leaned over in the saddle and whispered to him.

'Be prepared for this. Caesar's got something up his sleeve. I don't know how or what, but something's about to happen. Keep your eyes and ears open.'

Fronto frowned quizzically at the older legate as the general spoke once more to the German King.

'I will not leave, German. Neither I nor any of my officers would leave a deserving ally in need. *Rome* would not leave them. Your threats will bring you nothing but death. You think to frighten me with tales of my enemies in Rome. Those men of whom you speak would think of you as an animal and would be less inclined to parley with you than I. Beware of them, for they are not as friendly as I. Gaul does not belong to *you*, any more than it belongs to us. Our Provinces in the south and east are longstanding and peaceful, and we are not seeking new lands. Quintus Fabius Maximus subdued the Arverni *and* the Ruteni, but he did not attempt to turn them into a province, nor did he demand tribute. I...'

The general was interrupted mid-flow by the voice of Longinus.

'General!'

The various officers looked around at Longinus, who was pointing down the hill to the plain. Below, a large number of the German cavalry had swept around the side of the mound and were hurling stones at the mounted Tenth. As Fronto watched, a large rock came hurtling uphill, whizzing past his horse's head and missing by only a few finger-widths.

He turned and looked back down at the Tenth. They had formed lines with their shields facing the Germans and were readying their pila. Wheeling his horse, he charged down the hill toward the column.

'No! No one shoot back. This is a conference and a truce. Let them break it, but not us!'

He called out to a nearby centurion.

'Keep the line tight and slowly retreat from the field, keeping the shields to the Germans.'

The centurion nodded and began to relay the order down the line, while Fronto turned to climb the hill again. As he turned he saw the other officers descending at a steady pace. He fell in beside Caesar.

'I've had the Tenth fall out slowly without engaging the enemy, sir.'

Caesar smiled.

'Quick thinking Fronto. Now we are in the right and he's broken a truce. I think that will put the Gods on our side, don't you?'

Fronto nodded.

'It'll put our army in a real bloodthirsty mood, too. Not just the Tenth, but the other legions once they get to hear of it. I can't help but wonder how you arranged this?'

Caesar's irritating knowing smile crossed his face again.

'How I arranged *what*, Marcus? Events just sometimes have a fortunate way of turning out in my favour.'

Harrumph.

As Caesar laughed, Fronto dropped back to where Balbus and Longinus rode side by side.

'Alright. Which of you knows what happened there and is going to explain it to me?'

Balbus shrugged, and Longinus narrowed his eyes.

'What makes you think either of us was involved in this?'

Fronto growled.

'One of you has to have helped Caesar do this. He's devious enough to do it, but it has the hallmarks of a Longinus plot. Bear in mind that it was *my* legion that just got pelted with stones. There may have been fatalities; there were certainly casualties. Unless you want me to go round inflicting those injuries on *your* men to even up the score, tell me what happened.'

Longinus looked at Balbus and then sighed.

'Fine. It was my idea. Caesar wanted something that would incense the army. It really *had* to be the Tenth. I'm afraid that you've made them the most high-profile of all the legions, Marcus. If it's any consolation, Caesar wanted us to use German spears, but I managed to barter him down to rocks. That way we could keep the casualties to a minimum. I know you're angry, but you'll accept it later.'

Fronto cleared his throat in annoyance. It was true that no *real* damage had been done. For all his comments, he could not believe there had been bad casualties and he had not seen anyone left for dead. Longinus had only done what Fronto might have come up with had he been involved. The only thing that annoyed him was that it was the Tenth.

'I need a drink!'

Longinus smiled at him.

'I happen to have a small stock that I brought from Vesontio. It's not fantastic, but it's quite an acceptable taste. Care to join me when we get back?'

Fronto nodded and the first hint of a smile played across his lips.

'So how *did* you get the Germans to throw stones at my men?'

Longinus grinned.

'Auxiliary cavalry, Marcus. I sent them to infiltrate three days ago. They were in among the men when Ariovistus brought them to the meeting. They managed to manoeuvre not only themselves but even some of the real Germans into shouting angrily at the Tenth and then hurling rocks at them. When Ariovistus leaves the field, he won't have a clue who it was who started it, but he will feel like a truce-breaking idiot. *And* he will know that he's given Caesar an excuse to destroy him now. Our auxiliaries will wait until the camp is quiet tonight and then slip back out and return to their units.'

'Oh you *are* a clever little bastard, Longinus. I'm glad you're on *our* side.'

'Are you really? It doesn't seem like so long ago when you said you wished I'd fall down a really big hole!'

Fronto laughed.

'What makes you think I don't wish stuff like that now?'

Balbus coughed.

'When you've finished, I think we need to go and see our legions. News is going to spread like wild fire now, and we want to make sure it channels into controlled aggression aimed at the Germans, and not into stupid outbursts. We don't really want a riot at the moment.'

The others nodded and began to pick up pace.

A short while later, Fronto entered the gate of the camp and made his way to the praetorium. The Tenth rode in behind him, some a little battered and bleeding, but no one seriously hurt. They were the last of the party to arrive. Caesar had made sure that Fronto rode his legion in full view of the rest of the army before they could settle into camp.

Fronto dismounted in front of the valetudinarium, a joint temporary hospital for the use of all six legions and manned by staff from them all. He saw two capsarii lowering a man onto a stretcher just outside.

'Capsarius!'

The nearest turned and looked up. He smiled.

'Legate Fronto.'

Fronto blinked.

'Florus. How's the medical life treating you?'

'Very well sir. I'm now officially a capsarius. No more trench digging for me, sir. What can I do for you?'

Fronto gestured at the dusty troops behind him.

'Just cuts and bruises really. Lot of them though. I'll come and chat while they work if you've got the time.'

Gaius Valerius Procillus sat in a campaign chair and sighed contentedly. He reached his arm to the left and waggled the goblet. With audible grumbles, Velius reached down for the jar of wine and the jug of water and refilled the staff officer's drink. Procillus smiled down into the red liquid and shook his head as if in a daze.

'And what did you do then?'

Fronto grimaced.

'I suppose I just shut up. Velius definitely knew what he was doing and I think I was really in far over my head. If you know Velius, you'll know that if he's right it doesn't do to argue.'

Procillus frowned and glanced sideways at Velius.

'I'd not met him before.' He gestured at Velius. 'You honestly talk like that to a senior officer.'

Fronto smiled as Velius growled gently.

'Only when I deserve it.'

Balbus cleared his throat.

'I used to worry about Velius' attitude but I think now that it's people like him that are the main reason the army works. He's quite reasonable when you get to know him.'

Procillus shrugged.

'I try not to judge anyone on a first impression. That's just stupid. After all, if I did that I'd never have invited Mettius to a drink. Look at him. Looks like he fell off an aqueduct and landed on his face.'

Marcus Mettius grunted.

'At least I'm not effeminate.'

Balbus spluttered over his drink.

'Effeminate?'

Mettius grinned.

'He once got dragged off the street into a house and nearly got a nasty surprise on the Aventine.'

Fronto smiled at the two. He had not met them before, though he had seen them a few times at staff meetings. They seemed to be quite reasonable for high-class Senatorial officers. Fronto leaned forward in his chair.

'So you two are to be Caesar's spies then?'

Procillus put his finger to his chin.

'Spy is an ugly word, Marcus. We're information gatherers, scouts, observers and, at times, diplomats.'

Fronto smiled.

'Perhaps. Caesar seems to think that the two men camped on the other side of the stream are German ambassadors, and I tend to agree. *He* thinks that Ariovistus sent them to apologise and set up a new meeting. I don't think Ariovistus cares enough to apologise. To my mind, the only reason those two haven't crossed the dip and come to see us is because they're worried about whether they'll be murdered by the soldiers as soon as they do.'

Balbus nodded sagely.

'They're right, too. The Eighth are ready to tear the Germans limb from limb. I can only imagine how your boys feel, Marcus. I don't know why Caesar wanted the five of us here, but I think we'll all be summoned any time now to go see them. If I were the general, I'd send them back with no communications, but he doesn't think like that. I think you two are going with them.'

Procillus and Mettius glanced at each other and then at their companions.

'Look. We're going as ambassadors. We can observe and scout while we're there, but we're just ambassadors. I can speak three or four different dialects of Gaulish and German, and Mettius has stayed with Ariovistus years ago when we were first in contact with him.'

Fronto nodded, smiling.

'I thought I hadn't seen the two of you much during the campaign so far. You were pointed out to me yesterday and I didn't even know you. So have you been creeping around among the enemy all this time, or have you just been being nondescript and hiding among the staff waiting until you were needed?'

Procillus' face took on a serious slant for a moment.

'Marcus, be very careful. *I* know you're only joking, but what we do is very serious, very useful and very, *very* above board. We're ambassadors, remember? Nothing more and nothing less.'

Fronto nodded.

'I didn't mean to wind you up. I'm just intrigued. I'd expected Labienus or Brutus or maybe even Sabinus to do it if there were any more talking.'

Mettius opened his mouth to speak, but was interrupted by the general's voice from outside.

'Gentlemen.'

As the five of them filed out of the tent, Caesar, astride his white charger and wearing his scarlet cloak, smiled at them.

'Let's go and make life uncomfortable for Ariovistus.'

The six officers made their way down across the stream and up the other bank to where the two German riders sat patiently waiting. Caesar dismounted and stood among his officers.

'Speak.'

Ariovistus' men shared a private look and then one of them cleared his throat.

'King Ariovistus want new meeting. Want Roman general to come.'

He sat back in his saddle and made a gesture indicating that he had finished. Caesar shook his head, a stern look on his face.

'After the last conference and the German treachery of breaking a truce I am disinclined to meet with him again except on the field of battle.'

The German looked puzzled.

'King want Roman general to come.'

Caesar sighed.

'I am willing to send ambassadors to speak to your King and to make one last attempt to resolve this peacefully.'

Fronto smiled inwardly. There was no hope and indeed no desire to resolve this peacefully. Caesar had always wanted war, and all visible attempts at diplomacy had been just one ruse after another to buy time or to boost morale. He wondered what the general's ulterior motive was *this* time. Something that revolved around his two 'scouts'. Caesar indicated the two with a sweeping gesture of his arm.

'I will send two of my staff. Gaius Valerius Procillus speaks your language, and Marcus Mettius was once a guest of your King beyond the Rhine. They may speak for me. If there is a way to end this peacefully and acceptably, they will achieve it. I need to discuss a few matters here, but they will set off shortly. Please be good enough to go and inform your King of their imminent arrival.'

The Germans nodded and, wheeling their horses, galloped off to the north east. Caesar turned to face the officers.

'We need to give them a little bit of a head start. Mettius? Procillus? You know what you have to do. Fronto, Balbus and Velius, you are going follow them with an honour guard of cavalry. I don't want to provoke an incident yet and I don't want a skirmish, so I'm only sending twenty men with you. See them safely to the German camp and then leave them alone.'

Fronto frowned at Caesar.

'Shouldn't Longinus and his men be doing this?'

The general smiled.

'I've got other tasks for Longinus right now, and the Tenth will make a good honour guard. They were the reason the last conference collapsed, and the Germans have to be aware of that. By all rights they should expect you to go a little mad and kill a few of them. Your presence should discomfit them, and I like that.'

Balbus frowned now.

'Why me, Caesar? I've nothing to do with the Tenth.'

'But you are a level-headed tactical officer and that's an attribute that, for all his ability, Fronto sometimes lacks. Go with Fronto and Velius to the camp of the Tenth and pick twenty cavalry who look glorious and have exemplary records. As soon as you're ready, pick up Procillus and Mettius from the praetorium and get going. Any questions now?'

Fronto and Balbus looked at each other and grumbled, but there was no point in arguing with the general when his mind was made up.

As they wandered off toward the Tenth, Balbus shrugged.

'Pointless.'

Fronto gritted and ground his teeth.

'Not just pointless, but dangerous too. Two senior commanders and a high-ranking centurion just to baby sit ambassadors on the road? It's asking for trouble.'

Balbus shook his head.

'Not trouble. You heard what he said. There's to be no skirmishing or trouble. We're just an honour guard.'

As they crossed the rampart, Fronto shouted to the primus pilus.

'Priscus, get twenty clean and neat men on horseback as soon as you can and send them to the praetorium.'

Priscus raised an eyebrow.

'Just do it.'

A glimpse at the look on Fronto's face brooked no further argument. Priscus nodded and dashed off into the camp.

A short while later, as they stood in the praetorium with Mettius and Procillus, the Tenth Legion cavalry escort arrived, leading their horses. Priscus had done well. Fronto recognised a number of them and knew their courage, but they were also smart, right down to the crests on their helmets.

Fronto, Balbus and Velius hauled themselves up on to their mounts and joined the already seated Procillus and Mettius.

'Let's go.'

The column left at a gentle walk through the north gate of the camp, Velius shouting commands at the men, Fronto muttering and the two ambassadors whistling a catchy and happy tune.

It was early afternoon in a defilé between two ridges when Fronto felt the hairs stand on the back of his neck. He pulled his horse forward to fall in line beside Balbus.

'Quintus?'

'Hmm?' Balbus turned his head lazily, a happy smile gracing his lined face.

'How far do you think we are from the German camp yet?'

Balbus shrugged.

'According to the last reports, it should be about seven miles away I should think.'

Fronto lowered his voice.

'If that's the case, their pickets are a long way out aren't they?'

As Balbus raised an eyebrow, Fronto leaned slightly closer.

'I've seen men moving in a dozen places while we've been speaking. I have a bad feeling about this.'

Balbus glanced ahead to where Procillus and Mettius rode side by side chatting, and whispered back.

'We need to pull the ambassadors back then, into the protection of the cavalry.'

Fronto nodded.

'Damn that Caesar. We're not allowed to fight them. I'll move slowly and casually ahead and get the others back with us.'

Balbus nodded and slowed his pace slightly, allowing Velius and the guard to catch up with him.

'Velius? There's men around us.'

Velius nodded with the slightest movement.

'I've been watching them for a while. There's got to be at least a hundred of them. Germans. What do we do, sir?'

'Fronto's gone ahead to get the ambassadors. I think you need to pull the column into a four-by-five formation. Two lines is too flimsy if we're attacked. Once they're back, we'll get them in the middle of the column and move on. If we meet too much resistance, we'll turn round.'

A shout from ahead caught their attention, and they glanced up to see Fronto and the two ambassadors unhorsed. Balbus turned and cried to the troops.

'To arms, four columns and...'

His sentence uncompleted, the legate was hurled from his horse as it reared. Men on either side of the defile had hauled on ropes, and the lines had tightened and rose, sometimes under the horses' bellies, sometimes across their chests. As Balbus rolled painfully and came up to his feet, he realised that the whole column was in turmoil, horses rearing and wheeling, some riders unhorsed, others clinging on for dear life. He looked around quickly until he saw Velius, also climbing to his feet.

'Centurion! Help me cut these ropes.'

Velius staggered round for a moment, dazed, before drawing his blade and laying into the ropes that had halted the column. Near him, Balbus sawed at ropes. Gradually the cavalry untangled themselves and remounted. Fortunately, the Germans seemed to be interested only in stopping the unit, and not a single warrior entered the defile.

Balbus reared up suddenly and turned to look ahead. There was no sign of Mettius or Procillus, and the figure of Fronto lay in a heap in the middle of the path. Balbus started to run. Moments later Velius overtook him and the thundering of hooves announced the cavalry.

Balbus was still second to reach Fronto, though Velius was already crouched over him.

'He's alive, but there's a lot of blood.'

One of the cavalry dismounted and rushed over.

'He's quite stable, but we need to get him back as soon as possible. He's had a nasty gash to his leg, probably tipped him out of his saddle and there's a fairly nasty wound on his skull from where he landed.'

Balbus squinted at the man in the bright sunlight.

'You're a capsarius?'

'Yes sir.'

'Take my horse. Get him back to the camp immediately.'

He turned to face the centurion.

'Velius, you go with him. Get him back and tended. The rest of us are going to check around and see if we can find out what happened.'

Velius nodded and, helping the capsarius manhandle Fronto onto the legate's horse, he turned to face Balbus as he began to mount.

'Be *very* careful sir. This was organised well in advance, and I wouldn't be at all surprised if they hadn't moved their camp closer to us. You could wander into it without even realising in these hills.'

Balbus smiled.

'I know what I'm doing, Velius. I'm no green recruit. Just take care of Fronto.'

He turned and walked off down the defile, followed by the cavalry leading their horses, as Velius and the capsarius led Fronto back toward the legions.

CHAPTER 18

(IN CAMP BETWEEN VESONTIO AND THE RHINE)

'Fossa: Defensive ditches, such as those constructed round a Roman camp or fort.'

Fronto reached gingerly to the back of his head and prodded the wound. Shining shards of glass exploded in his brain, and he almost blacked out. Leaning forward with his hands on his knees, he vomited copiously on the tent floor before Florus could get to him with the bowl. The young capsarius had insisted on dealing with the legate personally.

'With all due respect, sir, if you keep prodding it, you're going to pull your brain out soon!'

Velius frowned at the young man.

'What is it with you medical types? You were a nice quiet lad when you were a legionary. Now you're a capsarius, you'd talk down to a bloody God!'

Florus turned to the centurion.

'Why are you here again, sir?'

Velius harrumphed but fell quiet. One of the senior medici had already ejected him from the tent twice. The sound of voices outside came to his attention and moments later the tent flap was hauled back and Balbus, Caesar and Longinus entered.

'Fronto, you look terrible.'

Velius grinned.

'He just tried to stir his brain with his finger, sir.'

Longinus smiled.

'I brought you some wine, but I think I should keep it for a day or two until you're a bit better.'

Caesar looked down at the capsarius as he finished cleaning up and rose.

'How is he? Is he going to be fit for active duty soon or is he out of action now until next season?'

Florus looked up at Caesar. Gone was his wide-eyed deferential shyness. This Florus was far removed from the young man on the hill before the battle with the Helvetii. Months of dealing with horrifying wounds, up to his elbows in blood and guts had hardened him. He regarded Caesar with a very professional look.

'It appears worse than it is sir. In a couple of days he'll think he's invincible again. The actual physical damage is remarkably light. He'll have a slight limp with the wound on his leg, but it should barely slow him down. The blow to the head created a hairline fracture, but doesn't appear to have done too much. The bone's thicker there for some reason, and it seems to have helped protect him.'

Velius grimaced. He remembered the day Fronto had found the body of Cominius and the blow he had received when he slipped on the blood. He looked up as Florus was still talking.

'Now he's mostly suffering from a concussion. It'll be at least a day before he starts making real sense.'

Longinus laughed.

'My dear medicus, you don't know Fronto. It'll be a miracle if he does make sense; he's never done it before!'

Caesar smiled down at the wounded legate, who was gazing in a confused way at his own knees. He had started to drool a little.

'Well I was thinking I'd best update Fronto with what we know, but I'd obviously better leave that until later.'

Velius stood and approached Caesar.

'Sir, with Fronto out of it, the primus pilus will be in control of the Tenth again, and I'd best report anything to him.'

Balbus nodded his agreement.

'Best keep Priscus informed, general.'

Caesar sighed wearily.

'Balbus found the camp not a quarter hour from the ambush site. They were nine miles from here then. Subsequent scouts have recorded it as little more than five miles away now. If you look hard, you can see the smoke from their fires. They're at the foot of a hill and I cannot fathom the man's intentions. If he were going to attack, he could have been on us long before now. They must be playing for time, waiting for reinforcements or some such. Anyhow, it seems that Mettius and Procillus were alive yesterday at least. They were spotted chained up near the camp's centre.'

Velius interrupted the general in full flow.

'Permission to put together a rescue party?'

Caesar frowned at him.

'Interrupting me is a good way to find yourself in trouble, centurion. No, you may not have permission. I'm not wasting valuable men on a foolhardy mission into the middle of the German army. I realise that it was your escort duty and you probably dislike having lost them to the enemy, but the field of battle is the place for retribution. The two of them know that and they won't expect a rescue attempt.'

Fronto looked up at the general, his eyes swimming.

'M'alright. Rescue.'

Longinus crouched down by the legate and whispered to him.

'Can I have all your money?'

Fronto nodded and smiled.

'Money for Longinus.'

Balbus grinned and gripped Longinus' shoulder.

'Gaius, it's not nice to mock the afflicted. Come on, let's go and make the most of your wine. You don't mind if we drink the wine for you, do you Fronto?'

Fronto smiled happily at Balbus, his head wobbling a little.

'I'll take that as a no.'

He turned to Caesar, Velius and Florus.

'Who'd like to join us?'

Caesar shook his head.

'I'm afraid I have far too much to do, but thank you for the offer, gentlemen. I need you to stay relatively compos mentis, however. Depending on what Ariovistus does in the next few hours, we need to be ready. I assume both your commands are standing to, along with the other legions?'

Balbus nodded.

'The entire army's on a war footing sir. We can be ready to move into battle at a quarter of an hour's notice.'

'Good. I want a meeting in my headquarters at dusk, regardless. You had best find Priscus and tell him. I'll send word to the other legates.'

Balbus turned to Florus and Velius.

'You two coming?'

Florus looked up and shook his head.

'Love to sir, but I'm not leaving the legate at the moment. Perhaps later when he falls asleep.'

Velius' face split with a wide grin.

'Why not? I think I have some wine myself somewhere. Where are we going?'

Balbus and Longinus looked at each other and Balbus turned back to him.

'Longinus and you are supplying the wine, so I'll supply the tent. My quarters in a quarter of an hour. Just give me time to put away the maps and the kit and requisition some more chairs from the quartermaster.'

As Balbus jogged off at a speed that impressed the others, considering the legate's advanced years, Longinus turned and grinned at Velius.

'Well I've got nothing to do for quarter of an hour. Shall we go back in and torment Marcus for a while?'

'Tempting, but I've got to go via our billets and warn the primus pilus about Caesar's meeting later. He never said whether he wanted *me* at the meeting. D'you think he does?'

Longinus smiled.

'No idea. I suggest you go anyway and then if he doesn't want you, you can always leave again. Better to be present when unexpected that absent when expected, yes?'

'Aye.'

The two of them crossed into the area of the camp set aside for the Tenth, and a number of the men saluted and greeted the two as they made their way to the praetorium. Priscus stood on a patch of bare earth with three of the Tenth's centurions and optios. As the men watched, the primus pilus drew a tactical plan of battle lines in the dirt and motioned where the individual cohorts and centuries would move with his vine staff. The two officers could not hear what he was saying as they approached, but he lashed out with the staff and caught one of the men a ringing blow below the ear before pointing back to the earth. Longinus raised an eyebrow and looked at Velius.

'That's Arius, our most junior optio. I don't think Priscus likes him much; thinks he's thick. He might just be right.'

Longinus frowned.

'He's *going* to be thick if he keeps getting clouted round the ears. I might have to have a quiet word with your primus pilus sometime soon. Or maybe with Fronto.'

Velius shook his head.

'I wouldn't worry over much about it, sir. Priscus knows what he's doing. Young optios get hit on occasions. It's part of the training and promotion process. When I started out in the Tenth the primus pilus was an evil old bastard who treated me like something he trod in. In fact, he did tread in me occasionally. Tremendous old sod, though. It breeds tough men.'

Longinus smiled at the grizzled centurion. It occurred to him that everyone who met Velius seemed to complain about him vehemently for a while and then began to appreciate the man. If he'd had that kind of officer in the Ninth, he might have been tempted to make a go of his legionary command. Still, he was happy with command of the horse. He reined himself in from his wandering thoughts as the two of them reached the primus pilus.

Priscus turned and saluted at Longinus.

'Morning sir. Touring the camp?'

'Just dropping by with a message, Priscus. Caesar's called a meeting at dusk and you're going to have to attend.'

Priscus frowned and shifted to Velius.

'Why, how's the legate?'

Velius grinned.

'Confused. And very prone to suggestion. If you want anything at the moment, I'd go and get him to sign it over. He'd probably sign away his year's pay if you asked him.'

369

Priscus laughed.

'I could do with a few things. Might go and see him in a bit. Still, I guess that means that I'm in sole command for now. Seems to be happening quite a lot at the moment. Where are you two off to then?'

Longinus waved the jug of wine.

'Going to Balbus' tent to test the quality of this. Coming?'

Priscus wavered for a moment, then shook his head.

'Can't really, sir. Too much to do without Fronto here.'

Velius winced.

'Need me here?'

'No, I'll manage. Just don't get plastered. I'll certainly need you later.'

Velius nodded as they turned and made their way toward the area allocated to the Eighth. Balbus' tent would be in the praetorium. As they approached the periphery, the guards assigned to patrol the edge moved forward to challenge them. The pila were levelled and then one of them said something to the other, and they were lifted again.

'Pass, friends.'

Longinus cocked an eyebrow at Velius.

'What do you suppose that was about?'

The centurion grinned.

'I've noticed that a lot of the Eighth's officers avoid eye contact with me. I think I might have frightened them a little when we defended the wall at Geneva.'

A voice behind them pulled them up short.

'Longinus!'

They turned to see Crassus marching at high speed toward the Eighth's camp. As he approached the perimeter, the guards stepped forward and levelled their weapons.

'Halt! Who goes there?'

'Get out of my way you idiots unless you want to be beaten to death.'

The two men dithered for a moment and, Longinus noticed, both looked at Velius who gave a barely perceptible nod.

'Pass, friend.'

The pila were put back up.

Crassus walked straight up to Longinus, apparently ignoring Velius altogether.

'Longinus, I want to talk about the cavalry.'

Longinus glanced sidelong at Velius and then sighed.

'What about the cavalry.'

'I've been thinking about it and I think you need to reorganise.'

'What?'

Crassus grounded his staff and leaned forward on it, emphasising his words with a waving finger.

'You're going to be up against around six thousand cavalry when we meet the Germans. I know they're only barbarians, but that's far more than we've ever fought in one group.'

Longinus growled.

'I'm aware of the odds, Crassus.'

'Are you also aware of the danger of having your auxiliary cavalry so separate from the regulars?'

'Crassus, I'm tired and I'm bored and you're annoying me. Get to the point.'

Crassus' face was slowly gaining in colour.

'Nearly all of your auxiliary alae are controlled by Gauls. They've got more in common with the Germans than with us. What makes you think they won't just turn round and join Ariovistus? You should split your regulars among the auxilia to keep them in line. Use your prefects and decurions to lead them.'

Longinus sighed again.

'Crassus, the auxilia fight much better under their own leaders than under ours. They feel more loyalty and the Gauls understand their troops' fighting techniques better. *And* they hate the Germans probably more than we do. You may be a big man in Rome, and you may even be a competent legionary commander, but you're not a horseman, and you don't understand the cavalry. Kindly stop sticking your nose in where it's not wanted and go put it back up the general's backside, where you habitually keep it.'

As Crassus' mouth opened and closed, trying to find words through his rage, Longinus turned his back on the man and walked off. Velius trotted to catch up and, once they were out of earshot, turned to Longinus, grinning.

'I'm fair impressed. It's not often a man comes out with a more outrageous line than me, but I like that. Don't you think he's a dangerous man to cross, though?'

Longinus shook his head.

'The man's an arsehole and he wants my job, you mark my words. I'll talk to Caesar later. I'm not having that man running any of my cavalry. Let's go find Balbus. I *really* need that drink now.'

The morning dawned bright and pale, a heavy dew still resting on the grass and the leather tents. The legions were now on permanent standby. Five days ago, Ariovistus had marched his army in a wide arc past the Roman camp and settled on the other side, effectively blocking the supply route to the Sequani and the Aedui. For the last five days, Caesar had brought the entire army out in force onto the field between the two camps. The men were marshalled and ready for battle; even eager. The last four days the army had waited, taunting the Germans, trying everything they could to draw Ariovistus out of his camp and onto a field of battle, but the German leader had not yet moved from his camp.

At the rear of the lines of men, Fronto sat on horseback next to Caesar and Longinus. His head was sore, but he was in full command of his faculties again.

'Can we not just go in and take him in the camp sir?'

Caesar shook his head.

'We can't take them effectively in their own camp, and I won't risk the casualties we'd receive doing it that way. We need to draw them into the field.'

Fronto sighed.

'They won't *be* drawn. We've done this for days. I reckon we've got maybe a week left before the supply situation becomes dangerous, then we'll *have* to take them in their camp. Supply wagons aren't even *trying* to get to us now.'

Longinus tapped his temple and smiled. Leaning forward in his saddle, he gestured to Fronto and Caesar.

'I think I might be able to draw the cavalry out. They're not coming out as long as the legions are here. We've established several times now to what lengths Ariovistus is willing to go to avoid an engagement with the legions. If you pull the legions back to camp I might be able to get the German cavalry to commit.'

Caesar looked unsure.

'There are supposedly six thousand of them, and they'll almost certainly bring some infantry support out with them. How many horse have *we* got?'

'Some nine or ten thousand at the moment. To be honest, I haven't had a chance to take an accurate census since we left Bibracte. Extra units were still drifting in from various tribes when we left Vesontio.'

A frown.

'Do you think it's wise, Longinus? You outnumber them, but not if they bring out enough support. Are you willing to take the risk? I don't want to find myself in a few days fighting the entire German army with no cavalry support.'

Longinus smiled.

'Fronto?'

'Mm?'

'How long d'you think it would take to get two legions out of the camp and to our current position?'

'If we were prepared, quarter of an hour at the most.'

'Right. If we need any kind of cover, we'll sound the retreat and start to pull back toward the camp. You can come out from behind us and give us the support we need to escape the field, yes?'

Fronto nodded.

'Fine by me. Balbus and I'll have our men on standby. One sound from that horn and we'll be out to protect you.'

Longinus looked at Caesar and shrugged.

'Well sir?'

'I still don't like it, but if you think it will gain us in any way, do as you see fit.'

Longinus grinned and rode off to the cavalry, massed at one end of the Roman lines. Fronto nodded at Caesar and then approached the staff cornicen.

'Sound the recall. Get everyone back to camp.'

As the cornicen began to play, Fronto rode along the lines looking for Priscus and Balbus. Spotting them relatively close together, where the Tenth stood alongside the Eighth in the line, he called out to them.

Fronto explained the contingency plan to the others as the legions backed in perfect unison from the field. Longinus, however, reached the cavalry as they were starting to pull back. Looking around, he spotted Varus and Ingenuus and waved them over.

'Right, lads. We've got permission to draw the bastards out and give them a beating. The legions are heading back to camp, but the Eight and the Tenth will be on standby to help if we need them. I need you to relay all the orders to the native contingents and to the regular officers. We're going to split into three wings. Varus, you take the right. Ingenuus: the left. I'll lead the central unit. We should have around six alae each, and probably more auxilia besides.'

Varus, the prefect of the Ninth and a longstanding companion of Longinus, sat up straight in his saddle.

'What's the plan sir?'

'We're going to move to just outside missile range of the German camp. When we're in position, each of you is going to make one major sweep into range with all of your troops carrying spare spears. A volley at the defenders will hopefully incense them enough that they'll come out and attack. Make the sweep quick, though, and then pull back to the line. I want minimal losses.'

Ingenuus nodded and gestured to the commander.

'And what will the central section be doing sir?'

'I'll be dividing my unit into two and doing the same as you, but in both directions at once.'

Varus smiled. It was a little disconcerting, due to the unfortunate scar that gave him a lopsided mouth and a slight hare lip.

'We've got a lot of people among the auxilia that will speak their language, sir. Maybe we should get them to egg the Germans on; insult them and so forth?'

'Good, yes. Pass the word around the auxilia. Caesar's worried that we'll all vanish under the weight of Germans. Let's show him just what cavalry can do, eh?'

Varus looked up again.

'One last thing sir, just for clarity. Formation? Are we going to do the bull horns? Closing the door from either side? A feigned withdrawal?'

Longinus smiled.

'We'll be starting in bull horn formation. We'll stay like that as long as it's advantageous, then feign a withdrawal and hopefully draw them in so that you two can come round and finish them.'

The three men grinned at each other.

'Let's go irritate some Germans.'

Within moments the field was clear of foot troops, and the cavalry had separated into three wings. The thousands of horses trotted gently and slowly across the field as the German camp came gradually into full sight. Caesar had been right. Marching on the camp would have been extremely costly in men. For all its lack of adequate defences, the camp was huge and very well-defended, positioned perfectly to allow little chance of breaking an easy way in.

The enemy cavalry were not immediately obvious, with individual pockets of warriors defending the woven stockade and the cavalry further back and out of sight.

Longinus watched as a few missiles started to hurtle through the air, falling short of the Roman force. Nice of the Germans to help him judge a safe distance. He rode forward a little longer and held up his hand. The wing came to a stop, falling into prefect lines. Behind him, two alae of regular cavalry sat between slightly larger numbers of auxiliaries. The wings under Ingenuus and Varus pulled slightly further forward, though at an oblique angle and still very much out of the range of German missiles. Both the outer wings ran with only one regular ala and large numbers of auxilia. Along the lines of men, Longinus could just see the other two commanders. Each held up an arm, indicating they were in position and awaiting the order. Longinus watched the missiles continue to fall short and smiled. No rush. Might as well let them use as much ammunition as possible.

It took a while for the more important German warriors to stop their lessers wasting ammunition. Finally it stopped altogether and a mass of cries and jeers rose from the camp. Longinus made a gesture with his hand and the Gaulish auxiliaries let go with a mass of jeering of their own. The noise for a few moments was deafening and, somewhere near the height of the racket, Longinus made another tugging gesture with his raised arm and the cavalry swept forward on all sides.

To either side of the commander, one veteran ala and well over a thousand Gauls charged obliquely forward, sweeping off to the flank, parallel with the fort front.

Though only a half of the cavalry at best had a spare weapon for a missile, each one was hurled or fired into the camp and the collective screams of hundreds of Germans reached the ears of the Romans even above the thundering of hooves.

Longinus wheeled the two units and brought them back out of range of the enemy missiles just as the irate defenders began to launch their ammunition impotently across the turf. Once they were back in position, he glanced to either side and was satisfied to see that his two lieutenants had performed their manoeuvres admirably. Precious few Roman bodies filled the intervening space, though the German defenders shouted defiance from among hundreds of dead and wounded. Longinus began to consider returning to his own camp for more missile weapons. The effect had been very impressive, but the chances of them pulling off the same manoeuvre twice with such success were too small to contemplate.

He was just considering how his cavalry could further aggravate the Germans when noises from either side of the camp announced the release of the enemy horse.

The Germans came bolting through set positions in their defences to either side. Thousands of them hurtled out in an unruly mass. Longinus smiled. Disorganised cavalry were as much a danger to their comrades as to the enemy. With two more signals, he gave the order to fall back and the entire Roman line turned and rode several hundred paces across the field before falling back into line facing the Germans.

Longinus was impressed, though a little disconcerted, to find that the cavalry had not charged en masse after the Roman line, but had formed up in front of the fort. Since they were still well spaced and unruly, he wondered what they were waiting for until he saw individual warriors who had climbed over the barricades falling into position beside the horses. The men were varied in height, colour and dress, but were uniformly well built and impressive. The commander guessed that these men were specifically attached to the cavalry, and he was intrigued as to what the cavalry could gain from such a hampering addition.

Slowly, once they were in position, the Germans started to move forward. They moved purposefully, not in a charge, but at a steady pace that suited both horses and footmen. Longinus gave the orders with gestures and the left and right wings under their prefects began to drift a little further away from the central body.

Longinus watched intently as the Germans made for the centre, devoid of tactical inspiration. This, of course, was why the Roman cavalry was so much more effective. Rather than acting on individual whim, they worked on the organised manoeuvres set by tactical officers. Admittedly most of the auxiliary cavalry broke down into their own fighting styles as soon as the initial moves were made, but by that time the strategy would have paid off and the Romans would have devolved to following the commands of their decurions in small units.

The Germans moved in resolutely, shouting curses in their guttural language. Once Longinus judged the position correct, he held up his arm and the two wings came around into the sides of the German mass.

Under normal circumstances, a manoeuvre such as this would confuse and dishearten the foe, and the bulk of the surviving enemies would turn and bolt through the remaining space. Perhaps Longinus had underestimated the Germans. With a footman attached to each cavalryman, the horses made a lunge at the Roman line and then pulled back next to their guardian footmen. When the Roman cavalry came to return the favour, they were faced with two opponents.

Longinus thought quickly. The initial volley had done a lot of damage, but here and now, with the current tactics of the Germans, there could be a massacre. He was interrupted from his train of thought as a German lashed out at him with a spear. The man was too far away for a truly effective attack, but the tip of the spear dragged across Bucephalus' shoulder. The black Galician reared and Longinus held on tight to remain in the saddle. He glanced down as he calmed to horse and saw the fresh blood flowing from the horse.

'Bastard. Come here!'

He set Bucephalus into a run and reached his long cavalry sword up and out behind him. He had, as he often did, elected not to take a shield into battle, and his other hand reached down into the pouch at his side. As he neared the German, the spear was levelled at his chest. The footman stepped forward and swung back his heavy Celtic blade. At the last moment, He pulled his fist from the bag and flung a handful of pebbles at the enemy rider. The spear wavered as the man rolled back in his saddle, stunned for a moment. A moment was all Longinus needed. The footman was unprepared, believing his opponent was reaching for the rider. Longinus' sword swept down and the German's head leapt from his shoulders and disappeared in the mass of men and horses. As the momentum of the huge swing carried the blade round, he swung the tip up and, still slick with the blood of the footman, it scythed into the back of the rider. His arms flew up, the spear discarded, and flopped backwards into the saddle.

Pausing only to reach down and pat Bucephalus on the shoulder near the wound, he pulled himself together and surveyed the field.

He shouted at the top of his voice, which was becoming hoarse and scratchy trying to reach over the din of battle.

'Sound the fall back.'

Somewhere near the back of the unit, the man sitting with a straight horn blasted out several notes and the Roman column pulled back. The Germans seemed uncertain for a moment and dithered as Longinus wheeled his men and rode off in the direction of his camp. As he went, he shouted orders to the prefects and decurions. Each turma of men separated and made off in its own direction. Jeering, the Germans followed the small groups, splitting off into similar sized units themselves.

At a further blast from the horn, the fleeing turmae led by Varus turned and engaged the Germans who, surprised, suddenly realised that they had outpaced their footmen. As he ordered the men into the fray, he surveyed the field and was satisfied to see that the manoeuvre had generally paid off, with few groups hard pressed. He joined the men, swinging with his cavalry sword and watching the spray of German blood arc through the air like a fountain. A moment later, the couple of dozen footmen attached to the cavalry arrived to discover that only three or four riders still sat their horses.

Varus grinned and shouted to his men.

'Sound the retreat. Time to head back.'

Across the field turmae were sounding the retreat and men were wheeling and heading for the camp before the footmen could get close enough to engage. Here and there a unit failed to pull back in time and met with a gruesome end at the ends of spears and swords but, on the whole, the Roman forces pulled out with little trouble and rode back across the turf. The more brave or foolhardy of the Germans chased the Roman units across the field but pulled up short when they saw the cavalry units passing through the widely spaced ranks of the Eighth and Tenth Legions. As soon as the horses were through, the wall closed and thousands of men began to bang the hilts of their swords on the rim of their shields.

Longinus reined in beside Fronto and Balbus.

'Well that was fun!'

Fronto took a look along the line.

'You came back a bit of a shambles. How'd it go?'

Longinus grinned.

'A bit hairy at times, but I think we got at least two kills for every one of theirs! Now let's get back into camp and I can tell the general how it all went before we go back to your tent and celebrate with that nice little hoard of wine I *know* you keep behind the chest!'

Velius was grumbling as usual.

'Why the hell we have to do this is totally beyond me.'

Priscus rolled his eyes skywards at Fronto and then turned to the training centurion.

'*Because* it's important that we get more grain, so we need to control the route for supplies.'

Velius looked around at the column, dropping their kit and separating out into the appropriate units.

'But it's *stupid!* We build a camp, so the German builds a camp between us and the supplies. Then we come round them at a hell of a distance and build another bloody camp between them and the grain. What's to stop them moving the next morning and building a new camp and doing it all over again?'

Fronto sighed and reached over in front of Priscus to gesture at the older man.

'*Listen!* We're building a new camp. The position's perfect. They *can't* get round this one to cut us off again. Once we're in there we'll have two camps, one on either side of them. There's no discussion; no argument and no chance of changes, so stop moaning about it or I'll have someone bury you up to the neck while the fossa's dug.'

The Seventh and Eighth Legions had been left at the large camp, along with half the cavalry under Varus. The rest of the army had left while it was still dark, and by dawn they had already skirted the German camp and were beyond it. The Germans became aware of the Roman column only when they had no hope of preventing them passing. By the time the alarm had gone up and the few skirmishers had come out, the legions had reached their new position less than a mile beyond the German camp. Now the engineers were unpacking their gear ready to build the new fortifications.

The few German skirmishers had made a feeble attempt to stop the Roman line forming, but they had been caught enough by surprise that the legions were forming before more than a score of Germans could muster. Fronto knew that a more concerted attack would be coming, but not yet. Ariovistus would have to try and stop them building a camp here, and so the four legions were deploying in Caesar's favoured formation. The first four cohorts of each legion would create a front line against German attack. They would be supported by a second line of three cohorts from each legion, slightly wider spread. The third line would carry out the construction of the new camp under the watchful eye of the senior engineers.

And so it stood now. The cohorts were deploying in formation, while the engineers marked out the dimensions of the new camp, smaller than the original, due to the terrain and the planned occupants.

Longinus' cavalry were set in two wings, one at each end of the line, with the commander himself on the left and prefect Ingenuus leading the right.

Fronto, his head still tender and his shoulder and leg sore, sat between the two lines of defence astride his horse. From here he could clearly see the half mile to the German defences. The few skirmishers were still visible, but staying well out of the way of the auxiliary slingers and archers that graced the Roman defensive line. He could see a force building up at the wall of the German camp like a wave behind a dam.

'Steady lads. Close up the formation. Any moment now there's going to be a flood of the bastards pour across that grass and into us. We've got to hold 'em off until the engineers are finished.'

One of the optios near the back of the first line looked around and up at Fronto. The legate recognised the junior optio from somewhere.

'How long d'you think it's going to be, sir?'

'We'll be here a couple of hours and the bastards will keep coming at us until we're done.'

'What happens then, sir?'

'Us and the Eleventh get to settle into the camp and dig our heels in. We'll have some of the auxilia with us and half the cavalry will be staying. The rest head back to the big camp. We're going to guard the supply line.'

From somewhere near the front, Priscus' voice sounded across the troops.

'Arius, do you never stop asking bloody questions? Concentrate on the job at hand.'

Arius jumped at the primus pilus' voice and jerked straight as a rod. Fronto smiled.

'Relax lad. Just do your job.'

A voice from off to one side of the line called out.

'They're coming!'

Fronto put his hand to his brow, shading his eyes from the early morning sunlight. Sure enough, the wicker walls had opened and men, both running and riding, came pouring through, though it would take them long moments to cross the field and engage. Fronto turned to look over the second line and saw Tetricus giving out instructions to a number of engineers.

'Tetricus! Make the front bank wide enough to support artillery!'

Tetricus shouted back over the mass.

'Already on it, sir.'

'And get the front bank built first.'

Tetricus grinned.

'Already *on* it, sir. And before you ask, the ballistae are here and ready to be put in position as soon as the bank's up.'

Fronto grinned back at him.

'I'll just let you do your job, shall I?'

He turned back to watch the advancing Germans. He would have very much liked artillery support from the start, but in less than an hour they would be in position and ready anyway.

'Centurions! The first volley of pila at thirty paces. Second at twenty.'

The front ranks of men drew back their arms, preparing the pila for attack. As the Germans pulled closer and closer, Fronto was surprised to find that Ariovistus had been very careful and reserved with the force he committed. Plenty of horses, so probably all his cavalry, but only enough foot to make it even with the Roman defence. They were light skirmishing troops too so, as long as the shield wall held, they should be able to keep the enemy at bay for hours.

Arius, the young optio in front of Fronto, craned his neck and addressed his commander again.

'Sir? Why aren't the cavalry coming forward to engage the enemy horse?'

Fronto smiled.

'The cavalry are here to provide support. They had a hard fight yesterday while *we* supported *them*.'

'So we're facing the cavalry on foot?'

'Don't worry lad. Just listen out for your centurion's orders.'

The young man turned back to face the enemy as Fronto watched the cavalry getting closer. Soon they would crash into the front ranks of the legions. He judged the distance. A little closer perhaps...

'Priscus, *now!*'

All along the front rank, centurions called out orders and the front rows of legionaries separated out, leaving gaps. In the spaces between, the Balearic slingers attached to the legions stepped into the field and fired off hundreds of lead bullets that crossed the intervening space at head height. Most of the German footmen were lagging a little behind and few of them were struck by the shot. Most of it struck horses on the chest and shoulders, making the animals rear.

All across the line, men were thrown or forced to hold on for dear life as their horses bolted madly from the field. It was a small blow really to the German army and even to their cavalry, but they would be a lot more cautious with future charges. At a further order from Priscus, the lines closed up once more and the slingers clambered out from between the ranks into the intervening gap between lines of cohorts.

Fronto scanned the field. Far more cavalry were coming at the sides, but they would be caught by Longinus' men and herded into the melee. There were still a number of horsemen in the field, but the majority of the centre were now warriors fighting on foot. In his head he counted 'Three... two...' Before he reached one, the volley was released.

Several thousand pila arced out over the field and came down among the mass. The hissing sound of the flying missiles disappeared to be replaced with the metallic and organic noises of their impact, along with a great deal of screaming. Moments later the second volley was released, too early for Fronto's liking, but the effect was still good. The mass had barely moved beyond the initial line of pilum casualties when they were struck by a second rain of deadly points.

Fronto watched the carnage from his mounted position with satisfaction. The initial volley was a shock tactic designed to terrify the enemy and break their spirit. In this case, it had also done a great deal of damage.

The German warriors were still coming on but were now advancing with a slower and much more reluctant gait.

'Steady lads. We've shaken them, and when they hit the shield wall they'll break. Just hold the line.'

The front runners of the German horde had now come within a few feet of the Roman line. They seemed reluctant to launch an attack on the shield wall and only once there were a reasonably large number of them did they turn, screaming, and run at the Romans.

The first point they hit was up by the Eleventh. Fronto could hear Crispus' precise and well-educated tone even over the vast noise of the clash.

'Maintain formations everyone! Rufus! Be sure your boys don't break out forward. Keep the line. Rear ranks move forward and support!'

Fronto smiled. The man was young and very inexperienced for a military commander, but his innate good sense and his knowledge of military history gave him more of an edge than many of the experienced commanders he had known. Moreover, Crispus had taken a newly-formed green legion with an officer corps drawn from all over the provincial military and had given them self-respect and honour. In no engagement since their formation had the Eleventh run or failed. Fronto felt confident with them on his flank.

Drawing his eyes back from the Eleventh, he paid a great deal of attention to the front ranks of his own. They had been hit fairly hard in a number of places but, even where the initial shield wall had buckled under the onslaught, the second or third row of men had pushed the enemy back out or maimed them and let them fall beneath.

All in all, the line was holding very well and already in places the Germans had given up on the assault and were drawing back toward their camp. The legions were, of course, very lucky in that they had made their way early and taken up the perfect position. The Germans had had precious little warning and had marshalled a small force to try and drive the Romans away. Had they been prepared or committed their whole army, things could have been *very* different.

Fronto became aware of someone calling him. He turned to see Tetricus waving and pointing to one side. Following his gesture, the legate could see one of the ballistae still on its cart. Tetricus shrugged. Fronto shook his head.

'We've driven off the first assault. By the time they're ready to come again, you should have the bank built. Nice thought though.'

He turned back to see most of the Germans now pulling back from the shield wall. Somewhere off to the right there was a disagreement going on within the German attackers. A particularly large and well-dressed warrior was halting fleeing Germans in their tracks. Though he could not understand what the man was shouting at his fellow warriors, Fronto could easily imagine what it was. The German warrior was unsuccessful in rallying the men and shouted something at them in a derisive manner. Turning, he stamped resolutely on toward the Roman line.

Fronto was impressed with the courage of the man, but his lack of foresight and common sense would be his undoing. He hesitated for a moment, toying with the idea of ordering the man be brought down with pilum or arrow. It would be ignominious and teach a very pertinent lesson, but a better lesson awaited.

The German stopped his advance around five feet away from the tips of the Roman swords. Holding his sword high above his head, he bellowed something at his enemy. A challenge, obviously.

One of the centurions called out 'He's mine!'

The man barely got to move out of the shield wall before Priscus' voice, harsh and powerful, carried along the line.

'Flaminius, if you so much as *think* of moving out of line, I'll take your vine staff and wedge it in your arse. This is the Army of Rome, not some Greek heroic epic!'

The eager centurion faltered and then stepped back into his position. The German grinned at him and then bellowed his challenge at the legions again. Along the Roman front, centurions called out 'Hold the line.'

After a moment more of shouting, the German warrior seemed to be shifting between dejection and derision. He appeared to be undecided as to whether he should attack the line on his own or return to his own camp.

Velius' voice could be heard from the left.

'Castus, you still got that unsightly boil on your arse?'

There was a small outbreak of laughter and an affirmative from among the Second Cohort, followed by muttered planning. Fronto did not generally like being left out of any tactical discussion, but Velius was a special case. Fronto trusted him implicitly and was intrigued.

Moments later, a rather chubby legionary stepped out to face the huge German and, turning to face the shield wall, raised his tunic and dropped his breeches. The warrior, who had been expecting a challenge, stopped in his tracks, faced with a legionary's afflicted rear end.

He dithered for a moment longer, undecided, and then gestured derisively at the Romans, turned away, and walked back to his camp. Fronto grinned.

'Alright, lads. We can hold anything they throw for now. A few more hours and we'll be back inside the wall and protected by artillery. Velius, have that man report to the medicus!'

He smiled, certain in the knowledge that today would be a walkover.

CHAPTER 19

(AROUND ARIOVISTUS' POSITION, IN BOTH ROMAN CAMPS)

'Equisio: A horse attendant or stable master.'

'Haruspex (pl. Haruspices): A religious official who confirms the will of the Gods through signs and by inspecting the entrails of animals.'

Fronto and Crispus sighed as two legionaries helped them settle their cloaks into place and tie the military knot around their cuirass. Longinus smiled from his seat in the corner.

'Your cloak's looking tattered and worn, Fronto. You're either going to have to buy a new one or start wearing that abominable glittery one.'

Fronto grinned.

'Blind the enemy? I'll buy a new cloak this winter when we're not campaigning. Might even be back in Rome, so I can leave the bright one with my sister then.'

Crispus raised his eyebrows.

'*Might* be in Rome you say, Marcus? Where else would you possibly be?'

Longinus interrupted as Fronto opened his mouth.

'Marcus here's one of those that likes to stay with his men. He'll probably spend most of the off-season with the Tenth in their winter quarters. Apart from a few trips back to see family, that is.'

Fronto nodded.

'These days Rome leaves a bad taste in my mouth. It's all politics, greed and power. If I don't stay with the Tenth, I'll probably go back to Puteoli.'

Longinus smiled at the other legates.

'Actually, I'm thinking of spending some of the winter in Spain. Probably in Tarraco or Saguntum, buying horses. Maybe you'd like to join me for a while. You remember how mild the winters are around there, Marcus.'

Fronto returned the smile.

'Sounds good. I'd like to see Tarraco again. It's been a few years now, but I'd lay bets all my favourite inns are the same as ever. You starting up a stable, Gaius?'

Longinus shrugged.

'Already got stables Marcus, but there's precious little good Spanish stock in them, and I rather like my Spanish horses. If you want to join me for a month or two, I've already got a villa being built near Tarraco. You too, Aulus, if you want.'

Crispus beamed at them.

'I've never visited Spain. In fact, this particular command is the first time I have left the familiar shores of Italy. Good grief, I've precious rare been out of Rome itself. I'd be enchanted to join you.'

Fronto glanced out of the tent doorway at the distant sound of the cornicen.

'Sounds like Priscus has given the call. We've got maybe a count of a hundred before they're fully standing to.'

Crispus squinted out of the doorway and into the sunlight.

'Regardless of the events of yesterday, I find it impossible to believe that Ariovistus will commit his forces today. How many times have we presented ourselves before his camp and all but *begged* him to engage us? I am certain of one thing: he will refrain from attacking either of our forces as long as he is under threat from both sides.'

Fronto nodded his agreement.

'I'm no student of grand tactics, but I agree entirely with Aulus. If he's going to attack us at any time, I'd look to our defences at night, when the two forces are harder to combine. Still, Caesar wants that we present ourselves for battle, so present ourselves we shall.'

Longinus gave them both a crafty grin as he tightened the belt around his chain cavalry shirt.

'We'll see him today alright. I can guarantee you.'

Fronto furrowed his brow and squinted suspiciously at Longinus.

'Alright Gaius, what do you know?'

Longinus stretched, watching the arming process appreciatively; quite grateful he had to wear only a standard cavalry mail shirt.

'Ariovistus has a very few long-range cavalry scouts still outside the field that come and go at night. He's now well aware of the train of supply wagons that should reach this very spot not long before dark. He won't attack until he's sure he's only fighting on one front, but he has to destroy this camp by nightfall, or he's failed to stop our supplies.'

Crispus grinned.

'So he's definitely coming, then.'

Fronto's furrowed brow had not moved.

'How do you know all about the German's scouts and what they've seen?'

Longinus tapped him on the head and made a hollow sound in his cheek.

'How do you think I know, Marcus? I've had my own scouts marking theirs one-on-one for days now. I know everything they've seen and done.'

Slowly the frown on Fronto's face fell away, to be replaced with a content smile.

'I'm going to rip the bastard German's face off if I get hold of him.'

'You and every other Roman on the field. Come on, or we'll be late for your primus pilus, and he takes the piss even when you're on time.'

Making a few last minute adjustments to the uniforms, the three commanders stepped out into the sun, along with the two legionaries. As the men fell in with their units, Fronto, Crispus and Longinus clasped arms.

'How long shall we remain in position before we retire to the camp?'

Fronto shrugged.

'Caesar will give it until noon and then pull the other force back. I would give the Germans maybe an hour after that before they come. It'll give the men a little time to eat. When we *do* fall back, allow them to go off duty, but make damn sure they're ready to fall in at a moment's notice.'

Crispus nodded and Longinus, hauling himself into the saddle, addressed the two legates.

'Both of you'll need to be ready, but the cavalry can eat in the saddle. I'll pull them back to the camp at noon, but I'll keep them poised and mounted and out of sight. Then, if an attack comes at short notice, we can harry them while the legions fall in.'

With a slightly unsettling smile, Longinus set off for the cavalry on the wing. Crispus saluted Fronto, unnecessarily he thought, and headed off toward the Eleventh.

Fronto turned and walked between the lines of men to the front, where Priscus stood with the tribunes and the signifers and cornicen of the First Cohort. The Tenth, like the Eleventh next to them, were in full battle formation, each century in position within the cohort, each cohort in position within the legion. With half of Longinus' cavalry on each wing and numerous foot and missile auxiliary units in position behind and beside the legions, they were ready to move.

He glanced briefly behind him at the front rampart of the fort. Tetricus was the only officer not in position with the legion, having volunteered to man the walls and the artillery with the crews. They would doubtful be of any use this morning, even if the Germans *did* attack, but were a gratifying support. Should the legions *be* engaged and have to pull back toward the fort, the ballistae would take on great importance.

With another glance up and down the lines to be sure that the army was in position, he signalled Priscus and held his arm up, motioning down the front at Crispus. Moments later, horns blew across the field, and centurions gave the order to march.

One of Longinus' men had made a daring dash for the German fort in order to judge the maximum range of their missiles. He had marked the range with a cavalry spear plunged into the turf bearing a fluttering pennant.

The Tenth moved out in formation with its allies and marched purposefully across the field. Rarely when moving into combat did Fronto suffer from nerves, but he was uneasy with this situation. Splitting the army may be helpful in protecting supplies, but if the *full* weight of the German army fell on the Tenth and Eleventh, they would be fighting for their lives, hopelessly outnumbered. The only thing that kept him reasonably confident was the fact that Ariovistus had proved time and time again unwilling to commit his entire force in one engagement. With two thirds of the Roman army behind him, he was again unlikely to commit everything to destroy Fronto's force.

It seemed such a short distance. A few moments later, he spotted the cavalry spear that marked the limit of German missile capability. With a signal to both Crispus and Longinus, he drew closer and closer to the spear and called a halt six feet behind it.

The figures of the German army were clearly visible moving around behind the defences of their camp. As the legions came to a halt, Fronto craned his head and looked along the line. One of the legionaries hefted his pilum and stared off into the distance. Fronto could understand how he felt, weighing up the distance to the Germans and wondering how strong his arm was. Unfortunately, even if they wanted to unleash a volley or bring up the archers, it was extremely unlikely that a single shot would pass beyond the defences. If they *had* kept the ballistae on the carts and trundled them forward, they could most certainly have landed a number of heavy bolts within. Still, he had his orders, and they were to occupy the field and offer battle, not to run harrying attacks on the enemy position.

He could see, even from this distance, the unhappy and bored look on the face of Aulus Crispus; a look that was reflected all along the Roman lines. No one liked standing here at attention for four hours on the off chance that the Germans might feel like leaving their rat hole today. They would be feeling complacent due to the repeated failures in drawing Ariovistus out to fight. Fronto was torn between giving orders to stand at ease and remove helmets and maintaining discipline. If they were more relaxed now, they would fight better later, when the Germans *did* come against them. On the other hand, if they let the troops relax and Ariovistus changed his mind and took advantage of the opportunity, then they could be in worse trouble. Damn Caesar for this ridiculous show of military power. Having spent much more time among the lower ranks in the less savoury areas of cities, and among the Gauls and Germans out here, Fronto knew much better ways of starting a fight.

Ridiculous. Turning, Fronto shouted to the equisio who held the reins of his horse toward the back of the legion. The soldier brought the horse forward and Fronto mounted. Looking to the side, he saw Priscus looking up at him, eyebrow raised.

'Going to check something out.'

'Don't get into trouble this time sir.'

'Trouble? Me?'

Grinning, Fronto trotted off along the front of the army. Reaching the Eleventh, he reined in beside Crispus.

'Fancy a little ride?'

The young legate smiled.

'I'd rather like to ride into that infernal pit of Germanic excrescence and lay about me with a sword. I would presume, however, that this is not the ride to which you refer?'

Fronto shrugged.

'I want to take a look round the other side and see what's happening with Caesar's force. I don't like this being out of touch. And I might be tempted to do something a little stupid and reckless, yes.'

Crispus smiled happily and waved his equisio over. Once he had mounted, he joined Fronto and looked back at his primus pilus.

'Felix, I'm just going for a little jaunt with the good legate here. We shall return forthwith.'

The two officers trotted off past the cavalry and up the hill among the scattered trees.

'Wish I had a man called Felix in my legion.' Fronto muttered. 'Could do with a bit of luck!'

Crispus smiled.

'Perhaps not. Despite having carefully pored over all of the records of my officers, I can never recall the man's real name. Everyone calls him Felix, though I rather get the impression that it is sarcasm. I don't believe in luck anyway, Marcus. The centurion *is* first-rate at his job, and I hold that it is fate and choice that make or break.'

He glanced sideways at Fronto and smiled.

'Although it is men like you that make me doubt my creed on occasion!'

Fronto grinned back at him.

'*Look* at me. Do I really *look* lucky?'

'Everyone to whom I speak believes that you may be the luckiest man in the Roman military!'

'Huh!'

'Or do you make your own luck, Marcus?'

Fronto growled.

'Aulus, I'm not very wealthy. I'm not very talented in anything but killing. I've not got enough patience for the cursus honorum and position in Rome. My sister and my mother think that I'm a waste of family blood and that the line will die with me. Indeed, the line probably *will* die with me, as the closest I've been to a good woman in years are ladies of low morals in Tarraco or Aquileia. I'll most likely die in a fountain of blood on a field hundreds of miles outside Roman territory.'

He realised he was starting to feel angry and that Crispus might get the impression it was aimed at him, but the ball was rolling downhill now.

'You and Balbus and the others have a chance. Balbus has his family back in Massilia. You are a very educated man and will go a long way in Rome. Longinus will retire some time to Spain or Umbria and live with his horses; his one passion. Galba will probably own a gladiator Ludus in the end. Crassus will probably rule the empire unless Caesar beats him to it. Me? I'll be up to my elbows in blood and guts and drunk every night.'

He was worried for a moment that he had gone too far. Crispus' face was mortified. The young legate looked as though one of the Gods had died in front of him. Then he smiled slowly.

'I'm stuck for words to describe adequately how I feel about that, Marcus, so let me borrow some from one of your men: Shit! Absolute unadulterated drivel. I know you better than you think I do, Marcus Falerius Fronto. You may not be from a ludicrously wealthy family like Crassus, but your family are not poor. After this campaign is over, you will return to Italy a very wealthy man. You have enough reputation that you could secure a very nice post by then. You could be a governor. Perhaps Spain, since you know it well. Balbus has told me several times what his daughters thought of you. You can have any future you choose Marcus, and I won't listen to any more self-deluded rubbish.'

Fronto blinked. For a long moment, he stared, and then he laughed; laughed so hard he almost unhorsed himself.

'Well I can see the other legions from here and they're just standing there. Let's get back to our units and let them stand at ease for now. Ariovistus isn't coming until after lunch.'

The early afternoon sun beat down on the defences where Tetricus chewed on a strip of pork, leaning on one of the ballistae. Squinting across the field, he stopped chewing, the pork forgotten for a moment. His eyes strained, unsure whether there was anything out there or whether heat haze and bright sun were playing tricks with his mind and his eyes. Swallowing the mouthful, he leaned across the mechanism to the optio who controlled the ballista.

'Optio, look over toward the Germans. Can you see anything?'

The soldier leaned forward and strained his eyes, raising his hand to ward off the sunlight.

'Don't think there's... Wait. Cavalry.'

Tetricus followed suit to confirm the soldier's report.

'Shit.'

Thousands of cavalry were hurtling across the grass. They had left their camp and marshalled their force before their charge, all unknown to the Roman defenders due to the hazy conditions. Now they would reach the defences in moments. Tetricus ran to the cornicen.

'Sound the alert.'

As the notes trumpeted out across the camp, the sudden sound of thousands of heavy infantry falling in filled the air. The Tenth and Eleventh would be very lucky to have a reasonable force in position to defend the camp. Glancing to the far left, Tetricus heaved a sigh of relief as Longinus and the cavalry swept around and forward toward the enemy. All they had to do was buy enough time.

The German force was massive. Perhaps not the full weight of Ariovistus, but certainly a sizeable part of it, greatly outweighing the Roman defenders. Again, the cavalry came at the front, supported by swift warriors on foot, one running with each horseman. Behind them came the mass of footmen, all armed and armoured according to their own individual whim and status.

Tetricus had been confirmed as commander of the artillery and had three ballistae set up on platforms along the front rampart. In between, the first reasonably prepared centuries of the Tenth and Eleventh moved up to the rampart and into position. With a quick glance back at the camp, he could see Fronto and Crispus and the various higher officers manoeuvring their men into place.

The men now in position on the wall watched the two cavalry forces hurtling toward one another. There were cheers and shouts of encouragement all along the walls as the Roman and German cavalry hit each other with a sound like a collapsing building. The dust raised by both groups of horse was phenomenal, and for long moments the entire engagement was lost to view at the defences. Then, gradually, the cloud settled and just a thin haze remained with the occasional small billow as horses manoeuvred for position.

As Tetricus scanned the battle, he spotted Varus, the cavalry prefect from the Ninth, slashing maniacally to left and right with his long cavalry sword. The prefect was causing such devastation that the Germans were starting to give him a wide berth. Tetricus grinned. Without having had to give the order, the crews had loaded the ballistae and moved all the ammunition into ready position. He would love to start them loosing, but it would be too dangerous at the moment, with the Roman cavalry so mixed in the melee. He took another look behind him, to see that the legions were now almost in position. Nodding briefly to the cornicen, he jogged to the other end of the artillery platform, to where Longinus had stationed his signal group.

'Time to sound the cavalry recall, I'd say, centurion.'

The man nodded and moments later the call blared out across the field. The cavalry began to return to the camp as soon as they had enough room to turn round in the melee. Varus and two other cavalry officers formed them up and restored the line as soon as they were detached, retreating slowly, but in formation, to the end of the fortifications.

Tetricus scanned further across the field. Still perhaps a third of the cavalry were involved in close and heavy fighting, not having enough freedom to disengage and return. He chewed his lip, wondering whether to seek permission from his commanding officer, but a tribune was a senior officer and should be allowed to make command decisions when he deemed fit. Besides, the trapped cavalry were running out of time.

'Ready the ballistae. Be *very* careful and *very* accurate. I want you to loose into the mass and try and give our cavalry some room to manoeuvre. If any one of you hits one of our men, I'll personally kick you up and down the wall.'

With grim, determined expressions, the ballista crews began to loose their shots, taking considerably longer than was customary. To begin with, their shots fell largely wide or short due to the care they were taking to avoid Roman casualties. Slowly, the shots began to pick their targets and here and there, hard-pressed Roman cavalrymen found room to turn and retreat as Germans were plucked from their horses and hurled into the mass, leaving a vapour trail of blood through the air.

Tetricus became aware of someone standing next to him on the platform. Fronto's voice was low.

'Well done, man. They're as accurate as I've ever seen. Where's Longinus?'

'I don't know sir. Haven't seen him yet.'

Fronto frowned.

'Why does the bastard always have to lead from the front? That's what the centurionate do, not senior staff officers.'

Tetricus smiled at the legate.

'Nothing *you'd* do at all then sir?'

Fronto grunted.

'There he is!'

The tribune followed Fronto's gesture. Longinus had carved a path through the German cavalry and was behind them, among the non-mounted warriors. Now he was making for the edge of the force. Though he was too distant to see clearly, he was obviously unhurt, as his sword rose and fell like a bird of prey swooping down for the kill. Moments later, he was out and riding along the edge of the German force, occasionally taking a swipe as he made for the defences.

All along the front of the enemy mass, cavalrymen had fallen, both Roman and German, though many had made it to the safety of the walls.

Fronto grinned along the line of the tenth.

'Ready yourselves lads. It'll be our turn in a few moments and we have to hold this wall.'

The tense, expectant feel among the men was tangible as the legate turned once more to face the Germans. A small party of Ariovistus' cavalry had broken off from the main force and were chasing Longinus as he ploughed his way toward the south corner of the fort. Fronto felt his heart falter for a moment as a thrown spear passed by Longinus close enough to shave with. He turned and slapped his hand on the ballista.

'Tetricus, get this thing trained on that group and give him some support.'

As the tribune and his men reoriented the weapon, Fronto returned his gaze to the chase. There were seven of them. Longinus had come out of the German force on a different side to the majority of his men, and had been far too deep among them to receive sufficient support. He was on his own, racing for the fort and nothing anyone on the wall could do would help. Even Tetricus' ballista would be unlikely to hit such fast-moving targets.

He felt himself swallow nervously as the watched and realised that everyone around him had fallen silent. He whispered under his breath, too quiet for the men to hear.

'Come on you bastard... come *on*!'

Suddenly from behind the fort's south corner, two more cavalry troopers appeared, making a bee-line for the German pursuers. Fronto thought he recognised Varus, but the other was unknown. The two raced toward Longinus, but they would not reach him in time. Though Longinus' favourite black Galician was a beautiful horse, the German horses were larger and faster. With a fresh wave of horror, Fronto realised what he was doing.

Longinus, with no hope of outpacing his pursuers, reined in and turned to face them. The two supporting cavalrymen pushed their steeds as hard as they could to reach their commander. Four more cavalry were now leaving the safety of the fort to support him. The commander, as was his wont, bore no shield but, as Fronto watched, he drew his pugio dagger with his second hand and rode at the Germans.

The legate barely dared breathe as he watched. Longinus hit the front two Germans with tremendous force, their horses smashing into each other. As the horses fell and rolled, Longinus was first to his feet, though one of the Germans had apparently died in the clash. Longinus' dagger glinted red and the body lay on its side, curled tight. The other German pulled himself to his feet and reached for his fallen sword. He looked up just in time for Longinus' blade to cut clean through his neck, and his head rolled away across the grass.

The five other Germans were on him now, though Varus and his companion were only moments away. The first German to reach him received a slash across the stomach that threw him from the horse. Almost simultaneously, his dagger found the leg of the next, plunging deep and ripping open the man's calf.

Turning to face the next, drenched in blood, Longinus failed to see the man behind him; the one with the torn leg. The German wheeled his horse round. Fronto stared in horror as the man brought his huge Celtic blade down in an over arm sweep and cleaved deep into Longinus' shoulder. The commander cried out in pain so loud that Fronto swore he could hear it even over the din as the dagger fell from Longinus' useless hand. He staggered and turned, raising his sword to the wounded German, blinded by blood and rage. His sword swung, off-target, and a spear thrown by one of the remaining pursuers caught him beneath his shoulder blade. The commander jerked straight, his sword toppling from his fingers, twitching violently, as the one with the wounded leg smiled a vicious smile and brought down his blade once again, ending the life of Gaius Longinus, Master of the cavalry.

Mere moments later, before even the commander's body had hit the floor, Varus and his companion fell upon the Germans, carving them repeatedly, driven by rage and grief. The other four cavalrymen joined them and the sight of their rage being taken out upon the bodies of German warriors already dead sickened even the most veteran of the watching legionaries. For a moment it looked like the troopers were going to ride on and attack the entire German force, though Varus motioned them back. He was the last to leave the site, dismounting, heaving the body of his commander on to the Galician and leading it back with his own horse.

Fronto, stunned and shocked, realised that he was standing like a gawping idiot while the Germans were already engaging further along by the Eleventh. Here by the Tenth, they were still thirty feet or so away. He turned, wiping his face, and looked down at the pale and anguished face of Priscus.

'Do you feel like defending today?'

'No bloody way sir.'

He shouted above the noise of the oncoming Germans.

'Cornicen: sound the advance!'

The musician, taken by surprise, put the long, curved horn to his mouth and blew the call.

Crispus heard the bleating over the sounds of combat and glanced to the other end of the wall in surprise. The Tenth were swarming over the wall and toward the Germans. That was not the plan; they were to defend the fort. Longinus and his men had done their job well, and the legions had been prepared. The Eleventh had been hit by them a couple of moments ago, but why the hell would Fronto abandon the plan and go for such foolhardy actions?

For a moment Crispus was dumbfounded, totally unsure what to do with this change of plan. He knew that the Roman position was strong; that they could hold the wall for ages without falling and that a march into such a large army against unknown odds was risky at best. All of his knowledge of tactical histories urged him to sound the Tenth's recall. For some reason, though, he found himself shouting at his cornicen 'Sound the advance!'

The Eleventh, deep in the bloody business of Roman frontline warfare, heard the call. Despite their situation, the shield wall pulled a little tighter together and, slowly, smashing at German arms and faces with their huge, bronze shield bosses, they pushed the mass back from the slope.

Crispus smiled. Fronto would not be alone. The Eleventh would be there to defend his flank, as they always were. He had disagreed with everything Fronto had said this morning and was damned if he was going to see the man lying dead on this field due to lack of support.

All along the fortifications, the legions had swept forward into the Germans. Fronto had been the first down the bank, in front of the Tenth's leading centurions. He had been the first member of the Tenth to take a German life. After almost an hour of brutality the news had reached Crispus, standing on the wall behind his troops and cheering them on, of the death of Longinus. He had been ashamed later for having temporarily left his legion, but he *had* to see. Varus, the cavalry prefect, had brought the body back, and had laid it on one of the platforms, where the body was in full view of the field. Crispus had looked down at the corpse and had felt something harden inside; a knot of twisted pain and cold anger.

The young man had fought in the engagements of the Eleventh before, but had fought carefully and calmly and usually at the edge or the rear, when only rarely the enemy actually reached him. Now white, cold, icy fire flowed through his veins and his senior officers, tribunes and centurions alike were shocked to see the young, educated, well-spoken and noble Crispus hauling his own soldiers out of the way in order to get to the enemy, growling like a starving wolf.

Fronto and Crispus met up as the sun began to sink behind the hills. The Germans were finally retreating into the safety of their camp, though many of their army's rear ranks had returned considerably earlier. Countless dead of both sides lay strewn across the battlefield and as they walked, the two legates had to stumble and sidestep the grisly remains. The two, blood-soaked and grimy, walked stiffly, tired and with no smile playing across their lips.

With the centuries of their legions moving slowly, victorious, across the field back to their camp, the legates paused at the embankment. Varus sat on the platform next to the body of his commander, drinking unwatered wine directly from the jug. He looked up as he saw the two approach and held the jug out wordlessly. Crispus reached out and took the container, upending it and pouring the wine into his mouth and across his face in a torrent, washing the blood from his skin. He threw the empty jug onto the platform. Fronto looked around at the Tenth, dragging themselves back to camp, and grasped the mail shirt of one of the immunes legionaries.

'Find me wine. Plenty of wine.'

The soldier took one look at Fronto's face and hurried off into the camp as the legate turned back to see Crispus crouched by the body. He tore a long strip of blood-soaked tunic from the commander's corpse and tied it round his upper arm. As Crispus turned back, there was a tear in the corner of his eye. The legates of the Tenth and Eleventh dropped heavily to the turf platform.

The sound of hundreds of hoof beats distracted Fronto from his train of thought, and his voice trailed away. He dropped the wine jug to the turf, and he, Varus and Crispus all turned to look at the new arrivals. Caesar sat astride his white charger, with Crassus beside him and Ingenuus with a number of the cavalry.

Crispus struggled to his feet and stood roughly to attention, faltering a little. Varus followed suit. Fronto merely hauled himself around to face the general and remained slumped. Caesar looked down at the scene with one eyebrow raised.

'What...'

His voice tailed off as his wandering gaze took in the body on the platform behind them.

'Longinus?'

Fronto sighed deeply and took another swig of wine.

'He fell protecting the legions while they got into position. We've been mourning him, as you can see. I've read his will. I think you should look too.'

Caesar dismounted and strode up the bank. Standing before the body, he lowered his head in respect and then sat with the others, motioning Varus and Crispus to do the same. Looking up briefly, he noticed the other riders. Crassus wore an impatient frown, Ingenuus a look of genuine distress.

'Crassus? Ingenuus? I think you should dismount and join us. The rest of you, go report to your comrades.'

As Ingenuus dismounted, Crassus coughed.

'Caesar, the cavalry is without a commander. Most of them are Gaulish levies. Perhaps I should go and make sure all is in order? They may desert without command.'

Varus rose to his feet, shaking.

'They are not cowards or animals, and they do not need shepherding! Will you not join us and drink to my commander?'

Crassus glanced at Caesar and then back at Varus.

'He is not *your* commander. He's gone. When *I* am your commander, you will not speak to a superior officer like that. Caesar? Permission to take command of the cavalry?'

Fronto jumped to his feet just in time to wrestle Varus back to the grass.

'Don't do anything stupid. Let the mindless fop make a fool of himself,' he hissed in the prefect's ear. Turning to Caesar, he spoke in a more audible tone.

'I presume you have no intention of putting *him* in command of the cavalry?'

Caesar cleared his throat.

'I'm making no decision about it now. Longinus is still warm. Crassus, if you're not joining us, you should head back to your legion for the time being.'

Crassus grunted.

'Yes, general.'

Turning, he rode off.

Fronto suddenly realised that Ingenuus was leaning over the body. He wandered over to the young prefect and patted him on the shoulder. The man had risen high in the ranks, but he was still very young, inexperienced and impressionable. He glanced up at Varus.

'Can you take him somewhere and talk to him?'

Varus, his face still red, nodded and beckoned to Ingenuus. The two wandered along the bank. Caesar looked at Fronto and Crispus.

'I want to see any prisoners you took. Just a couple, if you have lots. Can they be brought out here?'

Crispus and Fronto shared a glance.

'There aren't very many sir, if you get my drift?'

The general nodded. Crispus stood, shakily.

'I need to exercise my muscles for a moment anyway and perhaps dip myself in a horse trough. With your permission, Caesar, I'll bring you all the prisoners. Both of them.'

As he staggered off down the inside of the bank, Caesar looked at Fronto.

'*Both* of them?'

Nod.

'I see that you were well in the middle of the action, by the state of you?'

Nod. Swig of wine.

'The corpses and line of battle across the field show that you didn't exactly *defend the wall*, am I right?'

Nod.

'Marcus, you're one of the best. Certainly the best I have in *this* army, but I can't have you endangering the entire campaign through insane stunts brought on by grief and rage. And I *particularly* cannot let you lead Crispus down that path. He's young and naïve. He's lost a figure he respected today. You are the nearest thing he has here to a father, and how *you* treat *him* will affect his whole future. Are you going to speak to me?'

Fronto looked up and took another swig of wine.

'Longinus is gone. We couldn't get to him in time. Don't underestimate how well-liked he was.'

'You and he used to hate each other.'

Fronto glared angrily at Caesar.

'Don't pick apart what you don't understand. We never hated each other. We were just different, and there was a resentment. We were both mature and sensible enough to overcome our differences, and he became a damn good friend. One of the best. And a good cavalry commander. If you let Crassus run amok with them, our cavalry will all either die or desert. Here.'

He held out a parchment that Caesar gently took from his hand and unfurled before letting it roll up again a moment later.

'His will? It wasn't meant for me to read. What do I *need* to know?'

Fronto sighed.

'He left me his best cloak. Bit of a joke I think, the old bastard. Left me his horse too, would you believe it? Other than that, he appears to have left his sword to Varus, though I haven't told him yet. The rest of his stuff goes back to his family in Italy.'

Caesar nodded.

'He obviously held you in more esteem than I thought. He loved his horse a great deal I understand. Other than that, fairly ordinary, yes?'

Fronto nodded.

'Apart from one thing. He wanted me to propose Varus as his replacement should this happen. He specifically stated him in the amendment he made at Vesontio. Surely you can't select Crassus.'

Caesar sighed.

'I cannot always do what I wish, Marcus. I am not a God, so I must sometimes do as I am required. I have to give Crassus a chance. I can stop him doing something if he does it wrong, but I cannot prevent him from trying. I owe his father much too much for that.'

'So you're going to ignore this?'

He waved the will at Caesar.

'It is *my* prerogative and *my* duty to assign commanders, not their own. I would be happy to accept Varus and would go with the recommendation were he the only candidate. He has proved himself a number of times. However, Crassus *wants* it, and he's currently got the more important claim. Things may change, Marcus. There's a long way ahead of us yet. Crassus will get his chance to prove he can do it, but only one chance. No more.'

Fronto nodded unhappily.

'If you'd like, I'll speak to Varus and tell him all about it.'

'Thank you Marcus. Here comes Crispus with the prisoners. Before he gets here, I want you to remember one thing. Crispus is going to look to you now. He's very young, and he takes inspiration from the other commanders. Be sure you inspire him correctly and not toward chaos, yes?'

Another unhappy nod.

The two surviving prisoners of the German attack were dumped unceremoniously at the foot of the bank. Crispus indicated the auxiliary soldier standing beside him.

'This is one of our Aeduan allies who speaks both their language and ours fluently.'

Caesar looked down at the Aeduan cavalryman.

'You'll translate for them and I?'

'Yes Caesar.'

'Ask them why Ariovistus won't come out and fight me.'

A brief and garbled exchange followed between the prisoners and the auxiliary, after which he turned to face the general.

'It's a little hard to explain, Caesar, but... well you know how before the legions are committed, a Haruspex is consulted, and the entrails of a bird are opened in order to determine the auspices for the day?'

The general nodded. 'Yes.'

'Well, Ariovistus has his own Haruspices to consult, but his are Matrons of the tribes; revered old women. They cast bones and determine the will of their Gods from how the bones fall and, if they fall wrong, Ariovistus will not commit.'

'And the bones keep falling badly for him?'

The auxiliary exchanged brief words with the prisoners again and then addressed the general once more.

'They do not need to, Caesar. They cast their bones once when they first arrived and they informed the King that if he attacked before the new moon, the Gods would not let him win. Thus he has committed to small actions only and won't commit his main force until then.'

Caesar frowned.

'How long to the new moon, Crispus?'

The young legate shrugged.

'A little over a week, I suppose.'

'Too long. I won't let their barbarian superstitions prolong this standoff.'

Crispus cleared his throat.

'Sir, we are just as superstitious in our observance of ritual Haruspicy before taking action.'

Caesar nodded.

'Yes, but frankly, I've never believed in them. I go along with it to keep people happy, but life is what you make it, Crispus, and I intend to make it difficult for Ariovistus. We hold Longinus' funeral tonight. I want everything out of the way before tomorrow because in the morning we set upon the Germans.'

He turned and called over to the two cavalry officers. Varus and Ingenuus walked over to the general and stood side by side.

'Sir?'

'Gentlemen. I want you to arrange a pyre for your commander. This ballista...' he patted the weapon that stood next to Longinus' body 'will be removed to the camp interior. The pyre will be built here on this platform, and it should be high. I want the Germans to be able to see it burn quite clearly. Have torches lit all along the defences.'

Fronto glanced over at Caesar, a sad look about him.

'You can't even give Longinus a sendoff without making a statement with it, can you general?'

Caesar glared back at Fronto. The man was usually only this bold when they were in private. It could cause trouble if he started questioning his commander in front of other officers. Still, Caesar was aware of the grief clutching him at the moment and, whether he should have said it or not, he was, of course, correct. His glare lessened.

'Marcus. Anything that might give us an edge could save other lives. Besides, Longinus would have been the first to agree.'

Fronto snorted.

'I suppose so. If you're going to do it like this, though, do it properly.'

He turned to Varus and Ingenuus.

'Go and find Priscus of the Tenth and get him to send a forage party into the woods. We want thousands of torches making. One for every spectator when we burn Gaius.'

Varus and Ingenuus bowed and, turning, went about their tasks.

Fronto turned round to see Crispus and Caesar look at him.

'We line them all up on the field before the pyre, but also before the German camp. Can you imagine what a sight eight thousand burning torches will be? Shame we haven't got the rest of the men here.'

Caesar nodded.

'Still, it will be a great send off for Longinus and a sight to behold for Ariovistus. And, in the morning, we will force the man to fight us. If *he* will not come *out*, *we* will go *in*!'

CHAPTER 20

(THE FIELD BEFORE THE SMALL FORT)

'Actuarius: Clerks, both civil and military. In the legions, Actuarii existed from the very top command levels, down to century levels, where excused-duty soldiers served in the role.'

The pyre burned bright on the wall. There was a slight wind disturbing the smoke, though it blew high and away above the soldiers. Two legions and all the attached auxilia stood before the wall with burning torches held high.

Fronto stood with the two cavalry officers and Crispus, Crassus and Caesar on the platform near the body. He could see Priscus down below in front of the Tenth. The primus pilus was sweating with the heat and the effort of continuously holding the torch high. The rest of the men would be suffering in much the same way. The pyre had only been lit for short while, and they would have a long time to go yet.

Fronto wore Longinus' good dress cloak that had been left to him and Varus bore the good quality Spanish cavalry sword that had been willed to him. The rest of his goods had been packed to send to his family, along with a letter from Fronto, one from Varus and one from Caesar. As a last gesture, before Varus lit the wood of the pyre, he laid his own much-used blade at the commander's side. Fronto had caused much raising of eyebrows among the command when he brought forth his resplendent red and gold cloak and covered the torso with it.

Now they all burned together. Caesar had made a speech and then Varus had added his own words.

In the silence, broken only by the crackle of burning wood and the spit and hiss of flaming fats, Fronto suddenly put his hand to his brow, shading his eyes from the glare of the fire. Trying not to cause too much alarm, he sidestepped toward Crispus and whispered to him.

'Can you see movement out to the left, beyond the ridge?'

Crispus sheltered his eyes and gazed out.

'Yes. What's happening?'

Fronto, still squinting, shook his head.

'Don't know. They're not Ariovistus' men, though. They're moving in legion formation. It must be the rest of the army.'

He glanced up at Caesar to see the general smiling at him.

'Absolutely, Marcus. What a distraction, eh? While the Germans marvel at the bright lights, four legions and thousands of cavalry walk right past them in the darkness.'

Fronto gawped.

'The whole army here? Now?'

'They will walk right around the edge of the field and into your camp. If all goes well, Ariovistus will not know that they've even moved. It should throw any tactics he has planned completely out of the window when the entire army forms up here at first light.'

Crispus shook his head.

'The other camp must be occupied or at the very least maintain the illusion of occupation. Otherwise Ariovistus can retreat and occupy *our* camp.'

Caesar smiled.

'Yes Crispus, I've thought of that. There are around four thousand men still there, two cohorts from each legion. They should make a good show of it and, if Ariovistus decides to try and retreat that way there will be a force to prevent him.'

By now a number of the men attending the funeral on the field had noticed the army on the move past them. Fronto looked around at Caesar.

'Best tell them what's happening.'

Caesar nodded and stepped to the front of the platform. With them on the wall, Varus and Ingenuus wore grim expressions and at the front of the two legions stood their tribunes, twelve in all.

'Tribunes, to the platform.'

With much confusion and apprehension, the twelve men approached the pyre. Once they had struggled up the bank, they came to attention in front of the senior officers. Caesar looked along the line.

'Gentlemen. The figures currently moving along the periphery of the field are your fellows from the Seventh, Eighth, Ninth and Twelfth Legions, along with the rest of the cavalry and auxiliary units. They will enter this camp shortly and will stay out the rest of the night here with you once the pyre burns down. In the morning, we will be moving on Ariovistus and battle will commence. Return to your legions and inform the centurions of this.'

The tribunes and prefects saluted the general, the tribunes with looks of eager anticipation, the two cavalry prefects with grim satisfaction.

'Go now.'

As they made their way down the grassy slope to the troops below, Fronto stepped toward Caesar again.

'Are the other legions properly informed or still in the dark?'

'I sent a courier out to them hours ago. Balbus, Rufus and Galba have had their orders delivered and should have addressed their troops. The pyre should be starting to collapse in less than half an hour. Once that happens, dismiss the troops and send them to their tents. The legates, prefects and primus pilus of each legion will join me in the praetorium for a command briefing. I'm going now to meet the commanders when they reach the camp and give further orders.'

Fronto nodded unhappily. He could understand the tactical advantage of all this, but it seemed dishonourable to use the funeral of a well-respected Roman nobleman to pull the wool over the enemy's eyes.

Fronto stood side by side with Crispus and Crassus as Caesar left the platform, staring at the burning timbers and the leaping flames now entirely obscuring the body. Ahead of them, spread out across the grass, the men of the legions stood silent, watching the last moments of the commander.

Less than an hour later, the troops had been dismissed for the night and twenty five men sat around the edges of the large tent at the praetorium of the camp. Caesar entered last and walked through the officers to the empty campaign chair.

'I see we're all here now. Good.'

He looked around. Fronto sat with Balbus and Crispus with Varus and Ingenuus close by. Crassus stood with the staff. The beam of self-satisfied smugness on his face irritated the general, and he could see the rift between his senior officers widening by the moment. Something would have to be done to bring Crassus down to the level of everyone else, and yet without provoking his father into withdrawing support. He sighed.

'Very well. Firstly, due to the recent morale problems among the legions and the need to give them as much support as possible, each of my senior staff will be taking a position with the legions and the cavalry tomorrow. No one will stay behind safe and sound.'

There was a general rumble of assent from the officers.

'I will assign my staff after the briefing. They will act as lieutenants for the legions' current commanders. The cavalry will be split into two wings. Publius Crassus will command the left wing and I will personally command the right.'

The general became aware of unhappy grumbling among some groups, so he pressed on before anyone could speak.

'I have not yet decided who will take a more permanent control of the cavalry. Crassus and I will control a wing each tomorrow and both of us will have the close support of three regular cavalry prefects. When tomorrow is done with, I will consider the question more closely.'

He glanced around. The grumbling had died away, but the silence that replaced it was equally filled with distrust and discontent.

'In respect of the infantry, the six legions will all commit side by side, advancing in three lines as per our previous engagements. The first two lines will carry out the attack, with the third in reserve to support any weak area. I will leave it to individual command units of the legions, though I would recommend that the legate moves with the first and second lines, while his lieutenant remains behind the second line, with the third. Again, that is your decision. Officers who are stationed at the rear will be able to identify weak spots and draw support from the third line.'

'The non-mounted auxilia will be split into six groups, each with one of my staff to command and each assigned to a legion. They will move with the legions, though the exact nature of their placement I will leave to the commanders of the units involved. The only men left behind here will be the actuarii, the quartermasters, the medical units and a small guard to protect them and the pay chests.'

Nods and murmurs of approval.

'At first light, the troops will come to order within the defences and will then cross into the field, falling into position as fast as this can be achieved. As soon as the last unit is in place, we will move on the German camp at a steady field march. I hope to draw them out rather than fight them across their defences, but if they are still reluctant I will press them. I intend for this to end tomorrow. If Fortuna is with us, they will be surprised at the size of the force on this side and will be unprepared. Does anyone have anything to add, ask or suggest?'

The room stood silent for a moment before Ingenuus raised his hand.

'Caesar, I would like to formally request assignment to the right wing.'

The General nodded, entirely prepared for this,

'I understand. Granted. Do I presume the same request goes for you, prefect Varus?'

Varus shook his head.

'My unit and the others that have seen action under my command work best on the left wing. It would be foolhardy to ignore the benefits of their experience for the sake of a grudge.'

Crassus looked up sharply and then nodded.

'He's right general. I do not have a great deal of experience at cavalry command and having an officer who knows the strategy of a left wing offensive would be invaluable.'

Caesar smiled.

'Then I hope you're both very successful.'

Balbus coughed and gestured to the general.

'What about the artillery? Are we leaving them on the wall here or are we going to try and take them with us?'

The general raised his hands in a gesture of defeat.

413

'I don't see how we can realistically take them. We'll be on the offensive and moving fast. I think we have to discount artillery support this time.'

Balbus nodded.

'If that's all then, I suggest you retire to your units and get as much sleep as possible before dawn. It's going to be a busy day, gentlemen.'

The officers bowed as they left the tent, dispersing and heading back to their own men. Varus jogged and caught up with Balbus, Crispus and Fronto.

'Pardon me for interrupting sirs, but I'm going back to the pyre. It's still a long way off burning out and I'd like a chance to sit and drink a few toasts to him. Would any of you care to join me? I'll understand if not; there's not a lot of time left for sleep.'

Fronto smiled at the cavalry prefect.

'I'll happily join you, Varus, so long as you can get the wine. I ran my stock dry earlier.'

Balbus and Crispus glanced at each other. The younger of the two yawned and then smiled.

'Oh who cares? If I'm this exhausted now, what difference can an extra hour make? Count me in, and I *do* have almost a full chest of good wine. I'll send someone for it.'

The four of them made their way slowly to the now bare artillery platform upon which the embers of the pyre were burning down low, still warm and orange. Soon the detail would gather up the ashes and the bone fragments and put them in a ready-prepared funerary urn for transport back to Longinus' family.

Crispus looked over at Varus as they sat.

'You held the commander in very high esteem, did you not?'

The prefect nodded.

'He was the man who assigned me as prefect of the Ninth's cavalry while we were still in Spain. He's been my commander ever since I joined the Ninth, and he always looked after the cavalry something special. He taught me everything I know about horse tactics.'

Fronto smiled.

'And I gather that's quite extensive knowledge; I hear only good things. You'll command the cavalry yet. Caesar would have passed it to you purely on Longinus' recommendation if it weren't for the all-glorious, sunshines-out-of-my-arse Crassus and his father.'

Varus laughed, as did the others. Balbus was first to straighten his expression.

'You *do* realise, I presume, that Crassus is going to do something horribly wrong or stupid tomorrow. He doesn't know the first thing about a cavalry battle and he has absolutely *no* respect for anyone below Senatorial level. I'd have preferred it if you'd taken Caesar's offer and stayed on the right wing. Caesar *is* a good horseman and a good tactician.'

Varus shook his head.

'I *need* to be near Crassus. If anything's going to go wrong, the cavalry are going to need someone they know and trust to put it right. I have to be there to make sure he doesn't kill everyone in a mad rush for glory.'

Fronto gestured to Crispus and pointed at Varus.

'*That's* what makes a good commander. The men should always come first.'

Balbus shook his head sadly as he reached out for the jug of wine.

'I don't know, Marcus. I keep feeling it's getting close to my time. Longinus was not far off half my age and look at him. I can't afford to die out here in the field when my wife and daughters are back in Massilia waiting for me. I might see out this season and then give it up; become a gentleman of leisure. I own an extensive estate near Massilia, not to mention property in Rome and Campania.'

Fronto smiled.

'I hate the very idea of carrying out this campaign without you around, but I'm forced to agree. You're a good friend and the only one of us who really has something that counts to go back to. I'd hate to have to visit Corvinia the way I'll probably do for Longinus' family. Do you realise I don't even know whether he was married?'

Balbus nodded.

'He was. Didn't see her very often, but I gather it was a match of choice rather than convenience. He told me she was in Spain with his father, supervising the building of a villa. He...'

Balbus trailed off as Crispus leapt to his feet.

'Look, out there...'

The others followed his pointing and saw the figures, scattered and few, but darkened and definitely German, running across the field back to the camp.

'Scouts. They'll have seen everything.'

'There goes the element of surprise!'

Crispus frowned.

'Can we load one of the ballistae and get them before they escape?'

Balbus shook his head.

'No way we've got time. We can't catch them now. We'll just have to go ahead anyway. I'd best go let Caesar know though.'

Fronto glanced over his shoulder.

The field was full of men and metal. Six legions, even depleted as they were, numbered over twenty thousand and, with the auxilia among them, they more than doubled that. Thousands of cavalry sat on the wings neighing and prancing expectantly. Archers and slingers filled the rear of the force. Each legion had its own commanders present in all their glory. In all, the formation as a display of military might was a great deal more impressive than the carefully organised hilltop formation at Bibracte.

On the right flank, Caesar sat astride his white charger, the red cloak picking him out as an obvious target. Whatever Fronto might have to say about the general from time to time, the man was certainly not short of courage. A well-placed arrow could soon cut short his career in Gaul once they started moving forward. Beside Caesar sat Ingenuus, proud on his dappled grey, red cloak flapping in the breeze. Divitiacus, the most senior of the Aedui present, sat in his traditional armour on the other side of the general.

On the far left, Crassus sat on his brown and white, looking pompous to Fronto's eyes. In the centre Priscus was the front man of the Tenth, for Fronto and Varus were here, two hundred paces ahead of even the foremost of the army. Varus sat astride his white horse, some Gallic breed that Fronto did not recognise, while Fronto rode Bucephalus. He had to hand it to Longinus, this was a lovely horse. Comfortable and steady, but fearless and strong. There were a network of small scars on the horse's shoulders and flanks; signs of the situations in which the commander and the horse had both been in trouble and both come out to tell the tale. The scar on the horse's shoulder from the recent cavalry engagement was still fresh and livid. Fronto made a mental note to have someone look at it later.

The sun was already fairly high. Once word had reached Caesar that the massing of his troops was no longer a secret from Ariovistus, he had set back the assembly time to give the troops and officers a full night of rest. Consequently, when the legions had begun to move into position, the Germans were also already on the move.

Much as the German King obviously did not want this battle, he had been left with little choice. Knowing that the entire Roman force was in position, well supplied, and intending to march upon him, his only option had been to prepare for battle.

Fronto glanced along the German lines, not very far away at all. He was grateful that Ariovistus had chosen to make an open fight of it. The man could easily have stayed within the camp and made Caesar besiege it. Fronto knew they could guarantee a greater loss of life if that were the case.

'They're split up into different groups. Not tribes, but thingies, like the Helvetii did. What d'you call them?'

Varus smiled. Fronto made him chuckle even when blackest vengeance was gripping him from the inside.

'Cantons.

'Bless you!'

Varus grinned as the iron grip on his heart faltered again. Fronto was a rare breed among senior commanders. He and Balbus were very similar in many ways, and the effect that the two of them had on the other senior officers was noticeable. Varus could only imagine what the atmosphere among the men would be like now if Crispus, Galba and Rufus had come under the influence of Crassus from early on. Men who improved the morale of the army did it credit and Varus was determined one day to be one of those men.

'I can see seven cantons. That means the Suevi must have joined up with them on their march.'

Fronto sighed.

'Doesn't surprise me. If they moved as fast as the rest of the Germans did, they probably reached them before even we re-joined the army. Can you see what they've done at the back and the sides?'

Varus squinted into the haze.

'Are they fortifying around behind them?'

Fronto shook his head.

'They're stopping their own men from running. That's a good sign for us. Probably a lot of them are unhappy about being made to fight against the whim of their Gods. Ariovistus is making sure the only way they can get out is through us.'

Varus shaded his eyes.

'I think you'll find there's something else going on. They appear to be loading all those wagons around the back with women and children!'

Fronto stared.

'Now *that's* interesting. I wonder whether they're meant to encourage them to fight or to prevent them escaping. No one's going to flee the field if it means cutting through your womenfolk. Interesting. I think we should be in a good position today. Our men are riled and ready for a fight. If theirs are suffering that badly with morale problems, we should be alright.'

He leaned back in the saddle.

'We should probably get back and tell Caesar now.'

Varus waved him down.

'In a moment. Look at their cavalry, heavy on either side. D'you see?'

'I see cavalry. Why?'

'There's a weakness on the right. Look at them. They've concentrated around two thirds of them on the left. On the right they don't have many foot supporting them. They could be broken easily. The other side could be a problem. I need to speak to Crassus. He's going to have to pull in extra support on our left. Perhaps from Caesar's cavalry, perhaps from the legions.'

Fronto shrugged.

'Either you really do know your stuff or your eyes are better than mine. Looks the same to me. Still, I'll tell Caesar about the general situation. You tell Crassus about your cavalry, yes?'

As Varus nodded, the two of them turned their mounts and rode back toward the Roman lines.

Moments later, Caesar leaned forward in his saddle.

'Fronto. What's the situation?'

The legate grinned.

'They look a little unwilling. Ariovistus has them surrounded by wagons and women to stop them running. They're all drawn up in seven cantons and the Suevi are there. The legions should be able to take them so long as the cavalry are alright on the flanks.'

Caesar smiled at him.

'Oh, I think we'll be fine, Marcus.'

'Yes, I think you will. Varus said the cavalry element's much lighter and weaker on this side, like maybe it's a feint.'

Caesar frowned.

'What does he plan to do about it?'

Fronto growled.

'He doesn't command the cavalry if you remember, sir? He plans to warn Crassus.'

The general directed a warning glance at Fronto.

'Very well. We'll give a count of five hundred before calling the advance. I want Crassus and Varus to have enough time to adjust their attack.'

The two stared across the field to where Crassus and Varus sat astride their horses, facing each other and talking.'

'Varus, *I* am in charge of this wing, and *I* will decide whether we're not up to the task.'

Varus slapped his hand down hard on the saddle horn.

'*Sir!* If you don't arrange to bolster our wing now, we could find ourselves very deep in the shit when we meet the enemy. You said you wanted me here for my experience, and you're not *listening* to me. I *know* what I'm talking about!'

'We have the strongest cavalry force that's been fielded in this entire campaign; possibly in the history of Roman warfare. We have experienced troops fighting in Roman armour and style and vast amounts of barbarian levies fighting in the same style as the Germans. We could beat them if they were ten feet tall and I *will* not go to one of my opposite numbers and beg for help.'

'You don't *have* to beg for help, sir. Caesar knows all of this and he has the cavalry to spare. The third line of each legion is a reserve force for just such emergencies.'

'Get back to your ala, prefect.'

'If you order me there, I'll go, but you're going to kill a lot of people if you don't change the plan.'

'I *said:* Get back to your ala!'

With a face like thunder, Varus kicked his heels and turned to ride to his men.

'Yes, sir!'

Crassus stared off into the mass of Germans half a mile away. They had not the heart or the stomach for a proper fight.

'Germans! I'd take one Roman over a thousand of them.'

Toward the centre of the line, Priscus looked over his shoulder at the Tenth, behind him. They looked eager; angry even. He turned back and muttered to Sabinus, assigned as lieutenant for the Tenth and standing beside him.

'We're not going to have much room to manoeuvre, sir. Half a mile. If we run and so do they, we'll barely have time to draw swords!'

Sabinus nodded.

'Caesar wants two full pilum volleys before we meet them. You don't think we'll have time?'

Priscus snorted.

'Unless something miraculous happens, we'll not get a chance to let off *one* volley or, if we do, it'll have to be so early it'll be a pointless gesture.'

Sabinus raised an eyebrow.

'Fronto lauds your abilities as a commander to everyone. I've seen my fair share, but mostly from a nearby hill and directing grand plans. You're the one with the experience, Priscus. Do what you think's best.'

Priscus nodded and turned to face the Tenth.

'Disarm your pila. Pass them to the back of the legion and stack them for later. Draw swords.'

He turned to Sabinus.

'Do you know anything about their tactics, sir?'

The staff officer smiled and shrugged.

'I would expect more of what we've seen before: cavalry with individual infantry support, but what we'll meet in the middle is a different matter. They have a similar tribal and military style as the Gauls, and they've been fighting with and against them for many years. I wouldn't be at all surprised to see phalanx, shield wall or even squares.'

Priscus nodded.

'Some kind of shield-based defensive formation, then, eh?'

'Something like that.'

Priscus turned once more and shouted across the front line, in the centre of which stood the First Cohort.

'Remember the Helvetii lads?'

There was an affirmative murmur.

'You remember how they broke our square? How they got in among us?'

Again, an affirmative murmur. The First Cohort would clearly remember that moment, trapped among the Helvetii, trying to maintain their formation while the rest of the Tenth arrived. Next to Priscus, a signifer gripped his slightly dented standard very tight.

'If the Germans are in a line when we get there, we're going to do *that* to *them*! As soon as I give the word.'

A low approval hummed across the crowd.

Sabinus stamped his foot impatiently.

'Why aren't we moving?'

Priscus grinned.

'Dunno sir, but I'd make the most of it if I were you.'

Titus Balventius growled.

'I can lead 'em myself sir and you know it.'

Balbus sighed.

'No more argument Titus. I'm the commander of the legion and commanders should command from the front.'

'No sir. Centurions should lead from the front. Commanders should sit in shiny armour on a nice looking horse at the back, like a good gentleman.'

He rolled his one good eye toward Balbus.

'If you get yourself killed it'll only make my lads worry.'

'I'm touched by your sentiment. I am, however, staying right here. Even Caesar's leading from the front.'

Another growl. The primus pilus of the Eighth turned to face his men.

'See them? They're Germans, and they fight nasty. The only way to deal with them is to fight nastier. If I see any of you showing any kind of mercy or pity, I'll tear your arms off myself. I want to see you stab, slash, gouge, shield barge and kick and punch. When you're too close for that, I want to see you knee, head-butt and bite. Make the bastards afraid of the Eighth. Everybody else is.'

Once again, Balbus found himself looking sideways at his primus pilus. Balventius would get his honesta missio shortly, but he would probably turn it down. The grizzled centurion would likely stay in his current position until an enemy blow finished him. He was the kind of man that would make a good camp prefect when the time came. The legate made a mental note to have a word with Caesar.

Crispus smiled. To his left Felix, the primus pilus of the Eleventh, stared at him with a puzzled look. The young legate had taken on the hard look of an embittered veteran. Felix cringed. He had seen that look on plenty of men just before they got themselves killed on a revenge attack. He would have to look after this one. Aulus Crispus was young enough to be Felix's son and far too educated to talk to comfortably for any length of time, but he cared about his men and had a knack for last-moment strategy. He had the making of a fine commander. Felix wished he would shave, though. The lad was too young to grow anything but wisps, and he seemed to be modelling himself on the rarely shaven Fronto.

To the other side of Crispus stood Quintus Pedius, a staff officer roughly the same age as Crispus but already tanned dark and with a permanent five o'clock shadow. Pedius had served before as a tribune and travelled with his father on campaigns. Crispus felt oddly inferior when standing next to him.

'They don't look at all bad for a fledgling legion, do they Pedius?'

The staff officer smiled.

'They look like veterans, Aulus, and they soon will be. Remember, they're nearing the end of a full season of campaigning now, and they've fought several battles. I don't think you can really call them 'fledgling' anymore. And look at you. You look different to the young administrator who arrived fresh from Rome.'

Crispus shrugged.

'I'm that very same person, though I *am* starting to learn what it is to command men. I'm not entirely sure that I am the best choice. *You* were wanting a commission to command a legion, weren't you. Maybe after this battle you can take on the Eleventh.'

Pedius grinned at him and then looked across him at Felix.

'Centurion, what would you say if Crispus here were to step down as commander of the Eleventh in favour of someone like myself?'

Felix grinned his lopsided grin.

'Respectfully, I'd say stick it up yer arse sir. The lad's ours now. 'E took us as new and made us 'eroes sir.'

He turned to look at Crispus.

'You're me commander, lad. Don't ye dare step down. That's worse than getting' yerself killed.'

Pedius grinned at the primus pilus.

'My thoughts exactly.'

He smiled at Crispus.

'You're their commander until you or they die or until Caesar sees fit to replace you. Me? I'll wait 'til next year. There'll be more legions raised next year, you mark my words, and I've got my sights set on one of them.'

Crispus frowned.

'Do you know, Pedius, I've actually given not a single iota of thought to the future ever since Bibracte. I'd not set my mind at all to next year.'

Pedius smiled again.

'For now, just get through today, eh?'

———————————

Across the lines, the signal to advance was given. The legions moved forward at their steady fast march, shields locked in front, bristling with the points of swords and pila. On the wings the cavalry kept pace with the line.

The blaring of horns announced the attack of the Germans. Like two opposed waves, the armies moved across the grass, the Romans at a steady, unstoppable gait, the Germans in an unruly charge. Balbus shouted along the front of the Eighth.

'Ready pila. Volley at two hundred paces.'

As the legionaries raised their pila, Balventius shouted out louder.

'Drop pila and draw swords!'

Balbus had barely time to wonder about his order being challenged as he saw the wave of Germans swarming toward them and realised there would have been no time for a volley. The enemy closed in a phalanx formation and at a ridiculous rate. Further along the line, the primus pilus of the Seventh gave orders to cast pila. The missiles arced out over the German lines, finding their targets only moments before the shield walls of the two armies met with a crash.

Most of the legions had cast their pila with the exception of the Tenth and the Eighth and, from the occasional glance Balbus managed, he realised that the legions had encountered difficulties. Many soldiers in the front line were fighting off the enemy with their shield bosses while desperately trying to draw their swords in the midst of the melee.

Balventius, fighting like a furious madman at the front of the First Cohort, kept the line straight. He shouted over his shoulder.

'Stop pushing the line. Wait for the signal.'

Slowly things began to right themselves along the line. The legionaries had managed to draw their weapons and were now settling in to their standard shield wall tactics, though the phalanx formation of the Germans was seriously reducing the effectiveness of the Roman attack. The two armies fought from behind their protective shields and little headway was possible.

Balbus held his shield high and protective as he stabbed rhythmically with his blade. The men of the Eighth would be proud to be fighting alongside their commander, and he was glad to be with them, but having tremendous trouble trying to think of a solution to their current problem. The lines were locked into a stalemate; a war of attrition, and something had to be done to break it. Damn it, he could not think straight with having to concentrate heavily on warding off blows from the front.

Further along the line, Crispus had dropped back from the front line. He had been cut by a German blade along his upper arm, but not badly, and had bloodied his own sword. The Eleventh had seen him fighting among them, and that was what was important. Now he had to be somewhere to think and direct his men. All across the field, the legions had barely moved since the two armies met, and stood little or no chance of advancing yet. He flipped through the mental pages of military history. His mind whirled through the battles of Alexander, Hannibal and Scipio Africanus, trying to find a way out.

Balbus gave a sharp intake of breath as the German spear point glanced off the rim of his shield and dug into the pteruges hanging at his shoulder. The tip tore through the leather and scraped across his upper arm, drawing blood. Lucky! Had it glanced to the left instead of the right, it could easily have gone through his chest. A distant call came from the right, where the Tenth fought alongside them, and a roar went up from the men of that legion.

Priscus waved the men on around him while the butchery continued. The front few ranks of the legion continued to stab at the enemy, while the rear ranks opened up, leaving space for manoeuvring. One of the centurions called out to the primus pilus.

'Ready, sir.'

Priscus smiled and raised his voice over the din of battle.

'Break ranks!'

The front lines of the Tenth pulled aside for a moment. Pockets of legionaries continued to fight the phalanx of Germans, while gaps opened along the front. The Germans, surprised by the sudden withdrawal of sections of Roman shields began to surge forward, only to meet groups of legionaries from the rear lines, who were now charging shieldless through the gaps at the enemy.

The groups of men hit the German phalanx with the force of a charging bull and, rather than stabbing with their swords, began to wrench the German shields down and to the sides. Others vaulted over the top and came crashing down among the press of barbarian warriors. Instantly the order and formation among the Germans collapsed. Their phalanx front had been broken in several places, and now there were legionaries in among them. The formation turned into a melee within moments, whereas the Roman line had formed once again, the gaps closing with drilled precision.

Nonus had not had so much fun since he had raced up the hill with Velius and a few others to take out the last of the Helvetii so many months ago. It was gratifying that his reputation had been so confirmed that day that he was immediately called upon whenever anything slightly insane and dangerous was suggested. He had been the first among the Germans, vaulting so high he had come down several rows back. He had been lucky, really. The man who had leapt over just to his left had ended impaled on a raised German spear point.

He grinned like a savage as he stabbed again and again into the flesh pressed around him. The Germans had been so tightly pushed together in their formation that they had no room to manoeuvre. Their long spears and long Celtic swords were all but useless in such a confined space.

'Eleven. Twelve...' he counted as he systematically exterminated the men around him. He crouched low, turning as he went. Slowly a space was opening around him as bodies hit the ground, spraying him with their lifeblood.

He smiled again, wondering where Curtius, his friend and colleague, was. Curtius had been in the next group down and should be somewhere in this press of men. All he had to do now was keep going until the Tenth had broken enough of the front line to reach him. He would...

Velius was with the first few of his men to push into the broken phalanx. They surged forward, breaking their own formation and moving into a man to man melee, the Germans fighting back desperately and trying to make enough room to fight effectively. Pushing as hard as he could into the press of barbarians, he had not even noticed as he stepped over the fresh body of Nonus, the Tenth's wrestling champion, lying twisted among the enemy corpses.

Balbus' arm shuddered under every impact of the German blade, his shield fracturing and cracking, held together by only the bronze edging. Glancing along the line, he saw Balventius fighting like an enraged animal and cursing the barbarians as he plunged in repeatedly with his gladius. Belting an unwary tribesman with his shield boss, Balventius stepped back and craned his head over the melee. Balbus turned momentarily to follow his gaze, but a heavy blow pushed him into the man behind him.

'What's up?'

The primus pilus smiled, the effect as disconcerting as ever as the lines and scars on his face joined in places.

'The Tenth have broken them. We need to push hard. Now.'

He turned away from the enemy warriors and shouted to the Eighth.

'Push! Push the bastards back. They're breaking!'

The German he had been fighting took the opportunity to swing the heavy sword at the primus pilus' upper back. The sword edge sliced from his right shoulder across both blades, cutting through chain, scale and the man's subarmalis. The blade continued on its relentless swing leaving a trail of blood droplets, shattered links of chain mail and scales from the centurion's armour flying through the air. Balbus watched the blow in horror and disbelief.

For a moment Balventius staggered forward into the ranks of Romans, lurching, as the protective armour on his back neatly separated and most of the torso hung from one armpit like a loose rag. The veteran's knuckles tightened for a moment and then twitched, almost dropping the sword. The shield fell forgotten to the floor.

Balbus watched as the centurion almost toppled, then righted himself. As the grizzly Balventius turned back toward the Germans Balbus saw both the cut across his shoulders, which was deep and vicious, bleeding profusely down his back, and the look in his eye. Far from knocking him out of the fight, the German's blow had enraged him.

Balventius squared his shoulders and the blood from the cut splashed the men behind him.

'You little German whore-dog son of a Greek catamite! I'm going to tear your liver out with my teeth!'

The barbarian had drawn the broad blade back for another swing at the Roman. He grinned and let fly with the sword, swinging round like a pendulum, heavy and unstoppable. Balventius ducked and, as the blade carried on its arc above his head, stabbed with his blade into the man's gut. As his right hand twisted the hilt, he reached up with his left hand and gripped the terrified German's windpipe.

Balbus turned his head away just too slowly to miss the grisly sight as his primus pilus wrenched out the man's throat. Balventius held the lump of meat high as the German toppled forward.

'At 'em now, men.'

The Eighth surged past both of their commanders, piling into the enemy, Balbus pushed through them to his primus pilus. Balventius stood erect, head held high, as the men charged but, as soon as Balbus reached him, the two of them made their way slowly back through the ranks. They passed the main attacking force by and entered the gap between the second and third line, where the Eighth's capsarii sat, tending to the wounded. Balbus, knowing his officers very well, surreptitiously held Balventius' arm as he staggered and sank to his knees.

'Your primus pilus needs you.'

The capsarius examined the wound closely.

'That's going to need some serious work. I need you to get to one of the tents and lie face down on a cot. Legate, would you help me with him.'

Balventius spat on the floor and rolled his eye at the medicus.

'If I were going anywhere, I could do it myself, but I'm not. I need you to stitch me up right here and now while I sit.'

The capsarius opened his mouth to speak, but Balventius overrode him as he called over one of the orderlies on the rise nearby.

'Get to the quartermaster and requisition me a new mail shirt.'

Balbus shrugged as he turned and walked back toward the melee. Capsarii usually won arguments with the wounded, but he could not imagine Balventius giving any ground. The man was clearly insane and, given any leeway at all, would be back in the line as soon as possible, hammering at Germans, held together with twine if necessary.

Glancing from the slight rise across the field, he had, for the first time, a clear view of what was happening. The centre was moving now, the Germans falling back under the combined weight of the Tenth and the Eighth. The other legions were beginning to make some headway, and the cavalry were tied up with the enemy on both wings.

In the distance, at the far right, he could just see Caesar in his red cloak on the white horse, deep among the enemy cavalry.

CHAPTER 21

(THE BATTLEFIELD)

'Patrician: The higher class of Rome, often Senatorial.'

'Equestrian. The often wealthier, though less noble mercantile class, known as knights.'

'Nobiles: A noble Roman descended from a Consul.'

The German cavalry had moved in for the kill at both ends of the phalanx, in much the same fashion as the Roman line. Caesar had ridden at the front of the wing right in among the enemy. Most of the cavalry troopers and auxilia had been awed and impressed by the sight of the general charging among his men and subjecting himself to danger. Prefect Aulus Ingenuus, however, commanding the regular cavalry on the wing, had his own opinion.

He had been close enough to observe the combat most of the time, and had not yet seen the general actually physically engage a German warrior. Indeed, with the exception of occasionally brandishing his cavalry sword high, Caesar seemed not to have been involved at all. The few times German riders had been close enough to pose a threat to him, a number of auxiliary cavalrymen would rush to his aid and dispatch the enemy immediately.

These saviours of the general did not seem to be attached to any of the auxiliary units on the field and Ingenuus could only imagine that Caesar had organised and authorised a private bodyguard in the fashion so often favoured by Roman generals.

The two forces had met on the right wing with a thunderous crash. The report they had received from Varus had proved to be wholly accurate. Ariovistus seemed to have forfeited strength on this wing, presumably to create a strong position at the other side. The fighting had immediately become bloody and violent, with most of both forces armed with spears and a smaller proportion with long swords. Here and there among the Germans were footmen, attached to the cavalry as they had been before, one man to one horse.

As Ingenuus glanced around, looking for any enemy that was not already engaged, he suddenly spotted the German warrior out of the corner of his eye. The man had managed to get round behind him and lunged with his spear, jabbing deep into the horse's flank. As he tried to bring his sword to bear on the man, his horse bucked and jumped. The barbarian tried to land a more fatal blow with his spear, but the horse's lashing hooves caught him in the chest and hurled him across the field. The prefect had little time to gloat, as his thigh came unhooked from the saddle horn and he was pitched high into the air when his horse bucked again before cantering off the field, leaving a trail of blood.

Ingenuus had been a horseman from his earliest memories, riding his steed around the countryside near Capua every moment he had free. His family were reasonably wealthy, though nothing like the Senatorial class in Rome and had had a stable with several horses. He had almost been paralysed after a particularly bad fall when he was ten and had been forbidden to ride for a few years. Flashes of these days and many others passed through the young man's head as he fell. Fortunately, with the memories came the knowledge of how to fall and roll and avoid serious injury.

He hit the ground hard and rolled several feet until he came to a stop, standing as fast as he could to avoid being trampled by the numerous horses of both sides. An auxiliary cavalryman swept around with his spear and made for a moment to impale him before realising that he was not a German footman, but a dismounted Roman. Before anyone else could deal with him, he crouched and hunted quickly for his sword. There was no sign. With the way he was pitched from the horse, it could have come down anywhere. He shrugged energetically and only then, with that moment, did he realise how badly he had hurt his shoulder during the fall. He bit off an unbidden cry and closed his eyes for a moment until the pain passed.

Looking around to try and grasp how the land lay, he saw a German nearby, sat astride his horse, fighting with an auxiliary cavalryman. He stepped forward, almost stumbling over a body. Acting purely on instinct, he reached down to the body and picked up the broken spear the dead German had been using.

With a couple more steps, he found himself within striking distance of the German rider and brought the spear round in a two-handed underarm swing. Though the movement caused screaming pain in his shoulder, he persevered and the point vanished into the man's side just below the ribs, running deep within. The rider jerked once, made a croaking sound, and then slumped in his saddle, dark gobbets of blood pouring from both mouth and wound. Ingenuus gave a heave on the man's leg and the body fell to the ground, the Germanic sword still grasped in his hand.

Crouching down, wincing once more at the pain, he tugged at the dead man's fingers, slowly prising them apart until he could remove the sword. Grasping the hilt he stood, weighing the blade in his hand. It was heavier than the Roman cavalry sword he was used to, but not unwieldy. Hefting it, he looked around.

Close by, two Germans were stabbing with spears at a Roman cavalry trooper who flailed with his sword, knocking one of the spears out of the way while protecting himself from the other with his shield. For a moment, the prefect wondered whether it was truly wise to push his already painful shoulder but decided that he would not be able to fight effectively with one arm using a blade of this weight. Taking a running step forward, he drew the huge sword back, gritting his teeth against the pain. A final step and he brought the blade around in a wide sweep, impressed with the devastation wrought by a blade this size and gaining a grudging respect for Celtic smiths. The sword, relying more on its weight than its edge, caught the German in the side, severing the spear-wielding arm instantly and continuing halfway through the chest. The pure momentum of the sweep ripped the blade out of the body, carrying viscera and chunks of bone with it. The German slumped forward, almost collapsing in on himself with the shattering of so many bones.

The pain in his shoulder all but forgotten, Ingenuus stared at the Celtic sword. It might be harder to wield on horseback, and it was certainly a slower weapon than the blades he was used to, but on foot, and with the room to swing, it was devastating. The beleaguered trooper, suddenly faced with only one opponent, swung his blade and shattered the spear. Moments later he finished the man off, while Ingenuus scanned the field. He reached out for one of the now many riderless horses and grasped the saddle before he realised that there was no way he would be able to haul himself onto a horse with his shoulder like this and still carrying the blade. He turned again to scan the field for any further trouble. Most of the action had now died down. On this side of the field the German cavalry had been weakened, and the Romans had caused devastating losses with comparatively few on their own side.

It was as he was surveying with an air of satisfaction that he saw the three horsemen bearing down on the general. Four of the 'bodyguard' were nearby, but only one was realistically within reach, and he was under attack by the footmen attached to those cavalry. There were so many Roman regulars and auxiliaries around, but they were all occupied with chasing down the Germans who were trying to reach the other side of the field to rally their compatriots.

Taking a deep breath, Ingenuus started to run. His legs felt like lead and his shoulder burned as he pulled the sword back behind him, ready for a huge swing. Moments passed as he saw Caesar for the first time during the battle hold out his blade and prepare to engage in combat. One of the enemy horsemen veered off to deal with the bodyguard who was racing in to protect the general, but the other two separated as they reached Caesar, attacking him from both sides. With blood pounding in his ears and his breath coming in rasping gasps, Ingenuus launched himself at the closest.

The general lunged at the other cavalryman, his sword flashing in the sun. He had taken his ornate gladius into battle, rather than a standard cavalry sword, and the reach was unrealistic. There was no way he would be able to fight off the enemy for long, and he could not lunge far enough to do serious damage with the short sword. The German swung his blade and the general was forced to throw himself forward, flat across the horse's neck.

The other German reined his horse in a little and pulled his arm back, the spear ready for an over arm stab. He reared back and Ingenuus swung with the heavy blade, feeling the muscles in his shoulder tear with the effort. Unused to the weight of the blade, his swing was lower than he had intended and dipped even further, losing power as the blade travelled. Far from hitting the man in the side and unhorsing him, the edge smashed into the man's leg just above the knee, severing it messily and smashing into the horse's side. The German slid from the other side of the horse, the severed leg falling to the ground and landing close to the forgotten spear. The horse reared in shock and pain, the wound in its side deep and long. The blow had certainly broken its ribs.

In pain and confusion, the horse blundered forward into the general's. Caesar, locked deep in personal combat, was caught unawares as his horse panicked and bucked. The general was hurled into the air and crashed to the turf close by. Both Caesar's white horse and the German's chestnut panicked and thrashed for only a moment before running from the scene. Ingenuus rushed to help the general up, pausing only to stick his large Celtic sword into the one-legged German who rolled around on the floor in agony. The general was unhurt, apart likely from a little bruising and a pulled muscle or two. He stood, brushing himself down. The second German who had been locked in combat with the general had finally righted his nervous horse, just in time to face two of the bodyguards who had reached the scene. Leaving them to deal with the enemy, Ingenuus dropped the tip of his sword to the ground and leaned on the heavy hilt, wincing and rolling his shoulder. He breathed out, a deep relieved sigh, and then realised that he was in the presence of the commander of the entire army. He straightened.

'Apologies, general. Can I be of assistance?'

Caesar smiled at the tired and injured cavalry prefect.

'Aulus Ingenuus I believe. You've already assisted me, prefect. Looks like we've broken the wing, wouldn't you say?'

The young officer glanced around at the scene wearily. There were shattered remains of the German cavalry force visible here and there through the Romans and Gauls. Few remained on the field, and those that did fought desperately for their life against tremendous odds. Some distance away a party of Germans fleeing the field were just visible over the trees.

'Yes sir. I'd say we've turned the wing. Permission to depart, sir? I need to find a horse and a Roman sword.'

Caesar frowned.

'You're wounded, prefect. Look at the way you're standing. You need to get to the valetudinarium, not the stables.'

Ingenuus raised his eyebrows in surprise.

'I've a few aches and pains, sir, but I've no intention of leaving the field before any of the Germans.'

Caesar laughed.

'Very well. Shall we rally the cavalry and support the main push? Harry the enemy on the flanks?'

The prefect was opening his mouth and drawing breath to speak, when a regular cavalry trooper thundered to a halt next to him and saluted the general wearily. Glancing up, Ingenuus realised this was a decurion he used to serve with, one of Varus' men now. The trooper was spattered with blood; some of it his own. A grisly sight. The man straightened, wincing at some invisible pain.

'General, Commander Varus wanted me to tell you that we ran into real heavy resistance on the left. We're deep in the shit sir. Any help you can throw our way'd be real handy, sir.'

Ingenuus looked up at the general who tapped his lip.

'What does Crassus suggest?'

The trooper looked taken aback for a moment.

'*Crassus*, sir? Never stopped to ask. He's ridin' around at the back making sure no one retreats! Being an arse, sir!'

Caesar frowned.

'You mean he's led the cavalry into deep water and then left you there?'

'Not deep water, sir. Deep shit!'

Caesar leaned down to Ingenuus.

'What's your opinion of our situation on this wing?'

436

Ingenuus put his finger to his lip.

'We could push the remnants out, harry the flank of the infantry *and* chase down the escapees with only half what we have here, sir. Once the remnants of the cavalry are gone, we could try to remove some of their wagons and have a go at the rear, but it would be dangerous.'

'I tend to agree, prefect. You feel up to the job?'

'Yes sir.'

Caesar smiled again as the young man came painfully to attention.

'Good. And stop doing that... you'll break something. I'll take half the cavalry round the edge of the field to aid the left and pick up the third reserve line as I go. You take command here, but don't try for their flanks. There are too many wagons and defences round their sides and rear, and that's a job for the infantry. Chase them down. I'll join you as soon as I've seen to the left wing.'

Ingenuus nodded.

'Yes sir. With pleasure.'

Varus dared a quick look over his shoulder. The rear ranks of the left wing had thinned out rather seriously. Crassus had been pushing and driving all the time, sending forward any spare men he could find the moment he spotted a gap. There was no longer a reserve, no support. Everyone was on the front line and they were still outnumbered.

The enemy horsemen were, as previously, supported on a one-to-one basis by footmen armed with swords or spears, and there were a great number of riderless horses and dismounted cavalry littering the field. The prefect's attention was drawn back to the current predicament as the shaft of a spear drove past his shoulder. With a twist of his wrist, he flipped his sword and neatly cut the tip from the spear. Turning back to the man assailing him, he slashed twice in wide arcs, cutting the man across the chest and face. The German toppled from his horse, adding to the numerous bodies strewn across the grass, mostly Roman. He spotted one of the decurions nearby and shouted to attract his attention.

'Keep the line closed. No one's to be a hero. Just protect yourselves until help arrives. I'm going to see the commander.'

The decurion gave a barely perceptible nod and went back to fighting for his life, shouting orders out above the noise. Shaking his head with anger, Varus wheeled his horse and rode away from the danger toward Crassus, alone at the rear on his horse. The primus pilus of the Seventh was controlling the infantry while his legate dealt with the cavalry.

'Sir?'

'Yes, prefect?'

Varus came to a halt in front of the commander.

'Sir, you must pull in the third line of the legions; the reserve. We need them.'

'I won't have cowardice in my cavalry, prefect. We match them in strength.'

Varus growled audibly, the tip of his sword dipping dangerously toward his superior.

'If we weren't in battle, I'd kill you for that. We *don't* match them in strength. We're nowhere near. They outnumber us almost three to one with their infantry. We need to learn from *them*! We need infantry support!'

Crassus sneered.

'You are dismissed, prefect. You may leave the field.'

Varus growled again.

'*You* should leave the field, you puffed up, inbred, ignorant lunatic. I've got to look after my lads until support arrives.'

'There will be no support, prefect. I'll not beg for help.'

Varus wheeled his horse back toward the enemy.

'You don't need to call for help. I've already sent someone.'

And with that he charged off into the melee again.

Crassus watched with a rising fury as the prefect waded in among the enemy again. The man was brave, he had to admit, but he was just an equestrian. He would have to pay for talking like that to a superior officer; to one of the nobiles. After the battle, Varus would have to be removed from command, and beaten of course. He would have to speak to Caesar about the man.

Taking a deep breath, he scanned the rear of the field. He could not let another officer save his skin. He would have to do something himself. He looked around until he saw one of the irregular riders that carried messages.

'You. Go and find the commanders of the Seventh and tell them that their legate has ordered them to pull back and support the cavalry.'

The rider stared at the commander, a confused look on his face. Crassus sighed. The army would never be truly effective while they relied on barbarians for so many of their numbers.

'You go find big men in Seventh Legion!' He held his hands out showing seven fingers to emphasise the point.

'Tell them to come here!'

The rider grinned and said something unintelligible in his own language.

Another voice cut in.

'Belay that order.'

Crassus turned to see Caesar astride his white horse.

'General. We need my legion in support.'

Caesar smiled.

'I've heard. I've brought you half of my cavalry and the third line of infantry is wheeling left. They should be with you in a few moments.'

He gestured to the edge of the field, where hundreds of horsemen were appearing from behind a copse.

Crassus glared at Caesar.

'General, when I need reinforcements, I can call them myself, and I would have started with my own legion. I dismissed prefect Varus from the field and he insulted me and disobeyed my order. I shall be requesting the harshest of punishments for him.'

Caesar sighed and pointed into the distance.

'D'you see that, Crassus? That is a dangerously thin front line, near to breaking point. If you fail to hold that line, the German cavalry will have a clear run at our flank and our rear. Have you any idea what that means?'

'General, I...'

'It's a rhetorical question, Crassus... I'm known for my rhetoric. You're an able enough legionary commander I suppose, though too harsh. In time, you could even be a great commander, but you need to forget your pride, swallow your fear of failure and trust in your men. You're in danger of losing me half my cavalry and that man,' he pointed at Varus, hacking away among the Germans, 'is the only one holding that line together. Take the reserve cavalry into battle; I'm going back to push our advantage on the right. Win me the left, Crassus.'

Grinding his teeth, Crassus nodded curtly. Behind him, he could see several thousand heavy infantry. He would have to risk everything now to save face. As Caesar cantered back toward the remains of his wing, Crassus shouted out to one of the regular cavalry officers with the reserve force.

'Prefect! Order the reserve forward, then take charge of the infantry support and bring them up to the front as fast as you can.'

'Yes sir.'

The prefect saluted, turning to the reserves, as Crassus squared his shoulders and drew his sword. Nodding to the servant who held his gear for him, he retrieved his shield. With a deep drawn breath, he rode for the front line.

He saw Varus straight away. His attention was, however, drawn by an impressive fountain of blood and an airborne lower arm. He grumbled again, knowing that he had to make a magnanimous show here, or he was in danger of losing all the men's respect to Varus. Gritting his teeth, he rode directly for the prefect. The urge to 'accidentally' remove the man from the grand picture flashed momentarily through the legate's mind, but then professionalism took over. Waiting a moment for a gap to open, the legate hefted his blade and rode in alongside the prefect.

'Varus. Take all the men to your right and reform. I'm taking the left and the reserves are going to bolster the centre.'

Varus heard the legate's voice and glanced around in surprise in time to see Crassus lean forward over his horse's neck and drive his blade through a German footman. The prefect grinned maniacally.

'With pleasure, sir.'

The legate pushed forward, his bright, ornate armour now spattered with viscera. Looking out across the line, he saw the reserves almost upon them and the third line of infantry closing at the back. Turning his horse, he rode along the line toward the edge of the field.

'Left flank! Reform on me!'

Slowly the cavalry detached and withdrew to the commander. The Germans tried desperately to make the most of the gap left by the two forces separating, but those who rushed ahead to widen the breach merely came face to face with the reserve cavalry, fresh from the opposite wing. Not enough of their countrymen had seen the opportunity and rushed to seize it. As the few who had sought the advantage met their fate at the hands of cavalry swords, the third line reached the scene. Eight thousand heavy infantry; the trained elite of the Roman world, marched in unison, bearing the standards of six different legions. For the first time on the left of the field, the Germans knew panic.

Varus grinned as his men hacked, stabbed and slashed at the enemy, trying to carve an inroad into the main force. While he was under no illusion that Crassus actually trusted him, the legate *had* once more authorised his command. He raised himself as high as he could in the saddle and tried to look over the immediate area. The German wing was gradually beginning to give ground. He could not see the other wing, but the presence of half of Caesar's cavalry on this side could only mean that the right had punched through Ariovistus' defence. From here, Varus could see the centre and the advancing Roman line. The German infantry were giving ground with every moment, and only a few hundred cavalry lay between him and them. He shouted to his men.

'Push hard and push right. Try and join up with the Seventh!'

Sending some of the cavalry who were free of the melee toward the right hand side, Varus began to push for the main mass of Ariovistus' force.

As the Roman infantry finally hit the front line, the cavalry in the centre disengaged and moved to the sides to join Varus and Crassus. The infantry reserve, led by Quintus Tullius Cicero, smashed into the Germans like a hammer on an anvil. The power with which they hit threw many a German rider from his horse and Ariovistus' men finally gave ground, unable to bear the weight of such a heavy force.

Separated now by the infantry reserve, the two cavalry forces on the left fought independently, Varus pushing for the centre of the field and the main mass of the enemy, Crassus harrying their flank and pushing them from the field.

Varus caught only one more glimpse of his commander as Crassus, his shiny white and bronze armour now stained and spattered with blood and gore, wheeled his horse and fought off a German spearman. The man finally looked like the soldier he should be as far as Varus was concerned.

As the German cavalry finally gave, riders at the back fleeing the field, accompanied by their footmen, Varus could see the mass of the Seventh Legion only ten paces away.

'Let the reserves deal with the centre. We need to clear these bastards away from the edge, then we can start work on their infantry; give our lads a bit of a break.'

He looked around. The mass of German cavalry was now well and truly broken. The rear half of them had turned and were fleeing for their lives. Footmen were being trampled as their cavalry escaped. Those that were left at the front were no longer even attempting to push forward; they fought for their life and nothing less.

On the very edge of the field he could see Crassus' men harrying the fleeing cavalry. They were already half way off the battlefield in their pursuit.

'What the hell's he doing now? The battle's still happening!'

Returning his attention to the task at hand, he spotted a small knot of German riders at the rear of the enemy cavalry, jeering at their companions as they fled. They were surrounded by footmen with long spears, but they wore a great deal of gold and bejewelled and decorative armour. Blinking at a close call from a German spear and retaliating without even thinking, he shouted above the din to his unit.

'There are chieftains at the back. Push for them... I want prisoners!'

As he kicked his horse forward, a number of his regulars and a host of Gaulish auxiliaries joined him. It was tough and bloody work hacking their way through the remaining milling cavalry, but slowly and relentlessly they closed on the small knot of German commanders. Varus could not believe his luck. It was very unlikely Ariovistus was among them, but to take captive chieftains was not only a lucrative move on a battlefield, but would also break the Germans' spirit and increase the likelihood of a permanent surrender.

As the last horsemen in front of them broke away or died, Varus and his small unit reached a charge and spread out enough to allow a sword swing. He had to give credit to their opponents. The chieftains did not run, merely readying their weapons for combat. The footmen, presumably their own guard, levelled their long spears. As he bore down upon them, Varus recognised the danger. The bristling long spears would wreak havoc with a charge. Pulling hard on the reins, Varus stopped in his tracks, shouting out a halt to the rest of the unit. The regular cavalrymen reined in sharply after their commander, as did many of the auxilia. Some of the Gauls, eager and undisciplined charged straight at the group.

Varus turned his head away from the grisly sight. He hated to waste men or horses. Both were valuable.

Glancing around, he could see the situation was turning grave for the German chieftains. To his left the reserve force and a few of the cavalry were driving the German wing from the field. To his right, the German mass was being forced back into the 'U' of their wagons. Varus turned and lowered his blade.

'Do any of you speak Latin?'

One of the horsemen manoeuvred his horse out ahead of the others.

'I talk little.'

Varus nodded.

'You are finished here. Over. Understand?'

The German grinned a defiant grin.

'Many of us. Much left.'

Varus shook his head.

'You are finished. Surrender now. There's no need for you all to throw away your lives. Surrender and I'll guarantee I will do my best to see that you return to your lands across the Rhine.'

There was a great deal of conferring among the barbarians, and then the spokesman stepped his horse further forward.

'We not surrender to you. You fight us.'

Varus sighed. So much for diplomacy. He called out a number of orders very quickly in Latin; too quick, he hoped, for the German to have followed him. Behind him the regulars and some of the Gauls formed up with their swords at the ready. The rest of the auxiliaries moved out to the edge and levelled their spears.

'One more time. We don't need the bloodshed. Will you surrender?'

The barbarian chieftain merely snarled in response and threw his horse forward into a charge. Varus, disciplined as always, waited for the man, neatly sidestepped his mount and swung with his sword. The chieftain continued on between the regular cavalry as he slowly topped forward over his horse's mane and then slid from the saddle and bounced along the ground before coming to a rest finally in a broken and painful position.

Varus turned back to his men.

'Release!'

The Gaulish auxiliaries cast their spears in unison at the footmen protecting the chieftains. As many of the missiles struck home, the protective ring around the men fell away.

Varus held the chieftains in his gaze. Without a glance at his men, he gave the order in a low, quiet voice.

'Take them.'

Varus merely sat astride his horse, viscera still running down the blade of his sword and dripping to the turf. The cavalry swarmed past on either side, bearing down on the chieftains, intent on destruction. Varus knew when to take the lead and when to let his men off the leash. There were times when soldiers needed a free hand to take out their anger and hatred over the loss of comrades or personal injuries. He looked up only once at the destruction ahead of him. Afterward they would loot the bodies and carry the gold back to their camp for their own personal funds. Such was the way of things. Varus would go back empty handed and face the judgement he had called down. For all Crassus' change, Varus had disobeyed orders and had insulted a senior officer, and was under no misconception of what that would mean.

As his eyes gradually focused on the grisly scene, he noticed something he had not been able to see between the horses and men. A Roman. A man in a military tunic among the few survivors still fighting for their lives against his men. A momentary worry caught him and he called out at the top of his voice; a halt to the fighting.

As the cavalry drew back, surprised, the three remaining German warriors took the opportunity to drop their swords and surrender. Between them the Roman stood, his tunic dirty and bloody and torn, his arms tied together behind him. Varus rode forward, gesturing to his men to deal with the prisoners. He frowned at the Roman.

'Who are you?'

The man struggled to stand proud, though painfully and was still hampered by the way his arms were tied.

'I'm Marcus Mettius. Staff officer of Caesar.'

Varus stared. Everyone knew of Mettius and Procillus and their capture by Ariovistus, but no one had ever expected to see them alive again.

'What of Procillus?'

Varus dismounted and approached the officer.

'I don't know whether he lives or not,' the man replied. 'We were separated immediately. I must report to Caesar.'

Varus smiled as he reached round and cut the man's bonds.

'Caesar's chasing men halfway to the Rhine by now. I think you'd best come back and see the medicus before the general returns. Use my horse. I'll lead him and we'll get you some clean gear.'

Mettius smiled a relieved smile.

'Thank you, but I can walk. As we go, you can tell me who *you* are and what's happened since I was taken.'

Fronto had left Caesar and ridden round the back of the infantry to the centre where the third line of the Tenth had been massed. By prior arrangement with the other officers, and much to Fronto's personal dislike, he had agreed that, since he would be scouting for Caesar's staff, he would take position with the third line and command the reserves when they went in. As such, he had stood by his horse, holding the reins and talking to young centurion Pomponius throughout the entirety of the assault on the German line. He seriously doubted they would need the reserves. This

445

was it. Almost certainly the last action this campaigning year, and he had missed out. The legate spat on the floor and grumbled.

Pomponius waited until Fronto was looking away and then rolled his eyes skywards. He was getting sick and tired of the legate complaining. Most soldiers were happy to wait in the reserve. The chances of being skewered or sliced were so much slimmer.

'Sir, if you're bored why don't you go and see the support staff. I'm sure they're at least *doing* something, so you could get involved.'

Fronto glared at Pomponius.

'I'm not so desperate to shout at people that I want to watch quartermasters and medics screwing things up.'

Pomponius merely smiled and arched one eyebrow. He may be relatively new to the ranks of the centurionate, and even relatively new to the Tenth, but like all the officers of the legion, he knew the legate very well by now. Fronto saw the raised eyebrow and sighed.

'Alright, I'll go and see the support. If anything remotely exciting happens, have someone come and get me. At least someone back there's going to have some wine.'

As Fronto stomped off toward the rear, Pomponius smiled again and contemplated what life could have been like with a commander who *did not* care.

Fronto wandered into the makeshift hospital where the action was already fast and revolting. The battle had been going for less than half an hour, and casualties were not in short supply. Probably in the same amount of time the battle would be over, not like that protracted siege with the Helvetii. He cursed again and tapped irritably on his sword hilt. He was surveying the general carnage when his eyes lit on a familiar face.

Titus Balventius, primus pilus of the Eighth, sat on a slight hummock in the grass with a distressed capsarius tending to some kind of wound. Fronto grinned and made his way toward the battered old centurion. The man was covered in blood and clearly a lot of it was his, though beneath the crimson stains the man was as pale as a Vestal virgin at an orgy.

'Balventius. Been in the wars?'

He slumped to the grass next to the wounded man.

'Some bastard German got me when I wasn't looking.'

446

Fronto smiled again.

'I take it he doesn't look as well as you.'

The legate glanced over the centurion's shoulder to examine what the capsarius was doing.

'Sweet Fortuna, that's deep!'

As Balventius nodded, the capsarius tutted irritably.

'If you keep jerking around like that I'm going to end up sewing your lung to your heart, now will you *keep still!*'

The centurion glanced up at Fronto from his slightly hunched position.

'Are the Tenth not moving?'

Fronto gave his customary growl.

'Most of them are, but I'm commanding the reserve.'

Balventius turned his head, causing muttering from the man.

'How long are you going to be? I've got a unit out there with no commander.'

The capsarius almost dropped his last stitch.

'You must be bloody joking. You've lost enough blood to fill an amphora. You'll be lucky if you can walk fast without fainting. And there are twenty six stitches across your shoulders with a long, deep wound. The first time you swing or lunge, you'll rip 'em all out, and I'll have to start again from scratch. And *that's* if you don't lose enough blood to drop dead on the journey back. You're out of it centurion, I'm afraid.'

With an exaggerated tug that caused Balventius to wince, the capsarius finished sewing the wound.

'Does that mean you're done?'

'I've just got to bandage you now.'

Fronto leaned forward and spoke to the man.

'I'll help and, for the record, this man's almost certainly had worse wounds.'

Balventius nodded.

'Sorry, doc. There's no way I'd be staying back here unless I was missing a leg or something. Just get me bound.'

He looked up at Fronto again.

447

'If you really want to do something useful, sir, could you find one of these waste-of-good-air quartermasters and get me another mail shirt?'

Fronto nodded and, standing, wandered away from the valetudinarium until he found one of the quartermasters directing several immunes in unloading weapons and armour from a cart. Spotting mail shirts passing around, his eyes lit on a shirt of fish-scale mail.

'What's the chance of me getting hold of one of those?'

The quartermaster snorted derisively and then turned and realised he was speaking to a senior officer.

'Sorry sir. All the scale's spoken fer. Very popular with officers sir, and 'arder to get than chain. I can let yer 'ave some chain right now though. 'Ow many d'yer need?'

Fronto grinned.

'How many shirts have you got put aside to make a little packet on, though? Two? Three?'

The quartermaster, a slightly overweight centurion assigned to the Seventh, looked taken aback and wounded for a moment before a brief flash of guilt made it to his face.

'Well, I suppose I could let yer 'ave one o' the reserve stock, sir, but I'd 'ave ter buy another one in ter replace it, and they ain't cheap.'

Fronto nodded and grinned.

'I think I can probably cover it. You know me, yes?'

'Yer legate Fronto o' the Tenth. I seen yer sir.'

Fronto smiled again.

'Then put my mark against the shirt. I'll take it now and drop the money off after the battle.'

The quartermaster ummed and ahhed and dithered for long moments, contemplating being left one shirt down by Fronto, then sighed and reached over. Picking up the shiny scale shirt, he passed it to Fronto.

'Don't go getting' yerself killed today, sir. Yer owe me fer a good scale shirt.'

Moments later, leaving the unhappy quartermaster grumbling as his men continued to stockpile gear, Fronto wandered back in to the valetudinarium, the heavy armour, scales of steel sewn over leather and chain, draped over his arm. He wandered around until he found

Balventius, fully bandaged, struggling to pull a tunic down over his ruined shoulders.

'I don't know how you expect to fight when you can even dress.'

The centurion grunted.

'It's just a bit tight with these bandages on. The bloody capsarius refused to help me. Said he wouldn't help me hasten my own death. That's a nice shirt. What do I owe you?'

Fronto grinned.

'I've got a fair bit put away at the moment, so call it a gift.'

Balventius glanced out of the corner of his eye.

'Oh yes, the wager money from you and that Gaul. I made a packet myself. Well thanks. Soon as I'm suited up I'm off to the front again. You coming sir?'

Fronto shrugged and winced. It had been months since he had suffered his wounds to the Gaul in the ring, and they still ached most of the time and hurt like hell some of the time. He could not imagine what Balventius was made of to want to go back in like that.

'I guess so. I hate missing a good fight. You *sure* you want to go?'

Balventius nodded.

'Gotta show 'em you're indestructible when you're a primus pilus. Otherwise the moment you scratch yourself, all the other centurions start jostling into position for your job!'

Fronto laughed.

'Priscus once said something very similar to me.'

He helped the older man into the scale shirt and began to tighten all the fastenings. The capsarius, unwilling to leave until the primus pilus was definitely no longer his concern, stood close by, frowning and muttering to himself. Balventius looked round at the man and tossed him something. The capsarius looked down in horror at the lump of meat and gristle in his hand. Balventius grinned.

'See if you can put him back together!'

Fronto coughed.

'What *is* that?'

'It's a windpipe. Looks funny when it's not tucked away inside, doesn't it?'

Fronto swallowed. Balbus had told him that Balventius was a madman on the battlefield and he could quite believe it. A thought crossed his mind.

'You ever given any thought to what to do when you finish your next term?'

Balventius shrugged.

'Frankly I'm always surprised when I *finish* a campaign year. Never really occurs to me to think beyond that.'

Fronto fastened the last strap.

'Balbus thinks you'd make a good camp prefect.'

'Hah!'

The legate arched his eyebrow.

'What?'

'Camp prefects get to shout a lot and do too much record keeping. They get fat and slobby, coz they never leave the camp. They get rusty and weak coz they never get into a fight. I couldn't cope with being stuck that far from a fight.'

Fronto sighed.

'You're probably right. Better that than killed though.'

'C'mon sir. Let's get into the fight.'

The legate and the primus pilus strode across the field and reached the third line just as they were forming for movement. He found Pomponius shouting orders.

'Centurion? What's going on?'

Pomponius looked around at Fronto.

'Sir. Caesar's ordered the reserves to support Crassus' cavalry. We're heading for the left wing now.'

Fronto rolled his eyes.

'That retarded chinless wonder's going to get a lot of people killed today.' He glanced at Balventius. 'Want to head with the reserves?'

The primus pilus shook his head.

'Front or nothing, sir.'

The two of them made their way past the forming units and approached the rear lines of the Tenth and Eighth. The fighting had become thick enough that they could see from the slight rise that the

Roman front line was now a melee, Romans and Germans locked in small pockets, fighting like hungry wolves. The second line was still properly formed and held firm, striking out at the Germans when they actually reached the shields.

The battle was still heavy and dangerous, but to Fronto's practised eye he could see the way it was going. The Germans had broken early on the right and Caesar's cavalry were split between harrying them from the field and pestering the German flank. On the other wing, Varus and Crassus were managing to hold against heavy odds, but the reserves should even out that problem. In the centre the Germans could not break because of the circled wagons and womenfolk. Otherwise they would be ready to flee any time now. The legions had pushed the German infantry back almost to Ariovistus' camp, and the enemy were now hemmed in by their own defences. Fronto looked sideways at Balventius.

'You can head to the front and push, but I'm going to have to take some of the Tenth.'

'What for sir?'

'We've got to break their barricade at the rear, or they'll fight to the very last man. They can't run!'

Balventius nodded and shouted over to a centurion on the rear line of the Eighth.

'You! Take your men back from here and join with the legate here. You got a special mission, lads!'

The centurion saluted and his unit performed a quick about-face. Fronto nodded at Balventius.

'Thanks. That'll stop me thinning out the Tenth too much. Good luck. Don't get killed.'

'I'll try not to. You too, sir!'

Fronto turned to look along the rear line of the Tenth and, spotting Tetricus with two centurions, called over to him. The tribune looked around at the sound of his name.

'Sir?'

'Bring those two centuries out of the line and up here.'

By the time Tetricus and the hundred and fifty men of the Tenth made it to Fronto's position, the century from the Eighth had joined them.

Fronto glanced at the men, over two hundred of them and then over their heads to the front. He opened his mouth to speak, but his attention was momentarily distracted as he watched Balventius, having shouted and pushed his way through the lines of the Eighth, wade into the Germans, stabbing and slashing like a maniac. It was too far to see details, but Fronto could imagine the sounds of stitches popping and could almost picture the blood blossoming on the back of the man's shirt. He shook his head sadly and uttered a quick prayer to Nemesis under his breath.

'Right. This fight's going to go on for hours unless we do something, and far too many of our men will get killed for no good reason. We need to break that defensive circle of carts around their rear and flanks.'

He glanced at Tetricus.

'What's your opinion of the situation?'

'They've dug their own grave with those carts. They're almost built into a solid wall. Only a fraction of their army's going to get out alive. The rest are going to die in the centre. Those women on the top of the carts are goners. As soon as the centre panics, they'll be overwhelmed by fleeing infantry and probably trampled. They're fighting like caged dogs in the centre, and our infantry are paying heavily. We've got to help the Germans in order to help our own.'

'You're the siege man. Any ideas?'

Tetricus pursed his lips and tapped them with his forefinger, scanning the battlefield as he did so.

'First thing we'll have to do is get the womenfolk off the carts. Capture them, I mean, not kill them.'

Nods all-round confirmed his sentiment.

'That's got to happen first. Then we need to start dragging those carts out of the way and give them a path off the field. We'll have to be quick though; there's only a couple of hundred of us, and we'll be in the way of the entire German army when they run. We'll *have* to be quick.'

Fronto nodded emphatically. He could not agree more.

CHAPTER 22

(ON THE BATTLEFIELD IN FRONT OF THE GERMAN CAMP)

'Testudo: Lit- Tortoise. Military formation in which a century of men closes up in a rectangle and creates four walls and a roof for the unit with their shields.'

'Plebeian: The general mass and populace of Roman citizens.'

Fronto lined up his men. On the way round the field, he had collected two more centuries from the Eleventh, and his force now numbered almost four hundred. He held them at a safe distance on the wing where Caesar had first broken the cavalry. Caesar himself and a number of his men were more than a mile away now, pursuing and harassing the fleeing German cavalry. Ingenuus, on the other hand, had taken the rest of this wing and was picking off the few German warriors that stood on the outside of the crescent of carts. Some had been assigned by Ariovistus to protect the women. Many others had fled the centre of the field and crawled under the carts. Even as Fronto watched, more and more warriors were appearing from beneath the vehicles on their panicked passage out of combat, only to come face to face with Ingenuus' cavalry.

Fronto tapped Tetricus on the shoulder.

'You take command here for a moment. I need to get to the prefect.'

As Tetricus steadied the men and put them in a fighting formation, Fronto jogged across the field, trying to avoid stepping on, or even *in*, any of the grisly remains from the earlier cavalry engagement. Approaching the small knot of horsemen surrounding the prefect, Fronto realised that only that small group were regular legionary cavalry. All the swathes of men attacking the wagons were Gaulish auxiliaries of one tribe or another. For a moment, Fronto was challenged by a couple of the regular cavalry troopers until he was recognised and they saluted.

'Ingenuus. I need to speak to you.'

The prefect peered out between two of his men.

'Legate... I'll be there in a moment.'

Jostling his horse out through the men, he slid from the saddle and landed next to Fronto, wincing as he did. Fronto noted the way he held his shoulder and arm. The quantity of blood spattered across the man and the Gaulish broadsword he held clenched tightly spoke of a great deal of brutal action this morning. Fronto nodded at the man, a professional courtesy for someone with as much talent and guts as the young prefect.

'I appreciate what you're doing here, but we need to stop now. We've got to get that crescent of wagons broken down or opened up so that they can break and run; otherwise they'll be fighting our infantry until there's no one left.'

Ingenuus nodded and sighed.

'It'll take a few moments to round everyone up and pull them back, sir. What do you want to do about these odd defenders and the women?'

Fronto shrugged.

'We've got to give them the option of surrendering or dying.'

Ingenuus shook his head.

'No point, sir. I've been watching them. Even running away they won't surrender. You'll just have to kill them all, unless...'

His voice tailed away. Fronto frowned.

'Unless what?'

'Well it's just a thought sir. How much do we want prisoners?'

Fronto raised an eyebrow.

'You're proposing that we let them go?'

The prefect nodded.

'What else can we do, sir? We've got to let them go or kill them, so we can get to the carts. We want to let the women go anyway, surely?'

Fronto nodded.

'Alright then. Round up your men and find one of them that speaks the dialect. Get him to deliver an offer.'

As Ingenuus nodded and mounted his horse once more, Fronto jogged back toward the centuries under his command.

'Tetricus.'

'Sir?'

'If we can clear the people off those wagons, what do you propose to do?'

Tetricus smiled.

'That's easy sir. Look at them now. There's more coming out between and underneath the wagons every heartbeat. Some of them are even climbing over the top now; I've been watching the women beating them and calling them cowards or some such. I don't even know if we *need* to break the carts down now. Before too long the pure weight of men pushing at the inside will push them over.'

Fronto nodded.

'Not soon enough though. They're caught like rats in a trap, but they're fighting like men who have no way out. Every moment they stay trapped between the carts and the legions, they're butchering our men. I'm not having that. I'd rather see them run.'

Tetricus scanned the carts.

'Alright. We need to get some rope. Quite a bit of rope. There are three places where we could attach them. We'd have to get the prefect to give us horses. We can heave on the ropes and pull these three carts...'

He gestured to three apparently random carts in the wall. Fronto scratched his head.

'Why those three?'

'If you look carefully, you'll see that every other cart has been turned on its side. That's why it's a wall, not just a line. They're jammed against each other and none of the upright ones can move because of the upturned ones jamming them in.'

Fronto continued to scratch his head then slowly began to smile.

'I see what you mean. Those three are different. One of them's end-on.'

'Exactly. I'd guess that was the last cart they jammed in the line, but it didn't fit properly. If we heave on that one and the one on either side, it should give.'

'Bit of a narrow passageway for the entire German army to flee through, though isn't it?'

Tetricus sighed.

'Once that hole's opened up the whole lot will give under the pressure of all those men. How long are a few unanchored carts going to stand between thousands of men and their freedom?'

Fronto nodded.

'I take your point.'

Off in the distance, he could hear shouting. Shading his eyes and glancing over toward Ingenuus, he saw the entire force gathered behind the prefect, with the exception of two riders who sat out front, shouting at the wall in their unintelligible dialect.

'I wonder how it's...'

Finishing the sentence was unnecessary. The German response to the Roman offer was brutally obvious. While the German women spat in the direction of the cavalry, the men began throwing boulders, spears and anything they could find. The two auxiliary spokesmen disappeared beneath a shower of missiles and, as the barrage died away, their bodies lacked any movement. Tetricus shook his head.

'Why?'

'That's it, then. We'll have to do this the hard way. Follow me.'

Followed closely by Tetricus and the five centuries, Fronto moved at double time down to where the cavalry had gathered. He saw a regular decurion among the press and gestured to him.

'You. Go and find some rope. Lots of rope. We need six ropes; each at least sixty feet long.'

The decurion glanced only briefly at Ingenuus for confirmation before riding back toward the Roman lines. Fronto squared his shoulders and called over to Ingenuus.

'Prefect? We're going to have to take care of them I'm afraid. If they won't surrender and they won't run, they'll just have to die. D'you see the three carts over there, toward the centre?'

Ingenuus shaded his eyes.

'The one that's end-on? Yes.'

'That's where we have to hit. We need to clear everyone out of that whole area. I'll take the infantry into the centre and we'll clear the three carts and attach ropes to the wagons. You boys take the three of four vehicles to either side and then keep us covered. I'll need six of your men then, ready to take ropes and ride away with them. Once we've attached them, your horses will have to pull the carts over. As soon as the wall breaks, your whole unit's going to have to pull back behind the legions though, or you'll be caught when they flee.'

Ingenuus nodded and then frowned.

'What about you sir? If we pull a hole in that thing and you're all on foot, are you going to be able to get away in time?'

Fronto grinned.

'We'll be able to get moving as soon as the ropes are attached. I think we'll have time.'

Tetricus glanced off toward the Roman camp.

'I hope that horseman comes back fast with the rope. We've got to get moving.'

Fronto looked up at the cavalry prefect.

'Aulus, we're going to head in for those three carts now. As soon as your man comes back with rope, come and join us and sling the rope to us.'

Ingenuus nodded unhappily and, leaving the cavalry on the edge of the field, the infantry force moved on the wall in a column. Despite being drawn from three different legions, the five centuries under Fronto's command worked in perfect unison. Moments before the German missiles began to fly, the shields came up in front, then to the sides and the rear and, finally, over the top, in the traditional testudo. The five centuries each pulled the same manoeuvre at the same time, and the missiles bounced harmlessly from the shields surrounding them.

As the units closed on the targeted carts, the orders were given, and the front rank thrust their swords through the narrow gaps between shields. With synchronised precision, the centuries separated out into a wide line. Finally, a few of the German defenders began to consider the possibility that they had made a terrible mistake. They were now trapped between their carts and a wall of steel and bronze. Several of them broke and ran to

457

one side or the other. One or two actually laid down their weapons, only to be dispatched by the man standing next to them. Most of them resolutely stared the Romans in the face.

Fronto hoped the cavalry would move in soon; that the ropes would arrive. The testudo was good for protection, but any moment now they would have to reform in order to fight effectively.

Perhaps an early rush would remove their effective resistance long enough to take hold of the situation.

'Break ranks and charge!'

Chaos ensued as shields were dropped into their proper positions and the Romans hit the carts like a battering ram. A warrior standing between two wooden spars in front of the centre cart lashed out at Fronto with a spear, though the blow went wild, and Fronto easily brushed it aside with his squared-oval shield. Throwing himself in at the man, within the effective range of the spear, the legate continued to push the man's weapon arm to the left with his shield until he was almost on top of him. Bringing his arm up high, bent at the elbow, he brought his sword down between the man's collar bones and heard the crack of his solar plexus splitting. The body slid to the floor at his feet and he turned to examine the scene.

All around him now he could hear the sounds of furious combat. Shielding his eyes, he gazed out over the field at the cavalry. They were forming up into two units. Hopefully that meant the rope had arrived, and they were coming to help.

Suddenly a sharp pain shot through his heel. Fronto turned and looked down. One of the women, presumably driven from the cart top by panic, had been hiding beneath the vehicle and had sunk her teeth into his heel the moment he turned his back. Shit! She had nearly hamstrung him. Wobbling on his injured foot and trying to turn round without collapsing to the floor, he stepped back and tottered. Righting himself tenuously, he slammed the edge of his shield down onto her arms where she was trying to crawl out from her hiding place. He heard the bones break in her arms, but moments later slid and fell backwards, the reverberating shock too much for his weak and quivering leg.

No sooner had he hit the ground than one of the legionaries from the Eleventh bent and reached down for him. Gratefully he accepted the man's aid and pulled himself up. Horsemen were now visible around them and on both sides. He heard a length of rope whistle past him and the men started to tie the lengths to the carts. Briefly, close behind, a woman screamed. He closed his eyes and tried not to feel sorry for her, considering what she had done.

The legionary supporting him passed his shield to a colleague and sheathed his sword.

'C'mon sir. We'd best get you movin' before this place turns to hell.'

Fronto shook his head for a moment before realising that the lad was right. If he did not get a head start, limping like he was, he would be cut down by the fleeing hordes of Germans when the carts gave way.

The soldier half dragged, half carried the legate to the cavalry, where a few spare horses were gathered. Fronto kept looking over his shoulder at the fighting still going on by the carts. He also noted the remarkably visible trail of blood that betrayed where he had come from. The wound must be quite bad, he decided. After all, it had gone numb, and only really bad wounds went numb; the smaller ones hurt more.

'Best get you on a horse sir.'

The legionary looked over at Ingenuus.

'Can I leave him with you sir? You'll make sure he gets back, yes?'

The prefect smiled and turned to one of his men.

'The legate looks a little pale. I think you'd best get him to the medical staff quickly.'

Fronto sat up on the horse.

'I'm damn well going nowhere until I see Ariovistus leave.'

Ingenuus grinned.

'Then you'd best move your horse a little, sir, or you're going to be in the way of the ropes.'

As the cavalry beat an ordered retreat, Fronto scanned the carts. The infantry were pulling back in good order, around the line of carts and at an increasing distance from them. Tetricus had brought the units back together well, and they appeared to have suffered what even Fronto would term 'acceptable losses'. German warriors swarmed over, under and around the carts and began hacking at the ropes.

Ingenuus turned his crazy grin to the men around him.

'Heave lads. Pull the buggers over.'

The ropes tightened rapidly. As the first rope was cut by the Germans, two of the horseman had to correct themselves and were almost unhorsed. The other rope, however, held firm and the cart gave an ear-splitting cracking noise and then rumbled at high speed out of the wall. A number of German warriors were unfortunate enough to be in front of it, trying to cut the rope, and were lost with a sickening crunch beneath the heavy wheels.

As the central cart trundled to a halt some fifty paces from the wall, the ones on either side came away with just a few creaks, tipping first onto their wheels due to Tetricus' positioning of the knots, and then rattling away across the turf. A mass of Germans poured through the gap. For a moment Fronto feared they might wheel to the side and come after the mixed group of infantry and cavalry, but they were more intent on fleeing the death pit that was the centre of the field.

Fronto smiled. That was it. They had beaten Ariovistus. The Germans were fleeing the field in scattered panicky groups. Even if they ever managed to group together between here and the other side of the Rhine, the leaders of the other cantons would never follow Ariovistus against Rome again. Fronto found himself thinking deeply of drinking; drinking deeply. With a relieved smile, and heedless of his wound, he kicked his horse into life...

...and yelped.

———————

Fronto winced. The medicus dealing with his heel had all the bedside manner and gentle touch of a Numidian gladiator.

'When you've quite finished mauling and tenderising my foot, would you kindly tell me how long I'm going to be invalided?'

The medicus gave Fronto a look that worried him. No one this naturally unpleasant should be responsible for his wellbeing.

'You can hobble on it now, but only from seat to seat and so on. If you try walking any distance on it, you'll just end up in a heap and I'll refuse to redo it.'

460

'Thanks doc.'

Priscus grinned.

'It's alright. I figure you're getting used to sitting on your arse a lot nowadays.'

Fronto growled.

'You're almost as respectful as he is! Why is it that medici always treat me like a petulant child, but they never seem to argue with you and Velius?'

Priscus grinned.

'Medici aren't frightened of senior officers. They're generally sensible and well behaved. *And* medici know they're valuable. Centurions on the other hand have a reputation for being lunatics and don't take so well to being ordered around by medical staff. Take Balventius.'

'Why, what's up with him?'

Priscus' grin broadened.

'He's in the next tent with Balbus. The medicus had a go at him and when I last saw them, he was threatening the man with a sword. They won't argue with him anymore.'

A cough announced the arrival of Crispus.

'A very fine afternoon, gentlemen.'

'Crispus. How's things going?'

The young legate took a seat.

'The legions are once more in the camp, with the exception of the few centuries who persist in pursuing the Germans. Duty units are gathering the dead and still finding wounded.'

Fronto nodded soberly.

'And what of the Germans, then?'

'They continue their flight as though the very ghost of Scipio himself were after them. I am somewhat unconvinced that any of them will cease their flight until they cross the Rhine. They are, as I intimated, continually pursued by units of our infantry.'

Fronto glanced down at Priscus, who wore a confused frown. He smiled and translated.

'The Germans are running back across the Rhine, and we're chasing them.'

When he looked back up, Crispus now wore a confused frown. He sighed and glossed over the subject.

'Anyway, I presume the cavalry is still out?'

Crispus nodded.

'I very much doubt that the pursuant centuries will reach conflict at all. Varus and Crassus are already halfway to the Rhine by now, and Caesar and Ingenuus will not be tarrying. No one has yet found the King. Perhaps he died on the field, though I am more inclined to the opinion that he escaped.'

Without changing his expression, Fronto turned to Priscus.

'The cavalry are chasing them down. They haven't found Ariovistus.'

'Yes, thank you. I already got that.'

Fronto smiled.

'Crispus, you have a lovely turn of phrase but sometimes we mortals have trouble following you.'

Crispus smiled back.

'Indeed? Then I shall endeavour to paraphrase myself.'

Behind Crispus, a shadow cast on the tent leather indicated the arrival of another visitor. Leaning heavily on the medical table, still sticky with drying blood, Fronto heaved himself upright, gritting his teeth and closing his eyes. Immediate pain rushed through his heel and he almost collapsed. With a sigh he looked pathetically at Crispus and Priscus.

'Oh all right.'

The two of them half-lifted Fronto out of the tent, helping him across the threshold. Outside, Florus, the young capsarius from the Tenth, stood waiting respectfully. Fronto smiled.

'Busy Florus?'

The young man nodded.

'Fairly busy sir, though most of it's a job for the proper medicus now. We capsarii don't get much of a look in back here.'

Priscus looked the young man up and down. The fact that he was covered in blood was unsurprising, given his job, but the ripped chain mail he wore and the dents on his shield told a different story.

'I thought I gave orders that the capsarii were to stay behind the second line. And anyway, weren't you staying with the hospital, training to be a medicus?'

Florus shrugged.

'I'm a soldier first. Anyway, glory's quite hard to win when you're sat in a tent waiting.'

Fronto interrupted.

'Were you actually waiting for us?'

'Yes sir. A number of officers have gathered on the hill above the camp. Legate Balbus sent a message asking if you'd join them for a celebration.'

Fronto grinned. It seemed to have been a long time since there'd been anything worth really celebrating. Suddenly he found that he was missing that nice little tavern at Bibracte.

'I'd certainly like to. Best find a horse though; can't walk all that way with my war wound!'

Priscus stifled a laugh.

'War wound. I heard you were defeated in battle by an old woman using only her teeth!'

Fronto frowned and glanced around him. Crispus had erupted in laughter and was stifling it with his hand. Even Florus' eyes were watering.

'Fine, let's all laugh at the invalid. Somebody find me a horse. You lot can all come with me.'

They were halfway between the valetudinarium and the horse corral when the tumultuous sound of hooves brought them to a halt. They turned to see a group of a dozen auxiliary horsemen led by a regular decurion. The decurion was leading an extra horse with a young woman of perhaps fourteen tied by the wrists to the saddle horn. She was clearly Germanic and her wild hair and dirty face were matted with blood. She was unwounded, however, and stared arrogantly and defiantly down at the officers and men.

The decurion addressed the group, saluting at Fronto.

'Apologies, but could you direct me to the senior officer in camp?'

Fronto shrugged.

'That's probably me, decurion, on the assumption Caesar hasn't returned yet.'

The decurion nodded.

'Then I deliver into your custody one prisoner, taken by prefect Ingenuus. We've a number of others, but this one's important.'

'Important? How?'

'I believe that she's the daughter of the German King.'

Fronto's eyes widened.

'Ariovistus' daughter? Caesar's going to want to see her. She's royalty, so we'll have to treat her well. Honour of Rome and all that crap. Why's she tied to the saddle and gagged? Not good, decurion; not good.'

The decurion looked down at Fronto.

'With respect, legate, you haven't had to control her for the last hour. She's a biter sir. Got the prefect a good one on the hand. He lost a finger.'

Fronto shook his head.

'What *is* it with these German women? All right, give the reins to the centurion here and we'll take her.'

As Priscus took the reins in his left hand, the other hand still helping to support the legate, Fronto tapped Crispus on the shoulder.

'Mmm?'

The young man looked round.

'Aulus, I think you'd best go to the group on the hill and tell them we'll be delayed. Best tell them why too. I'll take the capsarius here with me.'

Florus looked up in surprise.

'Me sir?'

Fronto nodded and gestured at the prisoner.

'There's a lot of blood there and I want to make sure none of its hers. Priscus? When we get to the praetorium and you drop her off, can you go and see the quartermasters? See if you can round up some intact and clean clothing and a cloak for her?'

Priscus nodded.

'Anything else, your leglessness?'

'Funny.'

He glowered at Priscus as Crispus jogged away up the hill to see the rest of the officers. Turning to Florus as they headed for the centre of the camp, the legate gestured once more at the prisoner.

'Can you remove the gag, lad?'

With a considerable effort, the capsarius reached up and unknotted the military scarf that had been used for a gag. As he pulled it away, the girl spat on him, a mixture of saliva and blood.

'Charming.'

Fronto looked over at her.

'Do you speak Latin?'

The girl frowned and growled quietly, then took the opportunity to spit on Fronto, hitting him square in the face.

'Honour or no honour, I'm tempted to put the bloody gag back on! Listen, Princess: if you speak Latin, you need to tell me now. I'm actually capable of being quite nice and reasonable, and the young man here is a medicus who can help you with any wounds you suffered. When the general gets back, he's less inclined to be nice. In fact he can be a downright bastard. Now's your chance.'

Her third attempt at spitting on a Roman went awry. This time both were prepared and jerked out of the way.

'Very well. Let's get her to a guarded tent, and I'll leave her for the other staff. I'll be damned if I'm going to take my chances with another biter today.'

Ingenuus rode on, his left hand clutched tightly into a ball, with a scarf wrapped around it. The bloody witch had got two of his fingers. Two! He was no longer wielding a sword, just riding. The few pockets of fleeing Germans they came across either hurled themselves to the floor in supplication or hid in the brush. This was not combat; it was just making sure they left Sequani land. He kicked his horse a little and caught up with Caesar. The general rode at the head of his cavalry, not fast. He was happy to overtake a few survivors, but did not want to impede their flight across the Rhine.

465

As he pulled level, he became aware of shouting further back along the column. Turning, he saw two of the outriders heading toward the head of the line.

'Caesar, the scouts are shouting for us.'

The general craned his neck and then nodded. Holding up his hand he called a halt to the column and he and the prefect wheeled their horses and rode back along the line of cavalry to the scouts.

'What is it?'

The two auxiliary riders looked at each other, and one addressed the general in broken Latin.

'Caesar. Many German. In tree. Mile to north.'

Caesar arched his eyebrows and turned to Ingenuus, a question in his gaze. The young prefect shaded his eyes.

'There's a fairly large copse over there, sir. If we want to deal with them, we'll have to dismount. Unless, of course, they feel like surrendering.'

Caesar nodded.

'What do you suggest?'

'I'd take two alae and surround the place. Keep one mounted and use the other dismounted if we need to go in. I'd keep the rest of the cavalry at a reasonable distance. If the whole army were there I can't imagine why they would want to come out.'

'If you think that's best, Ingenuus, then see to it.'

'Yes sir.'

Nodding to one of his decurions and one of the auxiliary prefects that he knew quite well, he trotted out to one side. Once the cavalry had followed out of line and were assembled, Ingenuus called over the prefect and the decurions.

'We're going over to the copse that our scouts found a large number of Germans in. When we get there, I want the auxiliary cavalry to remain mounted and surround the place. The regular cavalry will dismount a short distance away and ring the wood within the line of the cavalry. If the order is given to advance, the regulars will advance on foot and the auxiliary will form a cordon to prevent escape. Inform your men as we ride. Time is short.'

As the various officers passed the orders on to their subordinates, Ingenuus kicked his heels and started the units moving. Once more he looked down at his bandaged and blood-soaked hand. The more he thought about it, the more he wished he had not. The loss of the fourth and fifth fingers on his right hand would create a few problems for him in the future, but he would still be able to carry out most tasks with reasonable ease. The main problem, and it was the brutal problem that he was trying to come to terms with, was that the loss of those two fingers would seriously reduce his effectiveness with a sword. Those two fingers gave you balance and stability with a sword swing, and the loss of that ability would make him considerably less effective in mounted combat. It was a painful possibility that his life in the cavalry was over.

On reflection, he had not quite realised how meteoric his rise through the ranks had been this year. A few months ago he had been a cavalry decurion with little prospect of advancement. After an almost instantaneous decision to go to the aid of a fellow officer, he had been raised to prefect, in charge of an entire ala of regular cavalry. Normally there would be no realistic place for him to go after that but perhaps into a non-cavalry role. Instead, however, some of the senior officers and even the general himself seemed to have taken to him. Here he was now, ordering prefects around with an authority granted by Caesar. Oh, he would not make it to controlling the entire cavalry force in this campaign, as there were Crassus and Varus both in line ahead of him, but one day he might have. Not now though. Once a medicus had pronounced him useless, he might as well sell his horse.

Muttering, Ingenuus tried hard to pull himself together. He was dangerously close to actual tears and that would be enormously embarrassing in front of so many hardened cavalrymen. He straightened in the saddle and drew his cavalry long sword. The agony as the sword dipped and pulled at his hand was intense, and this time tears did come; tears of sheer pain. Gritting his teeth, he laid the sword across his thighs and unwrapped the bandage. Blood trickled from the sodden scarf and ran onto his leg and the horse's flank. For a moment, he thought he might pass out, but his focus came back. Slowly and carefully he reached with his wounded hand and gripped the hilt. Fresh blood ran from the stumps of fingers as he applied pressure and, once more, he almost fainted. Sighing, he sheathed the sword, shook the excess damp out of the scarf, and reapplied it to his hand.

Looking up, the copse was now only a few hundred paces away. Holding up his maimed hand, he gave the signal and the auxiliary cavalry separated, riding out from both sides of the column to surround the wood. At his second bellowed command, the regulars reined in. For the next few heartbeats they could be seen all around the area, tying their steeds to the branches of lone trees or bushes. Once they were assembled again, he gave the third order and the dismounted regulars moved in, splitting off in much the same way in order to surround the wood a few paces forward of the cavalry. Ingenuus waited patiently for them to deploy into position. Once they were ready, two concentric circles surrounding a knot of Germans of unknown size, the prefect put his hands to his mouth and called out.

'This is prefect Aulus Ingenuus of the Eighth Legion. If any of you can understand me, I am offering you the chance to surrender. If you surrender peacefully, your warriors will be taken as slaves, but your women, children and old folk will be allowed to return across the Rhine. If you defy us, we will move in to take prisoners by force. If you understand, answer me now.'

The prefect sat tensely waiting. He would much rather they came out freely and he could let the women and children go. If the army had to move in, there would be a lot of unnecessary deaths. He listened intently, the whispering leaves in the trees masking any conversation that went on within.

Suddenly, he was sure he heard a voice begin to call out in Latin before being silenced quickly. Why did he always get to make decisions in an instant, when others got so much time to plan?

'Damn the consequences. Any German warrior to be killed on sight. Women and children are not to be harmed, but sent back to the cavalry as prisoners. Advance!'

The regulars moved into the trees in perfect order, as the auxiliaries behind them closed slightly to prevent escapees. Ingenuus sat for long moments, still tense, waiting for sounds of battle. After a count of a hundred, a shriek echoed through the woods. It had begun.

For several sickening moments there were loud cries, shrieks and clashes of metal from deep in the thicket. Ingenuus shook his head sadly, for clearly not all the cries were male voices. The prefect found that he was actually holding his breath when the first of his men appeared at the edge of the trees.

A few more men followed, and then a small group of a dozen came crashing through the undergrowth. Behind them others brought out the Germans taken alive, mostly women, but a few men, even ones of a fighting age. They would fetch a reasonable sum in the markets of Rome and would boost the already sizeable booty Caesar had squeezed out of the Tribes through defeat or protection. The individual soldiers of the legion would have made their own small profits from the battlefield before they received any gratuity from the commander. In all, a lot of people would be wealthy this winter, and the troops wintering in forts would have plenty of cash for women and wine.

All this flashed through Ingenuus' mind for only moments. He was too busy staring at the dozen or so soldiers that had come out together. They had separated once they were in the safety of open grass and the presence of the auxilia. Between them, sheltered and harboured among allies, stood a man in a military tunic and boots. Fashionable Roman hair style now ravaged and wild, boots worn, tunic dirty and torn, he still looked every inch the Roman Patrician.

As the men moved out of the way, and the prefect got a better view of the prisoner, he realised that the man's hands were shackled behind him. Dangling down by the side, Ingenuus could make out a triple-thickness chain, the three strands wound around one another. They had not meant him to escape. Ingenuus drew himself up and saluted, his bloody bandaged hand dripping onto the horse and the turf.

'Aulus Ingenuus, prefect of the Eighth.'

The Roman officer nodded, unable to raise his hand.

'Gaius Valerius Procillus, officer of Caesar's staff. Forgive me for not returning the gesture. No...' he interrupted as Ingenuus lowered his arm, 'you'd be better keeping that up. You'll lose a lot of blood with it down.'

Ingenuus grinned.

'Procillus. Amazing, sir. How long have you been held by them? Must be weeks now. And you're still alive and relatively well.'

The ragged officer smiled wearily.

'Relatively, yes. Borderline starvation I think, but I'm lucky. They won't do anything without the say so of their Gods and the old crones checked the auspices three times but still said no. Good job, really. They were going to burn me to death. I think they were trying to take me back across the Rhine to bargain with later.'

Ingenuus nodded.

'Seems likely. I take it that was your voice that I heard silenced in the woods then, sir?'

'That'd be me, yes. I need to get back to camp. Can you give me a horse?'

Ingenuus grinned.

'I'll do better than that. Caesar's less than a quarter of an hour away, so I'll take you to him. Then we'll get someone to crack those chains for you and I'll escort you back to camp personally. I need to have a medicus look at my hand, anyway.'

Several miles away, Varus kicked his horse to a greater turn of speed. Around him his own unit and one of the auxiliary alae raced for the river. They could see the small group of refugees ahead of them at the river's edge, pushing off in three small boats. Other, more desperate Germans were leaping into the strong, dangerous currents of the wide, powerful Rhine and trying to swim across. A few were making it; most were not. He could still hear the clash of weapon on weapon and the cries of the wounded and dying not far behind.

Crassus and his wing had chased down many of the fleeing survivors from the battle and had come across a large collection of German warriors that had turned and prepared to give their pursuers a fight. With the odds as they were, Varus could not in good conscience call it a battle. It was a slaughter and, to give him his due, Crassus *had* given them the opportunity to surrender. It had been in the depths of combat when he had realised why the warriors had given them such fierce resistance. Alone on the edge of the fray with only a couple of the auxiliary troopers, he had spotted a small knot of well-dressed and equipped men and women moving as unobtrusively as possible toward the river, covered by the fighting behind them. He had pointed them out to the auxiliaries, and one of them, a Sequani warrior fighting alongside the Romans had identified them as the Royal party.

They had been so close to the river by then that Varus had no time to draw this to the attention of Crassus and had instead gathered all of the regulars and auxiliaries he could find at the edge, racing off in pursuit of Ariovistus and his family.

Concentrating, he slowed his horse as they reached the edge of the river. He did not dare ride into the current. Looking up and down the bank for other boats, he was disappointed. Presumably the Germans had not expected to have to flee across the Rhine and had been woefully unprepared. With an irritated growl, he realised that the King had escaped.

Suddenly a number of spears whistled over his head, crashing into and around the boats. Turning angrily, he saw a number of the auxiliary troopers hurling their weapons into the boats.

'What do you think you're doing? You can't kill them all, and many of them are women!'

One of the auxiliaries looked down at him in surprise.

'They kill our women!'

Varus turned back to look at the boats and noticed that a few of the spears had, in fact hit home. The man Varus presumed to be Ariovistus himself stood nobly in the prow, shouting defiance in his guttural tongue. Slumped nearby were three women and two men.

Angrily, the prefect picked up a stone from the river bank and cast it after the boats, only to watch it fall short and sink into the water. Turning, he gestured to the men around him.

'He's gone. Back to your units.'

Varus mounted his horse once more and, with a last, longing look out at the small boats diminishing into the distance, sighed and wheeled his horse.

On the ride back across the hill and into the fray he kept berating himself for not having realised that the fight was a delaying tactic earlier.

471

Had he been a little sharper, they could have caught Ariovistus on the way to the river, and he would now be in chains on his way back to Caesar and, eventually, to Rome to be paraded before the public. Damn.

He looked up as they crested the hill and the bile rose in his throat. He was confronted with a scene of devastation. Without doubt the German warriors had surrendered, presumably when they had realised that the King was either safe or they had failed. There was not a single warrior offering any resistance and, too proud to run from Crassus' 'no survivors' policy were being cut down where they stood or knelt. With further horror, Varus realised that the auxilia was sat ahorse in formation watching the grisly scene. The perpetrators were the regular cavalry. *His* ala was murdering surrendering men.

His fury rising, he kicked his horse into a gallop and made for the commanders, Crassus and several prefects and decurions sitting in a group in the centre of the field. He tried not to look around as he rode, but could not fail to see the line of prisoners, a score or more, on their knees being beheaded systematically by *his* men. He fought the urge to draw his sword as he made for Crassus.

'What in the name of Mars, Jupiter and Fortuna is going on? These people are *surrendering*, Crassus. We need slaves, not corpses!'

Crassus merely turned his cold stare on the prefect and gestured to the officers around him. Obediently they rode away to attend to the butchery. Once they were alone, the commander trotted across to Varus.

'Don't ever speak to me like that in front of the men, prefect. It doesn't do for junior officers to question the judgement of their seniors, particularly in public.'

Varus stuttered, unable to believe the arrogance of the man.

'I'm not questioning your judgement, Crassus, I'm questioning your sanity! They're valuable property now, and they're people. Murdering them solves nothing.'

Crassus rounded on him.

'*I* am in command of this cavalry, Varus, not you, no matter how much you wished for it and angled for it. You may have been Longinus' pet, but you're an officer of the equestrian class, whereas I am one of the nobiles and a senior commander. I *will* not be questioned by my junior.'

Varus growled.

'Nobilis only tells us that *someone* in your family was great. It does *not* give you the right to treat the rest of the people as cattle. Without the Equestrians, the Plebeians and even the slaves there would *be* no Rome. No army; no merchants; no builders. What good would your rank be without them?'

Crassus smiled a dead smile.

'Exactly what I would expect one of your sort to come out with. Drivel. You don't understand how it works.'

Varus reached out between the horses and grasped the military scarf around Crassus' neck, hauling him closer and almost from his horse. Crassus' sudden look of surprise and, Varus thought, of fright was soon replaced by his usual arrogant and complacent smile. The prefect resisted the urge to punch him.

'Crassus, I am one of the *Patrician* class, not an equestrian. My father sat in the senate and so shall I one day, so don't you *dare* tell me I don't know how it works. To hell with you and your nightmare command.'

He let go of his commander and turned the horse.

'Men of the Ninth!'

Amid the slaughter, cavalrymen looked up at the prefect, blood still running from the tips of their swords and daggers.

'Form on the hill!'

He turned once more to face Crassus.

'My men will have nothing to do with this and neither shall I. I'll see you in the camp. This isn't over.'

Leaving a stunned commander sitting amid a field of bodies, Varus joined his men on the hill and began the ride back to camp.

CHAPTER 23

(EPILOGUE)

'Corona: wreath or crown awarded as military decoration.'

'Phalerae: (sing. Phalera) set of discs attached to a torso harness used as military decorations.'

Fronto glanced around the room happily before his attention returned to the table. Last time the legions had been in Vesontio, he had been in the middle of nowhere with one mounted cohort and had missed the place entirely. Priscus had told him it wasn't up to much, but had pointed out a bar that he said was quite reasonable halfway up the main street. And so he was now here. He had left messages with several people in the huge camp at the bottom of the hill to say where he would be if anyone wished to join him and had been most surprised when he actually found the place and strode in through the door to find Balbus and Crispus already seated close to a window. Fronto sighed contentedly as he dropped into the seat. He was able to hobble for short distances, but soon began to sway and topple if there was no one there to give him support.

Crispus stirred and put down his drink.

'The proprietor doesn't serve at tables, so I should be delighted to procure a drink for you, Marcus.'

Fronto smiled and reached out a restraining hand to stop the young legate from standing.

'He'll serve me, lad, don't you worry.'

Reaching down to his side, Fronto retrieved a leather purse and held it over the table. He upended the container and a large quantity of coinage dropped out, much of it in silver and some of it in gold. The ringing of coin on coin had certainly attracted the attention of the barman. Fronto smiled up in his direction.

'I'll have what these two are drinking. All drinks served to a Roman while I'm here go on my bill, and you can take it in silver and gold, with a little extra if you'll serve at tables. Ok?'

The barman nodded eagerly.

'Oh yes sir. I'll 'elp you s'much as I can.'

Fronto looked over at Crispus.

'What *are* you drinking anyway?'

Crispus smiled.

'It's a local brew. A little potent, but nicely tart and with a pleasing aftertaste. I rather favour it.'

Balbus snorted as he took a swig.

'Youth of today.'

Fronto grinned.

'You never cease to amaze me, Aulus. I take it you know about the award?'

Crispus nodded with a certain ambivalence.

'I cannot see how I particularly deserve it. I performed my duty to the same degree as everyone else. To be honoured above others such as the two of you makes me a trifle uneasy.'

'Don't be daft. You're still new to this game and already pulled a few manoeuvres that've got you a bit of a reputation. Be proud of that. Balbus and I already have awards from past campaigns. You've an empty harness. Time you got that corona. You *did* save the army after all.'

Crispus shook his head.

'Yes but what about all you've both done for this army?'

Balbus smiled at him.

'Don't kid yourself, Aulus. Caesar dangled awards in front of Marcus here, but he's refused them.'

'Refused? Why?'

Fronto shrugged.

'I'd rather they go to the men below me. They need them more. For me to be decorated above others more deserving isn't the sort of thing I do.'

Crispus nodded.

'For certain. I've have heard tell that both Velius and Priscus will receive phalera. Tetricus also, I believe.'

Fronto sighed.

'I've had the full list reeled off to me. I was one of the four who went through them with Caesar deciding on who was worthy of reward. Those three indeed, and you. Balventius is lined up for phalera, as are Ingenuus, Baculus of the Twelfth and your own primus pilus, Felix whatever-his-name-is.'

'Felix? Good. He assuredly deserves it. I have the niggling feeling at times that he tries to protect me. It can be a touch unnerving. For when is the ceremony planned, if you don't mind my asking?'

Fronto shrugged once more.

'Some time tomorrow. Can't remember exactly. We'll only be here a couple of days now and then it'll be time for us all to piss off back to our families for a while.'

'I...'

Crispus' voice trailed off and he stood suddenly and smartly at attention. Balbus hauled himself slowly to his feet and nodded respectfully. Fronto craned his head and slumped slightly further down. The door stood wide open in the warm late summer air and the general had entered unannounced. As he walked toward the table, Caesar gestured at the table for them to sit. He smiled sympathetically at Fronto.

'Is the heel still causing you trouble, Marcus? I thought you'd be sprinting by now.'

Fronto grunted and then turned his head again.

'Apologies, general. Please take a seat. The drinks are free at the moment and I suspect he's got wine if he looks hard enough.'

Caesar squared his shoulders and then unfastened his red cloak, folding it neatly and placing it on a bench near the fireplace. Behind him, three men entered and made their way over. Sabinus and Labienus were no surprise, but the inclusion of Varus in the general's entourage caused raised eyebrows around the table. Balbus nodded at them.

'Gentlemen. Please join us. I must say that I'm surprised to find you all frequenting a place like this.'

Sabinus laughed.

'Follow Fronto and you'll always end up in one of the best local drinking pits; this I've learned over the last half a year! As it happens, Caesar wanted to speak to you, so I just looked for your primus pilus. He always knows where you are. What's all the cash on the table?'

Fronto shoved the coins into a neater pile.

'It's our drinking funds. Should cover us all for however long we want to drink.'

He drew their attention to the barman who was standing helpfully and expectantly next to the table, waiting for orders. He was slightly pale, since he knew who the tall man with the receding hairline and the prominent nose had to be, Fronto guessed. As Sabinus ordered the drinks for the newcomers, Caesar took a seat and gestured for the others to do so.

'Marcus, I've deliberated further on awards and I've a couple of thoughts. One of them's really just a confirmation, but for the other I want your opinion and that of Varus.'

Fronto nodded and glanced at Varus, who just looked tired.

'Go on...'

'Well the second matter is that of young Ingenuus. I expect everyone is aware by now that I probably owe my life to his quick thinking and his selfless bravery.'

There were nods all-round. The young prefect had been the subject of a great deal of conversation after the battle. Saving Caesar's life, capturing a daughter of their enemy and rescuing Procillus, the young man had earned praise and respect from a great many sources. Fronto had wondered really whether even two phalerae were a gracious enough demonstration, when the lad probably deserved a corona. He looked up as Caesar continued.

'Varus, you're a long-serving cavalry officer and a commander of note. I have it on good authority that Longinus favoured you a great deal and his opinion of cavalry always swayed me. What is your opinion of the prefect?'

Varus stretched and took a swig of his drink.

'General, the lad's got the makings of a great commander. Possibly one of the best. I think another year of command in that position will be the telling point though. He has a tendency to leap into the fray both feet first and get himself into trouble, and he's very lucky he hasn't fallen foul of his own bravery yet. Basically, I think the wound he received was unfortunate. He'll never effectively wield a sword again in the saddle unless he has it strapped to his hand.'

Caesar nodded and turned to Fronto.

'You've served with him. What do you think?'

Fronto shrugged.

'He's actually got his head screwed on a little better than I think Varus gives him credit for. He's only got the same urge to do stupid things as the rest of us. And after this battle, he's reached the status of 'hero' among the men, so any accolade you care to give him will go down well with the troops. What are you proposing? Corona? Appointment to the staff?'

Caesar smiled.

'Actually, I'm thinking of transferring him to my personal guard as their commander. I would say that's a fairly high-status position.'

Fronto whistled through his teeth.

'I'd say so, yes. Probably a good man for the job, though.'

Varus nodded.

'I'd concur. It's a position I suspect he'll excel in.'

Caesar returned the nod.

'Very well. I'll make that official after the post-ceremony briefing.'

Crispus stuck out his hand.

'General, I think it would be of great use if you could inform us for when the ceremony is planned?'

Caesar raised his eyebrows in surprise.

'I'm surprised you haven't heard. First thing tomorrow morning. Labienus has been passing the word around to the senior officers.'

He smiled slyly.

'Perhaps he hasn't been round the bars yet, eh?'

Fronto grumbled.

'What was the other thing you meant to say; your confirmation?'

Caesar shuffled back a little in his seat.

'I'm sure you'll all be pleased to know that after a little deliberation, I have decided to appoint Varus as commander of the cavalry, with Crassus returning to the Seventh. I do hope you'll accept the position, Varus, as you come on the highest recommendation from the erstwhile commander Longinus who saw fit to request your appointment even in his will.'

Varus nodded, professionalism obviously overpowering his urge to smile and enthuse.

'I would very much appreciate the opportunity, general.'

Caesar smiled.

'Good, because I've already spoken to Crassus.'

The general reached out and drained the small goblet of wine, trying hard to suppress the look of distaste at the sharp local beverage.

'Very well. I'll leave you all to your carousing as I have a great deal to attend to. Varus and Sabinus, it's up to you what you do this evening but Labienus, I'm afraid I'll require your assistance.'

Caesar stood and, nodding, made his way out of the tavern, followed by Labienus, head held high. As he reached the door, the general stopped.

'I'll just remind you all that you'll be required for the ceremony tomorrow morning, so try not to get too inebriated.'

As the two left, Fronto turned back to Varus.

'Commander of the cavalry, eh? Well done man. I think we might as well stay here for the duration now. Everyone cough up. If we're to stay out the evening, we'll need to increase the size of our drinking fund.'

As the assembled officers dug deep in their search for money, a figure appeared at the door. They turned as one to the newcomer in surprise and anticipation.

Crassus strode in, slightly red faced and short of breath, looked around the dim interior until he saw the group round the table and then made straight for them.

Fronto drew breath to confront the man as Crispus and Varus both hauled themselves up. Crassus marched across the bar and to the table.

'I came to offer you my congratulations, Varus. I don't believe in grudges and there are more important concerns than personal aggrandizement. Will you take my hand?'

He held out his hand as Fronto blinked in surprise. Crispus slumped back onto his stool, though Varus remained half-standing, frowning and unsure. After a moment, he reached out and took the hand.

'I don't like your command style, Crassus, but then I suppose you probably don't like mine. I'm a cavalry man at heart and I suspect your talents lie with infantry strategy. Perhaps we'll work better together like that.'

Crassus gave a curt nod.

'Just prove yourself right and don't make me sorry I stood down. Here.'

He reached into his tunic and removed a small pouch. The leather clinked as he dropped it to the table.

'I have something to attend to currently, but have a drink to your success on me. Gentlemen, I will see you all at the ceremony tomorrow.'

And with that, he was gone. Fronto was still blinking in wonder.

'Do you think he's drunk?'

Balbus shook his head.

'He's trying to be professional. Hopefully that'll stick and he'll be different next year.'

Crispus looked up.

'Do you really think the general intends to recommence the campaign next year?'

Balbus smiled.

'Be sure of it. I expect Caesar will announce something tomorrow, perhaps at the ceremony; perhaps later at the command briefing. I'd lay my bet that the troops won't be returning to Cisalpine Gaul, and I'd suspect that's why Labienus and Crassus are rushing around like they are.'

Fronto nodded.

'I think we can safely say we're not finished in Gaul yet. I'm just intrigued to see how Caesar's going to engineer another reason to campaign. I do know one thing.'

Crispus turned to face him.

'What would that be?'

'I know I'm getting drunk tonight.'

Balbus smiled and nodded.

'Being the venerable old one here, I'll stay and keep an eye on you all. Don't be surprised if I drop off early though.'

With a laugh, Varus turned to face the innkeeper.

'Check and see how many amphorae of wine you have and bring the whole damn lot out.'

Crispus held his finger aloft.

'And the beer.'

Fronto could not help thinking that the ceremony had gone remarkably well. The sky was already darkening when he approached Caesar's command tent.

'Shit!'

Staggering to right himself as he tripped on a tuft of earth, he fell bodily against the leather, rolling for a moment before he picked himself up and tottered roughly in the direction of the door. On the third attempt he managed to open the tent flap and knocked on the wood behind.

'Come.'

Caesar's voice had a calm and soothing sound. Fronto smiled and wandered in.

'Evening sir, m'I first?'

Caesar glanced over from his desk where he was deeply involved in something and raised an eyebrow.

'I presume you've been drinking again then. At least you were relatively sober for the ceremony.'

Fronto grinned.

'Frankly sir, I's not that sober this M'ning. Moring. Morning.'

Caesar's knowing smile took on a hard edge.

'Yes. It doesn't look good during a major ceremony when several of the senior staff keep having to absent themselves to answer calls of nature. Still, I'm not about to discipline anyone when it's the end of the campaigning season, and I'm well aware of the fact that most of my army will be in a similar state tonight.'

He sighed.

'Never mind. So long as you can take in what we say tonight, you can go and sleep it off then.'

Fronto smiled at him.

'S'nice. Sleep. Off. Whatcha upta?'

Caesar closed up the wax tablet on which he had been writing and put away his paraphernalia.

'Finishing my diary.'

Fronto sniggered lewdly.

'S'nice.'

'Oh for the sake of Fortuna, sit down before you fall.'

Fronto sank gratefully into the seat, which rocked dangerously, threatening to pitch him face first onto the floor. He looked up at Caesar with a bemused expression and the general shook his head in benign resignation as the other senior staff began to file in.

Labienus and Crassus led the group of staff officers and senior centurions to the seats around the tent. Priscus made a point as he entered of treading fairly heavily on Fronto's toes.

At the end of the queue came the menagerie. Crispus tottered in with a slightly glazed and happy smile. He was bareheaded and the sword on his belt had been replaced with a small wine amphora. Behind him, Varus and Sabinus moved in concert, trying as best they could to prop each other up. At the rear came Balbus, looking slightly the worse for wear and rubbing his sore head. Crispus bowed deeply and halted for a moment, letting the world steady itself before he attempted to stand upright once more.

'Felicitations, fellow off'cers.'

Caesar sighed.

'It's a fine example of Roman civilised behaviour that my senior officers make to the local populace! I hope none of you have done anything to offend the Sequani?'

For a moment, Fronto and Crispus looked at each other blankly and shrugged. Balbus, the only one who had not now taken a seat, turned to the general.

'It's fine, sir. I've been keeping an eye on them. I think we've made rather a hit in Vesontio. Three innkeepers will be spending a very financially comfortable winter this year.'

Caesar nodded.

'Very good, Balbus. Do take a seat.'

With a piercing glance around the room to make sure that the more inebriated officers were awake and attentive, the general addressed his senior officers.

'Very well, now that we're all here, I am ready to call the season at an end. However, in order to protect our interests with our old allies and our new, I intend to winter the legions here at Vesontio, pending possible further activity during the next year.'

Fronto looked over at Crispus and nodded knowingly and with great exaggeration. Caesar gave the legate a sharp look and then continued.

'I have appointed Titus Labienus as commander of the army during the winter season while I and most of the officers return to Rome and our homes. Crassus has agreed to stay for at least some of the off-season as his lieutenant. I will be thankful for any volunteers to remain with the legions, and you can report to me at the end of this briefing.'

He gestured at Varus.

'As several of you are probably aware by now, Quintus Atius Varus has been assigned as commander of the cavalry for the next season. Crassus will continue in his role as commander of the Seventh Legion, but will also take on a more staff and strategy-oriented role.'

Crassus nodded as the general went on.

'Furthermore, is Aulus Ingenuus here? Prefect of the Eighth? I'm sure I asked you to bring him, Balbus.'

Balbus pointed over to one side where Ingenuus sat, holding his maimed hand high. Caesar smiled.

'Ingenuus. I have given great consideration to your future with the cavalry, and I feel that the position of cavalry prefect may no longer be suitable for you.'

Ingenuus' face fell and his arm wavered as he lowered it.

'Sir?'

The general smiled benignly.

'No need to panic, young prefect. This is not your medical dismissal, man; this is your promotion, on the assumption you accept.'

The prefect continued to look nonplussed.

'Sir?'

'I would like you to take command of my Praetorian Cohort. They are a mixture of Romans and some Gauls of differing tribes, all of whom have a reasonable command of Latin and a deal of experience and training in the ways of cavalry. I'd like you to take them in hand and train them in the ways of Roman tactics. You'll have to return with me to Italy over the winter, of course, and you can carry out your training on the fields of Latium. Do you accept?'

Ingenuus' mouth continued to open and close. He had gone quite pale.

Labienus, sitting slightly in front of the prefect, reached round and grasped his shoulder. The young man came out of a seeming daze instantly and blinked. Labienus chuckled and turned back to Caesar.

'I think he accepts, general.'

A snore and then a cough drew everyone's attention as Fronto blinked and hauled himself back upright.

'Sorry. Sorry.'

Caesar sighed and turned the other way.

'Still with the Eighth... Titus Balventius!'

The scarred and battered primus pilus of the Eighth shuffled in his chair. He sat stiffly and painfully, trying not to let his back touch the leather of the tent. He had spent over an hour in close consort with a medicus this afternoon following yet another reopening of his wound during the ceremony.

'General?'

Caesar smiled and held out a small tablet.

'Your honesta missio. You're due it, as I'm sure you're aware.'

Balventius stared at the tablet. He had seen many in his time. Money. Land. Probably, given his status and years of service, a reasonable plot. Perhaps even an estate. He mused for a moment. Titus Balventius: Farmer. Trying not to laugh, he held his hand out, palm facing the tablet.

'Sorry sir. I'm reenlisting for another term in the Eighth. Always meant to, just haven't had time to do the administration.'

Caesar glanced quickly at Balbus.

'I'm afraid that that will not be an option. I have discussed the matter with Balbus and he feels, as do I, that you have served your time on the field and should be offered the position of camp prefect. I have reassigned Cita and the position is now open'

Balventius grunted.

'Problem is: I don't want to be the camp prefect.'

Caesar sighed.

'I'm afraid it comes down to a choice, centurion. Camp prefect, or retirement. I can assure you that the terms of your honesta missio are *very* favourable.'

Balventius looked from the general to his commander and back again.

'Frankly, sir, I'm younger than the legate, for all my scars. I'm also, though he might disagree, fitter than him. My wounds are not severe enough to prevent me doing my job well, and this one will heal well before next spring.'

He narrowed his eyes.

'Without wanting to get your back up, sir, but I'd suspect I'm both younger and fitter than you as well. Both Balbus and yourself will be back next year and yet you ask me not to? No, sir. I don't accept there are only two options.'

Caesar frowned.

'Then what do you expect to do?'

Balventius grinned and shrugged, wincing only slightly at the new stitches.

'If you take this position away from me, I'll take my honesta missio, give it to my brother and then head off for the nearest centre of recruitment and sign up with someone else!'

Caesar's eyes widened and he stared at the man. To one side, Balbus burst out laughing.

'He'll do it too, Caesar. Fine, I withdraw my request.'

The beginnings of a smile began to creep across Caesar's face.

'Very well, Titus Balventius. You may return to the Eighth as their primus pilus and I'll have the records seen to. They'll be only one-year orders though, and this tablet is yours for the keeping. I would suggest that you go to your new estate over the winter and put it in order. Let your wound heal properly and then come to Vesontio when called next spring.'

The veteran centurion frowned and then nodded, accepting the tablet the general had continued to proffer. He sat, sighing with contentment.

Fronto leaned to Balbus and whispered loud enough to be heard across the camp.

'I'll bet he stays here anyway. S'a bet?'

Balbus nodded and shoved Fronto into a more upright position. Caesar drew a deep breath and then turned to other matters.

'As of tomorrow, the legions are being stood down for the winter, unless or until Labienus and Crassus require them. Anyone who intends to spend the winter in Rome, I will be leaving after lunch tomorrow, and I would suggest we travel together with our appropriate entourages.'

A number of the officers nodded, smiling.

Balbus glanced over at Fronto, who was now fully slumped in the chair, his eyes shut. He smiled and turned to Caesar.

'General, I will travel with you as far as Vienna at least, but I return to my family in Massilia. The legates Fronto and Crispus, I believe, have other plans also.'

Caesar nodded, glancing once again with mild disapproval at the slumped bodies of Fronto, Crispus, Varus and Sabinus.

'Quintus Pedius and Quintus Tullius Cicero, I'm afraid I will need you to report to me as soon as the midwinter festivities are over. You will find me in Aquileia.'

The two officers nodded.

The general stretched and then sat back.

'I believe that's everything, then. Unless anyone has a question?'

He was greeted with a snore. Balbus elbowed Fronto sharply in the ribs. And then swore and rubbed his elbow.

'Why does he attend late-night briefings in armour?'

———————————

Balbus kicked the cart's wheel.

'Fairly sturdy, I suppose. Don't think I'd trust it all that way, though.'

Fronto growled. His head still thumped like the hammering of Vulcan on his anvil.

'It's only carrying our gear. *We'll* be on horses.'

Balbus shrugged.

'Still, I hope it's light gear!'

Crispus looked up over the edge of the cart.

'We've hardly overburdened ourselves. Marcus is familiar with the locale, so it's only the necessities of life on the road. And Longinus' goods, naturally.'

Balventius, standing close by and leaning upon his vine staff, raised an eyebrow.

'Where are you both going?'

Fronto turned to the grizzled centurion and smiled.

'I'm going to take Crispus here to Spain and deliver Longinus' stuff to his family. They're building a villa near Tarraco, and I'm sure we'll find his family there. Besides which, I'm dying to show Crispus Tarraco and my favourite drinking pits. I'm going to drive that well-bred cleverness out of him with excessive carousing.'

Crispus grinned over the cart and Balbus laughed out loud.

'Don't forget you tried that the last couple of days. He's still just as nice and clever and verbose, but somewhere along the line he lost a valuable sword and helmet.'

Crispus waved a finger at his older friend.

'Ah, no. Waves of recollection hit me this morning. I'm certain that I sold my helmet in order to... to... do something or other. I'm not entirely sure what. I found my sword this morning. Almost severed my arm with it, in fact. Must have left it in bed.'

Balbus raised his eyes skywards and turned to Balventius.

'Gods, he even sleeps with his sword now. I swear that Fronto's becoming a bad influence on him.'

'Or a good one.' Balventius smiled.

Fronto finished securing a line and then glanced past Balbus at Balventius.

'What about you? Are you staying here, or checking out the nice little retirement nest that Caesar hand-picked for you?'

Balventius shrugged.

'Going to have a look. It's on the Rhone, just south of Vienna, so I can go with this lot. Big place, mind you... big place. I'll probably have a bit of a look round and then come back to Vesontio. Don't like to leave the lads alone too long. They go soft, like fruit.'

Fronto pointed over toward the rest of the camp.

'Don't rush back. Crassus'll probably have you all over Gaul in search of glory over winter. Unless Labienus stops him, of course.'

Balventius grinned.

'I've had a word with my juniors. I'd like to see any bastard get them moving without my say so, let alone that pompous prat. What about yours? Don't you worry about the Tenth?'

Fronto returned the defiant smile.

'I've left Priscus, Tetricus and Velius in charge. Can you imagine them doing anything they disagree with?'

'I suppose not. Well, I'd best get back. I've only got a quarter of an hour and I need to find that idiot stable master.'

Fronto frowned as Balventius left, and turned to Balbus.

'What's he doing with the stable master?'

'He bought a horse.'

'Why didn't he speak to Varus and borrow one?'

Balbus grinned.

'He doesn't trust ones that have been used in combat. Reckons they'll keep charging into trouble. He's a great primus pilus, but he's not exactly a confident horseman. I take it you haven't heard about Varus, then?'

'No. What?'

The grin on Balbus' face increased to a wide beam.

'After the meeting, when I brought you and Crispus back, Varus and Sabinus went back into town. Sabinus got into a bit of a 'thing' with one of the local girls. It all went a touch wrong and Sabinus ended up getting punched in the face. It might have broken his nose.'

'And Varus?'

'He didn't come back last night. We were about to send out a duty unit to looks for him, but Sabinus stopped us. When we asked why, he just kept laughing and saying 'he'll be fine."

Fronto smiled.

'Ah. Fraternising with the locals, I suppose.'

'I believe so.'

Tightening the last of the ropes, Fronto patted the horse on the flank.

'Well, that's it. We're ready for the off. We'll be heading for Narbo first on the way to Spain. The Aedui have offered to give us a small cavalry escort until we're back in the empire's borders. I guess we'll see you next spring. Unless you get bored of Massilia and fancy Tarraco for a while. We shouldn't be too hard to find.'

Balbus smiled.

'I think Corvinia'll want to go to Rome not long after I get back, and then out to the countryside. Anyway, I'd best keep my harpy daughters away from you. They were practically drooling over you at Geneva. I'm too young still to have you for a son, Marcus!'

Fronto frowned and then looked around to see the bemused question on Crispus' face.

'I'll tell you later.'

Balbus clasped hands with Fronto and then, shrugging, the two embraced before Fronto climbed onto his horse. Balbus grasped the reins for a moment.

'Take care of yourself. I'd hate to think how dull and straightforward next year would be without you.'

Smiling, Fronto looked round at Crispus and nodded. The younger man checked the securing of the cart reins to his own and then returned the nod.

'Ready.'

Fronto looked down at Balbus.

'I'll be fine. Same as always. Send my love to Corvinia and we'll see you next year.'

With a slapping of the reins, the two set off amid the buzzing of bees, the whistling of the wind and the song of avian life to the duty of delivering Longinus to his family, for the relaxation of the winter months, and for the delights of Imperial Spain.

END

AUTHOR'S NOTE

(Manuscript completed in 2003, author's note added at publishing in 2009)

It has long been a belief of mine that history is one of the most important subjects a human being can study. It is not only the story of where we came from and what created our modern world - and therefore essentially the story of us - but it is also an ongoing and deep parable from which we can, and should, learn.

It is also, however, one of the most difficult subjects to teach or to expound upon without boring the socks off the lay person. I had the privilege in my school days of having two history tutors who managed to bring life and personality to every nuance of their lessons, and that left me with a great conviction that the only way this fabulous, important and fascinating subject would ever ingrain itself into the non-fanatic was by being INTERESTING.

The Marius' Mules series began back in 2003 as an experiment on two counts:

Firstly, to see whether my storytelling was up to a full length novel. I had written a number of short stories, many of which are too geeky to expand upon now, but I was not sure whether I had the stamina to try a full length. Turns out, to my infinite pleasure, that I did!

Secondly, I was interested to see whether a dry historical account could be made exciting to the lay reader. At the time I was planning a holiday and it had led me through arcane channels of research to working through Julius Caesar's account of the Gallic Wars. I had the same problem with it as I have with many historical accounts in that the subject is fascinating and engrossing, but the text is difficult or dry.

Could I rework Caesar's own words and turn it into an exciting adventure/war story? In the process of attempting to do so, I discovered many things.

The genre's appellation 'Historical Fiction' is called just that for a reason. It is not simply history, as to write straight history with no imagination involved is to write a text book. There is the great need to make leaps and connections that are either vaguely alluded to or not there at all in the source. There is sometimes the need to slightly bend or shuffle events in minute ways in order to make history exciting. Historical fiction is not the retelling of history, but the telling of a story based on history.

Sources are not to be trusted. It became very obvious from early on reading Caesar's diary that the man was a gifted self-promoter. We know that Caesar was ruthless and ambitious, but I determined with Marius' Mules to try not to fall into the traditional portrayal of an all-round genius who has all the good ideas himself, while being ambitious to the end. To me it seems unlikely that Caesar did not rely on the experience and abilities of the men around him, some of whom had great experience in the field in different campaigns.

Then there is the matter of the vagueness of the late Republican world. We have a good knowledge of the Roman army of the Republic to the time of Marius and after, given his changes to the system, and we have an excellent understanding of the Principate army after Augustus' alterations to the system. The period from around 58 to 31 BCE, however, is a time of flux and change. The army after Caesar's death is very different from the one he takes command of in 58. I find it interesting trying to account for a few of those changes in this text as being the work of Caesar or his officers. A prime example of this is the legates of the various legions, who had always been temporary assignments, often for a single action, while later they are a term of office and a standard step in a noble's career. I see this as an opportunity to have Caesar be the one to begin assigning long-term commands.

Incidentally: one last comment. I have had it pointed out a number of times that since this book is called 'Marius' Mules', people have expected it to be about the great Gaius Marius. The title is based on a colloquial term for the men of the legions that was in use at the time of the Gallic Wars, since this is very much a book about them. To such comments I would ask whether you would expect the characters in 'The Green Berets' to be green?

Facetious. But that's me. I like a mix of violent, brutal action, exciting adventure, and irreverent humour. So, in conclusion:

I hope that everyone who reads this book enjoys it. If you did, please do drop me a line (details on my website www.simonturney.com) and feel free to leave a review for me to feed upon. If you didn't enjoy it you probably haven't got this far, but feel free to drop me a line and discuss why.

(2021 Addendum)

12 years ago I released this book (actually finished 18 years ago!) Much has happened since then. World changing Viruses, wars and historic accords, and perhaps more importantly the birth of my two children who are now being introduced to the world of ancient Rome, often against their will.

In that time I have made in the book world too many friends to even try mentioning by name, both readers and writers, agents and publishers. I value every connection, and if I do not stay in touch as much as I should, it is purely a time constraint and having the memory of a pregnant gnat.

Since this book, when I was astounded to see a paperback with my name on it, I have now written 46 more novels, some alongside fellow writers. I never tire of starting a new work, and I never tire of typing 'The End.' I am humbled and indebted to a readership who continue to enjoy my novels, not least this series, which is now approaching book 14 of a 15 book cycle.

I started as a self-published author, and some of my work continues to be just that, with me having the entire say over every aspect, but also full culpability for every mistake. But I have also had the honour of working with publishers such as Canelo, Orion and Head of Zeus, with some amazing people working for them all, and above the whole bunch my amazing agent Sallyanne.

Marius' Mules began as part of an Arts Council-funded project to release unknown paperbacks. After two such books, I moved to other systems, and thanks to the excellent Robin Carter nudging me in the direction of eBooks just at the time they took off as a thing, they exploded into the kindle market. I was well through the series before they were taken on as audio books, with a fantastic reputation thanks to the talented narrator Malk Williams. I had been asked many times whether there would be a hardback edition, but without the backing of a major publisher for this series it seemed unlikely. Now, however, thanks to that great 'river' who is a bone of contention among readers and writers alike, it can be done. This is the first Marius' Mules book to achieve a hardback edition. If it is well received, it is unlikely to be the last.

And so Marius' Mules begins a whole new journey even as I begin to bring the series to a close. It's been a wild ride, and there are a couple of years ahead of us yet, but thank you all for your support throughout. Historical Fiction, I have seen, has become a community of readers and writers together more than any other genre, and so I consider you all friends.

Thank you and I hope you enjoyed this first adventure.

Simon Turney, 12th March 2021

Full Glossary of Terms

❖ **Amphora (pl. Amphorae)**: A large pottery storage container, generally used for wine or olive oil.

❖ **Aquilifer**: a specialised standard bearer that carried a legion's eagle standard.

❖ **Buccina**: A curved horn-like musical instrument used primarily by the military for relaying signals, along with the cornu.

❖ **Capsarius**: Legionary soldiers trained as combat medics, whose job was to patch men up in the field until they could reach a hospital.

❖ **Contubernium (pl. Contubernia)**: the smallest division of unit in the Roman legion, numbering eight men who shared a tent.

❖ **Cornu**: A G-shaped horn-like musical instrument used primarily by the military for relaying signals, along with the buccina. A trumpeter was called a cornicen.

❖ **Curia**: the meeting place of the senate in the forum of Rome.

❖ **Cursus Honorum**: The ladder of political and military positions a noble Roman is expected to ascend.

❖ **Decurion**: 1) The civil council of a Roman town. 2) Lesser cavalry officer, serving under a cavalry prefect, with command of thirty two men.

❖ **Dolabra**: entrenching tool, carried by a legionary, which served as a shovel, pick and axe combined.

❖ **Duplicarius**: A soldier on double the basic pay.

❖ **Equestrian**: The often wealthier, though less noble mercantile class, known as knights.

❖ **Gladius**: the Roman army's standard short, stabbing sword, originally based on a Spanish sword design.

❖ **Immunes**: Soldiers excused from routine legionary duties as they possessed specialised skills which qualified them for other duties.

❖ **Labrum**: Large dish on a pedestal filled with fresh water in the hot room of a bath house.

❖ **Legatus**: Commander of a Roman legion

❖ **Mare Nostrum**: Latin name for the Mediterranean Sea (literally 'Our Sea')

- ❖ **Optio:** A legionary centurion's second in command.
- ❖ **Pilum (p: Pila):** the army's standard javelin, with a wooden stock and a long, heavy lead point.
- ❖ **Praetor:** a title granted to the commander of an army. cf the Praetorian Cohort.
- ❖ **Praetorian Cohort:** personal bodyguard of a General.
- ❖ **Primus Pilus:** The chief centurion of a legion. Essentially the second in command of a legion.
- ❖ **Pteruges:** Leather straps that hang from the shoulders and waist of the garment worn under a cuirass. From the Greek for 'feather'"
- ❖ **Pugio:** the standard broad bladed dagger of the Roman military.
- ❖ **Scorpion, Ballista & Onager:** Siege engines. The Scorpion was a large crossbow on a stand, the Ballista a giant missile throwing crossbow, and the Onager a stone hurling catapult.
- ❖ **Signifer:** A century's standard bearer, also responsible for dealing with pay, burial club and much of a unit's bureaucracy.
- ❖ **Subura:** a lower-class area of ancient Rome, close to the forum, that was home to the red-light district'.
- ❖ **Testudo:** Lit- Tortoise. Military formation in which a century of men closes up in a rectangle and creates four walls and a roof for the unit with their shields.
- ❖ **Triclinium:** The dining room of a Roman house or villa
- ❖ **Trierarch:** Commander of a Trireme or other Roman military ship.
- ❖ **Turma:** A small detachment of a cavalry ala consisting of thirty two men led by a decurion.
- ❖ **Vexillum (Pl. Vexilli):** The standard or flag of a legion.
- ❖ **Vineae:** moveable wattle and leather wheeled shelters that covered siege works and attacking soldiers from enemy missiles

If you enjoyed Marius' Mules I why not also try:

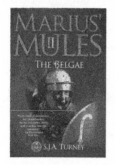

Marius' Mules II: The Belgae by S.J.A. Turney

57 BC. The fearsome Belgae have gathered a great army to oppose Rome, and Fronto and the legions assemble once more to take Caesar's war against the most dangerous tribes in the northern world.

While the legions battle the Celts in the fiercest war of Caesar's career, the plots and conspiracies against him, both at Rome and among his own army, become ever deeper and more dangerous.

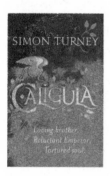

Caligula by Simon Turney

The six children of Germanicus are cursed from birth. Father: believed poisoned by the Emperor Tiberius over the imperial succession. Mother and two brothers arrested and starved to death by Tiberius. One sister married off to an abusive husband. Only three are left: Caligula, in line for the imperial throne, and his two sisters, Drusilla and Livilla, who tells us this story.

The ascent of their family into the imperial dynasty forces Caligula to change from the fun-loving boy Livilla knew into a shrewd, wary and calculating young man. Tiberius's sudden death allows Caligula to manhandle his way to power. With the bloodthirsty tyrant dead, it should be a golden age in Rome and, for a while, it is. But Caligula suffers emotional blow after emotional blow as political allies, friends, and finally family betray him and attempt to overthrow him, by poison, by the knife, by any means possible.

Little by little, Caligula becomes a bitter, resentful and vengeful Emperor, every shred of the boy he used to be eroded. As Caligula loses touch with reality, there is only one thing to be done before Rome is changed irrevocably.

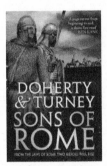

Praetorian by S.J.A. Turney

Promoted to the elite Praetorian Guard in the thick of battle, a young legionary is thrust into a seedy world of imperial politics and corruption. Tasked with uncovering a plot against the newly-crowned emperor Commodus, his mission takes him from the cold Danubian border all the way to the heart of Rome, the villa of the emperor's scheming sister, and the great Colosseum.

What seems a straightforward, if terrifying, assignment soon descends into Machiavellian treachery and peril as everything in which young Rufinus trusts and believes is called into question and he faces warring commanders, Sarmatian cannibals, vicious dogs, mercenary killers and even a clandestine Imperial agent. In a race against time to save the Emperor, Rufinus will be introduced, willing or not, to the great game.

Sons of Rome by Simon Turney & Gordon Doherty

Four Emperors. Two Friends. One Destiny.

As twilight descends on the 3rd century AD, the Roman Empire is but a shadow of its former self. Decades of usurping emperors, splinter kingdoms and savage wars have left the people beleaguered, the armies weary and the future uncertain. And into this chaos Emperor Diocletian steps, reforming the succession to allow for not one emperor to rule the world, but four.

Meanwhile, two boys share a chance meeting in the great city of Treverorum as Diocletian's dream is announced to the imperial court. Throughout the years that follow, they share heartbreak and glory as that dream sours and the empire endures an era of tyranny and dread. Their lives are inextricably linked, their destinies ever-converging as they rise through Rome's savage stations, to the zenith of empire. For Constantine and Maxentius, the purple robes beckon...

For something a little different why not try:

Daughter of War by S.J.A. Turney

An extraordinary story of the Knights Templar, seen from the bloody inside.
Europe is aflame. On the Iberian Peninsula the wars of the Reconquista rage across Aragon and Castile. Once again, the Moors are gaining the upper hand. Christendom is divided.

Amidst the chaos comes a young knight: Arnau of Valbona. After his Lord is killed in an act of treachery, Arnau pledges to look after his daughter, whose life is now at risk. But in protecting her Arnau will face terrible challenges, and enter a world of Templars, steely knights and visceral combat he could never have imagined.

She in turn will find a new destiny with the Knights as a daughter of war... Can she survive? And can Arnau find his destiny?